CLAW

VOLUME I

Edited by Kirisis "KC" Alpinus

CLAW Volume 1

Production copyright FurPlanet Productions © 2018
Cover artwork copyright © 2018 by Teagan Gavet
Contextual Intercourse © 2018 by Erin Quinn
The Beating of Wild Hooves © 2018 by Dwale
The Church Mouse © 2018 by Madison Keller
Tempered © 2018 by Crimson Ruari
A Simple Wager © 2018 by Holly A. Morrison
Support © 2018 by Kristina "Orrery" Tracer
She Who Wears The Mask © 2018 by Tenza
Trophy Hunting Blueseiryuu
The True Villain © 2018 by Dark End
Smokey and the Jaybird © 2018 by Slip Wolf
Frontier Living © 2018 by Jeeves Bunny
Roses © 2018 by Searska Greyraven
The Tutor Learns © 2018 by Skunkbomb

Published by Bad Dog Books
An imprint of FurPlanet Productions
Dallas, Texas
FurPlanet.com
BadDogBooks.com

Print ISBN 978-1-61450-443-6
eBook ISBN 978-1-61450-444-3

First Edition Trade Paperback July 2018

TABLE OF CONTENTS

To Blue Eyes, Fourpaws, Kitten, & Aunt Re-Re. Thank you ladies for living your truths so boldly, that you opened my eyes to a world outside my own.

To my loving boyfriend, Ocean, who believed in me and dared me to brave the unknown.

To Searska, Arara, & Gullwulf who helped beta read the stories awaiting you.

To my parents, for encouraging me to read and write every day.

And to you, the reader, for supporting the authors who have poured their hearts, minds, and souls into this anthology.

Thanks.

FOREWORD

"Hey Fuzz, do you think FurPlanet would ever consider having a female companion anthology to FANG and call it FUR?"

—Me, FWA 2015

When I posed that question to FuzzWolf in the Dealer's Den of Furry Weekend Atlanta, I didn't think neither he, nor Teiran, would take me seriously. For starters, I had just had my first two stories accepted into anthologies, had little editing experience, and had only been writing in the fandom for less than a year. I was a newbie writer and while my writing mentor, NightEyes DaySpring, could more or less vouch that I wasn't completely crazy, Fuzz really couldn't trust that I would be able to deliver. As I said, I didn't have a lot (read any) experience in editing stories and I was a relative upstart to the furry writing community. But what I lacked in experience, I made up for in ambition, dreams, and drive (or heaping helping of crazy).

What you are holding in your hands is the culmination of three years of planning, soliciting, reading, pitching, and research, and that's only on my part. The authors, who have so graciously submitted their works, have spent countless hours perfecting their stories (not to mention having me bork at them from Twitter) and they deserve your support. I truly hope that the ladies within these stories take you for a ride and leave you wanting more.

May you enjoy this anthology and I hope that it inspires, intrigues, but most importantly, turns you on.

Many borks,
Kirisis "KC" Alpinus

Contextual Intercourse

Erin Quinn

Her hands are magic. Gliding, sliding, and gently grazing those sensitive areas around her eyes, I question if what I'm watching is real. The nimblest actions my paws ever do is stuff vegetables into plastic cups for people to eat on their way to work; what she's doing is unfathomable.

"Now I gotta take a minute to thank my sponsor, FurNew, who supplied all this amazing shadow we're working with today. Thanks guys! If you'd like to see more videos just like this, use the code "CASS" at checkout at FurNew dot com. That's FurNew, for a new you."

I tap a claw against my laptop's spacebar, pausing the video so I can examine my attempts at mimicry.

"As if I can buy FurNew," I mumble while focusing on the drug store fur shadow wiped under both my eyes. A little foundation to prep the large black patches which take up way too much of my face, a few expertly placed wipes of white and gray powders, and I'd have eyes that would really pop. No thief mask for me!

I mean, that was the intention. Cassandra has a million online subscribers based on being able to help girls like me. Well, sort of like me.

"Blair, it's been a half hour. Can I please come in?" Dyna's baritone voice is sprinkled with that particular anxiety that comes from spending time in a public hallway in very, very, short shorts. I wanted this look to be a surprise. I want them to be proud of me. They were happy to wait.

For about ten minutes.

I close my laptop, resigning myself to the fact that a fifth view of "Popping Spotlight Eyes! Raccoon girl's BEST 2017 Look! *Sponsored Content" was not in my future, and march to the door. It only takes a few steps before the tight, awful, gross, one-size-too-small men's speedo I'm wearing rubs wrong against the bits and pieces I'm trying to ignore.

I think about the lacy black panties I'm wearing over the entire contraption, which brings out a smile.

"Oh? Done so soon?" They say, faux casually leaning against my door way.

"Just get your ass in here…" I say, then with a bit of dread, "and tell me what you think."

They spin around and I'm instantly jealous. Tight red latex shorts, perfectly shined, matching thigh high stockings accompanied by black heels, and a top which zipped down the front and left a bit of soft midriff visible, happily pushing over the brim of their shorts. It was a great look, even their antlers are accented with glitter. I'm jealous, and I miss Dyna's response to my question.

"Blair?"

"Oh yeah, I tried, but it's a mess, I know, I know." Makeup is hard, especially when it terrifies you.

"Sweetie," Dyna says, shooting me a confused look from their warm brown eyes, "your outfit is great."

I look down and am unmoved. I couldn't begin to count how many times they've seen me in this same combination of long puffy black skirt and tight black shirt with an indie band logo on it.

"These were from my laundry bin…the dirty one."

"Then all the more reason to get them dirtier tonight!" They stomp a hoof and I motion to watch the noise, pointing at the floor. I don't need any more notes from my landlord. Please, enough with the notes.

Despite my hesitation, I try and circle back to my original question.

"I meant my eyes," I ask them.

"They look pre—"

"I was following this video and I know I messed up and it sucks, but this makeup is junk and this fur is so black and gross and I'm gross and—"

They've placed a hoof on my muzzle. I sigh, inhale, and attempt to stop my racing, heart, mouth, and head.

"Let's just have fun. This party only happens once a season, and I'm not letting you miss it again. I promise, you are going to be bombarded with compliments and paws dying to get all over you," Dyna says.

"That…is my hope," I say to them and to myself. Maybe I have a shot at a sexy, fun, flirty night, even with the finger paintings under my eyes.

***

"You're with me, so shut up," Dyna says as we cross a set of railroad tracks. I'm secretly wishing we could have just stopped at my favorite bookstore, or coffee shop, or…oil change place? Yeah, that feels less nerve racking.

"But I look like a dweeb," I say, kicking a rock forward with my rainbow-laced pinked Converse.

"Doesn't matter. You're with me, so we're getting in." Dyna is nothing if not steadfast.

"Wait, so I do look like a dweeb?"

I motion. "No one says 'dweeb' anymore, we're not in junior high."

I punch their arm.

"You're still not answering."

They stop, taking my shoulders and making sure I face them. Well, I have to look up, and I'm seized by the fact that this deer, big antlers, glitter, and too tight shorts, doesn't give a fuck what anyone else is thinking about them.

"One, you look great. Two, I am proud of you. Three, you have a great butt. So, we are going to dance, and sing, and dance."

"You said dance twice," I say with a smile.

They lean down until our noses bop.

"Because I am excited."

I look down at between their legs.

"Indeed you are."

I am rewarded with a playful shove away and a companion who uses their superior stride to move ahead of me.

"Whatever, you ain't getting any from this deer."

"Don't flatt…oh whatever." I kick another rock. Lucky rock, they don't have to go out.

Maybe the confidence will rub off on me. Maybe that was the worst word choice possible. Maybe I should stop thinking about Dyna's pants. It's easier than thinking about mine.

Then my guilt catches up with me.

"I'm sorry," I call out, as they're still walking ahead, adding an effortless skip here and there.

Dyna stops and waits for me to catch up.

"About?" they ask.

"Making a sex joke?"

They shake their head, chuckling and somehow making me feel both more nervous and at ease.

"I've heard dirtier sex jokes. I've heard more offensive 'jokes', and I've had outright bullshit said to me. You know that. Relax, you're just all pent up and worried," they say.

"Just give me your confidence, I'll return it by the end of the night."

"Can't, I need it, desperately. Besides, everyone is different, so what makes me feel great may not work for you," they say.

"I guess so, I could never embrace my body like you do yours." I adjust my skirt and feel my chest. Long live A cups and padded bras. Very padded bras.

"You don't have to if you're not ready," they say, "We're both works in progress, especially me, okay?"

They smile, giving my paws a reassuring squeeze. Then there's a loud honk and a cup flying through the air, which lands right on one of Dyna's antlers, pouring soda down onto their face. They turn to the car before it accelerates away, tail flicking back and forth and legs tightening. If I didn't know better, I wouldn't put it past Dyna to charge and try to gore the car, but before they can even take a step forward, tail lights are disappearing over the horizon.

"Fuck you!" they say as loud as possible. A light turns on in the apartment building across the street, and my fur stands on end for a moment, but nothing comes of it. I'm quiet when I shouldn't be.

Dyna lets out one more swear and continues on, walking with the same long stride as earlier, only this time dragging me along. I stumble for a moment before I'm able to keep pace.

"Sorry—"

"No sorrys, you didn't do that shit. Fuck those guys, not worth my time. Couldn't handle this anyway and…" they trail off and stop.

"Damn right, you look so great, and like, they don't eve—"

They cut me off again, and I can hear cracks in one of the sturdier foundations I know.

"Could you just get this fucking cup off my antlers."

They bend over, and I take the cup off, tossing it in the waste basket outside our destination.

"Thank you, Blair," they say.

"Of course." I'm offered a hug and happily accept.

I want to enjoy the tenderness, but dubstep rears its thumping head. The door of the venue (a converted warehouse that still has the signage for a food packaging company that's long since left town) keeps opening and closing, giving our ears a preview of what awaits. If Dyna was a bit shorter, I'd be able to see inside as well, but that's fantasy talk.

I want to hug longer, but Dyna breaks our embrace and we head to the door. Their ID is checked, so is mine, and I'm quietly pleased that the incongruence of my gender marker to actual presentation isn't questioned. I think the staff is more concerned with getting our five dollars and putting on wrist bands. I'm considering this a little victory. I'll take any I can get.

I place a paw on the door to head in, turning to hold it open for Dyna. But they're still with staff, and it doesn't take me long to figure out the conversation.

"It's not she! It's They/Them, it's not hard, I just told you!"

"Sure, okay, just go have fun, dude," the wolf working the door says.

"Asshole," they shove their ID back into their purse, and I can hear a small hiss coming from Dyna. The wolf's grin hasn't disappeared, and I imagine how this will escalate. Dyna will verbally slap this guy down and I'm surprisingly excited for it; this isn't shit they take.

But it doesn't come. Their shoulders lower and they grab my paw, yanking us into the mess of smoke and lights. Maybe we both need to disappear for a night.

I hadn't smelled this many scents and musks mixed together since high school gym class, and even then, it wasn't this sexy. Every space on the dance floor is filled with people, by themselves, in couples, in triads, in masses of fur and tails and claws that I shouldn't even try to label. The stained concrete floor has been transformed into a canvas for physical expression. Near the far wall is a table and number of coolers stocked full of drinks, both alcoholic and not.

The dancers are observed by a brave few who have scaled leftover lifts and scaffolds from the building's industrial days. Lights have been set up, a mix between soft white lights and Christmas lights purchased on clearance. Pulled into it all, I'm easily overwhelmed by this makeshift menagerie.

My best hope is to stay next to Dyna. Keeping a firm grip on me, she wades through the crowd, while I throw out an "excuse me" to everyone even my whiskers touch. I don't think anyone notices or cares.

Hopefully someone finds that endearing.

We find open space and Dyna is comfortable enough to let go of me and start dancing. I shuffle my feet and wave my tail, but mostly watch them. They have a grace which would be noteworthy from here to a ballet stage, well, if you replaced a bump and grind with pliés. I'm thinking of this to distract me from checking out my best friend's ass. That would be weird, right? They like showing it off. I don't blame them.

It's easy to get distracted. A cute, short squirrel shakes her hips and sways her tail, which is being rubbed up and down by an adoring pair of foxes. Looks like one male and one vixen. That's a lovely sight.

Even lovelier, in my opinion, is the DJ. I watch the red panda on the stage as I try to twist and twirl along with her beats. She's moving between keyboards and her laptop, which is connected to a hard drive. Everything's outlined in neon lights, including her body; red lights around her ears and dangling from around her neck, green and purple glowing bracelets around her wrists, and a tail which has bright red rings fixed where the normal ring patterns in her fur would be. My knees would be turning to jelly if they weren't being powered by her music.

I hold my skirt and spin, letting it flare out, and drawing a whistle, which is surprising, but welcome. There's an urge in my throat to yell at the stage and thank her for coaxing some energy out of me or say anything at all, but my mouth is dry. Any wetness in my body has been transferred elsewhere. My exhales are noticeably louder and longer. The space between my legs is starting to ache in this sea of arousal.

While I can't yell a thank you, I can dance closer. I spin and skip closer to the stage, until I'm up against it and I can feel the heat increase. Bodies packed tighter together, sweat dripping from one's fur to another, and I worry my eye makeup might run and leave me with my everyday "bandit mask." The worries soon leave me, whisked away by the vision of the DJ, closer now than before.

And she looks back at me.

My tail curls around my hips, until the tip is pressing between my legs. She smiles, and I think I muster a smile back. She leans to her left and hits something on their set up. The lights change to different shades of red, the music slows to a pulsing thump. She takes a drink of water, and as our eyes lock once more, she lets a little drip down her front. I lick my lips. She does the same.

The squirrel pulls me from the moment, her tail moves in my direction. She smiles at me as well, and I wonder if this is how Dyna must feel, all this attention from all these beautiful creatures. The squirrel's lovely, lush, fluffy tail caresses down my front, against my shirt, against my skirt. I hope the DJ is watching.

The throb snaps me back. I crash against the conflict of what I want and what I am. Arousal flips into frustration, and I push away her tail. She stops smiling and goes back to the foxes.

My eyes dart around the dance floor. My body urges to respond to the pleasurable sensations all around me and I hate it for that. I curse myself, wishing I had a better solution than stupid speedos. Stupid tucking. Stupid body.

I look towards Dyna, dancing against a skunkette. They have seemingly danced off the troubles of earlier, once again fully themselves, fully confident. They push closer to the skunk, starting to grind against his thigh. Dyna doesn't fear whatever is in between their legs; they haven't bundled it up. They aren't adjusting themselves every two minutes in fear of someone noticing. They have a confidence I can only pretend to have; and while I found it inspiring just minutes earlier, now I can't watch Dyna without feeling my body tense, my eyes water, and my own confidence shatter.

It takes some pushing, but I make my way to the wall furthest from the dance floor.

This is Dyna's space. I'm glad they have it. I can stay on the fringes while cursing most parts of my body. I can observe, take in all the hotness, and there's a huge cooler of water next to me. See hot action, stay hydrated and cool, this is my motto to deal with my trembling knees and incessant foot tapping.

"You should go out there," I tell myself, taking a sip from my third cup of water.

"I agree, want to dance?"

How loud did I say that? Why did I say that out loud? I look to my right and find myself nearly nose to nose with a beautiful calico. She smiles at me, brushing a paw against mine, and I'm met with that bittersweet mix of 'this is already turning me on' and 'oh shit, I am feeling physical arousal'. I shift my hips to try and adjust my lower half without using paws. I don't want a repeat of the squirrel.

"You look a little lonely," she says, sliding a bit closer to me. Her jean-clad hips bump into mine and my eyes divert from hers to glance at what is a very slender figure and a bust I instantly envy.

There's a heat rising in my cheeks. I took more than a glance; I am obvious. My gray and black tail twitches. Am I sweating already?

She giggles and brushes a paw through the fur on the top of my head.

"You're a nervous raccoon, aren't you?" she says.

"It's my first time here. I'm Blair," I say.

She finishes the drink in her other paw and drops the cup on the ground. I watch it fall because it's less panic-inducing than looking at her. My tail won't stop swishing, and the tightness between my legs switches from annoying to uncomfortable as my arousal from these little touches can't hide any longer.

"You know, Blair," she says, pushing closer so we meet chest to chest; her curvy, voluptuous breasts pushing against my smaller, perky pair, giving me waves of excitement and jealousy, "first times have to be memorable."

I inhale sharply, working up the nerve to look up at her, just in time to feel her lips against mine. I close my eyes. Her rough tongue slips expertly into my mouth and begins to tussle with my own. The warmth from her body comes in waves, coursing through me with each pet across my muzzle, my face, and the back of my head. She scratches my ears in a way that goes further than any heavy petting I did in high school. She purrs louder, and it causes me to shudder. If not for the wall I had attached myself to, I'd be a puddle.

When she breaks the kiss, my knees bend, weighed down by the desire for more. But I keep steady, my paws in hers, allowing her to drag me from my hiding place and into the bathroom.

"What are we-wow...I mean," I stammer, blissfully disoriented from just a few moments of making out.

She can tell.

I let her lead, happy just to be on the ride. The restroom is small but empty, there's a counter with two sinks and two stalls opposite, the doors cracked open enough to confirm we aren't invading anyone's space.

"Up you go, cutie," she says while holding my hips and helping boost me onto the counter. Her paws reach my thighs, feeling over my skirt and making me yearn to feel her soft pads against my fur. I pull my skirt up above my knees, and she wastes no time rubbing my exposed thighs.

The warmth shoots up into my well-padded sex. I want to embrace it, I want to ignore it, this bittersweet throb which is both pulling me in and pulling me out of everything she does.

Then I feel it. Rough, lovely licks against my soft inner thighs. I pant and grip the counter, my back arching until the back of my head touches the mirrors. My mind ping pongs between excitement and panic. Maybe she won't say anything, maybe I should say something. I gasp, yelping and popping my hips up against her tongue. Her whiskers tickle me, my toes curl. She moves closer to what feels like, in this moment, the center of my being.

She screams.

"What the fuck?" her head shoots up as quickly as it shot down. She stands and backs up, fur on end and tail flicking.

I scramble and yank my skirt down, trying to sit up and ending up sliding off the counter. I catch myself before I land on the floor.

"I'm sorry, I can explain—"

"You're a fucking guy."

My eyes go wide, and I start backing up to the door.

"No, no, I'm transgender. We were going so fast. I'm a girl, my parts are just diff—"

"You have a goddamn penis," she hisses. "Fucking, like, how the fuck can you go around fooling—"

"I'm not fooling anyone, I'm trans and—"

"Trying to take women's spaces, you pervert!" She reaches into a stall, and a roll of toilet paper hits me.

My body has turned on me. The pleasure is gone, drained out in a matter of seconds. I feel betrayed. The door to the women's room slams behind me as I run outside, ignoring the staff. I want to run home, but my feet fail just as the rest of me has, and I tumble to the ground.

***

I've been crying in the grass and dirt, clawing into the ground in a vain attempt to hide myself. The music changes as the DJ ends her set and the dancers cheer. I listen to the doormen welcome people in and wish others goodnight. People pass by, and I'm sure most just assume I had too much to drink. I wish I had, then I could forget tonight.

"Need a hand?" My ears perk at the offer.

"Fuck you," I say in this half angry, half sobbing voice. I don't even look up, but I can imagine whoever offered is smirking, amused by this mess of a raccoon. I'll probably be on someone's social media in the morning.

Are the people by the door talking about me, the silly raccoon "girl" flopped over in the dirt? Has that calico told the entire club about me? Maybe Dyna will come find me once word of the guy pretending to be a girl spreads around.

I roll over and sit up in the dirt, bottles and cigarette butts scattered around me.

"Great, I'm literally surrounded by trash," I sob. Just another thing for someone to see and say about me. The normal thing to do would be to stand up and walk home, but I can't leave Dyna hanging.

I bring a paw up to my eyes and wipe them, cursing that I ever decided to come out. Maybe one of these bottles still has something in it? I reach out to one, which is reflecting a bit of a red glow. Which is coming from behind me, causing me to turn around and lean back on my paws.

"Blair?" says the DJ from earlier. The one I couldn't stop looking at. The one I'm sure already heard about the gender confused deviant who harassed a girl in the restroom.

"Okay, that's me," I respond. "Look, whatever you heard, I'm transgender and it wasn't—"

"I'm sorry about that bitch." She offers a paw and I hesitantly accept. "I talked to the event staff and we kicked her out for spreading that garbage."

"Um, thanks. Sorry I cursed at you just now," I say, looking in her dark, small eyes. She still had the neon necklace on, and the colored rings attached around her tail. "I liked your set, did more dancing than I thought."

"That's always great to hear. It's a really good crowd tonight," she said. "By the way, I'm Marcy. Do you want to go back in? I'm done for the night, so we could hang out?"

Her voice raises in a way I didn't expect, and I wonder if this isn't just a pity offer. I push out a smile and my tail joins hers in swaying. I nod, and seconds later, I feel her paw in mine.

"Oh," she giggles and yanks hers away, "I'm sorry, is that..."

I reach back out, "It's okay."

We join paws again and begin walking towards the door.

"I always work to make my shows inclu—"

I cut her off, and the words come out of my mouth like a star-struck fangirl, "I love your tail lights. They're so cool and sexy."

She looks at me. The door staff looks at me. My tail thuds on the ground. My fur stands on end. It feels like it takes her hours to reply.

"That's why I wear them," she laughs and pulls me through the door. There's no other reaction. Maybe the entire world isn't elementary school.

Once we hit the dance floor, both our paws lock together. Arms extending towards the ceiling, she pushes against me, keeping her eyes locked on mine as we settle into an embrace. She's already a mess of sweat and musk from performing, wearing a sleeveless shirt with her album logo hanging loosely from her shoulders, probably one size too big. I lean in against her neck and even with the music and chatter around us, I can hear her gasp as I sniff and lick. She already knows. She doesn't seem to give a fuck about what's in my pants. I feel bold.

Her tongue licks at my ear as I plant a few more kisses against her neckline. The rest of the room is disappearing into an anonymous silhouette of ears and tails, leaving me and this sexy, shining DJ. I taste her fur and skin, salty sweat and a scent dripping with energy. I want more.

When have I ever taken the lead? Not in high school, not in college, not earlier with the calico. So, what am I doing now, as I lead her off the dance floor back to the spot where I had previously enjoyed solitude? My mind tussles with itself, my instinct to guide her against the wall taking over as she's panting and nodding encouragingly.

She kicks a leg up and around my hips, using it to pull me tighter as she returns the neck kisses from earlier. My paws scratch the back of her head, leaning in close to lick and take a playful nibble on one of her ears.

"Is-is that…" I pant.

"It is-yes, please, more," she gasps while grazing her teeth against my skin. I lick along the angle of her ear, alternating kisses and the lightest of bites, while she does the same near my collarbone.

Then, my hips thrust. I can't help it as each touch, lick, bite, plunge through my body, dancing their way to the center of my arousal.

She moans. No screams, no cries, just a sexy, dripping, moan.

"I have a dressing room. Let's use it."

***

The dressing room door locks. It only takes Marcy a second to dive back into my arms, wrappings hers around me and walking us back until I'm the one against the wall. The privacy unleashes a more aggressive side, breathy moans turning into harsher whistles as she slides her dark paws under my shirt.

"So much padding," she giggles, and I'm not sure how to take it. I squirm and try to shrug, but she's already pulling at my bra, yanking it down, and I have to reach back and unclasp it to avoid anything ripping. A little more wiggling sends it to the floor, and Marcy looks up at me with a grin.

"Are you sensitive?" she asks. I nod. "Close your eyes." I comply with the request.

Then I feel the chill of an ice cube against my now exposed nipples. I moan as they harden, my muzzle closed, and head tilted back. My body arches against the wall as she runs it back and forth between my breasts, leaving my chest perky and wet. When the ice finally melts, Marcy then dives in with her tongue, lapping off the water from my wet fur, and giving my nipples quick flicks. It's a feeling I'm not familiar with, a part of myself that hasn't been pleasured by someone else. It doesn't appear to be her first time, though.

My shirt hits the floor, her shirt and necklace follow. There isn't a huge difference between the size of our busts, which honestly makes me feel good about my own. Marcy playfully pushes and swings her chest against mine, tickling for a moment as our nipples are in similar states of arousal.

"You look so good Blair," she says, squeezing my chest with her paws and kissing one side of my muzzle.

I try and form a compliment, but the words drool out. "You, yeah, so good."

She laughs for a second, but then changes her tone as she puts one paw on my shoulder.

"How do you feel about below the waist?" she asks.

"The sensations feel good, it's more, the equipment," I say.

She nods. "What would you be comfortable with? I want you to be able to enjoy whatever feelings you're getting."

I take a second, in a way I haven't before, to think about enjoying it despite shape or form. I look Marcy up and down and consider her acceptance of my body.

My skirt slides off easier than I imagined it would.

"Those panties look great on you," she says. I couldn't have wished for a better compliment.

There's a caution to her paws as they run down my sides to my hips, a tenderness which leaves space for me to stop the experience at any moment.

"It's like," she says, glancing up at me, "it's like I'm going to play with your clit, does that sound—"

"That's perfect," I say.

Her paw begins to rub against my panties, finding my clit already throbbing and eager. I'd thank her for this newer, sexier mindset, but I'm too busy gasping and moaning with each slide of her paw. She works herself up and down the front of my panties, moving her paw between my legs. I feel her little claws against the inside of my thighs, lightly scratching the skin before going gently against my clit, I yelp happily. The reaction only moves her to work her paw faster.

She then presses her paw tightly against me, pushing and pinning it between my legs. "How about you lay down?" She doesn't have to ask me twice.

There's little questioning the floor's cleanliness, but it's easy to ignore when you're looking up to see Marcy undressing. She slips off her black jeans, revealing a pink thong that doesn't leave much to the imagination. I take in her soft thighs, fluffy black fur going all the way to the small parts under her thong. It's difficult to hide how eager I am, and she easily picks up on it.

"This isn't too much?" she asks. I appreciate the check-in, but I'm shaking my head 'no' before she even finishes the question.

"Good, because I can't let you have all the fun," she turns to face my feet, giving me a perfect few of her ass. I adore how naturally round it is, shapely and formed from night after night of moving around on stage. I'd reach up and try to feel her legs and rear, except as I'm considering it, she's lowering herself onto my muzzle.

My first instinct is to breathe in, her sweat and wetness mixing into a delicious musk which makes my hips squirm, only to be met by her paws returning to massage the part of me now dubbed my clit.

My own cheeks clench as I arch up at her, loving each rub of her paw against me, worrying for a moment that I could burst from my layers of underwear and my favorite panties. It's a passing thought, however, as my senses bounce back to the curvy ass and wet pussy rubbing against me. She's soaked her thong, which I can feel slipping further between her lips and cheeks.

I begin to lick, giving her my tongue to grind against, and she responds by moaning louder and pushing down harder on my muzzle. In those seconds where air becomes scarce, I throb even more, and her paw responds by rubbing more against my clit. I feel the tip of my clit leaking, more than more, more than ever, as my lower half is nearly seizing up from all the heat and pleasure.

I take a long taste, my tongue licking her lips and then sliding between them. I feel her thong for a moment, then adjust my muzzle, which allows my tongue to discover her clit. At least...I'm pretty sure. She whistles loudly, nearly howling if she could, and she sits up straight on my face and bucks against it with all the raw desire I saw Dyna displaying earlier. I lick again, she responds even louder. Her scent gets more intense as I can feel my fur getting wetter. I adore her dripping on me.

As she grinds down, one of her paws reaches back, finding the fur on the top of my head and gripping it. I focus on the exact spot my tongue found, lapping at it like water in the desert. Except I'm anything but dry, and neither is she. Her ass clenches, and my paws reach up to feel her cheeks, rubbing them as I keep working my tongue back and forth, then swirling like around the tip of a lollipop.

Her body shakes like the dancers she inspired earlier, her thighs clenching hard against the sides of my heads, wrapping me in her sweat, her musk, her heat; I feel one last push against my muzzle, and then a wet rush against my nose and tongue. A little sour, a little sweet, the taste is overwhelming. I lap up what I can as she grinds and wipes herself on my face.

Eventually, the shaking subsides. She pants and slides down my body, sitting on my chest and looking over her shoulder. I greet her with what I'm sure is a dopey smile.

"Your makeup is beautifully ruined," she says. Drugstore powder mixed with Marcy's orgasm, way better than what any video could show me.

She then looks away from me, and in all the excitement, I had forgotten my own body. Was that an out of body experience? If it was, I'll take another dozen please.

My thoughts are cut off by her paws, as she goes back to work on my clit which is still hard, still pulsing, still aching for release. Especially now. Now more than ever. I can taste Marcy on my lips, smell her with every inhale I take. And I still have an incredible view of her ass.

It's the perfect mixture, as her paws expertly explore my body, feeling me, teasing, and then rubbing as fast as she can. My hips arch, my ass clenches like hers did, and I let out a low moan as I can feel myself spraying the inside of my underwear. Marcy rubs from the base to the tip of my clit, coaxing out as much as she can from me. I can feel my own wetness soak into my fur, contained as I desired, but released in a way I hadn't imagined until tonight.

"Oh wow," Marcy says, as she playfully spanks my crotch before climbing off my body and sitting next to me. I take a moment to soak in the moment, pun intended.

"How long have you been needing that?" she asks.

"Forever," I reply.

"I'm glad I could help," she leans in and kisses the side of my muzzle, then moves to my ear.

"And you were born to lick pussy," she giggles. She stands up, grabbing her pants and starting to slip them back on. I lay there a few more minutes. I'd rather this never end. I think she understands that, but still playfully tosses my shirt so it lands on my Marcy soaked face.

***

"You'll be back soon, right?" I ask. Marcy's typing her number into my phone.

"All I do is tour, so probably. Trust me, I'll let you know, cutie." She passes my phone back. I send her a quick text just to make sure we're connected.

Her phone dings. "Perfect! I always need people to talk to while I'm on the road. Especially when I'm alone, in a motel."

She steps forward, and we kiss. Arms wrapping around each other, I hold her tightly and hope it conveys to her how much tonight meant to me.

When we break the kiss, I can feel my eyes watering. She brings a paw to her mouth as she isn't meaning to laugh.

"Oh dear, that was wonderful," she says, brushing a paw against my eyes. I nod.

"Was amazing."

Eventually, we part. She mentions having to pack up her equipment, I mention having to find my friend Dyna. It feels like neither of us want the night to end, or maybe that's only me. But it does, and soon I'm walking across a less crowded, quieter dance floor.

Some are still dancing, the music has gotten slower and chill. Some have passed out on the floor with their partners. The bar is closed, it must be past two am. A few folks have taken to the stage, making out and rolling around in the glitter and streamers from an earlier set. The otter working the music doesn't mind. She's probably enjoying watching.

Dyna isn't with that skunk from earlier. I find them laid out across two chairs near the entrance. They tilt their head, as if forgetting I came with them.

"Where have you—what did—who did…that calico," they suddenly snap to life, sitting up and grabbing my paws. I'm sure they heard about the incident earlier.

"Oh no, it's fine, they kicked her out," I tell them. "I had a great night, as in, the kind of night I'll be masturbating to for…forever."

Dyna howls, pulling me in tight and shaking me. "Oh yes, yes, my child has grown up. Now you are a sexual misfit just like me! Yes, join us!" I have no idea where they found this energy.

"Okay, okay, yes, yes, that's me, big time heathen." I wiggle away. "Could we go home? I miss laying on a bed." Dyna can't get the smile off their face, and heads toward the door with me.

As we exit, they glance, looking for, but not finding the staff member from earlier.

"Damn, I think I had one kick in the dick left in me," they say.

"Save it for someone that wants it," I reply, and Dyna laughs, throwing an arm around me.

"You're filthy after whatever time this is. I have no idea, my phone died hours of ago."

"I'm a lot of things at this time of night," I say.

"You smell like—" Dyna leans in and sniffs at me.

"Stop that, geez, perv!" I playfully push them away. "It's red panda, for your information. That's what you're smelling."

"Red panda. Oh my god, no! You, you had sex with DJ Crimson Fluff?"

"I call her Marcy."

Dyna's eyes grow wider. "I'm going to be jealous of you forever. Ah! She's…she's gay? Queer? I, I mean, I assumed, but—" Dyna stammers, and it puts a pep in my step that I didn't know existed.

"It also turns out I have a clit," I say, as I wiggle my hips. Dyna turns me to face them, placing her hooves on my shoulders. They embrace me tightly, holding me close as our journeys intersect once more. I place my hands on their back and smile, feeling secure with their support, and finally, secure with myself. Dyna then leans her muzzle down, close to my ear.

"That's the hottest context I've ever heard."

THE BEATING OF WILD HOOVES

Dwale

Babs took the monitor from her pocket and unfolded it to check the time. Little thicker than a piece of paper and bearing a skin that gave it the appearance of such, the monitor showed twenty-three fifty-nine in the lower right-hand corner. She was going to be late to see Meg. If only there'd been someone else to watch her sisters, she might have been spared the tardiness, and the forthcoming chagrin.

"She was going to meet them sooner or later," was what she told herself. She stopped and turned back to look them over. The four lambs were sisters by a different father, and though largely of Scottish blackface stock, as she was, they'd inherited a white band across the dark fur on their faces, rather like permanent domino masks. Also unlike her, they let the fur on their bodies grow out eight centimeters or more from the skin, so they looked like puffs of bleached cotton with black pipe-cleaners jabbed in for arms and legs. Tonight, they were decked out in hooded polyester cloaks that shone wavy lines in the headlights of passing traffic. They were just a few hundred years behind modern fashion. The only way they could have stood out more was if they'd striped their coats with neon dyes, but it was Babs, and not her sisters, who had done this. People were beginning to stare.

"Please don't embarrass me," she said, then sighed. "I just want to talk to her for a few minutes, so sit in the booth, be quiet 'til I'm done, then I'll excuse myself and take you girls home. Alright?"

With one voice the chorus of ewes answered,

"Sister, our eldest, did swing by the diner at midnight,

Bade us to hush while she flirts with her feline girlfriend."

Babs took a deep breath and ran her hands down her face, resigning herself.

"Are you done?"

"Baa," bleated Agnes, largest of the triplets, who all three smiled. Little Phoebe, born a year later and forever a beat behind in their antics, followed suit as soon as she noticed.

Babs went ahead, grumbling. Her hoofcaps made muted thumps as she walked over concrete eroded to smoothness by years of transit, number untold. Fresher concrete, which is still gritty in texture, could grind hooves down to nubs in a short time if they weren't protected in some way, but even this polished type could cause cracking and chipping. Babs was always cognizant of that fact and took care to wear only the sturdiest hoofcaps that could be had, which involved black market military "surplus" and large withdrawals from her savings. Her hooves were how she made her living, after all, so she had every reason to foot the expense. Her sisters were wearing something more akin to house slippers, which didn't muffle their steps as much as her gear would have done, so their gait included a clip-clop that drew even more attention to their odd dress.

At least they would be inside soon. The diner's exterior of fake chrome, now peeling off in sheets the size of hand towels, was in view. It must have been meant to look old-fashioned, like an early mobile home, when it was new, but now it was becoming a ruin. The interior was however still clean and serviceable, if well-used, and kept busy at all hours feeding clientele from the bars and clubs down the block.

Behind it all, silhouetted against a sky of low clouds lit red by the broadcast towers, stood the tremendous wall that divorced the old world from the new one, where the bones of technology's golden age spun trash into electronics, while those without scavenged and improvised a slipshod facsimile of the world that had gone before. Babs paid it no mind. It was adamant as a mountain, and as final. If there ever had been a time when she'd entertained notions of trampling it down, then it was long past.

The greeter (Dorothy was her name, and she was also a server) was a chimera of harvest mouse stock, and with her granny glasses and stubby muzzle was the kind of cute that made Babs want to muss the woman's hair like she did with her sisters. Instead, she waved.

"Hey, guys," Dorothy said. "Just sit anywhere."

Music from one of the state AV broadcasts played from a wall-mounted monitor, a tinny, synthetic noise, void of expression, accompanied by a kaleidoscopic visualization in garish colors. The place smelled like grilled cheese and the air was always humid, taking into account already-high regional standards. Bab's coat was shorn almost to the skin, with some places shaven clean to show off her tattoos. Therefore, the moisture wasn't going to be as much of an issue for her, but her mind conjured up a vision of her siblings' coats frizzing out as though they'd all walked, hand in hand, into an electric fence. She had to stifle a laugh. Maybe the "grim reaper" cloaks hadn't been such a bad idea, after all. At least they could use the hoods.

Babs pointed to an empty booth with a sad plastic table, its blue textured coating scratched to baldness by tens of thousands of plates.

"You guys sit here," she said. "I'll be over there by the window, still in your line of sight. Just give me ten minutes. Order sodas or something." The triplets, trailing little Phoebe, slid onto the bench seats and didn't even pretend not to be staring as she walked away. She didn't have to look back for confirmation, she could feel the stares on her neck.

Meg had her computer out on the table, a unit the size of a bar of soap. She had a portable keyboard deployed and the output routed to her glasses; Babs could see glowing characters scroll across the insides of the lenses. She was a feline with straight, light brown hair down past her shoulder blades, with tawny fur that looked grey when in shadow. She was covered in spots like a wildcat, though Babs did not yet know her phenotype. When Babs drew near the table, she got up and the two exchanged cheek kisses before taking their respective places.

"My sisters' theater practice ran late," Babs offered apologetically.

"Oh," Meg said, and smiled. "Were they the ones in the—?" Here she mimed the outlines of a cape. Babs nodded.

"Mom had to pull a double shift, so I've only got a few minutes. I have to get them home."

Meg smiled, and there was enough regret in it for Babs' heart to flutter. She wasn't wasting her time with this person. There was a spark in her where Meg was concerned, one which threatened to kindle into open flame at every interaction.

Just then, Dorothy the harvest mouse took their drink orders, feeding them into a tablet with light, nimble fingers. Babs, being a sheep, had a wide field of vision. That was why she could watch Meg ask the mouse about non-dairy creamer, but simultaneously observe her siblings slipping from the booth she'd put them in and creeping to the seats directly across from where she and Meg were sitting.

"And what will you have, ma'am?"

Babs looked up at the waitress, then at the table where her hand had found its way to her knife and taken it up in an icepick grip. She put it back down and shot death at the triplets with her eyes.

"Seltzer and a packet of sugar."

"What?"

"Seltzer and a packet of sugar." She turned to the mouse. "Please."

"Sure thing, honey…"

Meg was grinning. Babs scratched herself on the back of the head as she sometimes did, unaware.

"I don't like to drink caffeine this late," she explained. "And I like the way the granules feel on my tongue. Listen, I'm sorry—"

"No, it's ok," Meg said, smiling still, and waved at the other table. Phoebe returned both gestures with vigor. "I guess the herd instinct is pretty strong?"

"Yeah," Babs said, covering the left side of her face with her hand. "In a sheep home, everybody drifts around the house together as people need to take care of things. Nobody stays out of line of sight for long, so privacy isn't…"

Here she caught a flavor of anxiety she'd tasted before: the awareness that she was saying the sort of thing that chases off prospective love interests. Her ears drooped, only to pop back up when Meg reached across the table and put her hand over hers.

"I see," she said, and grinned reassuringly, her green eyes flashing like gems. "But I already know you're not like other ewes."

"No," Babs admitted, voice flat. "I'm not." The corners of her mouth twitched upwards in spite of her sour mood. In fact, she might have forgotten her anxieties entirely had not the canid chosen that moment to interrupt.

He was slight like a fox or a small coyote, but his muzzle was too pointy to be either of those. He must have been a jackal, she decided, and not much more than a juvenile. His pants were beige where they weren't black with grime, and he sported a leather jacket with so many cracks and holes it looked like he might have snatched it off a drive-by victim.

Chimeras of herbivorous phenotypes often found leather off-putting, but not Babs. She was one of only a few who would wear it, and did so on the regular. So, it couldn't have been that which bothered her about this person. It must have been something in the way he carried himself, the hint of mockery behind his smile, or the stink of tobacco and beer rolling off of him. Whatever it was, he put her on edge, every nerve in her body tight and ready.

"You girls want to have a threesome?"

Meg clapped a hand over her mouth, lips forming words, though none got through her fingers.

"Dude!" Babs snapped. "What the hell? No, hell no."

"Oh, please," the jackal said. "Don't even try to tell me you two don't like cock."

Babs was on her hooves, fists balled up at her sides. She wasn't a big ewe, but she was a full head taller than this guy. With her close-cropped wool and sleeveless shirt, it was not difficult to make out the cords of her muscles straining beneath her skin, taut as guitar strings. The jackal could, apparently. He cowered backwards and turned away, muttering. She fixed her eyes on him until he was out the door, until she felt Meg's hand on hers. Only then did she realize that her date had been speaking for some seconds and she hadn't heard a word.

"Babs? Hun?"

"Yeah. Sorry." She sat back down. Meg regarded her with pert ears and a scrunched mouth.

"You were about to hit that guy."

Babs sighed. "Yeah."

"Are you always so quick to fight?"

The fire was hot in Babs' stomach, it wasn't until she saw Meg's frown that it was quenched.

"No, I—" she stammered, chasing the right words. "Look, that guy was an asshole." She buried her face in her hands, tormented by a fusion of shame, relief and unspent anger. Time passed, and Meg pried one of the hands away from her face, entwining their fingers.

"It's ok," she said. "I was just scared because I never saw you like that before. I mean, I know what you do for a living, but…"

Babs grinned ruefully. They'd discussed her career, and while Meg was inscrutable as any cat, Babs had learned to read her well enough to know that was going to be a point of contention in the future.

Just then, she snuck a glance at her sisters and noticed the quartet of Agnes, Sophie, Lydia and Phoebe had picked up a new herd-mate, a lamb who shared their "mask" facial marking. That would be Agatha, her cousin. She was holding a lollypop in one hand while Phoebe gave her a drink of soda.

"Oh, lord, they're multiplying."

Meg turned to look at what Babs had seen. Her eyes went wide and Babs had to laugh.

"We should probably get out of here. I need to get them home, and if my aunt's herd sees us they'll block us in."

***

The light from the inside of Meg's glasses caught in her pupils, vertical slits shining like slivers of green moon. She was checking her schedule.

"What about tomorrow?"

"Can't. Also, I think you should walk with us for a while."

"Hmm?"

Babs motioned with her snout for Meg to turn around. When she did, she saw the jackal from earlier skulking beside an alley. He made eye-contact, then ducked around the corner and was gone.

"Was that…?"

"Yeah. Let's get you to the tram."

The six of them went the other way from where they had seen the jackal, wary as rabbits, ears perked. They went without speaking, eyes probing for any potential ambush, but found only phantoms for half a dozen blocks. They passed convenience stores people ran out of their garages, a couple of strip clubs, a long, rectangular tavern that called itself "The Coffin" and more than a few buildings which had been hollowed out by fire or abandoned and left for the squatters. Meg sneezed twice at the smell of marijuana, although she couldn't have identified it. Babs could and did, however, and she could have named far worse substances in the air besides.

The attack came as they were traversing a space between a perpendicular road and driveway, from their right side. It was the jackal from earlier, who must have dashed or used a vehicle to get ahead of them. He strutted out from behind a dumpster, lifting his shirt to pull a pistol from his waistband, but Babs didn't give him a chance to aim. Her sisters were already bolting, and the jackal's posture, wide open, sure of himself, suggested that he expected Babs to run, too. Instead, she closed the distance in one step and snatched his hand and forearm, shoving her hoof-like nail into the tendons just above his wrist while also pulling back on his thumb; he yelped like a puppy and dropped the gun like it had burned him. It clacked onto the concrete.

Babs began the follow-up before the pistol hit the ground; she had pressed her hoofcap against the inside of his knee. It wasn't a kick, it was too gentle for that. The movement was almost casual: she put her foot up as one might have done to tie an errant shoelace and pushed. His knee bent against its regular plane of motion. There was a pop, and he crumpled to the pavement, thrashing.

No one saw the jackal's brother coming; it was as if he had materialized from nothing. A meter of steel pipe had appeared along with him. Snarling, he brought it down at Babs' head. Caught off-guard, she got a block up with not a split-second to spare. The pipe met her forearm with a muffled clank.

Her attacker must have supposed that her arm had been broken, or at least disabled, he certainly didn't expect it to snake around his weapon to yank him in towards her knee, which launched upwards and connected hard with his crotch. He expelled a choked squeak and collapsed. She kicked the pistol away as an afterthought, though neither jackal appeared capable of using it.

"Your arm! Are you alright?"

Meg's eyes had dilated to the point they seemed in danger of swallowing her face. Her tail lashed behind her in agitation.

"It's nothing," the ewe said, noting with some relief that her sisters had fled down the sidewalk and were safe. "I've had graphene lattice reinforcement on my arms and legs." She gave her arm a squeeze and winced. "Of course, the soft tissue is another story."

Babs smiled, but knew she'd be lucky to come off this with nothing more than a bruise. Her muscles could be pulverized under the skin, veins or nerves all but destroyed. And why did it have to be tonight, of all nights? That said, her arm didn't feel too bad, considering. Maybe it would be alright.

The jackal brothers writhed in the filth. Electric cars whined past them, some whose drivers must have seen all that had just transpired, but not one so much as slowed.

"Should we call the police?" Meg asked. Babs chuckled in response, but there was no delight in it.

"You don't get outside of the walls much, do you? Out here, 'police' are just thugs with state backing. No telling what they'd do." She took the gun and strode over to where the jackals were laying and crouched to look in their faces.

"I catch you trying to roll somebody again and I'll end you. You understand?"

They left their would-be assailants and went on their way. Later, Babs tossed the pistol off the side of a bridge as they crossed a river on the way to the tram station. Babs and her sisters were quiet and calm. Meg was alone in her shock, as much from their blasé reaction as from the violence itself. The group came at last to the edge of the depopulated tram station parking lot.

"So, day after tomorrow? I'll email you," Meg said. It felt corny given what had just happened, but it was all that came to mind.

"Sure."

They shared a kiss and held each other close, which set Babs' heart beating harder than the attempted mugging had done. With one voice, Sophie, Agnes and Lydia (and Phoebe, a beat behind on half the words,) said:

"Babs, in her power did smite the jackal footpads,
Now she's all hot like the loneliest Sapphic classmate."

Meg broke the kiss, eyes twinkling with confused amusement.

"They, uh…" Babs stroked herself on the back of the head. Meg could feel the heat of the ewe's blush on her ear tips, even if she couldn't see it under the dark face fur.

"They wanted to do community theater, but the only role that would put them all on stage at the same time was 'Greek Chorus.' So, they just kind of do that now."

Meg peeked over at the four girls and smiled. "They mean a lot to you." It wasn't a question, but Babs answered anyway.

"Yeah. I couldn't do what I do without them. And…" She gave Meg a squeeze around the waist, and whispered, "I have *you* now, too."

"Do you?" The cat slipped free of Babs' encircling limbs, an escape so smooth that she was left a moment hugging air while Meg capered up the path, twirling with wild grace like a fey dervish in the throes of an ecstatic dance. It would have been easy to picture her with gossamer wings, wearing nothing but jewelry and finger paint.

"We'll see," she taunted, though it was an invitation as well. "But I'll email you!"

She vanished into the station, leaving Babs to stand there with a dopey grin splashed across her face. Whether her girlfriend was an overgrown child or a crazy person, she couldn't say. Perhaps it was both. Whatever the case, her siblings' woops and jeers did nothing to spoil her humor as she rounded the four of them up and shepherded them home, the embers of Meg's kiss still smoldering on her mouth.

***

The coffeeshop was the kind that passed for upscale in that part of town. It was situated near the wall's massive western gate, which saw a permanent flow of soldiers and workers on business in the so-called "agricultural zones." As such, unlike the diner they'd patronized two nights before, its owners had access to better equipment and furnishings. Their seats and tables, even the coffee machine had the appearance of being manufactured rather than cobbled together from junk. The whole place consisted of polished surfaces and glinting metal.

Babs came in sporting a bandage over the outermost portion of her left eye, which was swollen to the point she could only open it with effort. Her forearm was bandaged, too; her opponent, spotting the bruise beneath her short wool and, seeking advantage, had targeted, expanded and worsened it. Now she looked like she was trying to walk off a car crash. The woman behind the counter, a corpulent rabbit by the name of Helen, grimaced when she saw her.

"Damn, honey! You alright?"

Babs beamed at her. Why wouldn't she, when she had the previous night's purse in her account? She waved her hand dismissively. "Better than her."

At that moment, another rabbit, a buck as hefty as his wife, emerged from the swinging kitchen doors with a stack of trays, which he set down on a counter.

"Hey, Babs!" he said. "Did you win?"

She nodded, and his face lit up; he returned the smile, and, after taking a moment to congratulate her, withdrew to the kitchen from whence he shouted the news to some unseen others.

Meg had arrived ahead of her and was already seated and waiting.

Now that Babs had turned to approach, her girlfriend got a good look at the pummeled eye for the first time and frowned, ears flattening. That frown was like rain on Babs' triumphal spirit; where she had come through the door elated, she took her place at the table sobered.

"It's not as bad as it looks," she began. "In a few days, it—"

"What happened?"

"I got elbowed in the eye," she said, fingering the bloody gauze and flinching at what she felt. "Five times."

"Oh no, is that legal?"

"It's standard MMA rules, for the most part."

There was no hint of recognition at what she had said, so she elaborated.

"Well, you know boxing has rules, and wrestling has rules, so in mixed martial arts it becomes more complicated still. And that's before you add hooves into the equation. The short answer is, 'Yes.' Elbows to the head are legal if both fighters are standing or on the ground."

The insides of Meg's ears blanched from base to tip.

"But you won."

"I caught her in the hamstrings. Hard. Repeatedly."

"I always thought 'hoofbeats' was just two people locking arms and kicking each other on the thigh."

Babs laughed and smirked. "If you ever saw anyone doing that, I guarantee you they were amateurs. No, it's a variation on standard mixed martial arts. It's what happens when you ban ungulates and tell us we're not allowed to fight."

She began her speech in good cheer, but was grim as death by the end, the shadows of a hidden resentment passing over her face like an abrupt summer thundershower. If she had possessed hackles, they would have been raised. Meg shrank at Babs' sudden intensity.

"Sorry," she said, catching herself and switching tones. She stroked her close-cropped hair, ears drooping. "It's just that when you have an ungulate phenotype, everyone expects you to be so docile. That goes double for women and triple for ewes. People don't respect your autonomy."

Thunder boomed in the east. Meg took the spoon out of her tea, it banged the lip of her glass mug, which rang like a bell.

"I might understand better than you think," the cat said, soft, even fearful, as though she were afraid someone might overhear. The room dimmed as clouds slipped over the sun. She took a hurried sip and looked behind her shoulder. Babs grasped her hand and squeezed it. Meg smiled, and her dazzling eyes shone, but the weight of an unnamed concern was evidenced in every muscle, from the splayed ears and downcast gaze, to the drawn and weary lips.

"Tell me what's wrong," Babs said, frowning.

"I want you to teach me. To fight."

The shift was so unexpected that she was startled by it and might have been intimidated had Meg not puffed out her fur, so that the hairs of her neck stood out like a mane, and the angry tail went bushy as a squirrel's. Babs snickered, and the usual color went back into Meg's ears, and more than the usual. She turned away and put her nose up, pulling her hand back to smooth down her ruff.

"Never mind," she said, wounded. "Forget I asked."

"N-no, it's…" Babs tried to swallow back the laughter. Alas, she couldn't reverse gears the way Meg had done. "It's not that. I never saw you like that before, you looked like a lion. But no, seriously, for hoofbeats…"

"I don't want to do what you do," Meg said savagely, her feline pride still smarting from the slight, "I don't have the time, nor the anatomy. And speaking of anatomy, how much of yours is real, anyway?"

Now it was Babs' turn to scowl. For a moment, she stared in disbelief, then, having confirmed to herself that she had heard right, she narrowed her eyes and sneered, nostrils flaring.

"*All* of me is."

Tense seconds ticked by while neither moved nor spoke. At last, Meg hung her head and exhaled, regretful of the line she had crossed and feeling her ire subside.

"I've had graphene lattice reinforcement on sixty-five percent of my skeleton," Babs said, voice even, but strained from the effort of keeping it so. "My knees, hips and elbows have been replaced. All this is standard at my level of competition. I'm sorry, I was going to tell you. It never came up."

"No, I'm the one who should apologize, that was a low blow," Meg said, and looked back up, pleading with her brows. "I've had a lot on my mind the past couple of days. I've got a problem at work."

"Well, what is it? Talk to me."

"I was trying to!" Meg shot, indignant, then cinched her eyes closed and had a deep breath before continuing.

"We got a new foreman a while ago. Some of the other girls told me he'd cornered them and tried to get them to..." She swallowed the last gulp of her tea and set the mug back onto the table.

"He hasn't done anything to me, yet. But today... There's this hallway that runs to the warehouse, lined with offices that no one uses anymore. I was on the way back and I saw him hiding in one. I mean out of the corner of my eye, you understand. I pretended I hadn't seen him."

"You're sure he was following you?"

"I'm sure. No other reason for him to be where he was."

"Damn."

There was silence, and time passed. The portly rabbit brought Babs a seltzer water and a packet of sugar without being asked. A convoy lumbered in, there in the day's leaden gloom, a column of steel behemoths up to four meters tall in some cases. There were armored tractor-trailers and half-tracks, personnel carriers laden with disposable fanatics. Autonomous helicopters with turrets hanging from their undercarriages like the stingers of wasps zigzagged over the proceedings, whisper-quiet. The pair did not speak until the convoy had vanished out of sight, as though they were transfixed in reverie. Only when it was gone did Babs resume.

"Can you report him?"

Meg shook her head.

"He's apparently tight with the block coordinator. I say anything, and they'll slam a lid on it and make my life hell." She took Babs' hand in hers.

"So, please."

Babs sipped her water and thought, and Meg was content to let her. It was dark now from the storm clouds, as dark as dusk, though that was hours away. The rain began to fall, a few drops at first, then it was like something broke in the sky and the water poured down, pummeling the roof, slashing at the windows. The sound seemed to start Babs out of reflection.

"If we do this," she began, cautious. "It won't be enough to show you a few moves, you'll have to train. And you must promise that you'll only use what I teach you as a last resort."

Meg squeezed her hand, the crescent of a wan smile taking form on the feline mouth, but more, Babs felt, from relief than from any jubilation.

"Thank you."

***

The zygomatic bone, the one which encloses the outer rim of the eye, was, in the case of felids, a thin protruding structure. From a fighter's point of view, it was just waiting to be caved in with a fist or elbow, and Babs had been forced to give Meg a few pops with an open hand to drive home the importance of keeping that area guarded. It was one of the reasons feline boxers were such rarities.

Meg lunged, and whatever nimbleness she possessed had abandoned her in that moment, the anxiousness and tension in her mind transferred to her muscles and stiffened them, squeezing the grace from her movement like juice from a grape. Babs slipped to the left and watched Meg sail past; she had overcommitted to the takedown attempt and was unable to stop herself. She hit the mat muzzle-first and came up with both gloves over her nose, spewing tears.

"Time!" she shouted, sounding as if she had a cold. Babs helped her to her feet.

"You ok?"

"Yeah. Let's take a break." She was panting and had been going hard for five minutes, so a breather wasn't a bad idea. They moved to the bench facing the ring in which they'd been practicing, one of three at the camp's disposal. From a room farther in, they could hear the clank of someone on one of the weight machines, and the hum of the heater, though to judge from the chill in the air, it wasn't operating at full capacity. The stink of sweat permeated the place, with hints of mildew. It was the pair's sixth session. Tonight, for whatever reason, they had the place mostly to themselves.

"Can't you go easy on me?"

"I have been."

"Well, go easier!"

Babs unstrapped her caps, the puffy variety hoofbeaters wore for training. They were ponderous things which reduced one's mobility to a frustrating degree, but the thinner type used in bouts carried far too great a risk of injury. They didn't represent the whole of the safety measures, of course; hoofbeats was notorious for its arcane rules about which kicks were legal on which parts of the body, at which times.

The matter was that she wasn't teaching Meg to do hoofbeating, which was sport, but to fend off an attacker, which was life and death. In a situation like that, there was no room for chivalry. Meg had to learn the unpleasantries of finger locks and eye strikes, of hair-pulling and tail-breaking. Otherwise, she would be forever at a disadvantage against those who knew.

"If I go any slower, I'll be standing still." In truth, Babs was tense herself. Although she handled it better than her sisters would have done, like all sheep, she felt most comfortable with a few others around for company. She had learned to accept outsiders as members of her herd, as sheep had to do to function in a mixed society, but only if she knew them well enough. That was why all their dates thus far had been at places where she was friendly with the employees.

She was still working on the discomfort that came from being separated from a larger group. Even though she had first stepped into the ring as a lamb on her school's wrestling team and was therefore at home with that sort of competition, her unrest at the empty room spoiled her flow. That could have made her rougher with Meg than she'd intended. She resolved to be more careful, though she was trying her best.

"Even so..." Meg felt along her calf, massaging it, and winced. "I don't understand how you can do this every day."

"I have to."

"No," Meg said, looking Babs in the face. "I know you worry about your sisters, but you could apply for citizenship, get on a work detail. You could provide for them without risking yourself like this."

Babs shook her head. "It's not about them. It's not about the money."

"Then what?"

"Well, it's like..." She looked down into her lap and squeezed her eyes shut. She did not speak for some time, and when she did, her words were careful and measured, as one might have spoken to inform a relative of a familial death. A lamp across the street shined through the front window and framed her in a rectangle of amber light.

"Life is always the same," she said. "There are those with power and those without. If you don't control yourself, someone else will, right? So, that's what it's about, for me. Through struggle, I learn to master my fear, my doubt. I take back the reins of my existence. And if I lose, then at least I have the scars to show that I tried." She rested her forearms against her knees and let her whole flesh sag.

"There's something else." She gritted her teeth, chasing her stoic center, the place of balance she kept inside. On an ordinary day she could have summoned it without effort, but now it was proving elusive.

"What?" Meg asked, her voice thin with worry, like a kitten's mewl.

"I can't get citizenship, I'm not eligible. You know Provision Forty-Five?"

Meg nodded, taking on a grave cast. Of course she knew, it was part of her work.

"My uncle used to hit me," Babs said, turning towards the window and clenching her jaw. Her eyes shone emerald in the streetlamp's jaundiced glow. "It was always me who got it, never my sisters, and never in front of Mom. I learned from a young age that telling on him just made it worse, so it went on for years."

A truck drove by the gym, in between Babs and the streetlight, so that a shadow overtook her features and extinguished the glow in her eyes, if only a moment.

"One day, Lydia was playing with this toy bird she had, just a cheap thing that chirped when you shook it. He had told her that he didn't want to hear it, but she forgot to switch it off and it triggered. He threw it on the ground and smashed it underhoof, then smacked her when she cried."

Babs laughed out of sheer nervousness. She could step into the ring with brawlers who trained several hours a day to pummel her face. She could do that without hesitation, but these memories had the power to demoralize her in a way that no beater ever could. She was still too close to childhood; the span of years was not so great that the wounds didn't ache afresh when she prodded them.

"Such a little thing, you know? It wasn't even that hard a slap, but I flipped out and kind of broke his shoulder with a rolling pin."

"I'm sorry," Meg said. She seemed unable to say anything else.

"Mom had us registered when we were young." Putting her hands onto the bench behind her, Babs arched her back. It popped. "You know what the application process is like. She was thinking by the time we reached working age, we'd be well along the way to citizenship. But since my uncle filed against us, it went on my record that I was prone to violent behavior. The short version is, my best options were marriage, prostitution, or combat sports. Back then I didn't draw much distinction between the first two, so I started looking for a camp."

"There must be a way to get you citizenship," Meg mused. "Maybe if I signed on as your sponsor…" She stared off into space without completing the thought. Some seconds went by before she realized Babs was peering at her.

"Does that mean you want to live together?"

"Oh!" Meg's jaw hung loose a moment, her pupils went from puddles to fine slits. She clamped her hands to her cheeks and whipped her eyes at the floor so fast that one might have thought it had burst into flames.

"No! No, no, I mean, no, but not, you know, *no*. So maybe? I was thinking about it." She nuzzled into her palms and squeaked, tail thrashing. She transferred her face to her lap, curling up like a snail to do so, and groaned miserably. Babs stroked her girlfriend's back and snickered, she couldn't help it.

"I feel the same way about you, kitten. So, maybe someday."

Meg nodded and uncurled. They sipped water for a while without speaking, enjoying their quiet respite. A few minutes later, a group of antelope bucks came in to use the space. Sleet began to fall outside. Thousands of infinitesimal shards ticked against the windowpanes and pattered on the frozen grass. The cumulative sound was a damp crackle, like the rustling of a plastic bag, but it was all-encompassing. Lightning struck; the sky rumbled like the lowing of some gigantic bull come to stomp the vestiges of civilization back into the mud.

"It's getting bad out there," Babs noted. "Let's hurry."

As they were about to make their exit, they were stopped by Otis, a russet Clydesdale about four times the size of either Meg or Babs. He must've been pushing two-hundred kilograms in weight, most of which was in his chest. He was the sort of fellow who needed to crouch and turn sideways to get through a common door and required as much maneuvering space as a forklift. His attire, a tunic and matching trousers of grey linen ("Fifteenth century accurate!" he had told her a dozen times), bespoke of a historical interest he had let bleed into his everyday life. That and the multitude of beads he wore in his hair gave him the air of a foreigner, though his twangy accent gave him away as soon as he opened his mouth.

"Got some news for you, Babs."

Meg had taken a step back. There wasn't much use for a chimera of that size in an office, so when Babs saw her take that retreating step, however subtle, she reasoned that Meg might never have seen such a large specimen up close. Citizens, those registered and permitted to live inside the safety of the walls, lead regimented lives, so it was possible that she hadn't. She put her hand on Meg's shoulder to reassure her.

"What's up, boss? Meg, this is Otis."

The Clydesdale offered his hand for Meg to shake. His enormous mitt swallowed hers when she accepted, though he gripped hers as gingerly as he would a child's.

"Pleased to meet you," he said, then returned his attention to Babs. "Need you to prep for another round of surgeries. We've got your next bout scheduled and your sponsors are buying."

***

Babs was on her side, straining against the onslaught. She thrashed and wriggled, grunting like a feral animal, but the positioning was all to her opponent's advantage and she couldn't get free.

I can't lose, she thought, clinching her teeth. *I can't!*

It was too late. She tried to turn her hips, but Meg's arms were clamped around her thighs so tight that they might as well have been bolted in place. Meanwhile, the raspy, unrelenting tongue flicked over her clitoris. These were the final steps of the deft and irresistible dance Meg had learned through trial and error over the course of many sweet, humid nights. Babs came, hard, on her lover's rough mouth, shuddering, hips bucking while her eyes clouded with the mists of euphoria, unaware of the small "mm, mm" vocalizations she was making.

"Six minutes, thirty-two seconds," Meg announced, checking her stopwatch. "At least that's one technique where I'm better than you."

"I was faking," Babs said, panting, and got grazed with a flung cushion.

"You *so* were not." Meg wriggled her way up the checkered bedspread to kiss Babs on the lips and see her face. Or maybe it was the other way 'round, since she did both, and Babs' muzzle was well-peppered by the end of it. In that moment, with the downpour pattering against the roof and darkened windows, the only other sound was what they made themselves. The mere act of drawing the curtains had shut out the rest of the world. It was as if the rain of judgement had fallen to cleanse the earth once more, while they alone had been spared, secure in the ark their mutual warmth had made. So absolute was her content that Babs was not even mindful of the distance between her and her flock. Meg must have felt similarly, as the slightest touch was enough to get a purr started up again.

Meg, at about forty-five kilos heavier than the wildcats from whose genes she had been created, had a purr like that of a cougar, a deep throbbing that Babs found she could reproduce by plucking one end of a metal ruler against the edge of a table. That exercise could not, however, replicate the vibrations that Meg gave off, which effectively turned her whole upper body into a massage pillow, or a sex toy.

She'd brought props as well, they were scattered around the mattress: beads, handcuffs, two examples of the ever-popular "novelty back massager," and Babs recalled some other items had gotten knocked to the floor. They hadn't stopped anywhere on the way to the hotel, so Meg must have had them in her gym bag the whole time.

"You planned this."

Meg shot her a devilish grin.

"I just like to be prepared. But then when Cletus said—"

"Otis," Babs corrected.

"When *Otis* said you were going to have all those surgeries, I..."

The purring stopped. Meg rolled away and sat up on the edge of the bed, the shapely back, draped with a curtain of straight, golden-brown hair, was left facing Babs. Glasses clinked.

"You want another one?"

"Sure."

Babs scooted up to rest her back against the wall, next to where Meg was, just to be touching her. They sipped room-temperature gin for a while, and Babs rubbed Meg's shoulders.

"They're going to spring for biotherapy," she offered. "They know I can't afford to be laid up in recovery when I need to be training. Not when the fight is coming so soon."

"I don't understand why you have to get them in the first place. Six surgeries just for one match..."

"It's like tuning a car," Babs said. "At strawweight, you have to account for every gram. My opponent is a low kick specialist, so it makes sense to go with lighter joints up top and put more armor in my legs."

"I suppose. But then between the surgeries and the training, you won't have much time for yourself."

By that she meant time for *her*. There was truth in the accusation, too. Already they seldom had more than a few hours a week together, and of late most of that had been devoted to training. At least Meg had improved enough to where she had something to show for her efforts, but a relationship needed to be more than that. She was glad then, and more than glad that Meg had suggested renting a room. Slipping her arms around the cat's slim, naked body, she pulled her into her chest and dappled her features with kisses of adoration from which the cat emerged chirruping.

"You won't be able to make it up to me in one night," Meg teased, tail-tip flicking at Babs' womanhood.

"No," Babs said, a smile creeping across her muzzle, "but I can try."

***

It was the first of the series, attaching support struts to the bones in her right foot (being unguligrade, this correlated with where the lower shin would be on a human, and was the portion of her leg used to check low kicks). The surgery had gone well. She was in convalescence now, quartered with seven other patients. While her sponsors had arranged a private room for her, she had shocked the staff by demanding a communal one instead. She felt well enough at ease, even if the people around her were strangers. The hospital blankets were almost white, so if she squinted, she could pretend the other patients were sheep.

The uppermost portion of the walls were also white but starting at about shoulder level they took on a yellowish hue that had not been part of the original décor. There was a monitor on either end of the room, muted, but streaming the state feed. At the moment they were on the "Terrorism Watch Minute," a fifteen-minute segment wherein they showed the faces of persons wanted by the authorities for whatever reason, the word "terrorist" having been stripped of meaning in the distant past. The threat level had been raised two levels to "turquoise," whatever the hell that meant, owing to a recent suicide photo-bombing that may or may not have really occurred.

No one was watching, but instead had their muzzles buried in their pocket monitors, texting, typing, reading, for the most part on illicit websites. The state did all it could to curtail the viewing of unapproved texts, but there were always workarounds and their dwindling supply of programmers had not the wherewithal to give their masters the information blackout they craved. Even a total shutdown of the main server complex would do little more than slow the local internet. That was one of the advantages of a distributed relay system, which had already been in use before the Overseers came to power.

It was an overcast day, and Babs, from her place in the far corner, lay looking out the window, into the roiling slate sky. The clouds were so low that, being on the second floor, she could have got her hand in them had she but opened the window and reached. Between her thumb and forefinger, she held her pocket display featuring an image of her future opponent, Chloe, a vicuna who claimed to be from the hinterlands. She was a quick, gangly fighter who had recently garnered attention for shattering another hoofbeater's knee a mere ten seconds into their match.

Babs had been watching footage of Chloe's bouts before her little sisters had stopped by to visit. They had departed again only minutes ago, so when she saw the figure in her peripheral vision, she thought it might perhaps be one of the triplets come to retrieve a forgotten item. Upon shifting her attention, she found that it was Meg, hair disheveled, cheeks matted with tears. She looked no less grey than the threatening storm.

She walked with purpose and ignored Babs' greeting while she busied herself drawing the curtain round her portion of the room. Only when it was closed did she sit on the edge of the bed and offer her hand to hold. She was trembling.

"What is it?" Babs asked. She had scooted upright.

Meg's eyes welled with tears and she gave a brisk shake of her head, regarding the curtain with distrust. She leaned in and whispered in her smallest voice.

"The new foreman, he snuck up on me and..." She sniffled and stopped to wipe her nose. "He grabbed me, and I just froze. I couldn't do anything."

With that, the tears she had been holding back came pouring out from between her eyelids, however tight she might clench them shut. It started to rain again.

"I couldn't do anything!" she cried as Babs pulled her to her chest, heedless of surgery, and cradled her head. Meg was too overwhelmed for quiet now, but repeated herself and wailed like a child realizing for the first time the unfairness of it all.

Babs' gown was sopping wet by the time she got Meg calmed down, stroking her hair and cooing. She had expected someone to complain and summon a nurse, but no one came. Minutes passed. They lay there amidst the drumming of the raindrops, the faint stirs of her roommates going about their business, and Meg's incessant sniffling. Every so often, she blew her nose.

"It's funny," she said, startling Babs out of her thoughts. "The things you remember sometimes. Did you have a crush when you were little?"

Babs thought about it, then shook her head. "I don't think so. None that I remember."

"I did. We had this framed print, thing must've been three-hundred years old, of a horse. Not a chimera, mind you, a wild horse. And I loved him. I wanted to be his wife, galloping around, eating grass, living out in the open, free. Just something I would daydream about, stupid kitten that I was. But now I can't stop thinking about it. I wish I still had that picture."

Babs gave her a squeeze. "I doubt you were ever stupid," she said. "I understand." In fact, she wasn't sure if she did. It seemed impossible, but might a younger Meg have longed for an existence beyond the onerous safety of the walls, the impositions of her society, without knowing it? And if so, might she long for that still?

"I don't know what to do," Meg said, looking downward. "I can file a complaint, but the block coordinator has ultimate control there."

"For now, you and the other girls need to start going about in twos or threes as much as you can. Don't let anyone go off alone if you can help it. And I think I need to have a little talk with your foreman."

Meg clenched her paws into fists and flared her nostrils. "You have to be a citizen to enter that part of the city. Besides, that wouldn't fix anything."

Babs cocked an eyebrow and flexed her arms. "I could fix *him*, at least. What's his name?"

Meg sighed and looked away.

"Well?"

There was no reply. She must not have wanted to talk about this anymore, which was understandable. Babs kissed the ends of Meg's ears. They flicked.

"Sorry, kitten."

A while later, Meg began to purr. Her hand crept under the blanket and up Babs' gown, who squirmed in response.

"Ok, this is weird, and we shouldn't—"

Meg shushed her, fingering between her thighs like a harpist on her preferred instrument. "Please, just let me. I'll be quick, but I need this, please." She repositioned and took the blankets by one corner and flung them aside, then nuzzled her way in-between Babs' thighs.

On some level, Babs recognized that what was happening was not born of lust, but of a desire on Meg's part to reclaim a degree of power, of control, which she felt had been taken from her. While Babs held the upper hand in defense training, it had always been Meg who ruled the bedroom. Now, in the wake of this vile intrusion she had suffered, she meant to reassert her sovereignty, as a monarch might have done in the wake of an indecisive coup.

The rest of the patients were off in their own worlds, so why not? A pleasant fire building in her loins, so fast she had scarcely noticed its kindling, all but ensured she would take the risk of getting caught. In the moment she had scant notion that this might even offend anyone, owing to her privacy-free upbringing. Hands tangled in her lover's hair, she rode her unrelenting mouth to climax, crying out a single time before catching the sound in her throat.

There was a series of echoing staccato pops, like firecrackers, which she at first mistook as coming from inside her head, from the rush of her violent release. As the haze cleared she felt Meg disengage. She looked down to find her staring back with stiff ears and pupils fine as razors, ears blanched white with fear.

"Just a drive-by," Babs said, laying a steady palm on her Meg's cheek. "Nothing to worry about."

"What? Shouldn't we hide?"

Babs laughed, almost a chuff. "Probably. We're used to it, though. They might lock the doors, but for the most part people just go on about their business soon as the smoke clears."

"That's horrible!"

"Oh, I agree. Yet, here we are." She realized that Meg was trembling again. The frightened eyes melted her heart and she opened her arms. "Come up here, kitten."

She clutched her against her chest again, cooing and smoothing her fur. She didn't understand how Meg could be alarmed so much by a shooting when it was her side who produced the guns in the first place, but the poor thing had already had a bad enough day without dragging politics into it. So, she held her there, petting her hair and scratching behind her ear until she got a purr going.

They shared what would be their last kiss for almost two months.

***

They had a decent crowd, judging by the clattering footsteps of the mostly ungulate attendance, which echoed from the cavernous arena into the converted office that now served as her changing room. It wasn't a true stadium, but the hull of a factory and its affixed business quarters, now given for rent to whoever might use the space, however unsavory. It had seen raves and porno shoots, chop-shops and, according to a persistent legend, any number of gangsters-turned-informants sealed into metal drums and buried alive on site. However, it spent most of its time as a windbreak for the homeless, as evidenced by a proliferation of graffiti and worn-out syringes. She'd fought in worse venues, though this one stank of urine more than most.

Babs' sisters, in Greek chorus mode, chanted:

"Weeks since she heard from her steadfast sweetheart,

Doubting her life, now she struggles to reach baseline."

"—baseline," Phoebe finished.

Babs flinched, stopping midmotion. That her sisters be allowed to visit her backstage, and to watch the fight from where she could see them, had been stipulated in her contract. This was one of the times she wished it hadn't been. And the play had come and gone, so didn't the theater want its cloaks back?

"Thanks, girls, you nailed it."

Otis the Clydesdale, in his best medieval regalia, hurried the four lambs out, either sensing Babs' annoyance or else because it was close to starting time. Evan, a greying elk and one of her coaches, was putting the last of the tape on her gloves/wrist protectors.

"You're a badass," he said, his rough voice somehow managing to qualify as a shout and a mumble all at once. "That's right girl, you're a badass! Yeah!"

"Hmm?" Babs looked at him blankly. "Oh, ah, right. Yeah." He had only been trying to get her psyched up for the fight, but, truth be told, she didn't feel like fighting. She didn't feel like doing much of anything. Where the hell was Meg? Why wouldn't she answer her calls?

"Close your eyes," Otis said from behind. It was time to put on her mask. It wouldn't do to have a competitor's face streamed onto the internet for the authorities to see, after all. Her cropped, bristly fur scraped the Lycra as Otis slid it over her muzzle. Some fighters spent a small fortune decorating their masks, which became a part of their persona, but Babs' was pure function, charcoal with a wide green band in honor of her camp's chosen colors. It left the end of her muzzle protruding. Next, he put in her mouthpiece.

"I know you're worried about your mate," Otis said, coming around to rest his huge hands or her shoulders. He looked her in the face. "But we need you to put it out of your mind for now. Keep your head in the game or that woman is going to wreck you."

"That woman" was none other than her opponent, Chloe the vicuna, who billed herself as being from the far west, but around whom there swirled a maelstrom of rumor. She had dark connections with the state intelligence service, it was said, and was the subject of classified technologies and high-level genetic engineering. Some of it may have been true but was more likely a marketing ploy.

Babs wasn't afraid of fighting Chloe, who was mortal flesh and thus could be vanquished, but she was terrified where it came to Meg and Meg's silence. Weeks it had been since that day at the hospital, without so much as an email. Her mind educed new horrors at every chance: Meg had been assaulted or killed by her foreman, or she had been kidnapped on the way to pay her a surprise visit or had been stripped of citizenship and cast out at the edge of the slums, lost and penniless. Most horrifying of all, she imagined that Meg had simply grown tired of her and gone on with her life. Her faith in Meg, however, was such that she could never quite convince herself of this, no matter how she despaired.

But despite that faith, she had thus far failed to shake off her disquiet. That apprehension was an opponent more than her match, one she could neither seize nor fend off with blows, who penetrated her guard with supernatural ease. She had been wrestling it all this time and was no nearer to victory than she'd been the first moment she had realized something was wrong. And yet the depths had failed to swallow her entirely, and now a thought emerged like a lantern against the darkness:

The prize money.

The night's purse was not an insubstantial sum. If Meg was in trouble, she would find out the how and where. There had to be a way. If she won, then she would have enough to hire someone to investigate, a hacker, maybe. She would play the part of a mercenary if that meant seeing Meg again. It was all that was left for her to do.

Something stiffened in her then, her eyes cleared and her doubts scattered like straw before a windstorm, crushed by the certainty of her mission, vaporized and let drift into the heavens. A smile spread across Otis' elongate face.

"Damn," Evan said, and whistled. "Ice cold." He and Otis exchanged a knowing look, then it was time to make their way to the ring.

The crowd, as mentioned earlier, was a big one, but still less than a thousand people, and those only by invitation: the bulk comprised industry insiders and high-rollers. While hoofbeats was not a primary target for law enforcement, it wasn't legal, either, so most of the audience streamed the event with a special keycode, purchased in advance, which could also be used for discreet gambling. The ring itself was lit in such a way as to deliberately obscure the attendees, while the doctor and judges looked like yuppie executioners in their black hoods and office wear. The referee and announcer resembled nothing so much as kabuki theater stage hands. Draped in black from head to foot, their attire revealed nothing, not a centimeter of fur. An observer would not even have been able to discern the length of their tails. Even their footwear, which might otherwise have revealed their phenotypes, was molded in such a way as to obfuscate the contours of the hooves inside.

Chloe was well down the aisle ahead of her, heading for the weigh-in and scan. The audience applauded, some stamped their feet or whistled, but that was the extent of the fanfare. There was no music, and the announcer was what one might term "utilitarian." Staff checked the vicuna over to make sure her gloves and hoofcaps were regulation, that her mask and headgear were tied to their satisfaction. The cheering settled to a quiet bustle. Something about the building, its high, lightless ceiling and rusted catwalks, seemed to deaden any clamor that arose.

She cleared the weigh-in and stepped into the scanner, a machine the size of a wardrobe. With its twin, gleaming-white panels, it looked like a cross between a refrigerator and a waffle iron. The ring lights dimmed when they switched it on.

The doctor crouched over the display, spectacles reflecting the screen through the eyeholes in his hood. He was looking for contraband, anything that might breach one of hoofbeats' most sacred tenets: that unnatural weaponization of the limb was prohibited. Whether by the addition of studs or spikes, internal or external, or through power return in the form of motors, springs, hydraulics, artificial muscle fibers or any other such mechanism, the rule against unnatural weaponization was absolute. Violation meant a permanent ban.

The scan wasn't perfect. Certain models of replacement joints, for instance, could be modified to accommodate and conceal a micronized torsion spring assembly that, when armed, would then whip the forelimb at prodigious speeds. The potential ban was oftentimes the least of the worries for those who used such devices, since a critical failure, as was wont to happen in a sport like hoofbeats, could blow out the back of their limb like a miniature grenade. Still, the profits were enticing enough that there were always a few fighters willing to take the risk.

Scan complete, Chloe hauled her lanky frame in through the ropes and paced the ring, stopping here and there to jog in place or throw a few punches, warming up her muscles. Babs was doing much the same as she waited at the gate to make her own entrance. From her point of view, every other person in the arena had vanished, except for Chloe. She watched the way she moved, as intent on her target as a dog on a piece of meat. The vicuna was taller than she was and swung with a deceptive sluggishness that belied the aggressive style Babs had seen in the videos she'd studied again and again.

"Babs? Babs?"

"Hm?" The rest of the world bled back into her awareness. It was Otis speaking.

"Remember the plan. We need you to start orthodox. She goes southpaw, use the jab and the left low kick. She goes orthodox, you wait for her to throw that power kick, take her to the ground. You get her down, you own her."

A hooded chimera to one side gave them a nod.

"That's us," Otis said, and they marched down the aisle.

She got through the weigh-in without any trouble. As she stood in the scanner, the lines of bright green light playing over her body, her mind turned once more to Meg. It would be alright, she would find out what happened, they would be together again. All she had to do was what she had come here to do. She made herself believe it, to do otherwise was to give herself over to doubt. That would flood her bloodstream with the material components of fear: adrenaline and cortisol, which would make her stiff where she needed to be loose and springy.

"*Wait for me, kitten,*" she thought, then shut the matter out of her consciousness. Once she had the go-ahead, she clomped up the steel steps and into the ring.

The announcer, in a voice suggestive of narcolepsy, went through his spiel. Hoofbeaters used pseudonyms so as not to bring the authorities on themselves; Chloe's ring name was "The Vicunannihilator," which was so bad it made half the audience groan when they heard it, whereas Babs went by "Shauna." She liked to think at least one or two people got the reference.

The other persons in the ring faded into shadows, only Chloe stood out from the rest in sharp detail. They locked eyes and now neither could look away without giving the other a psychological advantage. Striding to the center of the ring, they stared one another down as the referee went over the ground rules. Neither leant him more than half an ear. When it came time to return to their corners, Babs offered her gloves for the ceremonial tap, but Chloe walked away backwards without offering hers in turn. That was as an insult meant to get under Babs' skin. It didn't. She mouthed the word "bitch" and hoped Chloe could read lips. To judge by the glare she got in response, she could.

The bell rang and the two advanced, feeling each other out with jabs and low kicks, none of which connected. She could discern something of Chloe's status from her motions, the way she seemed to float over the mat like fog, not quick, but graceful and easy. It was time to turn up the pressure and change that. She remembered Theo the goat, her school's wrestling coach, saying that in their world "scared" and "defeated" were synonyms.

Chloe put her right leg up, as though for a snap kick, but appeared to think better of it and cancel halfway, then changed to the orthodox stance, left hand forward, right leg back. From watching Chloe's previous fights, Babs knew she was setting up for a power kick, probably to the lower leg. She didn't intend to let her do it, she circled to Chloe's left and threw a looping hook, as much to block her field of vision as anything. Chloe, though, had anticipated this and twisted her hips and torso, her whole being, into a roundhouse, one that Babs would have been able to avoid had it not come in a flash, like a gunshot.

The hoof connected with her left foot and she was glad of the reinforcement on her bones, as there was no question that they would have shattered without it. Although she wasn't yet aware of it, the sheer force of the blow had split her skin open. Meanwhile, her hook had landed, but only glanced the vicuna's snout and done no damage.

"*She has a spring in her right leg,*" she thought, backing Chloe off with a jab. "*She feints a snap kick to wind it. She arms it when she changes stance.*" And she smiled, because from that moment on, the only way Chloe could hope to win was to stop using the cheat. They continued to circle, sniping at one another's knees. Babs, the more experienced of the two, kept even tempo, waiting to see if her suppositions would be affirmed. As she predicted, Chloe's leg came up, went back down.

"Now!"

In mixed martial arts, predictability is death. When Chloe shifted the weight onto her leg to arm the mechanism, she had unknowingly backed herself into a corner. She now couldn't take a step with the full range of motion in that leg without triggering the spring, which would throw her off-balance. She could pivot on that hoof, or shift her weight again to disarm it, or she could throw a kick. But she could not take a step, and that was her undoing. When Babs, "Shauna" to her mind, juked to the side, she threw in precisely the same fashion she had before, a low snap kick meant to connect on or near the wound.

But Babs had been expecting it. Rather than check the kick with her foot, she lifted her leg over the kick completely and, leaning in, planted a clean right jab on Chloe's nose. It wasn't the kind of punch that would knock a person out, but sent pain surging through the sinuses, and that, in turn, flooded her tear ducts.

Half-blind and tasting panic, Chloe cocked her spring again in desperation, which only made her situation worse. This time, Babs rushed in before she could get the kick off; when it triggered, the sheep was already in too close for it to matter. She tried to push Babs away, but she was on her like glue, looking for the take-down.

Arms around Chloe's waist, she dropped her center of gravity and suplexed her onto the ground. With the vicuna's long limbs, not to mention the slight hooves that afforded her precious little ground contact, she offered next to no resistance. Now Babs, a wrestler first and foremost, was in her element. She mounted Chloe's side and rained fists and elbows onto her face, the only response to which was sightless, ineffectual groping. The Vicunannihilator had lost her head and with it, the match. Another moment and the referee forced his way in-between them, waving off the bout. It was a win via TKO for a fighter not being able to "intelligently defend," still the rule in mixed martial arts after more than three-hundred years.

Only when she went to take her victory lap around the ring did she realize she was bleeding everywhere, which was probably why the doctor kept trying to get her to sit down. Chloe was standing again, and apart from a thin trickle of blood from her nose, looked no worse for wear. When she saw Babs, her mouth wilted into a pout, like a sullen child. In a way, Babs pitied her. Chloe's build was well-suited to the sort of fighting she did, and she moved well, but so long as she relied on her cheat, her development would always be limited. And that was assuming she didn't get banned somewhere along the way. A few words with her manager were called for, in any case, but that could wait.

Pain shot up from her foot of a sudden and she went down onto one knee, finally understanding what the doctor had wanted to check. Although the graphene reinforcement held the bone together, a powerful enough shock could still cause innumerable hairline fractures in the gaps of the lattice. Her foot had broken under that first kick, but only now, with the excitement past, could she feel it.

***

The first thing Babs did when she got out of the hospital was to poke around looking for a hacker, but given the legality of their profession, she assumed it would involve more than a casual web search. It was two days later when she got the email.

The subject line was, *"I'm back."* The body of the email read, *"I have much to tell you. Can we meet somewhere? I'm sorry."* It was from Meg.

So, when Babs later asked herself how she ended up walking on crutches to a café at four in the morning, she had a pretty good idea of the answer.

Meg had changed so much, Babs almost didn't recognize her. The bones of her face showed clear through her fur, and her long hair was gone, shorn down almost to the scalp. Her tail dangled limp from her seat, like a hastily-hung scarf about to slip onto the floor. The brilliant green eyes were sunken into her head; when they came to rest on Babs, they filled with tears. Babs had been on the verge of crying herself, and when she saw that, it was enough to put her over the edge. They embraced there beside the table, weeping in something close to silence.

"I'm ok," Meg said, over and over. "I'm ok."

"What happened?" They took their seats, hands entwined in the middle of the table.

"I was in jail. That guy tried to grab me again. At first, I pushed him off, but he kept coming. I got hold of his fingers," she said, and tugged her hands free to reenact the motion, indicating the pinkie and ring fingers. "Pulled them back 'til he screamed."

"So," Babs began, but Meg interrupted.

"So, he flipped it around and said that I was the one who attacked him, and they arrested me." Meg's bitter tone sank like a weight through Babs' chest and abdomen, where it settled in her belly like soured milk.

"God."

"But I had gotten into the habit of leaving my smart glasses on 're-cord.' I think he must have realized it, because they vanished from the evidence room. But the data was already on the cloud. My sister uploaded it to her blog. It went viral."

"They let you go."

Meg kept her gaze trained on the table refusing to make eye-contact. "Eventually. The block coordinator released a statement on sexual assault and said the foreman was to be dismissed. Word is he just got transferred, though. And now the coordinator has the new foreman breathing down my neck, looking for an excuse to get rid of me." She sighed, clutching her weary head in her paws. "If I get demoted, I'll go down to 'menial.' Below that, it's euthanasia. I don't know what I'm going to do."

"You could come live with me," Babs said, giving her lip an anxious lick and leaning forward. "Convert your credits to something tangible, disable your infotack so they can't track you. People do it all the time." She remembered the story Meg had told her about the old photograph and quipped, "You could be like the stallion in your picture."

Meg smiled, weakly, but it was a true one, devoid of irony. She closed her eyes, imagining the beating of wild hooves, and her smile broadened like light on the dawn horizon.

***

Babs had been surprised at how easy it was to find a hacker, and even more by the reasonable prices. The amount a person could learn from a subject's data usage was staggering. A hacker in this day and age, she mused, was far better than a private investigator. True, it was a significant portion of her winnings to spend on an indulgence like this, but she hadn't spoiled herself in a while and felt it due.

She tugged a blonde wig over her head and checked the mirror to make sure it was on straight, then adjusted her corset. The faux dominatrix outfit, assembled piecemeal from her grandmother's articles, looked close enough to the real thing for her purposes. This wasn't going to be a photo shoot.

There was a knock at the door, which would be Owen, serial number 81819200, foreman and sexual predator. Meg had been right that Babs wouldn't be able to enter the city to confront him, but there was nothing to stop her if he should happen to leave, as he did every Saturday night to visit his mistress.

"It's open."

He paused, not recognizing the voice, but came in all the same. He was a cur with a splotchy red and black coat, taller than Babs, and perhaps twice as heavy, but soft and slow, like a newborn puppy. She popped her knuckles.

"Who are you? Where's Damara?" he asked.

"I'm Shauna, Damara's friend. She's a bit tied up in the bathroom at the moment, but if you're willing to give me a chance, I promise I'll work you over like you've never had done before."

He looked her up and down, then licked his lips and nodded. "Alright, little lamb, I'll play your game."

"Lock the door, then," she said. "I can't wait to get started."

The Church Mouse

Madison Keller

Anise tottered up to the votive candles, leaning heavily on her cane. The old mouse fumbled with the matches for a moment before getting one to catch. She lit a candle with a shaky paw. Then she bowed her head, closed her eyes, and whispered a brief prayer under her breath for her partner of forty years, dead as of one year ago today.

"Chandra, may the Lord watch your spirit. I miss you." Her large, round ears flattened, and her whiskers twitched in grief. A single tear rolled off her muzzle. Since Chandra's death, Anise's soft, white fur had become matted and her bones showed through her skin from weight loss. Without Chandra, it had been hard for Anise to find a reason to do day-to-day activities like brush her fur or eat.

The candle she'd lit flared up, the light searing her vision. Smoke from the votive candles began to burn her eyes, and Anise turned away, almost stepping on her own tail in her haste.

Might as well go to confession while she was here. Anise tottered up the nave between the empty pews. The old mouse stopped every few steps, as much to admire the old stained-glass windows of the savior in his mouse aspect that lined the hall, as to lean over on her cane, gathering energy for the next few shuffling steps. The floorboards creaked a familiar rhythm under her claws. Her sensitive nose twitched, detecting the lingering fragrance of incense from yesterday's ceremony overlaying the smell of dust and aged wood.

Eventually, she reached the confession booth. She tucked her cane under one arm as she slid open the door. The wood paneling clattered together, comforting and familiar. The sensation lasted only as long as it took her old eyes to penetrate the gloom inside the booth and for the coppery tang of blood to slap at her nose.

A body slumped over on the bench, white fur stained red. The tip of the mouse's naked tail rested in the center of a small puddle of blood.

Anise's eyes ran up and down the body, unable to comprehend the sight before her. She let out a disbelieving squeak, and then another.

The door on the other side of the confessional booth opened with a click. "Ma'am?" the soft voice of the pastor called. Claws ticked on wood. "Is everything all right? I heard—" He gasped.

Anise staggered back, eyes never leaving the corpse. Her cane clattered to the floor. Her back claw caught on the sanctuary steps and she fell back heavily against them. Her short hairless tail came up between her skirts, the end flicking wildly in her distress.

The pastor dropped down on the steps beside her, clutching the wooden cross that hung from his neck tightly in one paw. With his other paw he crossed himself. "God save us." His eyes were fastened on the body.

Anise didn't respond. Her eyes never left the corpse's face. A face she was intimately familiar with.

"Who is it?" the pastor squeaked, his voice breaking.

Anise's heart pounded in her chest and her breaths came out in short, harsh bursts. Anise shook her head, unable to respond to the pastor's question.

The pastor turned his muzzle towards her, his eyes wide. "Ms. Pentti!"

He scrambled to his feet, claws gouging the polished wood of the sanctuary in his haste. She heard his claws clicking away from her, the bang of the rectory door, and then a moment later in the distance heard him shouting into the phone about heart attacks, dead bodies, and ambulances.

Her face never turned, her eyes never wavered from the corpse. The young mouse had died a violent death. The blue eyes were open and staring, staring straight into Anise's own. Those eyes she'd seen in the mirror countless times over her long life. The cowlick between her ears, the one she plastered down with gel every morning to keep flat, was curling up now between the dead mouse's round ears.

Anise stared into her own face, dead in the confessional booth.

***

The wail of an approaching siren broke Anise from her stupor. She sat up on the steps and lowered her head between her knees, gasping. The fabric of her skirt pressed against her muzzle. The familiar smell enveloped her and helped to bring her back to herself by slow degrees. Gradually she became aware of the presence of others around her.

Someone was saying, "ma'am, ma'am, can you hear me?"

"Yes. I'm fine now." Anise lifted her head and blinked at the paramedic, a large brown mouse wearing a bright blue jacket. Her pastor stood in the aisle behind the ambulance personnel wringing his paws together, his nose twitching nervously.

"We're just going to take you outside to the ambulance and make sure," the paramedic said in a soothing tone.

Anise nodded and allowed the paramedic mice to lift her onto a rolling stretcher. They wheeled her down the aisle, bodily lifting the stretcher down the stairs to the street. Once at the ambulance, they checked her blood pressure, took her temperature, and asked her a series of questions about her name, age, allergies, and such, noting down everything in their tablets.

Despite being midday on a Monday morning in the middle of a mostly residential neighborhood, the flashing lights of the cop cars had already attracted a small crowd of mice, rats, squirrels, skunks, and stoats. Anise peered past the paramedics. Patrolmen were unrolling crime scene tape around the church doors. A black rat deputy, the badge pinned to his chest sparkling in the bright morning sunlight, spoke with the pastor on the sidewalk a few feet away.

A paramedic, the brown mouse who'd spoken to her in the church, cleared his throat. "Well, Ms. Pentti, you seem to be fine from what we can tell. However, we do recommend that you let us take you in to the ER for further tests. You received quite a shock in there and at your age..."

The young mouse trailed off to silence, leaving the rest unspoken but still ringing loud and clear. *At your age, you are a delicate fucking flower, to be coddled and swaddled like a baby,* she thought. Anise rolled her eyes.

"Thank you. No, I'm fine."

She threw off the blanket they'd thrown over her and swung her legs over the side of the stretcher. Before the paramedic could protest, she slid off and onto her feet. Anise strode away, ignoring the protestations of the paramedic behind her.

"You forgot your cane, ma'am!"

Anise stopped dead in her tracks, blinking down at her empty paws and then at her legs. The pain that normally wracked her knees and legs was gone. She swished her tail in irritation as she turned to accept her cane from the helpful medic. She really wanted to check on the poor pastor, but she was still shaken from finding her younger self dead, not to mention the strange lack of pain in her legs. So instead she hurried away.

For the medic's benefit, she pretended to use the cane until she made it around the corner out of his view. Then she clutched it to her chest and sped up. Her apartment building came into view a scant few minutes later. This morning on the way to the church it had taken her over half an hour to hobble that same distance.

***

Anise came in through her front door and carefully hung her keys on the hook before tossing her cane into the corner. As she entered the living room, the pictures sitting on the mantle caught her eye. Something about them seemed different, but as she moved closer the rattle of dishes from the kitchen startled her. No one else should be here; since Chandra's death she'd lived alone.

"Hello?" she called, wishing she hadn't thrown her cane away from her. She crept backward, heart pounding, feeling behind herself for a weapon. "Who's there?"

Chandra, as real as life, appeared in the kitchen doorway holding a tray of steaming cinnamon rolls in oven-mitt encased paws. Her brown fur shone in the sunlight coming in through the windows, the little splotch of white fur on her chest just visible above the cut of her blouse. She looked just like she had the last time Anise had seen her.

Anise's eyes widened, her ears flared, and her tail swished back and forth behind her widely, knocking a framed picture of them together at a local street fair off the side table beside her. It hit the floor, the glass smashing against the hardwood floor with a spectacular crash, sending glass shards in every direction.

"What?" Anise managed to gasp.

"Oh, I'm so sorry." Chandra set the tray down on the dining room table and peeled off the oven mitts. Her black eyes sparkled, letting Anise know that she wasn't angry about the broken glass. "I didn't mean to startle you," she said.

"Chandra!" she finally managed to croak out. Her front paws twitched nervously; she stopped herself from rubbing them through the fur at her throat only with an effort. "But, you're dead."

"Dead?" Chandra stopped in the act of pulling a broom out of the hall closet, concern etched in the set of her pointed muzzle. She looked over at Anise's cane lying in the corner, a smile flitted briefly across her face. "So, today is the day," she whispered, mostly to herself, her paws tightening on the broom handle as she swept up the mess. She put the broom away, and then knelt briefly in front of her bhakti shrine in the corner of the room.

Anise stepped back to give her privacy but couldn't tear her eyes from Chandra's form. She'd missed her lover so much that it hurt to not rush into her arms right then and there.

When she was done Chandra stood and turned to Anise. "Are you feeling alright?"

Anise shook her head and her muzzle split in a grin. "Yes, I'm wonderful." She danced lightly across the room and swept Chandra up in her arms, spun her about, and bent her down into a perfect ballroom dip that left them muzzle to muzzle. Chandra smelled just as Anise remembered, overlaid by sugar and cinnamon from her recent bout of cooking. No impostor then, this was Chandra, living and breathing, alive again by some miracle.

"So frisky," Chandra giggled and then licked Anise's muzzle affectionately. "Were your morning prayers so enlightening?"

"No, I've just missed you." Anise finished the dip and straightened, but kept her arms around her lover.

"You were gone all of an hour." Chandra leaned forward and gave Anise a peck on the cheek. From the kitchen a timer buzzed. She brushed her whiskers along Anise's muzzle as she pulled away. "I need to get those out before they burn."

As Chandra turned away Anise reached out and playfully grabbed her butt. Chandra giggled and gently flicked Anise's paw with the tip of her long tail from around the corner as she disappeared back into the kitchen.

Anise skipped after her. Who cared if the cinnamon rolls burned, she didn't want to miss a moment with Chandra, lest she wake from the glorious daydream. But before she reached the kitchen the doorbell rang. Anise sighed and walked over to the door. Right before she opened it she remembered to grab her cane and lean on it.

The door opened to reveal two massive brown rats dressed in perfectly pressed black suits. Her apartment building was mixed-species, both rats and mice, so the hallways were tall enough to accommodate their height, but just barely. The tips of their naked, pointed ears brushed the ceiling of the hall.

Anise kept her round ears rigid and upright, but her paws were trembling. Rats like these were government enforcers.

"Can I help you?" Anise squeaked.

In response both rats reached into their jackets and pulled out police badges. The leftmost one spoke. "I'm Detective Boom and this," he gestured to the rat on his right, identical almost in every way but for a notch on his muzzle, "is Detective Gruenhut. Can we come in?"

"Oh, of course, detectives." Anise limped aside, opening the door wide.

The two rats filed inside. They didn't sit, preferring to stand in the living room, looking at the pictures. Chandra appeared with a tray of steaming rolls, offering one cheerfully to each detective. They both declined, although their twitching whiskers gave away their interest.

"Detectives, this is my roommate, Chandra," Anise said, hobbling back into the living room.

Chandra gave a little nod to each of the rats, who gave her polite smiles in return. She set the tray down on the table and dusted some flour from her skirt, while shooting Anise a quizzical look.

"The detectives are here about the dead girl I found in the church this morning."

Chandra gave a little start and a squeak of surprise, her ears flattening to her head. "I'll just leave you to it then." With that she turned and scurried back into the kitchen.

Anise was grateful for the heavy smell of baked goods in the air that smothered the stench of fear that would be coming off both her and Chandra.

"Please, have a seat." Anise followed this up by sinking down into her favorite spot on the loveseat.

However, rather than sitting the rats continued looming about the room. Detective Gruenhut went over and picked up one of the framed pictures from the mantle. He held it up and squinted at it, snickered, and then passed it to his partner. Detective Boom laughed out loud.

Anise racked her brain trying to remember what pictures were on the mantel and why they might be funny but couldn't think of what they might be looking at. They deliberately kept the pictures in the living room bland, things like her grandpup's school photos.

Boom grinned and shook his head. "Where's this park at? I'd love to take my pups." He flipped the picture around to show it to Anise.

Anise had to stare at it for a long moment. It wasn't a picture she'd ever seen before. The picture showed her and Chandra riding a dinosaur, horns, frills and all. Chandra had a big grin on her muzzle and was holding a frilled parasol. The dino was in a running pose, their dresses were flapping, and their fur was plastered back, as if they really were moving fast.

"Ah," Anise stammered. "I don't remember."

Chandra bustled in with a tray of tea and teacups. She set the tray down on the coffee table, winking at Anise as she bent over, putting her back to the two suited rats. She straightened and smoothed her skirt. "Oh, that was in Ramoji Film City in Hyderabad."

The two rats blinked blankly at Chandra. So did Anise. She'd always wanted to take trips with Chandra as a couple. The entire idea made her heart ache at the fact that they had to keep their relationship secret from both their families.

"I'm from India. I went back to Telangana to visit my family, and Anise came along with me on holiday. Ramoji is where they film many of the Bollywood films." Chandra lifted the teapot. "Tea, anyone?"

Anise's head spun. That was a complete lie on Chandra's part. Yet, Anise could not explain the picture. This entire day just kept getting stranger.

Boom set the picture back on the mantel. "Yes, thank you," he said.

The two rats wedged themselves into the two wooden mice-sized rocking chairs while Chandra served them. Anise's china cups looked tiny in their massive paws.

Detective Boom took a sip of his tea and then lowered it. "Did you recognize the girl you found at the church today?"

Anise took a sip of her own tea, trying to think of what she should say. Thankfully, Chandra provided an excellent distraction by sitting down on the loveseat next to Anise

"Excuse me, who are you again?" Detective Gruenhut asked.

"Chandra Muni. We met in college. After Anise's husband died, she was raising three little pups all by herself and I moved in to help her out. We've been roommates ever since." Chandra gave an open muzzled smile.

"Ah." Detective Gruenhut narrowed his black eyes, staring down his long muzzle at Chandra.

Detective Boom, apparently playing the good cop today, gave a smile and continued his questions. By then Anise had settled on her story.

"Did you recognize the doe?" Detective Boom asked gently.

Anise shook her head, although her whiskers twitched, giving away her distress. "No, I'm sorry, detectives."

"She does look a lot like you," Detective Gruenhut said. "A family resemblance, if I'm not mistaken. Sure she isn't a niece or distant relative?"

Anise shrugged. Only when Chandra put a paw over her clasped fists did Anise realize she was shaking. "I know all my nieces, she isn't one of them." Anise kept her tone neutral. She was trying to keep from lying outright to the detectives.

***

After the two detectives were gone and Anise had shut and dead bolted the door behind them, she allowed herself to relax.

Chandra was in the kitchen, carefully washing the delicate china teacups. Anise came up behind her and wrapped her arms around the other woman from behind and pecked a kiss on one of her rounded ears. Chandra leaned back against Anise, lifting her butt to press the base of her tail firmly against Anise's crotch. Anise giggled as the tip of Chandra's tail snaked its way up her skirt and swatted her butt.

"You smell divine," Anise said, burying her nose in the ruff of fur at Chandra's neck. The cinnamon, sugar, and dough scent mixed with turmeric and Chandra's own natural musk to form an intoxicating scent. She let her paws drift down over Chandra's stomach and then lower, tracing a claw in a lazy circle around Chandra's crotch over the skirt's fabric. Anise still felt as if she was in a dream, but she was determined to enjoy every second of it while it lasted.

"Careful, *jaana*. I don't want to break the china." The china teacups tinkled together as Chandra brought out a paw to flick soapy water onto Anise's nose and muzzle.

Anise leaned close and began nibbling on the edge of one of Chandra's small, rounded ears. Chandra squeaked and wrapped her tail around Anise's leg.

"Leave the dishes," Anise whispered.

Chandra pulled a paw out of the water to rub the curl of longer fur between Anise's ears. Soapy water dripped down on her face, but she didn't care.

"I already started, so I may as well finish." Chandra said as she removed her paw and went back to washing.

"I have a better idea," Anise murmured. "You keep washing dishes and I'll keep you entertained."

Anise slid down Chandra's back until she knelt behind her, then draped Chandra's skirt over her head. A few quick nips of her front teeth shredded Chandra's underwear, and the scraps of fabric fell forgotten to the linoleum. She buried her muzzle in Chandra's bottom, licking and teasing. She reached one paw up between Chandra's legs and began running a finger around Chandra's now-exposed labia. Meanwhile, she shook her other arm free of the skirt and reached up to caress Chandra's breasts, teasing at the nipple through the fabric of her shirt and bra. Chandra shuddered with pleasure.

Paws shaking, Chandra picked up a cup and carefully scrubbed it while Anise fingered Chandra's labia, running her fingers up and down the opening. She waited until Chandra rinsed the teacup and placed it in the drying rack before parting the folds of skin with her ring and index fingers, soaking her middle finger when she placed it inside. She traced small circles around Chandra's clit, occasionally flicking the bundle of nerves.

Chandra thrust her butt back into Anise's muzzle and Anise used the movement to tighten her tail around Chandra's leg. The fingers of her other paw continued to rub Chandra's nipple while she teased the nub of Chandra's clit.

Grasping the edge of the sink with her breaths coming in ragged gasps, Chandra had given up all pretense of washing dishes. Anise could feel Chandra's wet desire slicking her pads, so she adjusted her paw, cupping her fingers to slip them up inside Chandra. Her thumb stroked the clit while she drove three of her fingers in and out of Chandra with increasing intensity. Anise lapped at Chandra's vulva, running her tongue along the sensitive skin and then up around the tight, puckered flesh of her anus.

A moan from Chandra turned into a shriek of pleasure as Chandra's vagina spasmed around Anise's fingers.

***

The next morning, Anise woke Chandra with sweet kisses. A year of waking to a cold bed left her even more appreciative of what she'd been missing. They had sex again, this time with Chandra on top, and then lay for over an hour snuggling together in the bed.

Much later, Chandra finally dragged them out of bed, first she said her daily morning prayers at her shrine and then made them a big pancake breakfast topped with strawberries from their window box.

"So, why'd you lie to those detectives, *jaanu?*" Chandra asked as they were washing the breakfast dishes.

Anise's paws started trembling and she dropped the dish she was drying. The plate smashed on the floor.

"Ah, I didn't mean to startle you." Chandra grabbed the broom and began sweeping up the pieces.

"How did you know I was lying? Oh, god, did those detectives know, too?" Anise leaned on the counter.

"No, well, yes, but it's complicated." Chandra dumped the contents of the dustpan into the garbage. "Do you want to talk about it?"

"I-I'll sound crazy." Anise picked back up the hand towel and began drying the pan.

"I assure you, you won't." Chandra put the broom back in the closet, brushing Anise's legs with her tail as she walked behind her.

Chandra led her into the living room and they curled up on the couch together, twining their tails. Anise told Chandra all about yesterday morning, starting with her lightning a votive candle for the anniversary of Chandra's death.

"I know." Chandra said as Anise finished up her story.

"You do?" Anise shook her head. "I'm not sure I believe myself and I was there." She jerked her head to meet Chandra's gaze. "How is it you say you know? Also, when did we get that picture taken, anyway? I've never been with you to visit your family."

Chandra ruffled the fur between Anise's ears. "That's a secret for now. I wish I could say more, but I can't. Not yet."

"Wait, what?" Anise protested, but Chandra held a finger up against the end of Anise's muzzle.

"That reminds me," Chandra said, unwinding herself from their pile on the couch and offering Anise a paw up. "I have something to show you."

She led Anise into their spare bedroom. As part of their cover, Chandra kept her clothes and personal effects in this room, although she slept in Anise's bed every night. From underneath the bed, Chandra pulled out a whiteboard covered in clipped articles and colored marker lines. Looking at the dates, some were over a hundred years old and others were dated for the future, but all the papers looked crisp and new.

"Wh-what is this?" Anise said, staring at the board with wide eyes. As she read the articles, she noticed a common theme: all of them were about the church.

"After you save me, this is the work we'll be doing," Chandra said, her eyes shining.

"But, you're already saved?" Anise asked. "And this, what is it that we'll be doing?"

Chandra shook her head while picking up her tail and fiddling with the end of it. "I'm not saved yet, but you will save me, and soon. As for our work, we're going to start a group to break the hold of the church, separating it from politics."

"Um," Anise raised a paw. "Why?"

"Let me ask something. Where was I buried?" Chandra dropped her tail and took Anise's paw in hers.

Anise frowned and looked away. "India," she whispered, unable to stop her ears from flattening and her tail tip from twitching. "In Telangana, in your family plot. That's why I lit the candle for you, instead of going to your grave. We were together forty years, yet I had no say in anything."

"I don't blame you," Chandra said softly, before her voice got a hard tone. "I blame the system, the influence of the church, for why we have to hide our love for one another."

"What does that have to do with what happened yesterday?" Anise's head spun. She sunk down on the bed, shoving the whiteboard aside to make room.

"Yesterday morning is when the church sends your past self to kill you. You have to go back and stop her," Chandra said.

"But she's already been stopped." Anise groaned and put her muzzle into her paws. This was all so confusing.

"No, but she will be." Chandra said.

"How?"

"By you, of course." Chandra looked at the clock on the wall. "This afternoon. We should get going. Don't want you to be late." Chandra paused and then added. "After you save yourself, don't forget to come back in time to save me."

"But how will I do that? And won't they just come looking for you again?"

Chandra smiled and shook her head. "You'll know how to do it when you get there. Trust me, your plan will be brilliant." She winked at Anise and then pecked her on the cheek.

***

Anise and Chandra walked up to the church steps. Anise gripped her cane tightly and glanced at Chandra.

"What do I do?"

"Go inside. You'll figure it out." Chandra turned to go.

"You're leaving?" Anise's ears flattened.

"I can't help you here. In your timeline, you haven't saved me yet. I'll be at home, waiting for you, when you're done." Chandra walked away, her round ears ramrod straight, her heels clicking on the sidewalk and her tail twitching giving away how worried she really was.

Anise took a deep breath and slowly made her way up the stairs. As she walked the light changed, the shadows shifted, until the stairs were in pre-dawn shadow. She'd stepped back in time, to early morning the day before. She wasn't sure how she'd done it, or how she knew with such certainty that she'd just stepped through the veil to travel back in time, but she trusted this new knowledge implicitly.

Inside the church, everything was still and quiet. No other parishioners were about at this early hour.

Confession didn't officially start until nine, when her past self would arrive. The votive candles were just as she remembered from the day before, except for one detail. Anise grabbed a match and lit a candle, giving thanks to God for Chandra's return. Now it was just as she remembered.

Anise walked about up the nave, her confident steps echoing off the walls of the church. She swung her cane, tapping on the floor only when it suited her.

She stopped at the confession booth and opened the door. Empty, as it should have been the day before. So where was the young version of herself?

There was a creak from the front doors. Anise slipped into the booth and held the door so that it shut quietly. She sat down on the bench, gripping her cane between her paws, trying to think. She wasn't going to kill her past self, but then, what was she going to do?

The door to the booth opened. Anise jumped to her feet, raising her cane like a baseball bat. Detective Boom grinned back at her.

"Hah, so it was you. Put that cane down, I'm not going to hurt you."

"Why are you here?" Anise narrowed her eyes, lifting her cane higher.

"I'm here to help you. Give you your welcome." Boom gestured and stepped to the side.

Detective Gruenhut slid his arm around Boom and pecked him on the cheek.

"Wait, you aren't really with the government, are you?" Anise set down her cane.

"No," Boom grinned at Gruenhut, who grinned back. "We're here to help."

"But Chandra said—"

"We were already both saved." Boom said as Gruenhut pulled away. "Now, some ground rules. We can give you advice, instructions, answer questions, but we can't do the deed. It's gotta be you."

Gruenhut nodded to the cane in Anise's shaking paw. "That the only weapon you have with you?"

"Weapon? Uh," she glanced at the two big rats still looming over her, blocking the only way out of the booth. If they wanted to hurt her, she mused, they already could have. "Yes, this is it."

"Here," Gruenhut reached one of his massive paws into his suit jacket. Anise squeaked and shrank back against the back of the booth. He pulled his paw out to reveal a tiny, mouse-sized gun. "You're shaking."

"Why me?"

"You were targeted by the Cross Auream, a secret society the church uses to eliminate the," Broom held up his paws and made air quotes, "gay problem."

"I expected them to come for me after they got Chandra, but it had been over a year. I thought—well, I didn't know. Maybe she didn't give me up?"

Boom shook his head. "She did, but you were slated for an experimental program."

"Apparently involving time travel."

"Yes," Boom said, glancing about. "But we're out of time."

Gruenhut held out the little pistol towards Anise. "You ever used one of these?"

Anise shook her head, almost numb as she took the pistol from Gruenhut. "No."

He pointed to parts of the gun. "This is the trigger. This little push-button on the handle is the safety. Gun won't fire if you aren't holding it down tight. Don't point the business end at anything you don't intend to shoot."

"Good luck." Boom said, lumbering away.

Gruenhut gave Anise a little salute. "See you on the other side."

"Wait," Anise said. "What do I do?"

"Kill or be killed."

Anise gripped the gun firmly. She peeked out of the booth and the two rats were gone. She just caught sight of Gruenhut's tail as it disappeared through the door at the back of the chapel that led to the offices. Just as the door clicked shut behind him, the front entrance creaked open.

Not wanting to be surprised again, Anise eased the door to the booth shut, leaving it cracked just enough for her to see. A slim form stepped through the door, pastel skirt swirling around her legs and showing off her high-heeled pumps. Anise recognized her instantly. Her younger self. From the sway of her hips and the sparkle in her eyes, she was her from right before the wedding. The sensation was surreal, like looking in a mirror at her past. She had a sensation of déjà vu, as if she'd seen this before, long ago in a since forgotten memory.

Anise shook her head to clear it and focused on the present, forcing herself to focus on the sensation of the gun in her paw. Scowling in disgust, she tucked it into her skirt pocket. This was herself. She couldn't shoot a past version of herself. The thought made her fur stand on end.

She took her cane back up, opened the door to the booth, and came hobbling out.

"Hello, dearie," she said as young Anise turned to look at her.

Young Anise looked her up and down, lips peeling up. "Ewww, I got so old."

Anise frowned. "With age comes wisdom. Why are you here?"

"I'm here to keep myself from making the same mistakes as you. They came to see me. Warned me that in the future I become," her eyes narrowed in disgust, "a lesbian."

"That doesn't answer my question." Anise took a few hobbling steps down the nave towards her younger self. "Why are you here? Who sent you?"

"The Aureum. I need to kill you, my lesbian future, to stop it from happening." Young Anise took a gun from her pocket of her skirt, holding it loosely by her side.

"And if you don't?"

"They kill me. And I won't miss my wedding tomorrow, for anything." Young Anise lifted the gun and pointed it straight at Anise.

Anise's heart sank. She remembered the time leading up to her wedding. She'd put her heart and soul into planning it down to the last detail. She'd been so excited, she would have killed if someone had tried to take it away from her.

Young Anise put her other paw on the gun and sighted down the barrel. Anise ducked and rolled between the pews just as the gun barked. Young Anise's shoes clicked on the floor as she ran down the nave. Anise laid down, scrambling under the pews towards the front of the church. She slid her cane out into the nave just as the Young her came running up. The girl squeaked in shock as she tumbled face first to the ground, snapping one of the heels off her expensive pumps. Her little gun popped free of her paw and skittered away.

Honestly, Anise thought as she stood and took her own pistol out of her pocket, who wears heels to go kill someone? She closed her eyes and turned her head away.

From this range Anise couldn't miss.

The shot was still reverberating from the windows when the office door opened, and Boom and Gruenhut appeared. They helped her carry the body over and hide it in the nave where she'd first discovered it.

While Boom and Gruenhut cleaned up the blood, Anise retrieved her younger version's gun. To her surprise, the gun was identical to the one that the rats had given her, right down to the serial number etched onto the barrel. Or, as she reflected, maybe it shouldn't have surprised her at all.

***

Boom and Gruenhut offered to walk her back to the apartment.

"What did I accomplish back there?" Anise asked them as they strolled along.

"To change the future, you have to change the past," Gruenhut said.

"Is that what the young me meant?"

"Time isn't a stream or a river," Boom said with a shrug. "Those targeted by the Cross Auream, if they manage to kill their future self, can change their future. Think of time more as a lake. Ripples in the future extend out in every direction."

Anise shuddered. The thought of being forever stuck in a marriage to a man she wasn't attracted to, never meeting Chandra. "How horrible. But then, what happens to me? I killed my younger self—"

Boom shrugged. "Honestly? We can tell you our theory, but that's about it."

"Alright," Anise hedged. "So, I take it the same thing happened to both of you?"

"Well, to Boom here first, then he got me," Gruenhut said, giving Boom a friendly punch on the arm. Anise noticed that he and Boom were just as careful as she and Chandra to avoid physical affection while out in public.

"So, what's your theory?"

"Well, you killed your past self, but you still have all your memories and the past didn't actually change, see?" Boom said. "Like, we went to the library and looked up newspaper archives. Nothing was different."

Anise nodded. "A paradox. That's why I had to be the one to kill my younger self. If one of you killed her, she'd have been dead along with me."

"Right," Gruenhut said. "We're living paradoxes. It's why we think we can move through time, and stuff."

"Ah, like why my joints don't hurt anymore or I don't need my cane."

"Gruenhut and I, we go to thinking about how to best use these powers," Boom said with a grin.

"The whiteboard," Anise whispered to herself. Louder, to Boom and Gruenhut, she said, "you want to stop the Cross Auream."

"Exactly!" Boom whooped. "So, you in?" He stuck out his arm, holding his massive paw in front of her.

"I'm in." Anise grinned up at him as she set her tiny paw in his big one. "We just have one stop to make first. I have to save Chandra."

TEMPERED

Crimson Ruari

Ok then, since we have a bunch of couples here today, pairing off for our stations will be easy." The golden retriever woman at the front of the room had one of those bubbly personalities that came out in her every word.

Kahina did not agree with the instructor at all. She was only at the stupid class because her coworker had to bow out at the last minute, and here she was, getting paired up with someone she didn't even know in a room full of couples. She was sick of couples—she saw them everywhere. Every meal for two, pair of seats, or bottle of wine. Well, that last one she could handle on her own. Not most nights, though. Getting hammered nightly and laying about, moping and drunk, was not the example she wanted to set for her daughter.

Finding a babysitter for Jaina at the last minute had been a challenge, and so the 'free class' had ended up costing her plenty already. Still, her therapist said that getting out was part of learning to be single again, and this was a chance to do that. Plus, Jaina didn't seem to mind babysitters too much anymore.

Kahina slunk carefully to a station in the back of the room. Couples filled every station in the room, and she hoped she'd be able to work by herself without anyone bothering her. That'd be nice, even if it wasn't exactly what her therapist had meant.

It was, however, not to be. When she reached the table, she found a dark-furred, painted dog woman standing there, grinning at her.

Kahina stopped. "I, uh-oh, is this one taken?"

The woman chuckled and waved at the station, with its collection of kitchen implements, some of which looked like they'd escaped a science class. "I don't have a partner yet, if that's what you mean. Please join me. Doesn't look like there are any other options, and she did say it worked best in teams." She gave a small wag of her tail and held out a paw. "I'm Retha."

Kahina shook, and noted the dog had a firm grip, but very soft paws. "Kahina. I guess you're not here with anyone, either?"

Retha shook her head. "Nope!" She grinned again and bounced a little in place. "But I like chocolate and that was good enough for me! Why are you here?"

Kahina blew out her breath and accepted her fate: a cheery partner for the class. It could have been worse, she supposed, and she did like chocolate herself. "My friend at work couldn't come, so she gave me her ticket. I barely made it, though; I had a heck of a time finding a babysitter."

The dog nodded. "Ah yes. I had to take my pups to my grandmother's, but she does love to see them."

"Oh? That's nice. Is uh—" Kahina glanced at the dog's paws, but Retha had placed them just to the other side of a scale when she leaned on the table. "Forgive my asking, but was your husband unavailable?"

Retha chuckled. "Oh, I don't have one." Her eyes flashed, as though she was enjoying a private joke. "It's complicated. Perhaps I shall tell you if our chocolate is good."

Kahina raised an eyebrow and flicked one of her ears. "I see."

"And you? No man in your life to care for the pups?"

"Just one."

"Oh, do you normally have more than one man?"

The hyena flicked her tail and blew out her breath. The woman was teasing her. "I mean I just have one pup. And no, no husband." She added, "Not anymore," under her breath, but not quietly enough.

The dog's tone changed. "Oh, I'm sorry. I'll leave you be. Let's make some chocolate, yes?"

The instructor gave them a welcome distraction as she welcomed them to "Chocolate 101: Chocolate for the Home Enthusiast."

***

The class turned out to be more fun than she'd expected. Her expectations hadn't been high, for sure, but by the end of it, they'd tasted half a dozen different preparations of chocolate and learned enough to be dangerous. That Retha had joked and snarked with her through the whole thing hadn't hurt, either; she had come to really enjoy the dog's company.

There was something in the way the dog's eyes flashed when they met hers after a joke that gave Kahina a little thrill. It was a small thing, but it made Retha's banter even more enjoyable.

As they were packing up, the instructor stopped by. She still looked annoyingly perky, even after a couple hours of wandering between cooking stations and talking almost non-stop. A stream of chocolate puns trailed off when they noticed her standing next to them, practically bouncing in place. Kahina wondered if she'd been taking stimulants when they weren't looking.

The hyena made the mistake of making eye contact, and the instructor took it as an invitation to chime in. "Are you two sure you're not a couple?"

Retha glanced between the two of them, then shrugged. "Pretty sure. I've never seen this woman before in my life." She paused, then looked at Kahina. "But y'know...I have pretty much everything we have here, if you want to come by next Saturday for a home study session."

The instructor bounced in place, arms behind her back as she looked expectantly between the two of them.

Kahina considered for a moment before agreeing. It hadn't felt like she'd had much choice. "Sure. Sounds like fun."

Retha grinned widely. "Count on it."

The instructor bounced off, looking entirely too pleased with herself.

***

The next day, Kahina received a text from Retha.

"Hey, I'm downtown for work tomorrow. Lunch?"

Kahina grinned; the dog had been rather fun during the class. And lunch? Lunch was pretty low-key, right? Nothing weird about having lunch with a new friend. She paused. Why did she think it might be weird?

Retha was cute, certainly. After all, she had that gorgeous, dark, splotchy pelt and those ears and that absurdly good grin. She couldn't deny that. And she was funny, without trying too hard – Kahina had found it entirely easy to laugh with the dog during the class. There was an easy-going sort of nature about her that Kahina found appealing.

The hyena scratched her muzzle. It was just lunch, right? She worked downtown, it probably wouldn't be out of her way. She had told

Retha that she worked downtown during the class. So it was convenient, she supposed. Too convenient? Probably not.

She typed out a reply.

"Sure! Got somewhere in mind?"

Retha's reply was almost instantaneous.

"I'm flexible. What works best for you?"

"There's a food hall at 33rd and Ashland. That's pretty convenient. 1215?"

"Sounds great! See you tomorrow!"

Seemed like an awful lot of exclamation marks. Maybe Retha was interested after all? Well, Kahina reflected, that was a given. She'd proposed the chocolate at her place. Which was... it was a big step for Kahina. She couldn't help but be nervous about that. It felt like more than a friendly chocolate class kinda date. In fact, it felt like a date. Kind of like tomorrow's lunch did.

***

Kahina found Retha waiting for her by a column in the middle of the food hall. The dog was sporting an ivory pantsuit that fit her very well, accentuating the power in her lean frame. She smiled widely when she spotted Kahina and waved. "Hey there!"

Kahina smiled – the dog's enthusiasm was infectious. "Hi! I uh, I feel underdressed." She was wearing a green sweater and a long, black skirt, something comfortable enough for the office, but not so dressy as to make the engineers she worked with look too sloppy.

Retha waved a paw dismissively. "Hardly! You look nice! And I just came from a meeting, so I'm dressed up. I can't wait to get home and get out of it."

Kahina coughed, and Retha chuckled. "I mean and get into something more comfortable."

Kahina coughed again and changed the subject. "So, food?"

"Food yes!" Retha's ears perked up and she looked at the shops. "Sandwiches and tea?"

Kahina considered the shop briefly. "Sure."

There was, fortunately, no line, so they got their food and found a table rather quickly. Retha paused between enthusiastic assaults on her sandwich. "I'm glad you could make it."

Kahina nodded. "Thank you. I-mmm, the class was fun."

"It was!" Retha's ears were perked and Kahina kept finding her attention caught on their broad, round shapes, so unlike her own, narrow, pointed ones. She couldn't help but find them cute, and the way they accentuated Retha's expressions only added to that.

"So," Retha continued, "What do you do?"

"I'm a technical writer," Kahina replied.

"Oh? Nice! What do you write technically about?"

Kahina snorted quietly and grinned. It was an obvious joke, but the dog delivered it well. "Whatever needs it, but mostly I write the documentation for our software."

"So, like, knowledge base articles?"

Kahina nodded. "Yeah, pretty much. Sometimes I whip up some ad copy for sales glossies. We're not that big a shop." She paused to work on her own sandwich. "And what about you?"

"I'm a financial auditor," Retha replied.

"Goodness, serious business." Kahina whuffed. She supposed that helped explain the suit.

"It is! But mostly the folks I deal with are nice enough. I mean, they know better than to get in my way." She grinned toothily, showing off a good set of pointy teeth.

Kahina matched her grin. The idea of Retha haranguing someone over a set of bad books flashed through her mind, and it was entirely amusing. "Yeah, you gotta keep 'em in line. Showing some teeth helps, right?"

Retha's eyes flashed. "Mmhmm. I like teeth."

Kahina coughed and felt her ears get hot.

The dog cleared her throat. "Ahem, where were we?"

Kahina took a long drink of her tea to collect her thoughts. "Ah, industry? What sort of books do you audit?"

"Education. I work for Hunter A&M, so I have to check in with campuses and extensions all over the state."

Kahina cocked her head to one side. "Oh? I would have expected they handled that themselves."

Retha nodded. "Oh, they manage the books themselves, but I work for the Bursar and we have to edit everyone's books annually. Central oversight, compliance, etc, you know?" She waved a paw vaguely.

"I can guess," Kahina offered.

Retha grinned. "It's not terribly exciting, but it keeps me employed."

Kahina nodded. "Yeah, I can relate! It's a bit dull sometimes, but there's something about taking a pile of notes from engineers and interviewing them and then turning it into coherent documentation that lots of folk scan use."

"Oh, I'll bet!" Retha leaned on the table. "You're quite an interesting woman, you know that?"

Kahina took another long drink of tea. "Oh, err, ah." Her ears flicked of their own accord. She had to admit the dog was pretty interesting herself, in a way she hadn't really considered before.

Retha leaned back quickly and brushed her suit down. "I'm sorry, was that too much?"

Kahina shook her head. "Mmm, no, no. I just, uh… I guess you caught me off guard."

Retha cocked her head. "Oh?"

"Well, I was married. To a man, I mean."

"But?" Retha cocked her head to the other side.

"But I mean, not anymore. And I don't know what I really want. It's been a while and I haven't thought much about it. I've just sort of been getting by."

Retha nodded. "Fair enough." She considered her glass for a bit, then took a sip.

Kahina tapped her claws on the table for a bit until the pause had dragged on too long for her. "So, uh…"

Retha considered her for a moment, then smiled. Kahina had to admit she liked being smiled at by the dog. "So, it's a friendly offer. I'd love to have you come over, we can make chocolate. If that's all, well, heck, you're good company and that's a good time!" She shrugged. "But if it's more? Well, I'd enjoy that very much."

Kahina nodded, eyeing her plate for a bit, then looked up at Retha and smiled. "Ok. I uh, hmm. I don't know where I am, but I want to try it out. Start with the chocolate and just see what happens, you know?"

Retha smiled warmly. "Makes perfect sense." Her phone buzzed, and she glanced at it. "Blast. I have to get back to work." She reached across the table and patted Kahina's paw. "See you Saturday?"

Kahina's stomach flipped at the dog's touch and she couldn't help but smile. *Oh, I'm confused something fierce,* she thought. *On the other paw, she could be a lot of fun.* "Yeah. See you then!"

Retha nodded sharply and walked off. Kahina sat there, watching her go, and found herself admiring the way the dog's suit hugged her rear.

She rubbed her muzzle. "Huh."

***

Kahina paced in front of her living room window, arms crossed tightly over her chest as she stared out at, well, not much, just the wall of the building across the way. If she went out on the small deck, she could look down at the street six floors below, but it was too hot for that. She was built for hot weather, but she had her limits.

She grumbled to herself about it. "It's not a dry heat. It's a soggy, wet heat and it sucks."

"What's that, Mom?" Jaina's voice came from her room. The apartment her salary afforded her was small, but at least the two of them had separate rooms.

She shook her head. "Nothing, hon. Talking to myself."

"Ok!"

She flicked an ear and could have sworn she heard a mutter of "yet again" drift out, but her daughter was wise enough to attempt at discretion.

The hyena stopped her pacing and eyed her laptop from across the room with a sigh. She hadn't found anyone available to take care of her daughter for tomorrow. All her friends had their own plans, which might have accounted for why there were no babysitters available. It looked like she was going to have to call Retha and reschedule.

Part of her really wanted to do that. What was she even doing, agreeing to go to Retha's place after that exchange? She huffed and lashed her tail. "This is crazy," she muttered to herself again, more softly than before, "I don't even like women like that. I'm not even looking for someone!"

She started pacing again. She couldn't deny that she'd said yes, or that she'd felt that thrill talking to Retha, or that she still wanted to see her again. *No denying you were checking out her ass when she left at lunch, either,* she thought.

Kahina coughed at that thought. She growled and stalked over to the fridge to pull a bottle of water from the fridge and pour herself a glass. The chill of it was refreshing and brought her focus more into the moment.

She had to call Retha. That was the first order of business. Thankfully, the wild dog had given Kahina her number.

Her stomach knotted and flipped while she waited for the call to connect. She rehearsed what she was going to say if she got Retha's voicemail. She hoped she got voicemail—it was a lot easier to get out of things if she didn't have to speak to anyone.

She was not so lucky. Retha's voice chirped through the phone, as cheerful as she'd been during the class. "Hey there! How's your day?"

Kahina was caught off guard by the dog's question. Retha was not making it easy on her, and neither was the way her stomach flipped back to excitement. Damnit. "I uh-it was ok. Yours?"

"Good! Or pretty good, you know. As good as work can be, at least. So, what's up? You're not thinking of backing out, are you? I just bought the chocolate."

Shit. "Well, uh-I was, actually. I haven't been able to find anyone to watch Jaina."

She was could practically see Retha's ears droop. "Oh no." There was a silence on the phone, and then a thoughtful hum. "How old is she, anyway?"

"Eight."

"Oh! Well that's no problem, then."

Kahina cocked her head. "Ah, what now?"

Through the phone, she thought she could hear Retha's tail wagging. "That's about my pups' ages. Bibi would not mind a third to watch after."

Kahina's free ear flicked as she pondered. "And who is this 'Bibi' who is taking care of your pups?"

The dog chuckled in her ear. "Bibi is my grandmother; I mentioned her during the class. 'Bibi' means grandmother. Her name is Imani, but she says that she has never been one for peace, but they didn't name her 'Askari,' and so she prefers Bibi."

"Askari?"

Retha chuckled on the other side of the phone. "It means 'warrior.' Bibi's hobbies since retirement seem to revolve around protest marches and picking up men too young to know better."

Kahina was pretty sure she could hear Retha's eyes rolling.

"I see. I'm not sure I want Jaina going to a march."

Retha chuckled again. "Bibi promises no protests or cruising while she is with the pups. My girls tell me she's been good so far."

"Well, alright then. That'll work."

Retha chuckled. "Good! See you tomorrow night!"

She couldn't help but smile. "You too. Good night."

Kahina ended the call and pressed her phone to her chest again, tapping her claws on the back. Oh, what had she gotten herself into? She eyed the small wine rack in the kitchen. A couple of bottles were in order for tomorrow night. She might need to stock up.

***

Retha had a townhouse in a relatively nice neighborhood. The houses were modest and seemed well-maintained; there was a house a few spots down and across that street that looked to have been remodeled recently. Retha's looked like it hadn't seen any major work in decades, but it was just as well-kept as the others.

She pulled her car into a well-maintained driveway, nosing up to the garage as far as she could. Two pups with the same dark coloration as Retha bounced out of the house as soon as the engine was off, showering them in a cacophony of greetings, their tails going a mile a minute. Kahina glanced at where her daughter sat in the back seat, but Jaina did not seem concerned. That was a good sign; she could get overwhelmed sometimes, and in this case, Kahina wouldn't have blamed her.

Still, her daughter proceeded to unbuckle herself, so Kahina set out to do the same. She opened the door and pinned her ears back—the pups were firing off a nonstop series of questions and seemed to repeat themselves quite frequently. Closing her door, and hearing her daughter's open and close, she addressed the two pups, "Hello! I'm Kahina, you must be Retha's girls."

They stopped for a moment, apparently collecting themselves, then the taller of the two answered: "I'm Miela and this is Hannah." The younger girl nodded confirmation.

Kahina offered a paw. "It's a pleasure to meet you. I'm a friend of your mother's."

She shook paws with the girls gently, and Hannah offered, "We know! Mom's been talking about you all week!"

Kahina felt her ears flick back against her head and flush. "Oh, has she? I'm flattered."

By this time, Jaina had rounded the car, and addressed them. "You've been the same way, Mom."

Kahina coughed. "Ah-hah. Yes, well." She held out her paw to her daughter. "This is my daughter, Jaina. Jaina, these are Miela and Hannah."

Jaina offered a wave, and Retha's girls waved back. It was, she reflected, a pretty good start, given her daughter's proclivity for quiet. She could relate.

"Girls, why don't you come get your things and wait on the porch for Bibi to arrive?" Retha was standing on the porch in question, and she smiled brightly and waved when Kahina looked up. The hyena couldn't help but feel her tail give a wag in response. The woman's enthusiasm was infectious.

The two pups ran off to the house, and Kahina looked at Jaina. "Hon, why don't you join them on the porch, while I get the wine." She kissed her daughter between her ears, which elicited a small wag, and then Jaina made her way to the porch, more sedately than the pups had. Kahina followed shortly with a couple bottles of wine.

Retha waved her into the house, explaining, "I'll wait out here with the pups for Bibi. The kitchen is down the hall and to the left. I put a wine opener out if you want to get a bottle started."

Retha's place was not especially large, and seemed to be about one room wide, with a set of stairs along one wall. The walls were pale earth tones, a soft gold here, a deep red there for accent. The kitchen owned the space at the far end of the house and opened directly into the dining room, which was open to the living room at the front. It was small, but efficient. The stairs suggested an upper story and a basement, so it seemed Retha and the pups probably had enough space to get by, if not by much.

Kahina opened one of the bottles to let it breathe—then took a moment to admire the efficiency of the kitchen's arrangement and the way it was presently occupied with bricks of chocolate, a scale, a collection of bowls, and a thermometer—before joining the rest of the crowd on the porch.

She stood comfortably, even pleasantly, close to Retha for perhaps a minute before another car pulled into the driveway. From it stepped a wild dog woman who Kahina would have sworn was perhaps sixty, at the most. She flicked her ears and waved at the group on the porch, prompting Retha to herd them all down to the car, Kahina included.

Retha provided introductions. "Bibi, this is Kahina, and this is her daughter, Jaina."

The older dog held out a paw, and Kahina shook it. She was surprised by the woman's grip, and the intense grin she gave. "Pleasure. Imani Sefu, but your daughter can call me 'Bibi' just as well as Retha's girls."

She squatted down, bracing her paws on her knees, and leveled that grin at Jaina. "I see you are getting tall already. Good, I don't bend like I used to." She flashed a look at Retha. "And I used to bend very well."

Retha grumbled. "Bibi! Why do you have to say these things?"

She stood and patted the younger dog's shoulder. "Because I can! And because it is true. These girls should not feel so constrained." She gathered the pups and ushered them down the steps. "Now, pups, to the car. I shall keep you entertained so these two ladies can have some quality time."

Retha covered her muzzle and coughed, managing to look abashed with her tail tucked against her leg and her ears pinned back.

Kahina's own embarrassment warred with amusement at Retha's. She waved at her daughter. "Have fun, hon! And thank you, Mrs. Sefu!"

The older woman tossed a quick wave as she herded the pups into her car—a small, practical SUV that seemed to have no trouble fitting the whole mob. It also seemed to have no trouble peeling out of the driveway backwards and zipping off down the street far faster than Kahina would have expected.

"Does she always drive like that?"

Retha simply shrugged. "Bibi drove ambulances for a very long time and she has never forgotten that. But she still drives better than most of the people on the road, so who am I to stop her?"

Kahina conceded the point, albeit reluctantly. "I see. Well, shall we? I saw you had quite a nice selection of chocolate."

Retha nodded and led the way back into the kitchen. "Why thank you! Three varieties for experimentation." She picked up the bottle of wine and eyed the label, then sniffed at the bottle and smiled. "Oh, very nice. Let's get this out, eh?"

***

"Hey, can you give me that spatula?" Retha waved her paw at the implement that was just out of reach.

"Oh, I'll give it to you alright!" Kahina grinned as she handed it over.

Retha's eyes flashed and her muzzle hung open in a grin. "Is that so? Careful, I'll hold you to that."

"Mmmm..." Kahina returned her grin but didn't push further. She'd found herself feeling more at ease the longer they worked, and as they cracked into the next bottle of wine, she was enjoying flirting with the dog. Retha had one hell of a wicked grin, and when her tongue lolled out, Kahina sometimes found herself thinking about just how good that tongue might feel.

It turned out that Retha's kitchen was a bit small for two people, but Kahina was finding she minded less each time they had to squeeze past each other. There was just no way one could avoid grinding her hips against the rear of the other, and she was pretty sure that Retha was going out of her way to make it extra difficult. Difficult, she thought to herself, adding heavy scare quotes. In a fit of whimsy, she 'accidentally' stumbled into the wild dog, and was rewarded with a sort of growl that was not entirely innocent.

Kahina had worried that working in such close quarters with someone as energetic as Retha would have been taxing, but she found that it bordered on intoxicating. Retha's focus was intense, her ears perked and her tail wagging as she stirred the chocolate in the double-boiler, pausing only to let Kahina probe it with a thermometer to see how they were coming along. The dog was just as intense and precise when they moved to pouring molds and rolling truffles, but she was never overbearing.

Thanks to Retha's prep work, the two of them managed to produce an appalling amount of chocolate, and she had just finished laying out the excess into bars. The dog scraped the bowl with a spatula and held up the chocolate-covered blade. "So, uh, there's only one." She grinned at Kahina, and judging by the sparkle in her eye and the set of her ears, it wasn't even remotely innocent.

The hyena could feel the wine singing in her blood as she leaned in, making eye contact as she licked it slowly. A thrill shot through her that she was sure had to do with more than just the chocolate, and she found herself panting softly. Retha grinned and held her gaze as she took her own lick, making it long and slow and lingering, the tip of her pink tongue curling around the lower edge of the blade before sliding upwards to end with a flick as she cleared the tip. The soft groan she gave as she pulled it into her muzzle, closing her eyes and clearly savoring. Her chest heaved as she stood there, muzzle separated from Kahina's by only an inch and a spatula.

She'd blame the wine if anyone asked, but it was more than old grapes that drove her to push Retha's paw down, clearing the spatula and letting her lean in to press her lips to the dog's. Retha's lips were warm and soft, which somehow surprised her, though, reflecting on it, she had no idea why. The response was less of a surprise, as Retha leaned into it, and snuck a paw around to cup the small of Kahina's back. The spatula clattered in the sink as Retha's tongue pushed into her muzzle, soft and dexterous and entirely sinful as it twined with hers.

Kahina shuddered, losing herself in the kiss for a few moments, or perhaps a few minutes, she wasn't sure. She returned the favor and pushed her tongue into Retha's muzzle, pressing the advantage to explore the dog's finer, thinner muzzle from within, tracing sharp teeth and ridged palate, tasting the lingering sweet and bitter hints of chocolate amid traces of wine and the overall taste of someone else's mouth, unique and familiar all the same.

Eventually, their muzzles parted, though they lingered close enough to feel each other's breath and for lips to brush as they spoke.

Kahina spoke first. "I uh-I don't know what just happened."

Retha grinned, and her paw curled against Kahina's back, pressing the tips of her claws through the fabric of her shirt. "Bullshit. That was hot as hell, and you know it."

The hyena felt her tail flick behind her as embarrassment flashed through her, but she nodded. "Ok, I guess I do. But like, I uh-y'know, I was married until not that long ago. To a man."

Retha's smaller paws trailed up the underside of the hyena's arms, holding her paws up for inspection. Retha turned her paws this way, then that, looking at all sides, then grinned back at Kahina. "Well, I don't see any rings on these fine digits, do I? You leave it at home or something?"

Kahina shook her head. "Uh, no. We uhh, sold them off as part of the divorce."

Retha hummed. "Good." She let Kahina's paws drop, and her paws slid over the hyena's shoulder, pulling her closer again. "So here you are, recently divorced and making out with a woman in her kitchen while both your pups are away. Does that seem accurate to you?" Retha's eyes dared her to deny it.

"Yeah, I guess it does. Yes," she corrected herself, "It's very accurate." Her paws found their places on Retha's lean hips, and the dog's tail swayed in response.

"So now that you know what that was, let me ask you this: what do you want from here?" The dog flashed her a grin. "Because I have some ideas, and I'd love to share them with you."

Kahina felt her paws clutching at Retha's hips as she pondered the question. "I don't know. I mean—" Her gaze flicked between Retha's, warm and inviting and maybe a lot more than warm, and the far side of the kitchen. She hadn't thought this far ahead. Not really. Not seriously. It was one thing when she was alone in bed at night to think about it, but it was another thing entirely when she was staring opportunity in the eyes. "I mean, I haven't been with a woman in something like twenty years and I hadn't ever really considered hooking up with one since then, not seriously, and I don't really know what this means for me in the long term and…" She trailed off, noting that Retha had acquired a smile. "What are you smiling at?"

The dog put a finger to her lips, gently closed her muzzle with a couple of fingers. She kissed Kahina briefly, then spoke. "My dear, sweet, sexy hyena, it doesn't have to mean anything other than that you slept with a woman twenty minutes ago instead of twenty years ago. You are cute and fun company and I'd really like to take you to bed and show you what a good time two women can have, but I'm not trying to convince you to trade your blouses for flannel." The dog leaned in close and slipped her tongue out, pulling it slowly over Kahina's lips, letting her feel the full, silken length of it before ending with another kiss. "So, what do you say? Come to bed with me and see where we go from there?"

"Is this what you had in mind when you invited me over originally?"

"I'd be lying if I said I hadn't hoped it would be the case."

Kahina's pulse was pounding as she considered the offer. It didn't take her long. "Ok. Let's uh-let's go to your bedroom and see what happens."

Retha's grin gave her plenty of ideas about what might happen.

"Excellent." Her tail lashed behind her as she bounced, quickly facing away from Kahina and dragging her out of the kitchen towards the stairs. It wasn't a big house, and it turned out that the upstairs was occupied by two bedrooms at one end and one at the other, with a short hallway and a bathroom in between. She was not surprised when Retha led her to the largest room. It was hardly gigantic inside but appeared to offer a decent-sized closet and direct access to the bathroom. An ample and loosely-made bed occupied the bulk of the space.

Retha turned and waved a paw. "Welcome to my inner sanctum. Can I help you get more comfortable?" The way her gaze flicked up and down Kahina made her meaning clear.

Kahina sensed the opportunity to claim it was all just a misunderstanding slipping away from her. She paused to consider that course of action, but after a moment's consideration, she decided to let the wine push her into just going for it. She smiled at Retha and nodded. "Oh, yes please."

The dog approached her, standing close enough that Kahina could feel the heat from her body. Retha's paws found the buttons of Kahina's blouse, wasting no time, and soon it was hanging open, leaving her belly exposed and her bra on display. It was a lightweight, teal affair, with just a hint of frill. The bra was practical, but it contrasted with her fur and made her feel a little extra sexy. She hadn't expected it to be on display tonight, but she was glad she'd chosen it and not one of her more subdued options.

Retha seemed to like it, too, as the dog smiled and slid her paws up Kahina's belly, pushing through her fur the wrong way with her fingers. A shudder ran through Kahina from rump to shoulders. When Retha's paws reached the hyena's breasts, cupping them lightly over her bra, she leaned in closely to say, "Let me know if I'm going too fast or if you're getting uncomfortable."

Kahina panted softly; she'd not felt anyone's touch in far too long, and Retha had such soft, delicate paws. She shook her head. "No. It's lovely."

Retha licked her lips. "Good." She smiled as she gave the hyena's breasts a gentle squeeze. "You have lovely breasts, you know. I'd like to see more of them."

A groan escaped Kahina's muzzle before any more cogent thought. Her ears flicked in embarrassment, to be so readily aroused, but she leaned into those paws anyway. "Ohh. Well, if I show you mine, will you show me yours?"

Retha's paws slid up over Kahina's shoulders to push her blouse off, then deftly snuck back to find and undo the clasp of her bra. Her quarry topless, the dog stepped back and spread her arms. "Absolutely." Retha licked her muzzle as she admired Kahina's breasts. "Goodness, you have nice breasts."

Kahina took that invitation to show her interest and closed the distance between them again. She pressed her paws to the lean dog's waist and slid them upwards, tracing the curve from Retha's hips into her waist. The hyena's stomach fluttered, warring with the growing warmth between her thighs as her paws neared Retha's breasts, exposing a dark-furred, spotted belly. She slid the dog's shirt off over her head and her paws found Retha's breasts, caressing their lean, modest curves through her bra. She kissed the dog again and rode the momentum, pushing her tongue into Retha's mouth, exploring that thinner muzzle, with its extra-pointy teeth and soft, warm tongue that welcomed hers, playing gently with it.

The depth of the kiss left Kahina short of breath and she panted as she withdrew her muzzle.

Retha grinned at her, tail wagging. "Well, that was a surprise. Just how far are you willing to go?"

Kahina let out a short yip. "I don't know, but I'd like to find out."

Retha planted her paws on the hyena's hips and walked her backwards to the bed. When Kahina ran out of room, her calves pressing into the bed, Retha paused. Her paws found the waist of Kahina's pants, and claw tips snuck in under it to trace the curve of the tops of her hips, while the dog leaned in closely. "These look too tight. We should get you out of them."

Kahina couldn't suppress another moan, and the flush in her ears deepened. "Only if you take yours off, too."

"Dying to," the dog breathed.

Kahina's fly was undone and her pants were pushed down past her hips within moments. A little gentle pressure from Retha and Kahina was sitting on the edge of the bed while the dog tugged her pants off. Her fluttering stomach warred with a growing warmth, and she crossed her arms under her breasts, inadvertently pressing them together and up.

Retha flashed her a grin, then shimmied out of her own pants, standing before Kahina in panties and bra. She glanced down at herself, then at Kahina. "I seem to be overdressed."

The part of Kahina that was thoroughly enjoying the view agreed, and she replied, "Very." Another part of her was reminding her that this was new and different and not what she was about. Or at least that she ought to be moving more slowly. Her anxiety wasn't being terribly consistent. Both parts had her pulse pounding and her tongue lolling out of her muzzle as she panted.

Retha's eyes flashed playfully, and she turned, facing away as she reached behind her and unclasped her bra. She swept her paws over her shoulders, brushing the straps off, and then Kahina saw only the dog's bare back, spots almost blending with the dark fur between them. Retha tucked her thumbs into the waist of her panties and pushed downwards. She followed by bending over in a simple, smooth motion Kahina couldn't help but appreciate. In much the same way, though quite a bit moreso, she appreciated the new view of the athletic curve of the dog's ass, tail waving over it as she gave Kahina an upside-down grin, her ears brushing the floor.

"See something you like?" The dog's ass wiggled from side to side, and Kahina could see the muscles under her fur flexing with the movement.

Kahina answered with a growl, following up with, "Hell yes." The tension in her groin supported this statement.

Retha turned and paused to look at Kahina as she lay on the bed. The hyena took the opportunity herself to admire Retha's breasts, with their small, pink nipples that contrasted nicely with her fur and were already perked. The dog looked like she might not even need a bra if she wanted to go for a run. Retha stalked to the edge of the bed where Kahina sat and trailed a claw over the hyena's shoulder, following a stripe. "You know, you still look overdressed."

Kahina tilted her head to the side. "I do?"

Retha sank smoothly to her knees, then licked her chin, her muzzle now just a little below Kahina's. "Yes." She lowered her muzzle and made her point by snuffling at the front of Kahina's panties.

The hyena twitched and let out a soft gasp at the unexpectedly intimate touch. Suddenly, she thought, as though we hadn't already been making out. She shook her head, then looked down at Retha, who looked up at her expectantly.

Kahina caught her breath, then replied, "Oh! Yeah, I am definitely overdressed."

Retha's paws found Kahina's hips and curled into the waistband of her panties. "Let me help you out of these." She tugged downwards, and when they caught under Kahina's rump against the bed, those same paws found an excuse to trail over the curves of her rear, claws dragging through her pelt before sliding under her and pulling the fabric away.

Her target finally freed of its constraining cloth, Retha leaned in, her nose brushing along Kahina's inner thigh, ruffling through the fur and sending little jolts through the hyena. It became even more intimate a moment later, when Retha's tongue pressed against her pussy.

Kahina felt another thrill run through her, cooler and clenching her belly, as she became viscerally aware of just what she was doing. Part of her wanted to stop, to dress hurriedly, and run away from the difference and change—a new person, and a woman at that.

Retha must have sensed her hesitation, because she withdrew her muzzle and sat back on her haunches, resting her muzzle on Kahina's knee. "Nervous?" It wasn't a tease this time, but softer, gentler. One paw brushed along Kahina's outer thigh.

She nodded, the motion short and quick. "Yeah, a bit. Just—I dunno. This has only ever been a fantasy to me. I've never been with a woman like this before."

Retha cocked her head. "Never? I don't mean to put you on the spot, but you seemed to play along pretty well earlier. I thought you might have done this before."

Kahina couldn't help but chuckle. "Well, hardly ever. I uh…college, you know? Some flirting. Some drinking. Some groping. Maybe a little more? It's a bit hazy, and it was ages ago. And not a regular thing!"

Retha kissed the inside of her knee. "Do you want to keep going?"

Kahina nodded again. "Yes! I just…" She paused, tapping her claws on her thighs. "I'm just really nervous. I guess I didn't have enough wine."

The other woman chuckled, then kissed her inner thigh, a little higher than before. "Oh, maybe, maybe not. Too much wine and we couldn't have any fun. We can stop at any time, but I have to say, I'm biased towards continuing."

The hyena reached out to rub Retha between her ears. "Uh-huh. Let's keep going, though, mmm?" She thumped her tail on the bed; she was still a tangle of nerves, but the part of her that wanted to keep going was starting to gain ground. It was a weird sort of jittery, inconsistent arousal, and it reminded her of nothing so much as her first few times with someone else.

Retha nuzzled farther up Kahina's inner thigh, then paused again. "You know, hon, maybe you'd be more comfortable if you closed your eyes. Just focus on how it feels."

Kahina nodded and closed her eyes. It seemed like very sound advice. As she soon discovered, this also meant she had fewer distractions from just what Retha was doing. The wild dog continued nosing up her thigh until her nose met Kahina's mons, where she snuffled through the fur over the soft flesh, and where her lips brushed over the hyena's. A surge of warmth rushed into her from her groin, and Kahina felt it chase away more of the cold anxiety in her belly.

She rolled her hips forward to give Retha better access, and then, as the dog's nose continued to brush over the fur of her mound and those lips found hers, she groaned and fell back to the bed. Her paws stayed on Retha's head, rubbing her ears, luxuriating in their soft fur and the way Retha's muzzle was very warm between her thighs. The thought sent a shudder through her, and then Retha's tongue sent another as the silken flesh slid across her folds.

Kahina let out a quiet groan that elicited another gentle lick from the dog. She found that the nerves were giving way to the appreciation of the dog's attentions, regardless of what she might be carrying down below. Part of her thrilled at the idea of being in another woman's bed, and she had to admit there were certain advantages. Retha had been nothing but a pleasure to be around and, well, if she pushed much harder with her tongue, she'd be a pleasure to be around.

She rolled her hips again, and Retha lapped harder. She gripped at the dog's head, pulling on it to keep that narrow muzzle in place and keep the tongue working across her pussy, basking in the warm rush she got every time the dog licked her. Retha shifted her attention, and Kahina gasped as the tongue went higher and caressed her clit. The dog had unerring aim, and Kahina suspected she'd done this trick before.

Small wonder, she thought between charges of pleasure, she certainly knows her way around a pussy. Kahina struck a paw out to grip the bed and dug her blunt claws into the sheets as she gasped at the dog, "Ooohh, fuck. Don't stop!"

She didn't. In fact, Retha redoubled her efforts, and her tongue flicked rapidly across Kahina's clit. The hyena writhed on the bed as every drag of that tongue sent a fresh jolt through her, intense and wonderful at the same time. Tension built within her, then peaked, and she gripped tightly at Retha's head and the bed as she came.

Retha proved herself attentive; she slowed her licking to a gentle, languid pace that let a panting Kahina ease her way down from that peak. The dog growled lightly, finally pulling her tongue back to lick all around Kahina's groin, teasing the fur of her outer lips, letting just a trace of silken tongue slide across lips and clit to send another, smaller shudder through her.

Kahina had begun to stroke Retha's ear when the dog rested her muzzle on her partner's mound and smiled up at her. Kahina smiled back, appreciating the view of those dark-furred, broad ears leading back to that lean muzzle, comfortably resting just above her crotch. "Hello there."

Retha cracked a grin and replied, "Hello there, yourself. Care for some company?"

Kahina rubbed one of those ears between thumb and forefinger. "Love some."

The dog wasted no time, and soon Kahina found her stalking atop her, then settling down, straddling Kahina's hips and draping her leaner, lighter form atop the hyena's. Retha licked her muzzle, then brushed it along the side of Kahina's face until it was tucked against the hyena's ear. Retha's voice was low, breathy, and very warm. "You're delicious, you know."

Kahina's ears flicked, and she squirmed under the dog. She licked Retha's lips, finding a trace of herself there. She wasn't sure she'd call it delicious, but she wasn't about to argue. "Yeah?"

Retha nipped the edge of her ear. "I mean it." She traced Kahina's side with her paw, dragging her claws along the side of her breast and ribs. "Cute, sexy, funny, delicious, and you moan delightfully."

Kahina squirmed under the barrage of compliments. It seemed over the top, but she couldn't bring herself to complain. "Well, thank you." She flicked her ears again. "You uh—is there anything I can do for you?"

A dark-furred head came into view as Retha propped herself up on one paw. The other used the newfound space to trail over Kahina's belly and then up to cup one of her breasts. "Lots of things, but it depends on what you're comfortable with, gorgeous. I'd be happy just to finish myself off next to you."

Kahina swallowed and thumped her tail consciously against the bed. "Well, I don't know if I'm ready to go down on you tonight."

Retha grinned and licked Kahina's chin. "Ooh, 'tonight', you say? What about tomorrow?"

"Er—I don't know if we have time tomorrow night. School night and all."

"Next time, then." She nibbled lightly at Kahina's throat.

Kahina felt a shiver run through her, and she let out a quiet moan. "Yes. Definitely. Maybe some more wine. Or liquor."

"A spoonful of liquor makes Kahina go down," Retha whispered it with a little singsong.

"I don't think that's how the song went." She tried to look serious but couldn't suppress a chuckle.

"I like my version better." Retha's paw left Kahina's breast, and the hyena could see it had disappeared between the dog's legs.

Kahina slid her paw down Retha's arm to join her paw. "Here, may I?"

Retha grinned widely. Her tongue hung out as she ground her hips into Kahina's paw, panting softly. "Definitely." Her paw slid away, brushing up Kahina's body to cup her breast again.

Kahina slid her free paw down to cup Retha's rump, finding it lean, but most pleasing to squeeze. She watched the dog's face, focusing on her reactions as she explored the area between her thighs. Retha had closed her eyes, but Kahina suspected she was putting on a bit of a show for her audience. Kahina enjoyed the way the dog bit her lip and the moan as the hyena's fingers found her lips, wet and warm, and then went higher to brush over her clit.

Kahina found herself fascinated by Retha's reactions. Her heart pounded in her chest, and she found she was enjoying it more than she would have expected. Her fingers, wet with Retha's juices, flickered over the dog's clitoris, and she watched as the dog shuddered and ground against her. In a fit of playfulness, she let her fingers slip off and traced the edges of the dog's sex, fingers rubbing through the wet fur and over the warm, soft flesh of her folds.

Retha panted for a moment longer, then growled mock disapproval.

"Tease," she managed.

Kahina took the opportunity to slip a couple fingers into the dog, giving a little shudder at the way those walls welcomed her digits and squeezed around her. "I couldn't help it."

Retha growled again, rolling her hips into Kahina's paw, pushing her fingers deeper. "I'm going to get you back, you know."

Emboldened, Kahina leaned up to whisper in Retha's ear. "I'm looking forward to it."

The dog bucked her hips sharply and she squeezed Kahina's breast, clawtips pressing through her pelt. "Good, but if you don't get back on my clit, I'm gonna bite you."

The hyena shuddered at the thought. She could do with more of the dog's biting. But, she thought, not this moment. She pulled her fingers from the dog's warm, slick canal and found her clit again, flicking her wet, soft pads there until Retha was panting and shuddering. That fine, lean rump flexed in Kahina's paw as Retha rolled her hips, grinding into the attention, and then the dog's body tensed above her. Retha's thighs squeezed tightly around Kahina's hips, and she uttered a breathless "Oh, fuck, yes," before her muzzle found Kahina's, tongue thrusting into the hyena's mouth. Kahina's tongue met it briefly, then slipped aside to let Retha fill her mouth with soft, exploring warmth.

Kahina's fingers continued to move as they kissed, until Retha pulled back, panting, and pushed her paw away. "Ok, that's enough," she panted, then sprawled atop Kahina. She panted softly, and her tail waved lazily over her rear. "Mmm, that was definitely enough."

Kahina couldn't resist squeezing her cheek again as she lay atop her. "Did you like that?"

Retha chuckled, licking Kahina's chin. "I fuckin' did. Did you?"

Kahina nodded. "Mmhmm."

Retha kissed her nose. "Good. Did you know you're pretty good at that?"

The hyena snorted. "I've had a lot of time for solo practice."

Retha growled and arched her back, pressing herself down into Kahina. "Well, I'm glad of it, even if you're an awful tease."

"I had to try." Kahina licked the dog's muzzle this time.

"I'm glad," Retha smiled at her, ears swiveling forward. "I'm glad you came." She coughed. "I mean, I'm glad you're here, not just in bed with me."

"I'm glad I am, too." She reached her paws up, stretching under Retha. She lay there silently for a time, pondering her next words. "I wasn't looking for a woman, but I'm glad I found you, anyway."

"Oh, going to keep me for a while?" Retha chuckled as she rolled off Kahina, slipping her smaller paw into the hyena's.

"At least until the pups come back."

"Oh, use me for Bibi's baby-sitting?" Retha tapped her muzzle.

Kahina leaned over and nipped the dog's ear. "Hey now. And your chocolate gear!"

"I feel so used." Retha stretched, and Kahina couldn't help but appreciate just how deliciously lithe the dog was, especially without her clothes. "But I'm ok with that." She was silent, then looked at Kahina. "See where it goes?"

Kahina nodded. "See where it goes." Her gaze drifted over Retha's bedside clock. "Which, I guess, is downstairs before the pups get back."

The dog gave Kahina a wicked grin. "I'll text Bibi to keep them for a while longer. I'm not done with you."

As the dog crawled out of bed to hunt up her phone from the pile of clothes, Kahina watched her lazily and reflected.

This isn't what I expected, but I want to see where it goes.

A SIMPLE WAGER

Holly A. Morrison

The door to the tavern swung open, revealing two women practically radiating triumph. On the left was a rabbit wearing the long, grey robes and carrying the stout wooden staff of a Kanly priestess. Her fur was mostly tan except for the velvety black on her face, paws, and large ears. Her hair was cut short, no longer than her cheekbones, and fell in a messy swoop that covered one of her purple eyes.

Her companion was a skunk in leather and steel brigandine armor over a tabard that might have once been white, but which was now thoroughly stained blue. A leather kilt protected her upper legs, while smaller pieces of steel covered her wrists and arms. Her fur was blonde-lavender except for a darker grey stripe that started at her nose and travelled down to the tip of her thick, bushy tail. Her hair, as blonde as her fur, was long and pulled back in a narrow ponytail. Green-black eyes glittered as she shifted the battle axe on her shoulder and lifted a large bag dripping some thick, blue fluid.

"We have slain the Great Moon Beast!" she announced as she tossed the sack into the corner. There was a polite cheer, but it died quickly. After all, slaying the Great Moon Beast was just a low-level prerequisite quest; nearly everyone there had completed it at least twice.

The rabbit, Aventine, rolled her eyes. She'd completed the Great Moon Beast Quest before and had only agreed to go again as a favor for a mutual friend. It had not been unenjoyable, though. Cora was cute, and watching her muscular body as they traveled to the Moon Beast lair had been a reward in and of itself. As they had become better acquainted, Cora had proven to be cheerful, upbeat, and willing to take chances. Aventine admired her bubbly attitude almost as much as her thick, twitching tail. It was a lovely tail, connected to an equally lovely rear end. Keeping it in her sights, the rabbit made a beeline to a table in the corner with a chess set on top.

Aventine set up the chess pieces while Cora accepted semi-serious congratulations from the gathered crowd. The skunk was getting into the spirit, but the half-grin on her muzzle let everyone know she was in on the joke.

After the crowd surrounding Cora filtered away, she swaggered over to the seat opposite Aventine. "Do you play?" she asked the rabbit, waving an ichor-covered paw at the chess set.

"Of course," Aventine said, a vague smile on her muzzle while her eyes met the skunk's. "Would you like to play a game?"

Cora found herself drawn into Aventine's coy, mysterious smile. The rabbit exuded an air of quiet self-possession, a gentle confidence that could be intimidating, but one that Cora noted as very attractive. She also favored Aventine's voluptuous body and soft, dainty paws.

Cora picked up the red queen to examine its rough-hewn shape. A devious idea began to form. "Sure," she said, drawing the word out as she set the piece back down. "But let's make it interesting, a simple wager."

"I'm listening," Aventine said, still smiling.

"How about loser shares a drink with the winner?" Cora hoped that a bit of ale might loosen them up to more personal conversation, something they had so far avoided.

"I see," Aventine said. "And the winner gets to pick the drink?"

Cora grinned. "Of course!" Aventine liked her grin. It was mischievous and playful, a nice contrast to Cora's warrior physique.

Aventine played white and got the first move. She did not get off to an auspicious start though, losing several pawns and a bishop. Despite Cora's kinetic personality, she had a head for chess and, in short order, had totally collapsed Aventine's flank, pinning her forces down in one corner. Cora plucked up her bishop, ready to trigger the end of the game.

Something plopped into Cora's lap and she dropped the chessman in surprise. Leaning back, she found her lap occupied by a wiggly-toed bunny foot.

"Sorry," Aventine said. The rabbit was the picture of innocence. "The floor's cold." Her other foot joined the first.

"It's fine," Cora said with a bit of a blush. She reached down to give the paw a gentle massage to demonstrate just how fine it was.

Aventine grinned, then turned her attention to the chessboard, and her grin widened. "Oh, dear, that was a very strange place to put your bishop." Cora looked and saw that when she had set down the bishop, she had missed the square she was aiming for. Instead of triggering the end game, she'd exposed her own side to retribution. To correct her mistake, she was forced to give up several valuable pieces. She thought this a perfectly reasonable exchange for continuing to rub the paws in her lap.

Aventine studied the now-evenly-matched board in silence for a while. "Mm. Cora? You would tell me if I were going too far, right?"

"What?"

"I mean, I don't want to overstep. So, you'll tell me if I go too far?"

"Oh. Well, yeah, of course." Cora smiled at the bunny. "Don't worry." In honesty, the evening was going far better than the skunk had imagined.

Aventine returned the smile, and then they both turned their attentions back to the chessboard. Cora snatched up her rook and was just deciding where to place it, when Aventine cleared her throat. Cora glanced up at the rabbit, paying not a whit of attention where she placed the rook.

"You stopped rubbing," Aventine said sweetly as she captured the hapless rook.

"I'm beginning to think you're cheating," Cora said, reaching for the board. She undercut her own grumpy manner by reaching down to rub the fuzzy paw in her lap. Her attention divided, Cora didn't notice until too late that her king was trapped behind her own pawns. Aventine slid her last rook down the file, checkmating the trapped king.

"Oh, I seem to have won," Aventine said, pulling her feet free. "You, dear, owe me a drink."

Cora's glare didn't seem to have much effect on the bunny, and she couldn't be that mad, anyway. "Fine," she said, summoning the waiter with a wave of her hand. "What do you want?"

Aventine wrinkled her nose. "Ew, no. You're covered in ichor. Bath first, then drink." She nodded to the waiter. "My friend here is going to take a bath, and then we'll need rooms for the night." He bowed and swept away without saying a word.

"What does that have to do with a drink?" Cora asked, but Aventine was already sweeping away.

"We'll have that drink in my room, if that's alright," she said, giving Cora a swift pat on the shoulder as she passed.

Cora stared after the bunny, half-formed protests dying on her lips. With a grunt, the skunk pushed herself away from the table, ignoring the stares of the tavern's patrons. She allowed herself to be shown to the small, steamy bathing room, complete with an oversized tub brimming

A Simple Wager

with hot water.

She stripped, her armor sticky where the ichor had dried to her fur, and then slid into the water. She soaked for a long while with the water lapping just under her chin. The big tub let her stretch out and so she did, closing her eyes as she just relaxed. Her thoughts drifted to Aventine. Amusement and exasperation warred in her as she thought about the rabbit's cheating. One of her hands drifted between her legs as she thought of Aventine's coy smile. Cora wondered how the bunny's little, pink tongue might feel where her fingers stroked.

With a start and a blush, she pulled her hand away. She didn't even know that Aventine was interested in her, or women in general, and there was no sense fantasizing. Though, she told herself, hand creeping down once more, a little fantasy wasn't totally improper. After all, if Aventine was uninterested, she would just tell Cora so. That would be the end of that. What harm would there be if she fantasized about Aventine while she pleasured herself?

Cora huffed and pulled her hand away and turned to the task of scrubbing her fur clean. She shoved away the tingling need and vague warmth in her loins and just worried about the Moon Beast blood that was still stuck in her fur. It took a good ten minutes of scrubbing to get the ichor off, by which point the water was a faint, luminescent blue. Her thoughts kept straying to Aventine, to the rabbit's warm paws in Cora's hand, to the cottony tail, to Aventine's voluptuous figure.

Sighing, Cora climbed out of the tub and rinsed herself with a bucket of water. Feeling better, or at least less sticky, she pulled on a linen shirt and a fresh kilt and headed towards the row of rooms to talk to Aventine.

Cora was making entirely too much out of this. She was agonizing over something that could be solved with two minutes' conversation. She would knock on the door and just lay it all out for Aventine and see where the two of them stood. And if things didn't work out, well, she could always get back into the bath.

She tapped on the door and heard a soft voice say, "It's open."

Cora stepped inside, her eyes closed as she steeled herself. "Aventine, listen, before we get that drink. It's just, I find you really attractive, and I was just wondering if, you know, you might want to see where things head and…" She ran out of steam, gave up, and opened her eyes to gauge Aventine's reaction. What she saw made her jaw drop open and caused

104

any lingering doubt over whether Aventine was interested in her burn away.

The rabbit was sitting on the edge of the bed, her head cocked to one side as she politely listened, that small smile playing on her lips. She, too, had changed. Aventine was wearing a shimmering white silk shift which hugged her hips and chest and seemed to strain whenever the rabbit breathed in. Her legs were crossed, but Cora could still see the matching panties, not quite shear, peeking out from under the shift.

"I see," Aventine said. She nodded to herself as she considered. "Yes, I think I would very much like to see where things head." Privately, she was more than a little relieved. She had half-expected Cora to take one look at her and just walk away. The skunk had seemed interested, but Aventine had misjudged such things before. "But, for now, you should come over here."

Cora shut her mouth before she settled herself on the bed next to Aventine. "So, uh, did you want to put something on before we got that drink?" She looked at the rabbit obliquely, enjoying the way the material clung to Aventine's curves but trying not to stare.

"Silly skunk," Aventine said as she sidled up to Cora. One arm slid around the skunk's shoulders and a hip settled into, almost on top of, her thigh. "Everything I need's right here."

"What're you doing?" Cora asked, even as she put her arms around Aventine's waist.

"Seducing you. Is it working?"

"Yes, I-I think so."

Aventine was so close, the warmth of her body making Cora's heart pound. Whatever nonchalance she affected, her pulse and the way she leaned into the rabbit, their muzzles nearly touching, gave her feelings away.

Aventine tilted her head up and smiled as she pressed her lips to Cora's. Their kiss was brief, exploratory, both women examining how they felt toward the other. They broke apart quickly, their gazes locked. Cora opened her mouth to say something, but Aventine silenced her with a soft finger.

The rabbit let her finger drift down over Cora's chest, her stomach, and finally settled at the top of her kilt. Aventine leaned in to kiss Cora again, letting this kiss linger while she found the strap holding Cora's kilt in place. Her small, nimble fingers quickly pulled it loose and tugged the kilt open. She broke away from Cora to admire the skunk's dark green panties, then swiftly did away with those.

Cora hiked herself up onto the bed, letting Aventine get kilt and panties out of the way. Excitement and embarrassment warred in her as Aventine slid her hands under her blouse and then helped her pull it over her head. She shivered, only partially from the slight chill as she sat there in nothing more than slightly damp fur.

"I think I'd like that drink now," Aventine murmured. Cora started to ask what she meant, but, for the second time, Cora shushed her. With a slow, sly smile, the rabbit sidled down between Cora's legs, then gave her the tiniest of licks. The skunk shivered, which had nothing to do with the cold.

"That is the worst joke ever," Cora said.

Aventine didn't respond, except to gently spread the folds of Cora's sex and run her tongue along it. Cora laid herself back on the bed with a moan. Aventine's tongue, small and nimble, teased along Cora's dewy folds, pressing as far into her as it could go. Her ears twitched lightly with every soft sound that Cora made.

That warmth returned with a vengeance, and soon Cora was forced to cover her mouth to keep from crying out. She nearly squealed when Aventine abruptly slid up, lips and tongue finding the skunk's clit, the rabbit's teeth not quite nibbling on it. One of Aventine's fingers replaced her tongue inside of Cora, then a second, wriggling inside of her, seeking out the spots that made the skunk squirm and whimper. Her tail, partially trapped underneath Aventine, lashed at the bed as the rabbit kept up her relentless assault on the skunk's clit.

Cora was getting quite damp, and Aventine slid down to lap between and around her fingers, still pistoning deep inside of her. Aventine shifted her other hand to tease Cora's unoccupied clit with her thumb, rubbing firmly over the skunk's button. The rabbit's nose was full of Cora's scent, her own panties dampening as she licked up every drop of Cora's juices.

It was more than the skunk could take. With a muffled cry, Cora bucked against Aventine's muzzle. Her body tensed, then shuddered as she orgasmed, her tail curling up. She dug the fingers of her free hand into the bedding, closing her eyes tightly as she tried to keep quiet. Waves of pleasure crashed over her while Aventine kept licking and rubbing, diving as deeply as possible into her, heightening and extending

Cora's orgasm. Aventine made an appreciative little purring noise but never slowed, even when the skunk's climax waned and finally ended.

In fact, Aventine continued to lick until Cora put her hand on the rabbit's head. Aventine looked up, licking her lips and grinning mischievously. Cora was too out-of-breath to say anything, but Aventine understood. She climbed up until she was snuggling against Cora's side, one arm and leg carelessly thrown over the skunk, muzzle perilously close to Cora's lips. Cora pulled Aventine to her, closing the last millimeters between them to kiss. She tasted herself on Aventine's lips, or thought she did, mingled with the sweet flavor of the rabbit's mouth and tongue.

Aventine murmured something into Cora's lips, but the skunk merely grinned. Her hands stroked over Aventine's back, first over, then under her thin slip. Aventine arched into Cora's hands, breaking the kiss.

"Did you enjoy that?" Aventine asked, leaning in just enough to brush her nose against Cora's.

Cora chuckled softly, her hands still running up and down along the rabbit's spine. "Very much so."

"Maybe we can do it again sometimes?"

"It's cute that you think we're done," Cora said then, when Aventine tilted her head, rolled over to pin the rabbit underneath her. Aventine squealed and giggled, pressing in for another kiss. She looped her arms around the back of Cora's neck and held herself into the kiss.

Cora kept one hand underneath Aventine, but the other slid around and up under Aventine's shift and settled on her breast. As far as Cora was concerned, it was the perfect size: just a little more than a handful. She gave it a squeeze, eliciting a squeak and soft moan from Aventine, followed by an excited shudder as the skunk's thumb found a nipple nestled in the thick, soft fur.

Aventine wrapped her legs around Cora's hips, practically hanging off of the other woman as they kissed and Cora played with the rabbit's bosom. Her thumb rubbed over Aventine's nipple, rough callous teasing the sensitive nub, making the rabbit wriggle about.

Aventine slid away from the kiss, struggling to catch her breath. She laid her head back on the pillow, which gave Cora the opportunity to leave a trail of kisses along the line of her neck. When she got to the hollow of Aventine's neck, she sat up and tugged at the shift. With a great deal of squirming, the two of them got the thin cloth off and into some corner of the room. Cora, her hand on Aventine's chest, grinned broadly as she admired the view. The soft, sweet rabbit lay before her, wearing nothing but panties that were now so damp as to be transparent.

"Like what you see?" Aventine said, the last word dissolving into a squeal as Cora dropped back and nipped at her neck with a little growl. "I guess that's a yes," Aventine murmured, lifting her head up to expose her neck to the skunk's playful bites.

Cora nibbled her way back down along Aventine's throat, then along her collarbone. Her muzzle slipped between Aventine's breasts, leaving a soft kiss there before she smooched her way along the one that she wasn't still playing with. Cora found Aventine's other nipple, giving it, too, a kiss before she wrapped her lips around it. She looked up, grinning, watching Aventine's beatific expression of pleasure as the skunk suckled on one nipple, while rolling the other through her fingers. Her free hand slid down, over the curve of Aventine's butt and then along her thigh and then it was rubbing, a little awkwardly, between the rabbit's legs.

Aventine moaned aloud, not bothering to stifle her cries. She jumped when Cora slipped her hand under the panties, pulling them down enough to give her room to rub Aventine's sex directly. The angle was all wrong, however, and soon Cora had climbed off of Aventine to snuggle in against the rabbit's side. Aventine turned so that her back was against Cora, her head on Cora's bicep. The skunk draped her long, fluffy tail over the rabbit, and Aventine hugged it to her chest, nearly purring. Cora pulled Aventine's panties down further and, with Aventine's assistance, they joined the slip on the floor.

With one arm holding Aventine close, Cora ran her fingers over the rabbit's damp sex, teasing around her entrance. She nuzzled into Aventine's ears, whispering how beautiful Aventine was, as her first finger slid inside of the rabbit. Aventine shuddered against her, her breath catching in her throat. A second finger joined the first, then a third, before Cora was sliding them in and out of the rabbit, letting her hand rub against Aventine's clit in the process. Soon, Aventine was squirming about in Cora's grasp, squeezing the skunk's tail close. Cora added little nips and nibbles along Aventine's long ears between whispered compliments on how beautiful Aventine was, how warm and soft she felt, and how fun it was to make her squirm like that.

Aventine's moaning was rising in pitch, her cheeks visibly flushed through her fur. She was grinding her hips into Cora's hand and had started to draw her legs slowly up to her chest. Suddenly, Cora pulled her hand away, wrapping her arms around the rabbit and hugging her close. It took Aventine a moment to realize that Cora had stopped playing with her, and she looked over her shoulder, her expression a mixture of confusion and reproach.

"I believe our bet was to share a drink of the winner's choice," Cora said.

"Oh, I see," Aventine responded, a little hoarse and out of breath while a light blush crept up her face.

With a grin, Cora directed the rabbit to climb up and straddle her face. Cora gripped Aventine's hips, holding her at just the right angle, while Aventine braced herself against the headboard with one hand, the other burying itself in Cora's hair. Unlike Aventine's small, nimble tongue, Cora's was long and broad, and instead of careful, targeted teasing, Cora simply lapped at Aventine's sex.

She took two slow licks over Aventine's entrance before pressing her lips against the rabbit's pussy and pushing her tongue deep inside Aventine. Her sex tasted as sweet as her lips had, Cora noted with pleasure. Her tongue delved far inside the rabbit, lapping at Aventine's inner walls over and again. As worked up as Aventine was, it only took Cora a few moments to push her over the edge. With a squeal, Aventine pressed herself into Cora's tongue. She shuddered as she orgasmed. Cora ran her tongue over Aventine's sex, slipping it back inside of her with each stroke, until Aventine's climax waned and, finally, stopped.

Cora helped Aventine drop to the bed in a kind of controlled fall. The two wrapped their arms around each other, lips meeting for another kiss, slower and softer than the others. When their lips broke apart, they nuzzled into each other, a tangle of limbs underneath Cora's tail.

"Yes," Cora said.

"Mm?" Aventine asked, her eyes closed while she nosed at Cora's cheek.

Cora grinned. "I would like to do this again."

Aventine answered with a lazy smile. "Any time you want." Her voice was soft, her breathing deep, if still a little fast. "But maybe a nap first."

Cora chuckled as she settled in with the rabbit for what promised to be a very lovely nap.

Support

Kristina "Orrery" Tracer

The trip home had started seventy hours and two continents ago, with a clean bill of health from the Bahuchara Center. Aqua cried when Dr. Kuchhadia pressed a parting gift into her paws, a hand-mirror in a carved wooden frame. She stared into its depths the whole time I arranged payment and got our luggage ready for the trip. She was on strict light-duty, no-lifting restrictions for the next three months, so I wasn't expecting her to help, but I was amused by how entranced she was. The newly-made mouse's teal-blue eyes glistened as she studied herself, staring past the surgical scars to the newly narrowed shoulders, lengthened muzzle, and smooth, sinewy tail that she curled and uncurled around her own wrist. Occasionally, she pulled her gaze away from her reflection to smile gratefully, gesturing towards her body as if to ask me if I saw what she did. If this was real.

Aqua's simple joy reminded me so much of my own, right after my reconstruction. The memories from my trip, from my lonely over-night in Amsterdam waiting for a morning flight to India, to the last exhausted steps back to my apartment, had been burned in my mind. I remembered my first taste of solid food: mattar paneer on rice, with mint water. I remembered Dr. Modi's frown and the twitch of his mus-tache when I told him I'd come alone. Even something as simple as put-ting slip-guards on my hooves for a morning run, could jog memories of my time in physical therapy, learning how to use my new body. It sometimes felt as if my trip hadn't just been yesterday, but could be to-morrow. Sometimes I wondered if I could wake up in the middle of the night and still be in the hospital bed, pressing the nurse call button just to have someone there. I smiled at my wife and gave her a thumbs-up to show her I understood how she felt. I wasn't going to let her face this alone.

It was oppressively hot and humid in Vadodara, the middle of mon-soon season, and the air was thick enough with moisture for it to bead on my fur just by standing still. It had been the middle of winter the

110

last time I'd traveled here, and even though it hadn't been any cooler, it had at least been dry. I wiped the sweat from my stubbly pelt and again thanked the travel guide's recommendation of a body trim. Aqua's coat wasn't long enough yet for her to feel it, but her constant complaints of itching were probably worse. After two months of hospitals, hotel beds, and foreign food, we were both exhausted as we stood in the line to access the terminal. The elderly couple behind us, a man in a business shirt and tie and a woman in a red-and-brown sari, waved away our apologies.

"Bahuchara?" the husband asked, and I nodded. "Good business, many tourists come to Gujarat," he offered in heavily-accented English. "Congratulations."

"Thank you," I said as I reached out for Aqua's paw. "She's the one to thank; this is her trip. I'm just here to help." Aqua just squeezed my hoof, then grabbed her crutch again.

The security officer at the transit line drummed his fingers on the podium, making a show of slowly reading Aqua's clinical release. The paperwork attested in English, Gujarati, and Hindi that the bearer was a recent patient, and the after photo was only a day old; the only difference was an extra night's sleep and the weariness of a walk from the taxi stand. "Do you have any legal identification?" he droned, equal parts bored and irritated.

"She shouldn't need that," I said, putting one hoof on my hip. "The clinic's paperwork was enough when I traveled. You know the photo's going to be out of date."

"New rules. This isn't legal ID." His tone told me *new* meant *five seconds ago*. He snapped his fingers against the paper. "I need proof of identity."

Aqua groaned. "Fine." She leaned heavily on one crutch and fumbled in the inner pocket of her jacket.

She hissed and I stepped in to help, holding out a hoof. "Let me?"

"I've got it." She waved off my offer and dug out her passport. Its photo—male human, brown hair, ears nowhere near as expressive—was a fairly close match with the before photo on the release. "This make you happy?"

The security guard took the passport and made a show of studying it. "Please have your photo updated within ninety days of return." She returned both papers to my wife, then turned to me. "Yours?"

I passed over my own passport; I'd updated my photo long back, and the impala in the picture looked remarkably like me, albeit with longer fur and several more hours of sleep. He gave mine the barest glance, then returned it as well. "Enjoy your trip."

"Asshole," Aqua muttered once we were through the scanners. "I hope his kids want to be cows when they grow up."

**

We'd been stuck on the bus for half an hour; neither of us had wanted to drive to the fitting clinic. Aqua sat bolt-upright on the seat next to me, clutching her documents folder in her fingers as if it might disappear if she took her eyes off of it. I put a hoof on her leg, trying to still the nervous bouncing. "I'm here."

"I know," she said, but the shaking in her voice belied her tension. "I keep telling myself this is okay, this is what I want, but I can't—" She closed her eyes and dropped her voice. "I can't know, you know? This is all guess-work, all of it. I'm thrusting myself into the void, running on a dream and a feeling. I'm so scared I'm chasing a fantasy."

"We've all been through this," I reminded her. "You're not going through this alone."

"I know, and that helps," she retorted. "There's just nothing I can do or say to prove any of this is real. It's all just… feelings, emotions. Sometimes that's not enough."

"Sometimes feelings are all we have." I shrugged. I'd given up trying to prove anything years ago. I just knew I felt better now. She'd figure that out in time. "This is our stop."

The secretary at the clinic, a brown-furred coyote named Melody, smiled as we approached. "Welcome back, Ndidi." She nodded to my wife, standing beside me, and flicked one ear. "And you are…?"

"A-Aqua," my wife said, her arms wrapped tightly around her chest, her folder clutched under her arm.

"It's okay, Aqua," Melody soothed. "We've all been there. I need a cur-rent ID and the reference pictures for the prostheticist."

Aqua passed over the folder, then shoved her hands into her pockets. Melody carefully opened it with a claw tip, then extracted the sheets within. The first page held reference pictures drawn by the reconstruction artist. The second looked like a blueprint of an anthropomorphic mouse, annotated with dimensions and color guides. The third was a familiar picture, an old draw-

ing of a pudgy murine figure, an array of rings decorating her left ear. The camisole the figure wore was teal instead of Aqua's current purple, and she had a leather jacket instead of a fleece vest. The jeans she wore were hip-hugging and fitted to the mouse's frame, instead of the faded straight-legs with the button on the wrong side that she was currently wearing, and where Aqua's feet were sandal-shod, the mouse in the picture's hinds were bare save a single toe-ring. The biggest difference, though, was the pose. Where the figure in the picture stood comfortably and relaxed, flashing a peace sign at the viewer; the person beside me shifted her weight from one leg to the other, hugging herself with her head hunched. Her eyes the picture's and her cheeks flushed.

Melody smiled and put the pictures back in their sleeve. "It's a lovely image. Have you picked a doctor yet?"

"Kuchhadia," she murmured. "I'm hoping I can get on her calendar; she's booked two years out."

"Lucky if you do," the coyote grinned, her ears perked upright. "I had to see Modi; his results are great, but his recovery time's longer. Just try go in the winter; Gujarat's miserable in summer."

***

The rainstorm that had started on the last flight followed us through landing, baggage claim, and the taxi ride home. All the way back, Aqua's head either lolled back against the headrest of whatever seat she was in, or rested against my neck. Now, at last, the cool rain seemed to welcome us home. She slid awkwardly from the front seat of the taxi and into my arms. "We're almost home," I murmured as I helped her into her crutches. "I'll get the luggage; can you pay?"

Aqua nodded, then moved around to the driver's side door while I started unloading suitcases. "We really appreciate this; the first two companies we called refused."

"Fluff's got money," the driver said with a shrug. "No sense leaving that on the table."

We both froze at the slur, and my ears shot upright. "Excuse me?" the mouse replied after a long second. "Did you just—"

"Don't make it personal," he replied. "I got a cousin that went fluffy. Big cat. He's alright." He swiped her card on his phone, then passed it back. "Sign here?"

We watched him pull away from the curb in awkward silence. "Asshole!" she snapped once he was gone. "He literally just pulled a some-of-my-friends on us!" She scowled at me. "Are most people like that around here?"

I shrugged. "Less so here than most places in the States."

She paused and flicked her tail. "Was I like that, before?"

"A long time ago, maybe," I chuckled, "but not lately. Let's get you inside. I'll get the luggage." The wheels of the suitcases grumbled against the cracked pavement as I walked up to the door. The mouse picked her way carefully along the driveway beside me to the front door of the apartment complex. Her tail curled and swayed behind her as she moved, reflexively trying to counterbalance her hesitant steps.

At the front door, she stopped and looked down. "Ndidi?"

"I'm here." I stepped over the threshold and blocked the door so that she could take her time. "What can I do?"

The mouse shook her head. "I just want a spotter. That's carpet in there."

I frowned and let go of the luggage. "Remember the rug? Let me help you."

"I've got this," she replied as she took the first hesitant step forward. The tips of her crutches sank deep into the plush pile. It absorbed my hoofbeats as well, and the suitcases slowed to a crawl across its expanse.

***

The gurney's wheels squeaked on the tile as it flew down the hall. Aqua whimpered, scrabbling at the railings, while two orderlies pushed her. I jogged behind, my hooves clacking on the floor. We pulled into a pre-surgical ward, and a small cloud of nurses swarmed into the room. Within moments, a bottle of water appeared, as did a paper cup of pills, and Aqua paused her crying long enough to swallow. I walked around the table and took her paw in my hoof, squeezing it carefully. "I'm here."

"Hurts." The tears on her face made the word redundant. "Can't move it."

"Hush, love." I stroked her arm with my fingers. "The doctor will be here soon."

It took six agonizing minutes for Dr. Kuchhadia to appear, an older

Indian woman wearing a bindi, her salt-and-pepper hair pulled into a tight braid. She nodded as she entered and walked right up to Aqua's side. "The nurses said you fell?"

"She did," I replied. "Right after—"

"I asked her," Aqua's reconstruction surgeon replied curtly, her lightly-accented English clipped and precise. "Aqua, can you talk?"

"Yes," my wife panted against gritted teeth. "After physio. I caught the edge of the rug in the lobby."

Dr. Kuchhadia hmmed and lightly stroked Aqua's leg, fingers feeling for signs of damage. "Likely just a sprain, but we should X-ray and confirm. I'll call Radiology and tell them you're coming, and the nurses will bring you an ice pack for swelling. One moment and we'll head down." She stepped out of the room, and a flurry of Hindi flowed in from the hallway.

I carefully brushed Aqua's forehead with my thumb. "I told you, love, I could've gotten the wheelchair."

"Told you," my wife breathed in response, "if I want help, I'll ask for it."

***

When Aqua cried out, I was ready. I stopped and half-turned, letting go of the luggage so that she could fall into my arms. I caught her weight and braced her, trying to make sure I didn't put any extra pressure beyond her own weight. The mouse's muzzle pressed awkwardly into my shoulder, but I just grunted as she stumbled into me, her crutches banging into my sides. "I've got you."

"Damnit, Ndidi!" My wife's response startled me enough that I almost dropped her anyway. She tapped her crutch against my leg, then groaned and pushed herself away from me. "I told you, I've got this."

A bellow down the hallway cut my response short. "Ndidi!" One of our neighbors, a grizzly bear named Lewis, barreled out of his room towards us, then snapped out his arms in a hug. I returned the embrace, then quickly pulled myself loose. As I withdrew, he turned towards the mouse beside me, his muzzle splitting in a grin. "Aqua? That you now?"

"It is, yeah." Aqua nodded and visibly leaned on one crutch, letting go of the other to hold out her paw.

"Oh, hell no," Lewis said as he dashed forward, faster than I'd ever seen him move before. His arms went around her shoulders, squeezing with eerie delicacy for someone so massive. "Welcome to the family, and welcome home."

I pushed a smile onto my muzzle. "Lew, we just got back. We could use a shower and a couple of days to sleep."

"Oh! Sorry!" Lewis leapt backwards, sending Aqua's loose crutch clattering to the ground. "Oh, let me, uh—"

He and I both stepped forward together and grabbed for the crutch, colliding with each other. "Sorry, I just—"

"Hey," Aqua sighed, making us both freeze. "You're going to knock me over. Let me?"

We both stepped back again, giving the mouse some space. With painstaking slowness, Aqua hooked the arm brace of her fallen crutch with the end of her other one, then carefully lifted it into her grasp. We both watched as she put it on again. "I told you," she said with an exhausted smile, "I've got this."

"You're not supposed to be lifting anything," I reminded her quietly.

"I have to lift myself and my crutches, at least," she replied. "Two walks a day."

"Only two?" Lewis said. "Dr. Modi had me on four."

"You probably have three times her mass," I reminded the bear. "And you went ten years ago. New procedures, new rules."

"Oh, yeah, fair enough." The bear nodded. "I'll go tell Dave you're back; he'll be ecstatic. Rest up, we'll talk later!" Then he waved and continued across the rug and out the front door of the building, leaving us to make the last long stretch home.

***

Thunder rolled in the distance as we opened the front door. I put a hoof on Aqua's shoulder and helped her across the threshold, transitioning from carpet back to tile. The crutches' rubber tips squeaked as she tottered back towards the bedroom, punctuating the rain against the windows. I abandoned the suitcases in the front hall, then shed my coat as I walked. "You're doing great, love," I encouraged. "End of the hall, right turn."

"I know our apartment, Ndidi," the mouse groused. Her voice was thin and strained from exhaustion. "I'm just tired."

"Do you need to sit?"

She shook her head. "No, I just want to lie down."

"Okay." I carefully stepped around her, then turned on the light in the bedroom. I quickly kicked the loose clothes strewn around the floor into a pile by my side of the bed, then turned back and motioned her to enter. "It's safe now. Carpet again, be careful. Almost there."

Aqua smiled gratefully and counted down the steps as she approached the bed. "Four… three… two—oof!" She stumbled on the last step, flopping heavily onto the foam mattress. With a groan and a clatter, she tossed aside her crutches, then rolled onto her side. "Home."

"Home," I repeated as I shed my top; the shirt was slick with rain and weariness, and it fell to the floor with a wet splat. "You made it."

"We made it," my wife concurred. "I couldn't have done this without you. I—" She stopped, choking up anew. "I'm home. I'm *me* and I'm *home* and… and you're still here."

"I'm still here," I agreed, tossing my rain-soaked pants into a pile. Dressed in just a trim bra and panties, I sprawled on the bed next to the mouse and grabbed a pillow for the two of us to share. "We're still here."

"We're here," Aqua breathed, clutching at me weakly. I pulled her into my arms and stroked a paw down the back of her head, rubbing with the grain as the nurses had showed us. We lay there for an endless moment, my wife's newly sculpted muzzle pressed the tan fur of my shoulder, shaking and sobbing with exhaustion and joy. "Everything's going to be okay."

"It will, promise," I said, holding out my hooves to her. "Want me to help you undress?"

She looked at me, then shook her head. "No, I think I just want to lie here for a bit, if that's okay."

I frowned slightly and flicked my ears again. "You're exhausted and you're sweaty. You should at least let me help you get undressed."

"I should, and I will," Aqua agreed with a sigh, rubbing at her muzzle. "If I need help, I'll ask."

***

"Ndidi?" my wife called out from the fitting room, her voice shaking. "I need your help."

"I'm here," I called back through the door. "What can I do?"

The latch unclicked, and the door swung open. "It doesn't fit right, I don't think. Maybe this is a mistake."

I stepped inside at the unspoken invitation and closed the door behind me. "Deep breaths, love. Don't tug on anything. It's going to feel a little tight and strange. What's wrong?"

Inside the fitting room, Aqua stood next to a table, staring into the full-length mirror and clutching a latex applique. She'd gotten the belt cinched around her waist, and the mouse tail attached to it hung behind her; it stuck out a little too straight to be organic, but the color was a close match for her skin-tone. One of the small breastforms she'd gotten had adhered, but the other had slid down her chest. She'd pulled her panties tight to hold her tuck, but her lower body contour was around her thighs. She'd managed to get the claws on her left hand, but the ones for her right still sat in their unopened bag. Smears of adhesive dotted her skin. "It's not working."

I chuckled. "Did you read the directions?"

"Directions?" She turned away from the mirror, eyes wide. "Were there—" She blushed. "I was so nervous. I tried to listen."

Carefully, I took her facial appliance in my hooves and set it down on the dressing table. "You've used way too much." I grabbed the paper towels and gum remover, then started cleaning up the excess adhesive. "It's okay; I did the same the first time."

"I can't do this alone," she said. "I've got gunk everywhere. Help me clean up?"

"Of course, love." Once I had her face clean, I moistened a fresh towel and wiped away the cleaner. "You're shaking."

"I'm nervous," Aqua repeated. "It's like I'm so close, but the closer I get, the more it hurts. Does that make sense? It doesn't make any sense to me."

"I understand." I put a few small dots of gum on the mask. "This is all it takes; more and it will run. Press and hold in place for ten seconds. See the guide marks?" She nodded and took the mask back from me, then pressed it to her face. A slow ten-count later, she removed her hands and looked in the mirror again. The mask was light grey, textured to look like fur and contoured to match the body-plan as closely as possible. Small fibre-optic whiskers splayed from the end. The illusion faded if I looked at her eyes, brown human ones staring back from open circles in the appliance, but a makeup brush and some time could close that gap. I smiled at the mouse in the mirror and took her hand in mine.

***

I rose from the bed and finished stripping off my clothes, the bra and panties joining the pile of discarded clothes. Naked, I sat beside her on the bed and watched her struggle to sit up. She fumbled with the buttons of her blouse, then slid it off her shoulders with a hiss. "Gently," I said, as much to myself as to her. I remembered how hard it was to move in the first few months after my change.

The mouse shot me a glare. "Why don't you grab my crutches for me?"

"But—" I cut myself off sharply at Aqua's whisker-twitch and held up my hooves. "Okay. You've got this."

I rolled over and grabbed the crutches from the side of the bed, then passed them to her so she could stand. She managed to get out of her camisole, revealing the small curves of her breasts, but her new body and her exhaustion were clearly making the skirt a challenge. She groaned as she reached behind her, fumbling with the flip over her tail-base, then rocked back and forth as she tugged the fabric past her murine hips. "You'll probably want to stand up for this part."

"Ndidi, will you stop?" she hissed as she squirmed. "You're right here. I know you want to help, but if I need it, I swear, I'll ask for it."

I raised a brow and folded my arms. "Like with the carpet in the front entrance?"

Aqua visibly blushed, her ears pinkening inside. "Touché," she admitted. "Still, if you hadn't been hovering over me the whole trip, I probably would have. By that point, I just needed to feel like I was in control." She cocked her head to the side. "Did whoever went with you act like this?"

I smiled sadly. "I went alone." I managed to keep my voice from cracking until the very end.

The mouse flinched. "Oh. Oh, Ndidi." She held out her arms to me. "I'm sorry, I should've realized."

"It's okay," I whispered as I pulled her against me. "It was a long time ago. I thought I was over it, but I guess I'm not." I hugged her carefully, mindful of her stitches, then let go. "I'll let you finish."

She kissed my muzzle, then smiled at me. "Would you help me with my skirt, then spot me to the mirror? I want to see how I look."

I smiled back and nodded. "Can you stand?" She raised herself onto her crutches, and I knelt to carefully work her skirt past her hips. The back of the bedroom door had a full-length mirror on it, and I escorted her over to it. An anthropomorphic mouse stood in its reflections, leaning heavily on her medical crutches. Teal-blue eyes darted about as she took in all her changes. Her light grey pelt was still awkwardly short and pink skin showed through in places, riddled with fresh, angry scars from the full-body rebuild. Her front teeth hadn't yet fully grown in, so her muzzle looked oddly bare as she opened her jaw and studied herself. She didn't look like the picture she'd shown me three years ago, the one that started this journey. Behind her, an impala stood, tan fur shaved oddly short, the white of her chest and black spot on her forehead pale against the skin beneath. "It'll improve in time," I cautioned her, remembering my own shock at seeing myself the first time. In the mirror, the impala's hoof gently gripped the mouse's shoulder with blunt black-tipped fingers.

"I read the guide," she said with a toothless smile, the sparse fur beneath her teal-blue eyes damp with tears. "I look… I look better."

I smiled at her confidence. "You do, yes."

She nodded again. "Help me lie down? I'm exhausted." I nodded again, and together we tottered slowly back and I helped her back to bed. "And ravenous," she added once she was prone. "Dinner, then sleep."

"I can accommodate." I went back to the hallway and got my carry-on bag, then sat down on the edge of the bed and opened it up. The first thing I pulled out of it was my laptop; ordering dinner took just a few clicks, and then I set it aside. "We'll have noodles in an hour. I'll answer the door," I offered unnecessarily.

"That, you can do," the mouse replied. "Pass me my mirror?"

I pulled the hand-mirror Dr. Kuchhadia had given her out of the bag, then lay down beside her and stroked the short fur of her tummy, sliding my other arm under her head. "I'm proud of you, you know. For making it." I hugged her close, pulling her against me and draping her tail over my leg.

She squirmed back in my embrace, pressing into me. "Thank you, Ndidi."

"You're welcome, love," I whispered into her ear. Silence settled in between us, the comfortable quiet of happy exhaustion as I traced my fingers over her front, occasionally brushing one of her nipples. After a few minutes, she shifted, then let out a sigh and squirmed a little. I lifted my head from the pillow. "Everything okay?" I asked.

"Everything's… um…" She squeaked quietly and ducked her head.

"I was just thinking about how this started, and the picture and… um." Her tailtip flicked against my ankle. "Could you help me, please?"

I smiled and kissed the back of her head. "I'd love to." I shifted my arm slightly, then cupped one of her breasts. Her nipple was already stiff under my blunt fingertips, and I ran a circle around her sensitive flesh, making her shiver. "This good?"

She nodded, then lifted her upper leg, bent at the knee, opening herself to my fingers. "Can I watch?" she asked, picking up the mirror.

"Please," I agreed, and I brought my other hoof to her mons while she adjusted her view. Her skin there was more sensitive, the rebuild more extensive, but she only nodded as I caressed her. "It looks rough, I know, but—"

"It'll heal," she hissed. Her breath sped up as I explored her newly-crafted flesh, gently stroking her outer labia. They were already swollen, and the scent of her anticipation clung to her skin as I started petting her in earnest. A soft sigh escaped her with every stroke, and she began to rock her hips in time to my motions, pressing herself into my touch. Her words carved a breathy stream through the silence. "I needed this. I've wanted this for years and I didn't know how to say it and I was so afraid and nowwww—" Her words slid into a groan, punctuated by a rumbling of thunder outside. "I have to know."

I teased one finger between her lips, brushing against the tender inner folds. "I want you to know," I breathed in her ear, tugging carefully at her nipple with my other hoof and rolling it in my fingers. "Tell me how it feels, Aqua."

"It feels—oh hell." She panted and scrabbled at the mattress with her claws. "It feels incredible." I rolled one fingertip around her clit, not touching it directly, and she let out a strangled gasp. "I… I don't have words, it's like… it's like a key in a lock, a missing puzzle piece. It's like… like I always needed this, it feels—" She shuddered in my arms. "Hell," she said again. "Nerve twinge."

I stopped my explorations and kissed the back of her head. "Should I stop?"

"No," she insisted. "In fact, would you… kiss me?"

"Are you sure?"

"I am." She squirmed forward, out of my arms. "Please."

I nuzzled the back of her head. "Okay, then. Careful when you roll on your back. Pillow above your tailbase." I grabbed a second pillow and positioned it, then helped her turn over. Once she was propped up, I slid off the end of the bed, kneeling between her spread legs. From this position, the recent scars of her surgery were unmistakable, the parallel rows of reshaped flesh running between her legs. Her labia were damp, the lips flushed and parted slightly. "Ready, Aqua?"

She drew in a deep breath, then let it out. "Please."

***

I opened the front door and held it open while Aqua darted inside, then closed the door behind us and locked it. "We're home now, love. It's safe."

"I was a wreck," she sobbed, leaning against the wall. "That asshole—"

I put a hoof on her shoulder. "I'm sorry that happened. Do you want some company? I can call Lew and Dave over."

The mouse shook her head rapidly. "I just want to lie down."

"Okay." I guided her back to the bedroom, shrugging off my coat as we walked. We got to the end of the hall, and I flicked on the light. Aqua dropped onto the edge of the bed, then sunk her muzzle into her paws. "I'd almost forgotten."

I sat down next to her and put an arm around her waist. "How did it feel, forgetting?"

My wife lifted her head and smiled weakly. The makeup just below her eyes had started to run. "Normal. Average. I felt like—" She stopped and sighed. "I felt like I was just being me, you know? Like I was what I looked like. Like I wasn't wearing a mask, that this was just how I looked, you know?"

I nodded and took one of her paws in my hoof. "I know. It is you."

"It's not, though, is it?" She hissed through her teeth. "It's all just make-up and rubber. It's not real."

I squeezed her paw and picked through my words carefully. "It's real enough."

Aqua frowned. "It's not real enough to avoid coming off when some asshole steps on my tail and then laughs when the belt breaks."

I sighed and nodded. "That's not what defines real, though, is it?" The mouse didn't answer; she just looked down at her paws. "Real is who you are inside. Real is what made you want this in the first place."

"I guess," she said after a moment's quiet. "I can't prove any of this. I just know it, and that has to be enough. And that makes every misstep ten

times worse, like I have to keep proving it's true. To everyone." Her voice dropped to a near-whisper. "To me."

"I believe you, Aqua. I have since you told me." I let go of her paw and stood. "I'd like to get comfortable. Want to join me?"

"No, I hate—" Her voice cut out suddenly.

I tossed my pants onto the pile of dirty laundry by my side of the bed and stood back up. "You hate what?"

Aqua was silent for a moment. "I hate getting undressed. I hate taking off the appliances. I hate… what's underneath."

"The trip's in three months," I reminded her. "That's not an illusion."

"And I hate it when you say it like that," my wife groused. "That just makes me feel like I'm faking it the rest of the time."

I stripped off my top and bra, then sat back on the bed in just my panties. "You're not a fraud, I promise. If you were, I don't think you'd feel this way. Also, you shouldn't sleep in your prosthetics," I said gently. "You don't want to have to replace them again this close to not needing them anymore."

"That would be dumb," she wearily agreed. "One sec." She stood up and stepped into the bathroom, while I curled up under the covers. She came back several minutes later, stripped of her appliques and clothing. Her human face looked so alien to me at this point, even though her eyes were the same. This wasn't her to my mind anymore, I realized; she was the self the prosthetics embodied, the self in the picture instead of her old human skin. She darted under the covers, quickly hiding beneath the sheets.

I scooted in close and snuggled up against her, wrapping my arms around her to try to stop her shivering. She folded her arms and turned away from me, so I pressed my chest to her back, the bare skin cool against my pelt. "Three more months. That's all."

"It's too long," she whimpered, shaking. "I'm not going to make it. I nearly broke down crying in the bathroom. I want this—need this—so badly. I can't explain it, any of it, and and I hate how I feel every time I look at myself."

"It's alright," I tried to comfort her as I rocked carefully. "You've made it this far. Soon this won't be an issue any more. I went through this; you can make it too."

"I hate it!" Her voice cracked. "I hate feeling like this. I hate having to wait. I hate how every time I look at myself in the mirror when I'm made up I get excited and then I have to take off the stuff and I just feel worse for liking what I saw because it doesn't feel real anymore."

"It's real," I insisted, reaching down to stroke her tummy. She was physically aroused, and her cock twitched when I touched her. "Do you want help with that?"

"Just hold me. Talk to me," she said. "Tell me it's going to be okay?"

"It's going to be okay, Aqua," I said softly, kissing the back of her neck. I felt her arm start to move, and I pulled her more snugly to my chest. "The flight's in three months, and then it's six weeks at the clinic, and then it's over." She whimpered softly in the darkness in front of me, nodding. "Smooth tail, and round expressive ears," I continued, describing her body to her. "Short little claws and light grey fur. Beautiful blue-green eyes, just like you wanted. It's all going to work out just fine." I kissed the back of her head and hugged her. "Pert little breasts and wide hips, and that long, sexy snout. Smooth between the legs, and such a sensitive—"

Her shudder cut me off, followed by a sob. I held her until the shaking stopped, murmuring softly to her while her crying subsided. Once she was done, I reached back and grabbed a towel from my nightstand, then discreetly passed it to her. "How do you feel now, love?"

"Bad," she said, her voice still shaking. "Broken." Her sigh was almost a whimper. "It'll be better in three months, won't it?"

"I hope so, Aqua," I replied, my own guts clenching. Even at my worst, I'd never been this bad, but I had less to change, less to fix to feel right with myself. "I hope so."

***

I nodded again, then leaned forward and pressed my muzzle to her sex. She jumped as if the lightning outside had struck her, letting out a long moaning sigh in response. Her scent was unfamiliar but not unpleasant, still very much her. I parted my lips and ran my tongue along her labia in the most intimate of kisses. She groaned and grabbed the bedsheets with her freshly sculpted claws. "Oh—" It was a cry of recognition, of understanding, a wordless acceptance that ran through her from crotch to head. Emboldened, I licked more deeply, probing between her netherlips, caressing her tenderly with my tongue. Her groans and squeaks became my guide, showing me how to help her discover herself with my muzzle. With each stroke, her breath rose, her sighs keening higher and higher. She gripped the bed to hold herself fast, driven past words, past thought, lost in the qualia of new flesh.

Her hips against rose to meet my muzzle, and she whimpered against the bed. "I—please, yes, I'm so close." With that, I let myself seek out her newly formed clit. That hot and sensitive nubbin of flesh was flush with nerves and sensation. When I licked it, my wife let out a squeal. She dug her claws into the mattress as I circled her, coaxing her closer and closer. Lightning struck outside, and her entire body shook in the moment of climax. The moment stretched into silent seconds, followed by the low rumble of thunder and the slow release of tension as Aqua slumped against the bed with a groan. "That's... that's enough," she moaned. "No more. No more."

I placed a last kiss against her mons, well above the overstimulated area, then rose and lay down beside my wife again. She rolled onto her side and hugged me tightly, then began to sob. "I'm here, Aqua," I soothed, stroking her bare back. "Did that help?"

She shook her head. "Yes," she breathed, tremulous and awe-struck. "That was... I don't have words for it. Thank you, love. That helped."

My own eyes grew damp at that, and I wiped at them with the back of one hoof. "I'm glad, Aqua, and thank you." I glanced at the clock. "Dinner will be here in forty minutes. Let's... let's just lie here until then." The mouse in my arms nodded and sighed happily, and I held her close as she admired herself in the hand-mirror, listening to the rain.

SHE WHO WEARS THE MASK

Tenza

B artender!"

"Yo."

"Water? The Fuck?" A cheetah woman in a cobalt dress shirt and black dress pants righted herself unsteadily. She pushed the bangs of her pixie cut away from her dilated, amber eyes.

"Look lady, you're done for the night and it's only 9:30." The imposing Kodiak bear slid a paper slip and pen to her. "You drive here? I know you came solo, so it's not like I can have a buddy take you home. We can get you stuff to nibble on to dry you up."

"C'mon! It's a bad day! You ever-ever have one those?"

The bartender didn't flinch. "A rough day at the office. Weekend's coming up. Throw back a few. Seen it a million times. But you are this close to falling out of your chair, that's why I'm cutting you off."

"I'm fine! I walked!" She fumbled around with the back of her cell phone's case until she pulled out a credit card. With a swift lunge, she slammed both credit card and tab onto the bar top. Nearby glasses rattled as a loud crack pierced through all the clamor. The card now bore a fissure along its left side. Patrons of the bar fell silent and focused their attention to the scene playing out before them.

He glared and folded his arms. "Do you want cops? I can make cops happen if you keep this up."

"No. I just—" She tried her best to fix a gaze upon the bear, but all she could do was rapidly blink. "I just—pay you." She placed a small ink blob onto the tab and attempted a signature but was only able to make a few unsteady strokes before tearing into the paper with the pen's tip.

"Look, you might have walked here, but you definitely are not walking home. The only place I know of close by that would be able to let you get it together is Cuppa, right there across the street. Do you want that?"

She nodded slowly but enthusiastically. "Good."

"Hang tight." He pressed a button on his lapel microphone. "Waitstaff, we've got to make a coffee run. Who's got a moment to do it?"

***

The cheetah slowly opened her eyes. Whatever was clinging to her body was plush, yet firm. *Where am I?* She took a moment to compose herself. She pressed her paws into the cushion of a cloth upholstered sofa and slowly began to sit up. The fragrant aroma of coffee lingered in the air. Next to her was a recliner upholstered in the same fabric as the sofa. There were magazines on the small table in front of her. In the adjacent corner was a collection of board and card games. Around her was a violet, translucent curtain; the railing it was mounted to showed a quarter-circle arc with respect to the walls behind her and to the left. She gained her footing and pushed the curtain aside. A small sign was taped to it: PRIVATE FUNCTION! DO NOT DISTURB! She made her way to the front counter unhindered as nobody was in line.

A middle-aged husky adjusted his glasses and fixed his gaze onto the cheetah. "She's alive! Do you know how much paperwork we'd have to do if someone actually died here?"

She glared at him. "Where the hell am I?"

"You're at Cuppa. Lou from across the street had you brought here. We don't mind looking after those that may have had a bit too much." The barista started to wipe a blending pitcher. "For most, it's just a cup of tea and maybe a snack until they start to sober up. We tried to give you a drink when they brought you over, but you started to dry heave, that's why we put in you in the Cozy Corner."

The cheetah pressed her paw to her forehead. "I've been saying that I want to come here, but these aren't exactly the circumstances I had in mind."

"Better here than in an alley."

"No argument there. Thank you for all your help..." She leaned forward, reading the lapel on the black apron. "Evan?"

"The only one here. How about you?"

"Annette."

"I can get you a mint tisane. Seems to work better than coffee. First one's free. Hot or iced?"

"Iced and I'll still tip you." Once he was finished, she took the cup from him and glanced over at a small group of people a few tables down. "It looks like they have some really interesting costumes."

"Them? Oh yeah, they come here the second Friday of each month and want to show off what they're doing. They'll stay here for hours. I've never had any big problems out of them and they buy lots of food and drink from us too."

She raised an eyebrow. "But why the costumes? Isn't this like something you see at one of those conventions?"

"They come to have fun. On the off occasion that we get kids here, they keep them entertained. The only time we've even had the faintest hint of an issue is when they'd gotten into some really heated discussion about comics and got loud. Otherwise? Nothing."

A raccoon got out of her chair. "You can tell her that we don't bite!" Her black hair was tied into a chignon with a decorative hairpin holding it together. Draped over her shoulders was a scarlet, waist-long mantle. Underneath the mantle, she wore a white vest which allowed her to be sleeveless. Her skirt was a deep crimson; a slit in the rear of it allowed her banded tail to move freely. At the end of her white stockings were single-strapped, black dress shoes with slightly raised heels.

"Madi!"

"Fluffbutt, she's curious. It's clear as day."

"It's 11:25."

The raccoon folded her arms. "Don't derail my train of thought!"

"Who cuts your checks?"

She groaned. "You Boss, but it's my night off."

"Just don't spook her, okay?"

Annette made her way to the back of the coffee shop. They appeared to be a group of about thirty with styles that ran a wide gamut: school uniforms, historical dress, elaborate costumes with a futuristic bend, and even some in casual clothing emblazoned with various creative franchises. Some even carried props such as enlarged jewelry or fake weapons. After looking at the group, she couldn't help but feel out of place in her office attire. "Just what have I come across?"

Seated again, Madi tilted her head slightly. "What's wrong? We're just having a good time."

"Nothing's wrong. I'm just taking all this in. Is this some kind convention thing? I mean, that's what I'm led to believe."

"We're a group of pop culture enthusiasts, some of us going as far to engage in costumed play of our fan interests. It's called cosplay for short."

"I see. And who are you supposed to be?"

Madi flittered her fingers as if she were trying to summon something from thin air. "I'm Hélène Cazalet, the sorceress that is duty bound to vanquish all those that wish to resurrect the dark forces of years gone by."

"That's a good character." Annette sipped her tisane slowly.

"She speaks to me. She's got a no-nonsense way of handling things and she's got such a strong determination. Also she can set things on fire with the wave of a finger!"

Annette scoffed. "That's not very diplomatic." She looked around at the group in more detail. A card game was in progress, but it looked a bit too complicated for her liking. One end of a table had three artists, each with a sketchbook but a common cache of drawing implements between them. Some in the group were freely conversing about life, others about what the next episode of Viking Overlords: 2089 would be about. Others still enjoyed a nice drink and snack while in the company of friends, saying hardly anything at all. "This is a big group. Who organizes this?"

Madi extended her paw to Annette. "You're talking to her."

Annette shook Madi's paw. "I gathered that you worked here from what you were saying to your boss, but this is your doing?"

The raccoon flashed a toothy grin. "Absolutely!"

"So do you do this as a hobby?"

"Yes! Very much so! Stay with us for a while!"

***

It's finally 6:00. Annette unplugged her cell phone from a charging cord attached to her work computer. She waved goodbye to her few remaining colleagues before descending a set of stairs. The downtown plaza bustled with activity as crowds would gawk at wares and enjoy treats from food trucks. Sometimes she would partake in this herself, but not this Monday night. After meandering her way through crowds and crosswalks, Annette opened the door of Cuppa.

The raccoon waved her over to the counter. "You came back!" Unlike the elaborate dress of the other day, she wore a simple black apron on top of a teal polo shirt and black pants. Her hair was restrained under a teal baseball cap.

"It looks a bit slow tonight. Customer retention is crucial in the success of any business. Therefore, it is imperative that I return."

The patches of black under Madi's eyes shifted as she furrowed her brow. "Huh?"

Annette smiled. "You saved my ass the other night, so it's only fair I spend a bit of money. That work for you? A large, frozen, almond chai if you would be so kind."

Madi smiled. "It's my pleasure. If you're willing to stay for a bit, I'll be on break in about 10 minutes."

Annette promptly paid and dropped a couple of bills into the jar at the counter. Once the drink was finished, she made her way to a small, round table nearby. She took a sip through the straw, savoring the spices on her tongue. With time to kill, the cheetah checked text messages on her phone until the raccoon joined her with a cup of hot black tea.

"Welcome back!"

"I remember from the meet that you said you were here Sundays to Thursdays and I've been meaning to come here. I just didn't plan on making my first visit the way that I did."

The raccoon shrugged. "These things happen."

Annette tapped the side of her plastic cup with her dull claws. "I'm sorry that I wasn't too talkative the other night. I was just absorbing everything and I wasn't really—"

Madi smiled. "You don't have to apologize so much. You were in rough shape and needed some time to decompress. I get that."

"You're right, I shouldn't beat myself up over it." Annette took a sip of her drink. "So, this cosplay meet is your brainchild. How did it come about?"

"We weren't doing too well about a year ago. Evan tried all sorts of flashy marketing things he'd see on the internet but all of them were just duds. That's when I pitched the idea to him of having a group of us create the monthly meet. He thought it was just going to be this random, one-off thing but he was desperate. Once we started coming regularly and bringing even more people with us, he warmed up to the idea."

"Nothing like bringing the customers in. Trust me, I know that a bit too well."

Madi leaned in closely, taking a sip of tea. "So, what do you do exactly?"

"I'm an accounts manager over at Zydestra. I'm the person that looks after the needs of existing clients, tries to figure out their buying habits, and how to get them to keep buying. I listen a lot and carefully assess people. I'm a lot of things to a lot of different people."

"That sounds important. You really have to multitask a lot, don't you?"

"That's the understatement of the century."

The raccoon laughed. "Well, I suppose so." She fixed her gaze on the cheetah's spots, mentally tracing lines together to see what patterns would emerge. "Battle princess."

Annette stopped mid-sip and flicked her ears. The straw slowly slid out of her lips. "Come again?"

Madi shook her head. "Sorry, just thinking out loud. I was trying to see what sort of costume would look good on you. I have an eye for that sort of thing and I think you'd make a great battle princess."

"You know, it's funny that you mention battle princess because fencing is a hobby of mine."

The raccoon's eyes widened. "Fencing? You mean with swords?"

"It's derived from a sword, but nothing like what most people think of when they hear the word 'sword'. What I use is called an épée. It doesn't have a sharp edge and has a grip somewhat like a gun, but it has a pretty big tip; that's how electric scoring systems know who landed the point. Duels are fast-paced and require a lot of precision. We wear protective clothing because the tips of the weapons move at high speeds and the blades do flex quite a bit."

Madi sipped her tea, glancing at a nearby clock to keep track of how long away she was on break. "How did you get into it?"

"One of my co-workers got free lessons from a contest and the prize allowed two people. He needed a plus-one and I took him up on it. After the free sessions were over, he quit but I decided to keep going."

Madi beamed. "That's awesome! Not only would you be a battle princess, but you could play the part very convincingly!"

Annette laughed. "I admit that your hobby is also intriguing, but to do it myself?"

"I recall clearly that you thought our costumes were cool. We can start off small if you'd give me the chance."

"Well, that's awfully ambitious of you."

The raccoon smirked. "Ambitious would be me asking if you're seeing anyone right now."

Annette coughed and almost choked on her drink. She squeezed her cup lightly. "Now that's outright bold. Take a girl to dinner first, won't you?"

Madi lightly brushed her leg along Annette's. "I can make you dinner instead."

The cheetah could feel the heat rush to her face. "Ambition indeed." She took a prolonged sip of her frozen drink, trying to buy herself time. "I'd be a fool to turn down a home-cooked meal." She smiled. "I'm open to the idea. Let's exchange numbers and discuss this further."

***

Annette swished her tail and looked up from her cell phone, making sure that the directions she'd been given were correct. She gazed at a sparsely decorated apartment complex. The cheetah didn't come directly from work but stopped at home to change into a black T-shirt with a pair of bright orange shorts. Black, ankle-length socks and silver running shoes adorned her feet. Not only had she gone home, but in her paw was a small cloth shopping bag. She jogged up a set of stairs and bore right until she reached door 226. She pressed the buzzer next to the door and it opened shortly thereafter.

"7:15. I love a woman that knows how to be on time." Madi smiled as she greeted her guest. "Please come in and leave your shoes in the corner." With no obligation to either cosplay or workplace, Madi's hair was down to her shoulder blades in waves of thick curls. She wore a loose-fitting blue T-shirt and cloud-patterned pajama pants.

"Well, I tend to be pretty punctual." Annette slipped off her shoes and placed them next to a smaller pair of plain black walking shoes that unquestionably had seen better days. She extended the bag to her hostess. "Here."

"You brought them!" She reached into the bag and produced a bag of white grapes.

"It would be really rude for you to make dinner and to have not brought what you'd asked me to."

Madi quickly popped them into the refrigerator. "I know but I just really like grapes!"

Annette pulled out an old camera, complete with telephoto lens. "As also requested, here is the relic that I've held onto for so long."

"You're such a darling!"

"It's broken. I got it cheap for an art class a long time ago and even then, it was kinda dodgy when it worked. Wound up with a B, so I can't really complain."

"Yeah, but I can gut it and make it into a killer prop. Speaking of props, did you want to see my little studio?"

Annette followed Madi into a room next to the kitchen. Against the wall was a table-mounted sewing machine along with multiple sewing patterns and remnant bolts of fabric. On tension-mounted rods were several coat hangers with miscellaneous outfits. Below them were transparent storage tubs containing various articles of clothing. On the opposite side of the room were a wide array of accessories and props arranged neatly in an upright cabinet. Annette looked around in awe. "Madi, I know you said that you enjoyed cosplay, but I didn't know it would be all this! I can tell you've worked hard at it."

"I guess when you get right down to it, it's more than a simple hobby." She placed the camera with the other items of her prop collection. "I know this is gonna sound really pathetic, but what you see here is why I get up every day."

Annette's tail swished slowly. "What do you mean exactly?"

Madi wrapped her arms around her chest. "I was actually a pretty sheltered kid, to be honest with you. Dad worked long hours and Mom was a busy body. Teenagers can be pretty cruel too, especially when you don't really fit in. I did everything I could do to get into college and with a little luck, I got in. Only thing is, I went from wallflower to life of the party. Next thing you know, I'm in the ER after getting scooped off the floor in a dorm room."

Annette's ears leaned back. "Madi, you don't have to—"

"That's when my folks yanked the rug out from under me. They let me come back home for a while, but I had to quit school. They didn't trust me. Not long after that, I got the job at Cuppa. It turned out to be—and still is—nice enough job and I tried to figure out what I was gonna do next. Then one day, I went to the Sci-Fest downtown. I see everyone dressed up and decided 'Wow, I want to do that too!' and that's when I found the very thing that could keep me going in spite of all the snide comments from my mom or dipshit customers. They let me take a few classes at the trade school and I'd read all kinds of things online. Eventually I saved enough and got the apartment. I took on small odd costuming jobs and started working on some projects. It really turned me around! If I hadn't taken part in cosplay and embraced my nerdiness, I'd be incredibly miserable or probably dead."

The only thing Annette could do was open her arms and offer Madi a hug.

The raccoon readily accepted, but then looked up at her guest. "People say that what I do, what my friends do, is nothing more than just a way to escape. It's not that people are thrilled about all the stressful stuff they have to go through, but they see people have fun and they feel left out because our fun isn't how everyone else has fun. When anyone comes over and asks 'Why?', I do my best to make them feel welcome, even if we don't get that level of compassion in return." She took a deep breath, then loudly exhaled. "Sorry for making it weird."

Annette patted her back reassuringly. "You're fine. Although it looks like you've got bigger aspirations than Cuppa. When do you think you'll leave?"

Madi stood on the tips of her toes and leaned into the hug a bit more firmly. "I don't know for sure, but the reality is that I need to start making some moves. With my ever-growing hobby, I feel like Cuppa's starting to wear me out and I just feel like I want to devote more time to making creative things. I do feel sorry for lying to you though."

Annette's ears pivoted forward. "About what?"

"That I tried to downplay this as just a hobby. This really is more than just a hobby."

"Hardly a lie. I can understand wanting to minimize as to not scare off a total stranger. I can relate to feeling like something's missing. My folks really wanted me to just go out there and be a career woman and just do the thing. I did and I am! But I'm pretty sure I've hit my plateau. I can't help but feel like I'm supposed to be doing something more than being stuffed in a cubicle, managing whole districts worth of customer accounts. My coworkers and superiors think I'm a real go-getter. Truthfully, I think people mistake competence with ambition."

Madi glanced up at Annette. "Yeah. When you came to visit me at Cuppa the other day, you looked like you'd been put through the wringer."

"Some days it's like that." Annette pulled Madi in a bit closer. "On really bad days, you get piss drunk and get dropped off in a coffee shop and black out."

"Don't beat yourself up over that. You met me, right?" Madi smiled. "Do you feel as passionate about fencing as I do with cosplay?"

"Maybe not as passionate as you are. I'm not trying to make it a professional thing because their routines are incredibly intense! For me, the appeal of fencing is that I know that I'm good at precision work and can quickly assess a situation. But unlike my job, I feel invigorated when I'm out on the piste. There's just that sense of thrill and achievement when you can best your opponent. The analytical appeal of chess with the brute force of combat."

The raccoon was in awe. "You have a way with words!"

"Thank you!" Annette wrinkled her nose and inhaled deeply. "Is something burning?"

Madi shoved the cheetah aside and dashed to the kitchen. She quickly took the stock pot off the stove and peered inside. "It's not ruined, but it's a bit darker than I would have liked. Please sit at the table and I'll have it to you soon!

Annette sauntered into the kitchen, peering curiously over Madi's shoulder. "It smells amazing."

The raccoon gently poked her guest's ribs. "Shoo! I will bring it to you!"

"But—"

Madi wiggled the spoon at her, a gold-colored broth coated half of the length of the handle. "You are my guest!"

Annette couldn't help but chuckle after seeing how flustered Madi had become. "Very well. I shall sit."

***

Annette bounced up the stairs and this time she brought a much larger cloth shopping bag. She rang the buzzer, and the door opened. The cheetah smiled, took out a smaller plastic bag and gave it to the raccoon.

"More grapes! You really know how to please a girl!"

"This is the fifth time I've brought you grapes. Wouldn't you like something else for a change?"

The raccoon smiled. "I've got complex interests but simple tastes."

Annette smirked. "Well, you were awfully cute when I kept feeding them to you."

Madi hid her face. "You treated me so well. For a moment, I almost felt as if I was being paid tribute."

Annette leaned her ears forward. "You were quite content. It was well worth pausing the movie for about an hour. I'd keep feeding you and you'd try to make me your pillow."

"You make a good pillow."

"But you have the fluffy tail. Do you grip your own pillows that hard?"

The raccoon smirked. "You didn't complain."

Annette gently bit her bottom lip. "No, I can't say I did." She jolted the large bag. "Oh! I brought the clothes!"

"Great! Just set them in my studio!"

After removing her shoes, Annette followed Madi to the studio. "How they escaped the thrift store is anyone's guess."

"I can put them to much better use."

Annette set the bag down and looked at one of the lower shelves. She spotted a stubby wooden dowel with a notch cut into it. Secured inside the notch was a long, narrow strip of acrylic glass. "Is that a sword?"

"Steve commissioned one from me at the last meet. I've never made one, so I would try it out."

The cheetah tapped her chin. "I want to know how that one turns out. I just might get one from you."

Madi squealed. "Battle princess! I knew you would come around!"

"You're slowly warming me up to the idea, especially after I did the sword lesson with Jake at the meet." She rolled her eyes and sighed. "If people actually fought with the techniques used in movies, you'd have a lot of injuries."

"Oh, no doubt." Madi peered into the bag, looking over the donated clothes. "Any one of those outfits you particularly hate? Any one of those you just absolutely loathe and cannot stand?"

Annette thought for a moment. "Well, there is the graduation gift many years ago. My Aunt Gladys had a pretty keen eye for fashion. By keen, I mean not at all."

The raccoon chuckled. "How bad?" She grinned. "Put it on!"

"Damn it Madi!"

"What? Just humor me!"

Annette mulled this over. "Only if you promise to make your crab bisque like—"

Madi didn't hesitate. "Deal!"

"Deal." The cheetah flicked her tail as she sorted through the various outfits until she pulled a lilac blouse and long mauve skirt. "The most questionable gift I've ever gotten. Just give me a moment while I go and change."

Madi smiled. "Don't mind me!"

"Are you serious?"

The raccoon lowered her voice. "You don't have to be the only one to undress."

Annette could feel her cheeks warming. She'd been put on the spot, yet couldn't help but feel this was some kind of ruse. "Do it."

Madi's voice regained its usual enthusiasm. "Now that's the spirit!" She slipped the loose T-shirt over her head, tossing it onto the floor. An unbuttoned denim skirt followed it. Hugging her body were a matched set of bra and panties. The aquamarine underwear accented her silver fur and was a striking contrast to her black hair, mask, and ringed tail.

"Your turn."

She should have known that if anything, Madi wasn't shy. Annette wrapped her fingers around the fringe of her shirt and lifted it over her head. She was about to drop it aside, but with a flick of her wrist, tossed it onto Madi's skirt. A tangerine bra restrained her ample bust, but it was soon concealed by the blouse. After unfastening her belt, she slipped out of her shorts and tossed them onto the growing pile; a pair of indigo panties clung to her. Without much fuss, she slipped on the skirt.

The raccoon leered. "The PTA mom look is absolutely hot."

Annette glared. "You cannot be serious."

"No. You're absolutely right. Your hair is cute, but with that outfit, it looks like you're going to complain to a supervisor about getting ice in your ice water. Ask me how I know."

Annette exhaled. "You aren't wrong." Her ears lowered and her tail flicked to and fro. "Madi, I've been thinking."

"Yes?"

"Last week was the first time in a long while I'd been able to feel just comfortable with somebody else. I mean, comfortable enough to feel intimate with them. I couldn't even remember when my last kiss was."

The raccoon raised her paw and pivoted her wrist into a salute. "I gave my word and stopped at third."

Annette cracked a smile. "Please Madi, not now. I still want to take this a bit more slowly." She sighed. "But at the same time, I feel like I want to go a bit further. In the last month-and-a-half, I've come to realize that I've been too good at being everything to everyone and all for the sake of keeping up appearances. Or rather, I guess I knew all along, but just now ready to admit it. With you, I can just be myself."

Madi leaned forward on the balls of her feet and looped her arms around Annette. She took a moment, studying the features of her face. "The lady who wears the mask decides to bare her heart."

The cheetah closed her eyes. "That wasn't an easy admission."

"And I know just how important of an admission that was. I know we're told time and again to keep an appearance and get into a relationship because it's what's expected of people. We're both near 30. We can approach this like adults, with no need of pretense. I know that I can be a bit immature at times, but I can be quite serious too."

Madi rested her paws on Annette's shoulders. "Ms. Account Manager, it's my turn to give you a proposal. Going head-long into a relationship right now would be too fast, but it looks like we'd both like some deeper intimacy. I would be willing to give that to you. Let's just try it and see how it goes. If that long-term chemistry's not there, we could part ways as friends."

***

Framed memorabilia, wall posters, and trinkets decorated Madi's bedroom. Two candle flames faintly glowed in pools of wax. With a pillow pressed against her back, Annette reclined against the headboard while Madi opened the drawer of her nightstand.

Annette smirked. "Going for the toys right away?"

The raccoon swung her tail onto the edge of the mattress with a loud thump. "Hardly. Even now, you're a bit tense and I'd like to help you with that." Madi pulled out a buffing brick and a pair of metal scissors. As she crawled onto the bed, she took Annette's right paw her own and lightly tugged on each finger. She slowly slid the black padding of her thumb along Annette's short, dull claws. After careful inspection, Madi set to work. She filed away any edges and buffed out any ridges she encountered.

Annette closed her eyes, sprawling more of her body against the pillow. The fragrance of patchouli tickled her nose as her ears fixated onto the gentle rasping of the block's cadence. Before long, both paws had been given Madi's attention.

Madi set the block onto her nightstand and leaned forward, whispering into the cheetah's right ear. "You hate these clothes? Let me free you of them." A metallic clinking echoed throughout the room as brief flickers reflected from the candlelight. She twirled the scissors around her index finger before resting them in her palm. Madi placed the blades at the bottom fringe of the skirt before stretching it tout and slid the blades along the fabric. With each tap of the scissors, she pulled the skirt apart. Reaching the waist band, she pressed firmly to ensure the skirt had been fully dismantled before peeling it away.

Annette's heart began to race and she shut her eyes tightly. She shivered as the cool air caressed her legs. Each tap of the scissors became louder as her blouse met the same fate. She was able to free herself of the sleeves once Madi tugged on them.

"A good artisan recognizes just how versatile her tools are." She slid Annette's right index finger into one of the finger holes and used the scissors as a lever, stretching the finger backward and held it in place. Madi repeated this for each of the remaining fingers and then for the cheetah's left paw. She then placed the scissors onto the night stand and began to massage Annette's paws, giving special care to deeply press into and knead her black paw pads. She smiled as the cheetah purred. "Of course, a good artisan also recognizes when to abandon tools and use her fingers." She placed her paws behind her back, unclasped and discarded her bra. Within moments, Annette's bra was on the floor as well.

"Diamond cutters." Madi teased.

Annette bit her bottom lip. Her nipples puckered in the brisk air. "I fear they are a bit cold. Would you warm me up?"

The raccoon eased herself onto Annette's lap. She traced a finger over Annette's nose and then her lips. She leaned forward and slowly licked Annette's right nipple while seizing her left breast, kneading it firmly. Madi could feel the cheetah shiver as she suckled, her curls ensnared and scalp kneaded by Annette's fingers. She finally relented, but only to switch sides. The raccoon slid off of her lover's lap and nibbled the base of Annette's right ear. She firmly kneaded the cheetah's shoulders before crawling down the length of the bed, slowly dragging her dull nails along the cheetah's sides. She leaned forward, nuzzling Annette's belly and kissing it gently.

Annette arched her back and could feel a warmth radiating from her loins as Madi's claws latched onto the waistband of her panties. The cheetah wiggled her toes as the fabric was slipped off her mound, eased down her legs, and tossed onto the floor. Her face blazed intensely as the raccoon's paw traced along her inner thigh. She could feel her folds become slick as Madi cupped her palm around them and began to trace her fingers along their contours. Annette's clit slowly emerged with each caress of Madi's fingers.

"Mmh! Madi!"

Madi began to flick against her lover's nub with gradual acceleration as the cheetah squirmed beneath her. She pulled her hand away and parted Annette's legs, sliding in between them. With the cheetah's thighs resting on her shoulders, Madi gently pressed her tongue to Annette's clit. She gave it a gentle kiss, then lapped at it slowly, tracing her tongue along the stiff flesh. The cheetah tugged on the curls of Madi's hair. She felt the raccoon's tongue press deep inside, then brush upward, but much slower than before. Annette's legs tensed and her toes curled as she neared her peak.

"Gods, yes!"

The raccoon pressed her tongue onto Annette's clit once more and began to purr. Unlike that of the cheetah, Madi's purring was in short pulses. What her purring lacked in duration was exceeded by the vibration her pulsing could achieve. She clutched her lover's hips as her muzzle was pressed tight to Annette's sex.

Annette moaned and arched her back as she reached her climax. She breathed heavily and felt a bit lightheaded. "Madi…"

The raccoon smiled. "Shh. Just relax and savor this."

Annette shook her head and as soon as she recovered, she lunged forward and pressed herself tightly against the raccoon. "I'd fancy you on my lap and I suggest you take your own advice."

Madi needed no further instruction; she turned around and sat on Annette's lap and leaned back. The raccoon had little time to prepare herself as Annette kneaded her shoulders. Her eyes clenched as the cheetah leaned forward and licked the base of her left ear.

"Ooh, that's…very nice."

Annette purred as she nuzzled the nape of Madi's neck. She leaned in for a tight embrace, sliding her paws down Madi's chest and resting her palms against the supple contours of her lover's breasts; nuzzling became nibbling, cupping became kneading as the raccoon bit her bottom lip. The cheetah let go of Madi's breasts, draping her fingers down the raccoon's sides and tucking her fingers into the waistband of Madi's panties. Annette firmly pressed her teeth against Madi's neck and suckled, careful to not bite through the pelt.

"Mmh!" The raccoon shuddered, pivoting her hips as warmth enveloped her body. She exhaled as Annette tugged on the waistband, pressing the panties against her sex. "So! Fierce!" Madi's heart raced and her folds tingled.

Annette let go of the waistband, draping her left arm around Madi's chest and tracing her right finger along the raccoon's chin before brushing it across her lips. She nestled against the raccoon's left ear. "Shall I unwrap you now or make you squirm a bit more?"

"Tease!"

"Oh come now, I think you can take a bit more squirming." Annette purred as she unlocked from the embrace and eased Madi onto her back. She peered at the raccoon's panties and grinned, lightly dragging her finger along the damp fabric. "My, what have I done?"

Madi smirked. "I'm still only half-naked, so clearly not enough!"

Annette sucked air through her teeth. "You've done it now." She slid her paws along her lover's sides and peeled away her panties. "Half-naked you say?" The cheetah lifted Madi's right leg, nuzzling along the inner thigh and easing herself between the raccoon's legs. She lightly kissed Madi's belly, resting her chin on her lover's mound. The cheetah slid towards the foot of the bed and slowly brushed her fingertips along Madi's wet folds. Her fingertips glistened with slickness as she spread her labia apart.

As Madi became more wet, she could feel the cheetah ease a single finger into her depths. Her muscles tightened around the finger as it pushed forward. She rocked her hips as the tightness began to ease and Annette was able caress her spot within. She felt a second finger work itself inside and her walls flexed to accommodate. The fingers thrust held a steady rhythm at first, but the cheetah increased the pace, and fell out of sync with lover. "Nnh!" Madi recoiled. "Claws!"

Annette eased her paw out slowly and her ears leaned back. "Shit. I got carried away."

Madi leaned forward and pat her on the shoulder. "You didn't hurt me. It was just a bit uncomfortable."

Annette nodded slowly. "A bit more carefully this time." She re-assumed the position from before, nuzzling the top of Madi's mound. She found the raccoon's nub once more and vigorously stroked until it stiffened. Reaching up with her left paw, she seized Madi's right nipple and felt it swell in her fingertips. Madi writhed and moaned, but the cheetah kept her well in place and at her mercy.

"Yes! More!"

Annette used her first two fingers to aggressively manipulate Madi's clit before sliding the two fingers slightly inside for careful stroking. She would alternate between these motions before her well-lubricated fingers and thumb seized the stiff nub, pinching and flicking with much vigor.

All Madi could do was roughly grasp the mattress. Her moaning grew louder until she screamed and felt an intense, tingling heat rush from her core to all corners of her body. Her hips bucked wildly before her climax finally subsided and she could steady herself.

Annette freed herself from the grasp of Madi's legs and scooted up to the headboard to join her. "Am I still a good pillow? You could probably use one right now."

Madi took a few deep breaths, crawled onto the cheetah and nestled the top of her head between Annette's breasts. "A fantastic pillow."

"But you should be the pillow, especially with that tail of yours."

The raccoon rested her paws on Annette's hips. "You make a compelling case."

"Madi?"

"Yes?"

"You ruined that outfit completely."

Madi closed her eyes. "Does the lady, now shed of her mask, long for it yet again?"

Annette tilted her head. "What do you mean?"

"That outfit was absolutely atrocious. You said so yourself."

"But to outright destroy it? Wasn't there something from it you could have used?"

Madi shook her head. "I can always use fabric scraps. But more importantly, that outfit was a projection of a person that you couldn't be comfortable with; it's the image of a person that isn't really you."

Annette sighed. "That's pretty deep."

Madi slid off the cheetah. She then eased herself back onto her lover, this time facing her. "It looks like we've gotten in pretty deep ourselves."

Annette adjusted her body position with Madi on top of her. "I know but let's remember that we're taking this slowly."

"I know and thank you for understanding."

"Don't get me wrong! I'm not saying we can't be an item, but let's just—"

Madi ran her claws through Annette's hair. "You're overthinking it. No judgments and no ill will. Just as we agreed to."

The cheetah smiled. "Yes, you're absolutely right."

"Warrior and sorceress" Madi chuckled. "A tried and true ship."

Annette blinked. "Ship?"

"I mean, making them a couple. Shipping. 'Relationship' is where the term comes from."

"Ah. I see that I'm going to be learning a lot of new lingo from you, but I'm up to the challenge. With that said, I would totally ship them."

The raccoon smirked. "Regular, priority or expedited?"

"Damn it Madi!"

The raccoon laughed, then leaned in for a deep kiss. "You're much prettier without a mask. Don't ever forget that."

Trophy Hunting

BlueSeiryuu

Sensitive ears twitched at the sound of sharp claws digging into her thighs, the nylon covering her curves splitting under the pressure of her lover's nails. She jolted and let out a harsh cry that made her throat hoarse. Her legs twitched helplessly in her lover's large paws, while the creature between her legs let out a soft chuckle—her hot breath and cold nose above the lover's labia making her squeeze her face in between her delicate thighs. The deer regained her composure and gave a sharp tug on the chain in her hand which earned her a half-annoyed huff.

The tigress beneath her smirked to herself as she rested her chin against the edge of the seat, she let out a couple of breaths against her lover's wetness, calming her before she finally settled to do what she did best. She grinned, tugging gently on her end of the chain before her tongue rolled out of her mouth. Her tongue was wider than her lover's vagina and as soon as she gently flicked it against the sika deer above her, she let out a moan. The tiger at the bottom ran her tongue from the bottom to the top, the sandpaper texture of her tongue causing her lover to jolt as it electrified every nerve in her body.

The recipient held her eyes closed for a brief second, the clinking of the chains on the leash she clutched keeping her grounded enough to feel the warmth spreading through her small frame. She squeezed her eyes tighter, trying to cast her mind back to the awkwardness that had led them to this moment. When had they first met again? It was at high-school wasn't it? A familiar sound of a throaty growl as her lover lifted her head and rested it gently on her thigh broke her thoughts.

"You ok?" A sharp tug at the tigress' neck made her wince. "I see, shall I continue then?" The feeling of hooves digging roughly in her shoulder blades answered for the one on top.

In truth, that initial fear she had felt when she first laid eyes on the creature between her legs had never faded. She considered it an essential part of the sex and perhaps, more integrally, a means of showing respect for her lover, Sheera. Impa tried to focus her attention back onto the computer—she was attempting to beat a personal record on her game, and such musings of her oversized lover were only causing a distraction.

She needed to get the trophy, she needed to maintain her place on the global leaderboards for the game, to make sure that her name was known on the online community. Sheera had once remarked in an argument it was because Impa had never been a popular child and she was trying to make up for it by being famous online—-that had been the night that Impa had decided to put a collar on the tigress for her insubordination.

She leaned back in the chair and felt as the tigress underneath adjusted herself. The tight space Sheera had crammed herself into beneath the desk had led her to be squashed against the edge of the chair, her entire body at an awkward curve in the desk cavity. Sheera initially thought it was punishment for the last time she'd distracted her small-hooved companion during one of her games—the tigress walked in, offering her a drink at the exact same time as a boss summoned a powerful attack Impa's avatar couldn't dodge.

The tigress didn't understand a lot about the wonderfully vibrant and musical world on the other side of the computer, nor did she understand why her lover would gasp at something on the screen in a similar manner as when the tiger lapped between her thighs.

All Sheera knew was that the game was important to the deer and that Impa had gained some fame online for her skill as a player. Impa had once suggested going 'pro' and doing such work as a career, but the tigress had no such interest in such follies, gaming was not a real job, and she only wanted to make love to the lover who she admired for so long.

The tiger's ears twitched as she waited for the noise that Impa told her signaled the beginning of a new round of gameplay and admired as the deer leaned forward in the chair, hooves tapping rapidly on the keys. She had found there was no sexier opportunity for making love to Impa than when there was a chance to distract her from that game.

It helped of course, that the game was a source of fighting in their daily life—-Sheera was intensely jealous of it, and found that her lover's affection for the online world meant less attention for her. Impa was also eager to tease the tigress with the game, making a show of deliberately ignoring when Sheera was groping her, growling lowly in her ears and nipping gently at the back of her neck when she was horny. The tigress often won Impa's attention after the game's end and after bickering, they'd make love far harder and rougher than normal, moaning each other's name as they ground against each other.

It was somewhat cruel of Impa to take advantage of Sheera like that, but the deer liked the thrill of making the tiger desperate, more loving, affectionate and eager to take advantage of their size difference.

"Don't you get bored down there?" The deer asked, waiting for her teammates to select their characters.

"I make my own fun."

The tiger felt a gentle hand caress the end of her nose and, despite herself, she flinched. She may be the biggest cat on the planet, but she had some unusual responses to silly stimuli, thus earning her the nickname "kitten" by her lover when they were out with friends. The memory of the nickname made her more anxious to continue, the wetness between her legs growing as her mind begged her to continue.

Then the sound of a distant gong echoed through the desk to the tigress underneath. The deer's game had begun.

The tiger grinned, the devilish voice in her head telling her that she needed to taste Impa. Her reward would come when she made the deer moan and a hoof would reach down to pull on one of her whiskers a little too roughly.

The tiger took a deep breath, nostrils filling with the scent of cherries from the deer's shower gel, mixed with the earthy scent of her desire. She grinned as she pressed her nose against the top of her pussy, chilling the skin and earning a surprised gasp from the deer who yanked roughly on her chain. The tiger chuffed before licking gently, the sandpaper texture making the deer squirm once more.

The deer tried to hold her nerve, her eyes squinting as she clutched tighter at her mouse. Impa's clicking was becoming more erratic on the screen with every motion of her lover underneath. She was trying her best to ignore the pressure in her groin and the warmth spreading from the tips of her hooves to her waist. The deer could feel Sheera's body trembling with anxious purrs. She knew that beneath her, the tigress had succumbed to satisfying her own needs - she could feel her pressing her head against her thigh and she could feel a deep rumble spreading up her body. Her lover's purring made her panic, missing another target and getting a derogatory comment from one of her teammates in response.

"You're...putting me off," she moaned. Her lover's cry of approval earned her another lick as the tiger moved for another taste of the honeypot. The heat creeping up her body was quickly becoming a fire and she found herself reclining back in the chair. The tiger beneath the table was still drawing tired circles around her own clitoris, the occasional tug against her collar making her press harder. Then she heard the sound that intoxicated her ears—her lover relaxed her legs and let out a soft moan as her concentration died and her thoughts clouded over. The tiger purred, tongue lapping eagerly as she pleasured herself in time with the gentle cries of the deer.

Sheera hated that game, hated the attention that Impa gave it, and there was a moment of decisive celebration in the back of her mind as she finally won the deer's attention.

The mist was growing thicker and the deer was finding it harder to focus, she tried to focus on the coldness of the chain, the task at hand on the match or how much she should instinctively despise the tiger. Anything to stop the tigress from getting the gratification of winning their power dynamic—she wanted to be in charge.

Then it hit. Like a tidal wave through a molten mass of marshmallows in her head, she let out a screech. She threw herself back into the chair, her mind flooding with a storm of emotions as she felt her body relax against her lover's face beneath. She was interrupted from her glow by the sound of a teammate yelling swears at her. Through the fog, she stared blankly at her screens—her mind sharpening as she hit a pained realization: she'd been kicked from the game she needed to desperately finish her trophy run.

"Gah stupid! I have half a mind to make you into a trophy now you've messed up my chances!" The deer pouted childishly and tapped Sheera on the shoulder blade making her growl. She let out a frightened squeak, slamming her legs together with a force that cut the tiger's air supply slightly. The tiger desperately shook her head until she felt the grip loosening and pulled back, slamming her head against the edge of the desk in the process. The deer giggled and tried to stifle the laugh behind her hooves. The tears forming at the edge of her eyes and the vibrating of her body as she tried to hold the giggles back betrayed her. She was about to put her legs against the desk and push her chair back so the tigress could crawl free from underneath when she felt two large paws stop her. Pointed nails dug against the delicate suede of her fur, and suddenly the tigress' maw was encapsulating the entirety of her pelvis.

She suddenly found herself holding her breath, the air in the room was suddenly tense and thick with fear and unspoken words. Sheera's teeth were on the verge of puncturing the deer's skin, teeth forming a bruise against the flesh and there was a sharp jolt down her back as a rough texture scraped against her clitoris. This was a dangerous game; one slip, and those teeth would drive straight through her pelvis and she'd be spending the rest of her night in the ER, trying to explain how their sexual games had resulted in an embarrassing injury.

"Make it up to me," the deer glowered. The deer willed her body to relax and leave her lover to her ministrations. The motions of the bigger mammal encouraged Impa to relax and the concern of injury dissipated, as if the deer had forgotten that in the wild, she was nothing more than an appetizer to a mighty beast like Sheera. She relaxed into the motions and closed her eyes.

Now she thought about it, she was rather fortunate—her lover was so relaxed about these beliefs, seeing them as almost trivial. She'd even suggested some of their activities contain this unusual dynamic—the chain around her neck a sign of trust for them both. The deer had first felt something akin to a power rush, their sex suffering as a result, but now, she found these playful sessions a source of entertainment.

There was something farcical about the acts. The idea of a creature twice her height and more than double her mass submitting itself too easy to her whim was laughable yet it seemed to come so natural to Sheera and her. Impa glanced back at her abandoned game and back to the tigress beneath her, there was something of a similarity between her relationship with Sheera and her relationship with the online community—she commanded power and it was dizzyingly exciting.

Her mind was a swell of chaos as she tried to sort through the jumble of emotions that always flooded her mind when the tigress decided that more exhilarating play was wise. She contemplated her anger over the lost trophy in her game and her hollow threat to turn Sheera into a replacement—it was certainly an exciting prospect, but those big brown eyes staring up at the deer were much better full of hunger and desire in Impa's opinion.

She'd become so consumed by those thoughts, that she'd failed to notice the sensation of breathing had receded away and that coarse texture of her lover's tongue was nowhere to be found.

"Back with me I see." The tiger made a false yawn, the sound of the chain against the collar making the big cat chuckle softly. "I'm sorry my musings were boring you, Mistress."

There was an element of mocking in that final word that the deer didn't let go unnoticed.

"Oh no." Her lover leaned forward, closing her legs and falling forward to land on the pillow of dense fur on her lover's head. "You were doing fine, I was just—"

"Daydreaming of all those times you thought I'd bite you or put you off your daft game?" The feeling of hot breath against her tummy made her feel strange, yet the butterfly sensation was welcome. "Perhaps you'd allow me to show you how silly you're being?"

Permit? Were they still playing with the idea of her being in charge again? She'd been so lost in her daydreams that she had almost forgotten the leash in her hand. It was just like her lover to continue the power dynamic until she had permission otherwise.

"I would like that." She leaned back, to find herself scooped up into those heavy paws that she knew were surprisingly deft and nestled into her favorite spot, just between the two large breasts that complimented the curves of the tigress so well. The gentle stubs where the deer's horns had never grown made the tiger gasp as she nuzzled her way into the fur.

As Impa found herself tenderly placed amongst the nest of pillows, she tried to swallow that sense of doubt in her mind.

You will always be the prey, never the predator. One day she will tire of you.

For the tigress, the next part of their game would be the most worrisome, but as was usual and expected of a predatory animal, she forced herself to conceal her concern. The deer was eager for more, the scent of sex permeating her nostrils and she could see the lust in her lover's eyes as she stared longingly at the bigger beast.

Drawing one of her claws from its hidden sheath, she steadied her breath before looming over the small deer. On good days, when the deer was relaxed this was an unnecessary risk.

Pressing her paw pad against her lover, gently circling her clitoris, she watched the anxiety on the deer's face melt back into lust. The pair locked eyes and Sheera licked her lips. Impa's legs were relaxing into the sensation, and the tigress could feel every involuntary twitch of the deer as she bucked up against her paws.

A finger slipped into the creature's dainty opening with surprising ease and the nervous screech almost made the tigress retract back entirely until she heard a shy whisper beneath her.

"No, I'm ok, just your fingers are cold." Her body was prickling with a mix of cold and heat as her nerves stood on end—she could already feel her muscles squeezing at the cat's intrusion desperate to keep it in place.

It was a deliberate slowness that the tiger moved with, one that made the ungulate beneath her hot and breathy as their dangerous playfulness resulted in a lingering heat throughout the girl's pelvis. The heat would grow intense until the deer grew frustrated.

"Stop it," she huffed, and the tigress paused like she had been caught in headlights. A glimmer of pain passed over her face before settling into her usual grin.

"Did I do something wrong?"

"Yes! You're going that slow on purpose, aren't you?" The petulant demeanor of the deer was best demonstrated in these moments. "Stop messing around and just give me the orgasm. You're obsessed with teasing me."

"Not at all, my love. In fact, I just like to watch you squirm beneath me. Giving you an orgasm is not as important to me as the act leading up to it, why shouldn't I draw it out?"

That moment of brutal honesty broke the deer from her dream-like haze and reminded her that she was a fortunate woman. The big cat leaning over her had always been much more patient a person than she. What the tigress had often thought was just the act of a slow-burning pleasure, had been interpreted by the deer as a mini-orgasm that was drawn out for her frustration.

The look of hurt splashed across the tigress' face also reminded Impa that her mind was often wrapped up in the fear caused by the predator-prey aspect of their love life. That she regularly forgot the cat had a sensitive streak, and merely pointing out that her pleasuring had caused upset, was causing her obvious pain.

"Let me do something for you, you're always so keen to make sure I'm happy, after all."

The awkward shuffling to get herself into the position she liked best always reminded her of something like a piece of abstract art—her large lover positioned on her hands and knees over a pillow—meanwhile the deer would find herself laying back, admiring the intricate patterns of stripes across the entire creature's body.

She wondered how the texture of her tongue must differ from her mate's, or if perhaps the tiger just wasn't as vocal as her, as every explorative lick merely earned her a sway of the tail. If it was Sheera going down on her, often the first lick would make her yelp.

The feeling of damp spreading on her muzzle, and the low purr that vibrated through the bed as she lapped with more urgency gave away her lover's desire, every lick earning more sweet stickiness to seep out. She'd often heard her taste described as nectar by the cat, she could see why every time her kitten offered her the chance to return the favor.

The tigress was a relatively silent lover in comparison to her and she'd always found it somewhat upsetting that her efforts weren't rewarded more with that adorable squeak her lover would make at the right angle—a sound she imagined to be more like her own—that made her feel as if she and her lover weren't much different.

Her lover's purring was making her legs quiver as she tried to keep lapping with eagerness. Despite the mysterious aura of the tigress and her relative quietness, that was a facade hard to maintain as her orgasm approached. She was struggling to keep herself upright.

"You can collapse down if you want, I can handle it." The deer quipped, nuzzling the joint of her leg as a means of reassurance.

"But—!" The nuzzling continued and the tiger's legs were beginning to buckle and the deer could see the effort the tiger was making to remain upright. At last, she relented, covering her lover's face. Sheera's paws fumbled for the sheets, grabbing fistfuls for anchorage.

"Feels good." The deer mumbled from under the nest of fur as the coldness of her nose chilling the tissue of her companion's vagina as her muzzle was coated with the sweet tasting nectar of her lover. The purring was quickly morphing into a low growl, and her orgasm was signaled by a loud roar and the feeling of the sheets being clenched tight.

Silence fell over the pair, the room covered in a warm hazy glow.

***

She felt herself being grasped by her ankles and pulled flush against her lover's body gentle kisses against her legs, torso and finally down to her face as she was pulled to meet the lopsided smile of the big cat, a look of glassy-eyed bliss over her eyes.

"Shall we continue?" The tigress purred, her tail swishing from side to side as that familiar devilish smile crossed her features. The deer adjusted herself to sit in the pillows, aware of the monstrous stature and that evil grin that in the wild would have meant that the tiny deer would be nothing more than a mere snack.

She could feel warmth in her cheeks, whether that was fear or desire was irrelevant to the deer as she moved across the pillows and fumbled for the drawers where the pair hid the myriad of toys that helped them cover the size difference without causing pain to either of them.

"I want you to be top!" The deer declared loudly and the tigress beamed at her, nodding quietly.

As the big cat fumbled with the straps on the strap-on that the deer had selected, the deer couldn't help but find the act funny. Whether it was the fact her lover always seemed to struggle with fitting it on, perhaps it was how she'd frown at her paws as she spread lubricant across the faux dick, or perhaps it was just the size of the penis in comparison to the seven-foot tall creature, looking more like a pin against the orange and black fur.

As her lover struggled, slipping the end of the strap-on for the wearer into herself with a low purr, the deer reached for the remote that made the device vibrate and readied herself into a position against the pillows. After a few more awkward fumbles with the straps and buckles, and a growl of irritation the tiger looked proud, the buckles and leather finally in place and the device ready for making love to the creature clutching the remote quietly.

Silence. Anticipation. Warmth.

On her knees, the tiger had to enter her at an awkward angle—one small slip and she would cut off her lover's air as they mated—the deer would be a sticky mass at the front as the tigress would try and fail several times to enter. Finally, she slipped in with the sound of a low groan beneath her.

Their position wouldn't be seen amiss in the kama sutra, the tigress having to arch her pelvis down towards her lover as she rested on her knees, arms stretched out to hold the bed board. Beneath her, the deer was trapped by their joining at the pelvis, her neck arching over the edge of the pillow mountain and her nubs, caught against mattress springs, holding her in place against the bed. From the deer's angle, she could make out the thick textured fur under her mate's chin; so soft she almost wanted to reach out and touch it, even though her mate didn't usually approve of such affection.

Then the movement happened, the first subtle motion of the hips and the deer found her mind back in reality.

Slowly and deliberately, the tigress moved and readjusted her position to give herself a better view of her lover, a big paw grasping around her hip as the other strained to reach out for the headboard, the predator arching her back and pelvis so she could watch the nervous peeking from the deer as her breath hitched in time with the deliberate rocking at her pelvis.

The deer focused her mind on the white underbelly and firm breasts of the tigress, and then at the chain and collar still hanging from the creature's neck as she twitched with the motion of the sex toy caressing sensitive tissues inside. The first squeak of desire left her lips with such a surprise she covered her mouth and blushed, earning a gentle chuckle from the creature above her.

With gentle tenderness that would be unbecoming of such a predatory beast, the tigress gave her hip a reassuring squeeze as she pushed harder against the toy, making the deer groan and clench as the sex toy slid deeper, disappearing at the hilt.

That was a cue for the deer to take control again, fumbling for the remote and steadying herself into a motion of mimicking the motions of the creature looming over her, a soft, lopsided smile making her relax as she thumbed the keys.

The vibrations spread through her entire body almost instantly, beginning softly and as her lover sank into her once more, the vibrations from her lover's side made the nerves in her clitoris jolt.

The motion pleased the tigress, who relaxed into her motions and let out a low meow and a smile graced her lips.

Weak hands pressed harder at the buttons, desperate to heighten the charged sensation between them, their bodies growing ever closer that you could almost be mistaken as to where the tigress ended and where her much smaller lover began.

Each increase of the strap-on's settings were matched with drawn out sighs and the increased sensation of slickness as the tigress increased her pace. Shortness of breath and growls and sighs that were quickly becoming desperate cries of pleasure were echoing off every wall in the room.

The deer's mind, once consumed with fear of her lover and frustration at the loss of her trophy could only feel submission to the desire, making her brain take on the texture of marshmallow; warmth spreading from the tips of her hooves up her legs and into her pelvis where it was matched with sensations of cool air between her legs and buzzing both from the toy and the purrs of the creature leaning over, the hand at her hip now balancing the predator's body clumsily as she increased the pace and pressure at which she mated the deer beneath.

A dangerous game with a deadly lover that made every nerve in the sika deer's body feel as alive as the first time they ever tried to make love—when the fear kept her from her pleasure and made her hungry for far more.

The fire spread between them, and every subtle brush at the hips seemed to only intensify the feeling of fire. The deer underneath holding her breath to make the fire burn even greater as she felt her lover's purring vibrate her entire body as she bore down on her.

Hips moving in tandem, the shock of their mutual orgasm would make Impa's ears ring and her sense of smell sharpen, above her, the tigress slumped forward, letting out a heavy roar that would almost certainly evoke fear in the creature beneath her.

Sharp nails were digging into the mattress only a few inches above and beside the deer's head, in order to maintain her balance and still permit her to maintain their conjoinment. The tigress panted heavily, the feeling of vibrations from the sex toy making her quiver as she tried to regain her senses.

The smell of sex and warmth around the room and across her lover's fur made the deer woozy. Her head rolled against something rigid, setting an alarm off in her head that something rigid should not be there.

As always the tigress made sure not to crush her lover beneath her as she left her brain to swim in the blanket of post-orgasm haze. Her nails still tore into the mattress around the sika deer's head. She had to bend herself into an awkward position to look down and see the tired eyes of the small ungulate stare up at her, head pushed against the mattress as her long thin neck strained to afford her a better view.

"You still fear me?" The wide eyes staring up at her had been misinterpreted by Sheera as fear, rather than bliss.

"You're just so good," the deer teased, tongue poking out from the upside angle only causing the tiger to chuckle to herself, the sound resonating down the sex toy still connecting them and the deer's body vibrating with the sensations.

She moved the deer as if she was unwrapping a delicate present, gently pulling free with a fluid motion—a reminder of the fact the deer felt just as safe in her presence as afraid—and after loosening the contraption, watched her lover move to a comfortable nest of pillows.

"I'd much rather nestle into your chest," she remarked.

Rolling her eyes, the tigress moved to lay back on her side of the bed; long muscled limbs stretching high above her head as she retracted her claws into their sheaths. The sensation of small hooves hoisting the fairy-sized deer onto her chest, and the feeling of the sharpened feet scratching against her dense guard hairs made her skin feel alive. She reached a hand down to caress the delicate back of her lover as she stretched and lay on her stomach, head resting between the delicate mounds of the tigress' breasts.

"I'm so jealous of you," Impa sighed.

"I'm jealous of you too," the tigress remarked.

"Why?"

"You're so small and delicate, so frail. You're plagued with insecurities about whether I will bring you harm. I think that's as important to our love as the sex!"

"How so?"

"Because you still laugh and smile with me." The tigress poked her tongue out. "You are my Mistress—I will be a better lover for any who command my respect like you do." She rubbed her neck where the deer had pulled the chain roughly for effect. "Do you not want to go back to your game, I thought you said your trophy was only available today?"

"I've decided, you're a better trophy than that one I wanted in the game anyway." Bleary eyes stared at the tiger as she moved around the room with a grace and sway like the character the deer loved so much in her game.

The deer would fall asleep last, the only thoughts that crossed her mind were a polite reminder to herself: that fear is what made their passion deeper, the predator-prey dynamic had once been a fight for survival and she and her lover—the perfect antithesis of herself—had harnessed that strength to not only find a constant want for each other, but a chance to poke fun at the other. To further solidify that point to herself, she leaned her head to one side, her stubby antlers digging into the tiger's breasts, leaving dents that would ache come sunrise.

That's what you get for having breasts when I am flat. For being my exact opposite. For making me feel more alive every day.

THE TRUE VILLAIN

Dark End

The door to The Hideout (16th and Oak) banged open, and a flash of lightning briefly illuminated the hooded silhouette of the fearsome Doctor Midnight. Villains and minions around the dimly-lit bar turned towards her and waited with baited breath to hear the outcome of the doctor's latest nefarious scheme. The skunk in the doorway knew how to milk the moment and casually plucked at the fingers of her right-hand glove until she could pull it off completely, and then she gave a dramatic sigh and said, "Foiled again," to a chorus of sympathetic groans.

Doctor Midnight swept off the doorstep, with far more swagger in her step than her recent defeat seemed to warrant. No matter what had happened, her head was held high, and her tail swept majestically behind her. When a drunken patron tried unwisely to flirt with her, the power of her glare alone sent him slinking into the corner. Who did he think he was, a voice whispered in her thoughts. She was Doctor Midnight herself.

It was as though an unseen power was propping her ego up and not allowing the night's events to wear it down.

Which was, in fact, exactly what was happening.

The black-caped skunk slid into a stool at the end of the bar, where Rochelle was already waiting with her favorite drink. "Thank you," Doctor Midnight said. "You always know just what I need."

"Psychic," Rochelle gently reminded her. The petite mouse drank in the last few luscious dribbles of confidence from the skunk and slowly closed off her mind from such voyeuristic pleasures. "Who was it this time?" she asked, after she was certain she wouldn't learn the answer before it had been spoken aloud.

The skunk, now free of both her long gloves, drummed her claws on the bar top. She had doffed her hood as well, revealing a mohawk of bright white fur. "Stardust," she said. "That skank."

Rochelle winced. "Really, now. Don't use that kind of language in my bar." She put her hands on her hips, trying to be as stern as she could in a loose tee with nerdy print and a pair of loose shorts to go with. She could, if she wanted, make everyone immediately terrified of her, but, really, where was the fun in that?

Midnight gave a quick roll of her eyes and tapped a tongue impatiently on her sharp teeth. "Have you seen her costume?"

The mouse shook her head.

"Boob window."

"What?"

The skunk gave an even longer roll of her eyes, as if accusing the mouse of not paying attention. "She dresses in skintight silver spandex from the neck down, covering every inch of her fur, except, of course, for a big patch right over her oh-so-fucking-perfect cleavage."

Although Rochelle had mental barriers up, the image in Doctor Midnight's mind was sharp enough to cut right through. "Really?" Rochelle said.

The skunk took a drink and hmmmed non-commitally in her throat. "We were finally making progress. No more stupid mini-skirts and close-cut suits. We could finally wear more practical clothing." She gave a tug on her own cloak, which rattled with numerous pockets filled with everything an evil genius might need, far more useful than any utility belt. "Then along she comes in that tight little number, as if the 90s never happened, flaunting herself all over the place like a centerfold starlet."

Rochelle now thought that Midnight was being far too unfair. "It's her choice what her costume is, Doc."

Doctor Midnight arched a single eyebrow and gave Rochelle a withering stare over the black bridge of her muzzle. She really had the imperious villain act down, even without Rochelle mentally boosting her ego. "Be that as it may be, she also gave an interview recently. And in that interview she talks about how her uniform is the one that is truly empowering women and that we should all be wearing one. She said that you or I only wear what we do because we are ashamed of how we look."

"That skank!" The words were out of her muzzle before Rochelle stopped to think about them. The mouse clapped a hand over her face, ashamed.

The skunk's face twisted in a sardonic smile. "You see what I mean?"

"Ugh, yes."

Midnight took another drink and steeled herself for a dramatic pause. "It is of no concern. I will get her… next time."

Rochelle nodded. It was a common enough sentiment in the eternal struggle between hero and villain. But then something tickled at her mind through the barrier she had erected. Midnight was focusing very hard on a single clear image and it was puncturing into Rochelle's own mind. "Wait a synapse," Rochelle said. "You're not really angry with her."

"Of course I am," the skunk said, more defensively than was wise. "I'm furious."

"No, you're really not." Rochelle had a cocky grin as she cast open her mind a little wider. "You want her."

The skunk scoffed. "I want her in a cage."

"No, no, no, you *want* her."

The carefully molded exterior dropped in an instant. Doctor Midnight's eyes went wide. "How do you—"

"Psychic," Rochelle again had to remind her.

"Damn it."

The mouse had to contain the bubbling squeak that threatened to pop out of her throat. She quickly pushed everyone else's minds away from herself and Midnight, so they wouldn't be overheard. "Don't worry. I won't tell anyone. I think it's cute. Midnight's got the hots for a heeeerooooo," she elongated the last word teasingly.

The skunk snarled and dug her claws into the lacquered wood of the bar. But the anger wasn't directed at the mouse. "It's infuriating. There I was, building my latest hero containment unit, and I realized that I was unconsciously designing it to put her on display, chest out so I could admire it. It was so, so inefficient of me. She was—she is!—a distraction. I can't wait until I can finally… I can finally…"

"Get her in bed?" Rochelle offered.

"Punch her!" Midnight snapped, and then added, "And then, maybe, get her in bed."

Rochelle slipped her hands in her pockets, biting her lip as she allowed herself to drink up the feelings of lust that were threatening to bubble up inside Doctor Midnight's mind. "Why don't I stick around on your next outing? I might be able to help."

The imperious look returned to the skunk's features. "Help how? You're a barkeep."

"Psychic barkeep," the mouse said, getting a touch more irritated.

"Oh, right. Sorry. Wait, are you making it hard for me to remember that?"

"Maybe. It's not intentional, Doc."

Midnight shrugged. "Oh well. Anyway, if you wouldn't mind coming along, I'm short on minions as it is. She tossed most of mine in jail, while I was… preoccupied. I think the next job needs to be to spring them."

Rochelle grinned, oddly happy to be heading into the fray for once.

***

Stardust was even more stunning than the picture Rochelle had seen in Doctor Midnight's mind: a coyote just shy of six-feet tall with a brilliant pelt of browns, tans, grays, and whites, hidden behind a mask and from the neck down by a layer of silver spandex. She was unquestionably beautiful, but it was a beauty that could not be attributed to any one trait, not her eyes, nor her smile, nor her curves. Instead, it was the sum of all the parts collectively, where not a single strand of fur seemed out of place. It honestly made Rochelle self-conscious of even the smallest possible faults in her own appearance.

And then there was the costume. It was twice as lurid as Midnight had described. The costume hid barely half of the coyote's breasts, and what was hidden wobbled and shook so much with every motion that Rochelle was honestly surprised they hadn't popped free already.

Doctor Midnight's so-called hero containment device (or HCD) was a massive metal ring with the hapless Stardust caught spread-eagled within thanks to electroschackles around her wrists and ankles.

You could also tell Stardust was a bit on the young side: she had an urge to make small talk with her captors that older heroes stoically avoided. "So," she said brightly, "I haven't seen you before."

Rochelle was impersonating a rather simple-minded minion and she wished she had some bubblegum to chew on so she could complete her look. As it was, she idly twirled a finger through her fur and sashayed a little closer. "Yeah, I'm new. You locked up all the other help, so I had to lend a hand."

Stardust thought for a moment. "I got it. You're side-kicking."

"We're villains, darling," Rochelle said in a squeaky voice a half-octave higher than her usual. "I'm minioning."

"Right. Sorry. Minioning." Stardust gave a sheepish, but genuine, smile. "Is that nice?"

"It's nicer when the captives aren't trying to distract me with small talk and hope I won't notice them trying to break their bonds." Rochelle flicked a lever and the electroshackles hummed, tightening their grip.

"Damn it. How'd you see that?"

"Psychic," Rochelle said, proudly.

Stardust screwed up her eyes to look straight ahead, took a powerful breath, and then belted out into song, "OH, THE CAMPTOWN LADIES SING THIS SONG. DOO-DAH! DOO-DAH!"

The mouse squeaked out a stream of giggles. "See?"

Stardust shivered and relaxed. "Wow, that was... Why did I do that?"

Rochelle giggled louder, trying and failing to stop herself from feeling every moment of Stardust's complete confusion. "Don't worry. I don't like doing that often. If I take full control over you, then it's hard to tell who I am anymore, you know? Also, don't worry about your secrets. I don't like learning them. Life gets too simple and... and..." Rochelle feigned not knowing the word.

"Predictable?" Stardust helpfully supplied.

"That's it! Yeah. Predictable." It was mostly the truth. With her abilities, Rochelle could easily be one of the most powerful supers on the planet, but she had no interest in the petty squabbles of heroes and villains. The constant fighting they did—so boring. The only reason she hung out with villains and managed The Hangout was because they tended to have more interesting emotions than heroes did. "I can still chat though."

That seemed to cheer Stardust up. "Anything is better than just waiting to see what Doctor Midnight's inevitable deathtrap will turn out to be."

The mouse flicked a hand dismissively. "Nah, the doc's not big on deathtraps."

It was true. Doctor Midnight was a notoriously practical sort of villain: "I don't want to rule the world," she was famous for saying. "I just want to make a few changes." She also knew that deathtraps were often a waste of mental energy. She preferred restraining heroes until she was far away and then releasing them. Death usually only resulted in avenging crusaders that were even more annoying.

"So what's your power?" Rochelle asked, genuinely curious.

Stardust actually had to think for a moment, and when she spoke it was intoning memorized words not her own, "Spontaneous generation of angular momentum with localized telekinesis. In other words, I can spin with incredible force and tow some things with me, before launching them out like a slingshot."

"How do you get a name like Stardust from that?"

"I wanted to be Comet," the coyote said brightly, and then soured, "but that was already taken. I figured Stardust was close enough. I suppose my ability to spin is why I'm locked up like this. If I could start to turn a little bit, I don't think this thing could stop me."

Rochelle giggled. This was a moment she had been waiting for. "Oh no, that's not why you're in that thing."

Stardust tried to twist, her coyote ears flapping about as she tried. "But... it's clearly designed to stop me from even beginning to spin. Once I start, she'd have a hard time stopping me."

"Yeah, but that'd be easy to do just by tying your feet and hands together. Single anchor point, everything bound there. Easy and efficient."

Stardust's mouth hung open a little, like she had a hard time believing this ditzy little mouse had said something that complicated. "Then why—?"

Rochelle covered her mouth as she gave the most innocent giggle she could manage. "You may be a hero, Stardust, but you're still a good-looking gal. I think she has a thing for you, even if she won't admit it."

Stardust took a moment to process that, and as she did, Rochelle kept her mind open wide. While Stardust's face stayed impassive, her thoughts were secretly pleased. Very pleased.

Maybe... maybe a little too pleased.

"Thanks for letting me know, uh..."

"Rochelle," the mouse said, and held out her hand as if dumb enough to not realize the hero's arms were shackled.

"Good to meet you. Maybe one day I'll get to toss you in jail myself."

Rochelle gave a wink. "Maybe. Anyway, can I ask another thing?"

Stardust shrugged and looked around. "Not like I'm going anywhere soon."

"Well, I was just wondering about your uniform and all, you see I was read—"

A sudden shudder went through Stardust's body. The coyote threw her head back and wailed as if Rochelle had just stuck a knife into her. "Daaaaaaaaamn it."

Rochelle blinked. "W-what?"

"The interview. You read it, didn't you?"

The mouse could only give a weak nod.

"Oh my God, I'm so, so sorry. I didn't mean to say all those things they just tumbled out."

Rochelle was still a bit stunned. "Tumbled out?"

Stardust nodded forlornly. "It was my first big interview. I was all stressed. I clammed up, I couldn't get the words out, and so I just said the first thing that popped into my head. It was so, so stupid. I didn't mean it. Please forgive me."

Rochelle felt her act starting to drop. She felt genuinely sorry for Stardust. A poor choice of words at the wrong time and it was going to hang over her head for months. Possibly forever. It wasn't like she was a psychic and could make everyone forget. "Hey, uh, what was the real reason then? I could maybe spread it around discreetly. I'm good at that." She flashed a winning smile.

Stardust flushed, her ears flattening atop her head and her tail curling between her legs. "I don't really feel comfortable talking about that."

Rochelle was about to protest when a single, clear word flared up in Stardust's mind. "Wait, what does fanfic have to do with anything?"

"How do you know about that!?"

"Psychic," Rochelle said, although a bit more apologetically than usual.

The coyote let out a whining howl of frustration. If she had been free of the electroshackles, no doubt she would be stamping her foot. "You can't tell anyone."

"I won't. Swear on my code of honor as a villain." There was no such code of honor, but she meant it all the same, and she pushed out the idea that Stardust should trust her.

"Okay..." the coyote said after a long pause and even longer sigh. Her tail hung limp behind her. "Tell me, did you get your powers slow or fast?"

The mouse shrugged a little. "Slow. Had 'em since I was born and they grew with me as I aged."

"Not me," the coyote said. "20th birthday. 7:00 PM on the nose. One second, middling college student. Next second, saving the world." She gave a little chuckle. "Before becoming Stardust, nobody really noticed me. I had two or three friends. I'd gone on two dates, if you could even call them dates. (That idiot Brian spent the whole time talking about himself.) Two days later, the whole city took notice of me. Everyone wants to have their picture taken with me. Little girls want to grow up to be me. I get a dozen offers to go out on a date a day now. People don't just want to be with me, they want me, if you get what I'm saying."

Rochelle did get what she was saying. "You've googled yourself, haven't you?"

"Helllll yeah!" Stardust said with a swoop of her head that send her long hair swirling around her head and with her voice echoing like she had just said her signature catchphrase. "There are at least two porno sites devoted just to yours truly. Fan art. Fan fic. Even fan vids."

"Really?" The mouse was wide-eyed. She'd never heard of that before.

"Sure, sometimes married couples do superhero roleplay. Maybe she's me conquering the villain in the best way possible or maybe she's me, tied up and helpless and ravished all night long." The coyote bit her lip and stared dreamily up at the ceiling.

Rochelle held up her hands in a T. "Time-out. Let me get this straight. After becoming a super, all the attention made you realize that you were actually an exhibitionist?"

A firm nod from the coyote.

"Well, then why not say that?"

Stardust hung her head to one side, muzzle tucked in against her collarbone. "The local hero league is way too conservative. We're not even allowed to be out of the closet in public. They'd throw me out for sure if they knew I was kinky too."

"Tried villainy? We don't care about any of that."

The coyote mock-scoffed. "I have a duty to the people."

"Uh-huh," Rochelle winked. "Well, should you change your mind, just let me know. Anyway, you became a hero, realized you were an exhibitionist, couldn't tell anyone about it because of League membership rules, made your costume so it would secretly feed your desires anyway, and then got flustered under your first big interview and blabbed out the first thing you could think of?"

"That about sums it up."

Rochelle cracked her knuckles. "No worries, hun. I'll start seeding thoughts that you didn't really mean that at the interview and you were just stressed by it. No one will think any different within, say, two weeks."

"Oh, thanks, how can I ever repay you?"

Rochelle smiled. "Just remember what I told you about the Doc. Be nice to her."

"Can do. As much as I can with me being a hero and her being a villain and all that."

Rochelle nodded and silently withdrew a key from her pocket. She set it down on a shelf just inches from Stardust's hands and winked before turning and whistling her way out of the room.

***

Doctor Midnight did not blame Rochelle for Stardust's escape: she told the mouse so frequently (and Rochelle made sure to reinforce that thought frequently too). All the same, she avoided The Hideout for a few days, quietly scheming in her secret laboratory. She was only drawn out when Rochelle sent her a message saying that something had been left at the bar for her.

The skunk appeared in a gloomy fog. A scowl seemed etched over her lips and her mohawk seemed to droop over one ear. Nobody tried to strike up a conversation as she stomped down to her favorite stool. A nice suite of emotions for Rochelle to enjoy, even if she felt guilty for enjoying Midnight's unhappiness. "Thanks," the skunk said, distractedly, "for helping me out the other day." She was forcing herself to be nice, Rochelle could tell.

"Cute coyote still on the brain?"

"Ugh." The skunk dropped all pretense of control and allowed her head to smack into the bar top repeatedly. "I haven't been able to invent anything. Not a single plan. Not a single device. No schemes, no ideas. Nothing."

"I'm sorry to hear—"

"Did you know she has a porn website?"

The words had been muttered into the bar directly. Rochelle barely heard them. But she could feel the images bursting into her mind. "Oh. You found that."

"Yeah," Doctor Midnight said, half in a breathless sigh. "Someone drew a picture of her and me together. Several someones."

Rochelle felt she had to be a little careful here. "You're not, uh, planning to burn anyone's house down, are you, doc?"

The skunk sat bolt upright, her mohawk quivering. "No. That is a thought. But no. They actually portray me rather well. Corset, most times. Very slimming. Very flattering."

Rochelle breathed a sigh of relief. "Then..."

"I can't get her out of my head!" The skunk tore at her cheekfur in frustration, then started biting at her claws. "It was bad enough when I could only imagine what she looked like under that costume. Now I've seen it. Or what it might look like. I've seen what I might do to her. I haven't done any productive work in three days." And then, almost in a whisper, she added, "I wore out my best vibrator."

"Maybe this will help then," she said and picked up the large manila folder behind the bar.

"Is that what you brought me here for? What is it?"

"It's a letter. Apparently a very large one."

"Who from?"

"Stardust."

Doctor Midnight actually leapt out of her chair, upper body straining over the bar, and snatched the folder from Rochelle's hands.

"Hey!"

The skunk ignored her as she tore into the folder. "Ugh, did that... that fool really write a letter to gloat about escaping? How prosaic."

Rochelle sighed and picked up a few dirty glasses and took them to the sink. She spun around when, only two seconds later, an emotional wave of shock slammed into her mind and Doctor Midnight's hands slapped against the bar. The skunk was standing straight, eyes wide, staring at nothing at all, the manila folder pinned to the desk with as much force as she could muster.

"What? What is it?" Rochelle said.

"Shhh," the skunk hissed, glancing around for any prying eyes.

"What?" Rochelle asked again, voice lowered.

"It's not a letter."

"Then what is it?" she asked for the third time, impatience in her voice.

"Photos."

"What kind?"

"Glamour shot."

"Seriously?"

"Breasts and nothing but."

"Naked?"

"Mostly..."

Rochelle reached but Midnight yanked the folder away, shoving it into an oversized coat pocket.

"I can't believe her," the skunk fumed. "Argh! I am going right back to the lab. I am designing a new doomsday weapon and this time I'm going to point it straight at her."

Rochelle barely had time to wave and call after her, "Have a good time!" Then, when the skunk's stomping footsteps faded from the alley outside and the tingling sensation of lust and excitement left with her, Rochelle said to herself, "Those two are coming along nicely."

***

"Success at last!" Doctor Midnight crowed. "How do you like my new freeze ray, Stardust?"

The skunk, coyote, and mouse were in the harbor district, surrounded by creaky old warehouses and mountains of shipping containers. Midnight had announced their arrival by blowing up the container they needed to break into in rather spectacular fashion. The resulting fireball drew the attention of every media helicopter in the city. It also drew the attention of the local hero league, who had dispatched Stardust right away. The coyote had come spinning gracefully through the air, landed ten feet away, and been half-way through declaring that Midnight and Rochelle were under arrest when the bright blue beam of the freeze ray struck her in the chest.

The coyote found herself encased in a crystalline structure from the neck down, unable to move more than a slight wobble. She opened her mouth, but the skunk cut her off with a wave of her hand and a tap of a switch at her belt. Midnight's voice was suddenly amplified, loud enough to reach the media circling overhead. "Today, you will all witness the downfall of one of your greatest heroes." She tapped the switch again and looked at Rochelle. "Too much?"

The mouse waggled her hand from side to side in a so-so gesture.

"Fine. Not too much grandstanding today." She turned the amplifier on again and cackled in magnificent fashion up to the swarming helicopters. "You fools. Time after time you throw Stardust here at me. Me! The greatest inventor the world has ever seen. So of course I designed a weapon that would neutralize her completely. No movement, no threat. I think I much prefer her this way." Her eyes slid over the trapped coyote's form and as she flicked the amplifier back off, she spoke directly to Stardust. "Consider this payback for those pictures."

The coyote growled and tried to free herself, succeeding only in wobbling a little more.

Doctor Midnight burst into laughter. "Oh that is adorable, dear. Keep it up."

Rochelle quietly sidled a little closer, mentally tapping into Midnight's sense of ego and delight. It washed over her with such power that she felt momentarily woozy, joining in the maniacal laughter until the skunk shot her a dirty look. Right. She was still playing the part of the minion.

Together they watched as Stardust tried to throw her weight around inside the icy prison. A sharp crack rent the air as it fractured near the base. Doctor Midnight leveled her weapon and braced herself as the coyote threw her weight against the prison again. This time the crack split wide and the coyote suddenly looked as if she realized the flaw in her plan just as the ice went tumbling over with her inside. She hit hard, recovered quickly, and spun her way back to a standing position, sending a torrent of icy slivers flying in all directions. "Now who's adorable, Doc?"

Rochelle and the skunk both looked up, having shielded their faces from the flurry. Their breaths caught in their throat and Midnight diabolical laughter reached a fever pitch. "Oh, I think it's still you, dear Stardust."

Stardust followed the skunk's gaze down and saw that she was standing there, completely nude. She slapped arms and tail over her body to cover herself.

"This is truly a treat," Midnight said. "My freeze ray must have made your outfit so much more brittle. Spinning at the speed you do, you tore it to shreds. A more perfect revenge I couldn't imagine." But something nagged at her, and she leaned down to whisper in Rochelle's ear. "But why does she look like she's getting turned on? Is she moaning?"

The mouse facepalmed.

And then she facepalmed Doctor Midnight, adding to the physical slap a mental one that imparted all that she had learned about Stardust directly into the skunk's brain.

Even with a genius level intellect, getting your memories broadsided with new information was a bit much for her to process, and Doctor Midnight stared blankly ahead for a good five seconds before her mind caught up. "Oh. My. God."

"Yep," Rochelle added.

"I've had this whole situation wrong from the beginning."

"Yep."

"And now, I may have inadvertently revealed her secret to the world."

"Yep."

"I'm a villain. But that's just… evil."

"Yep."

"Argh!" Doctor Midnight paced back and forth, clutching the weapon to her chest as though it were a lifeline. "What do we do? I'm not good at ad-libbing. I'm a planner, not a do-er."

Rochelle looked at Stardust. She could feel the worry emanating off her in waves, rapidly shifting to terror as she was realizing how her uncontrolled arousal would look to the hero league. "Well," she said, and cracked her knuckles, "Finally my turn to get to be the villain for real."

Doctor Midnight had half a moment of confusion plastered across her face before Rochelle's control asserted itself. Then she seemed to freeze in mid-air. *Don't resist*, she hissed into Midnight's mind. The skunk seemed to relax after that, a sense of trust in her old friend welling up inside her. She whispered the same message into Stardust's mind, soothing her worries and slowly guiding her hands down to her side, revealing her naked body to the cameras above again.

Rochelle reached out and popped the amplifier from Midnight's belt, holding it in front of her. "Hello up there!" she said with a cheery wave up to the sky. "I suppose I should introduce myself. They call me…" and here she paused, because she hadn't gone by a villainous name other than Rochelle. "They call me the Mental Mystic. I bet you think this meeting here was all a coincidence. I bet the hero league also thinks that it dispatched Stardust here of their own will. I bet even the great genius Doctor Midnight thought all these meetings with Stardust were pure coincidence. Nope. That's all me. I just thought these two would make such a great couple: the dark and mysterious Doctor Midnight and the bright and spunky Stardust. Oh well, that mishap with the freeze ray just means I have to work a bit quicker than expected. I hope you all enjoy the show!"

She could feel the pair of them both grow worried at the thought of them putting on a show, but Rochelle pressed down on their fears and nudged Midnight to step forward. Sluggishly, the skunk began to move, until she got the idea and practically sauntered up to Stardust.

Rochelle left the coyote's mind largely alone. Once she got the idea to not hide herself anymore, she started playing her part to a tee, squirming in place, tail curling over one hip as if wanting to hide her sex. When Midnight leaned in and met her lips in a deep kiss, the coyote moaned once and then joined back, kissing just as hard.

Rochelle giggled silently at how easy this all was. Changing what someone wanted to do took a lot of concentration and effort; it wasn't always possible. But this was the sort of thing Midnight had been dreaming of so the mouse didn't even need to push her mind that hard. Just a little nudge here and there and soon she was groping the coyote with wild abandon. The mouse may have been straight herself, but with Doctor Midnight's lusts warming Rochelle's own mind, at that point a show was a show. She slipped into the privacy of a warehouse office where the cameras wouldn't be spying on her and opened her mind completely to the two other women. She groaned at the phantom tongue she felt probing her mouth and the feel of Doctor Midnight's gloved fingers rubbing at her sex. She felt all the desires of both hero and villain crash into her and make her shiver.

But she wasn't yet done directing the action. Midnight's hands were fumbling with her own clothes, slowing down as she realized she was stripping before a very public audience, so Rochelle sent another psychic prod to make her ignore everything going on around her. So far as she and Stardust were concerned, there was only each other. At last.

Now both naked and given free rein to act out their own inner fantasies, their actions couldn't be more different. Midnight's touches were demanding, kissing ravenously, clutching at Stardust's fur, fondling lewdly. Stardust was far more gentle, stroking and caressing.

Rochelle shivered as she felt her nipples—well, Stardust's nipples really—brush through the rougher fur of the skunk. She bit her lip and clenched her thighs as Midnight's finger reached into her—no,

Stardust's—sex.

"Not so fast," the coyote said. She pushed the clinging Midnight a few inches away, enough to give her room to start snaking her way down her body, leading with her muzzle and kisses peppered through her fur. When she fell to her knees at last and ran her tongue once over the skunk's swollen labia, both Midnight and Rochelle gave a moan of primal desire.

That slim tongue slid out and caressed over Midnight's sex, while her hands and claws ran teasing furrows through the fur of her thighs. Each teasing slip of that tongue sent a shiver rocketing along Midnight's spine and made her fur stand out even straighter. Rochelle could feel her own heart pounding within her chest. She needed this now. She needed this just as badly as Midnight did. Finally, the skunk had had enough and gripped the base of the coyote's ears tight. "P-put it in me. I need it."

Stardust obliged, but even then, she gave the sly grin of her name-sake species and had to make even that a more teasing experience. She spread the skunk's labia apart with her thumbs and flitted her tongue over them, like a snake scenting the air. Midnight ground forward and hissed through an escaping moan. "More. More."

Rochelle squeezed her eyes shut as the coyote finally penetrated Midnight's sex. The tongue seemed to writhe within her, pushing deep, receding, flicking around then pushing in deep again. Rochelle was grinding her hips in the air but she could feel Midnight gyrating, pumping her hips forward as if that would make that magical tongue sink deeper, work harder, hit all the right spots within her.

Rochelle was panting now, cresting on a wave of sexual excitation from both hero and villain simultaneously. Her hand was locked between her thighs, rubbing at herself through her clothes to get that extra little bit of stimulation. It wasn't needed.

A moment later, Midnight had a knee-shaking, breath-catching, toe-curling orgasm that was so powerful it launched Rochelle right through one of similar strength, and she fed it back to Stardust who, without having have touched herself in the last minute, came just as hard, squealing in delight.

As she tried to find her breath, Rochelle quietly withdrew from the minds of both women and let them remember the cameras overhead. The two came to their senses in a flash, looked at each other, looked up, and dove for cover, cursing.

Rochelle smiled weakly and collapsed to the floor, thinking that she was going to have to wait for her thighs to be less sticky before she made her way home.

***

Doctor Midnight came stumbling into The Hideout a few days later. She wasn't her usual imperious self. She was relaxed, light-hearted, laughing with the other patrons. And in turn, many of them were encouraging her, telling her not to worry so much about what had happened. "You had a fun time," one of them said, "Last time a mind controller got a hold of me, they left me clucking like a chicken in front of central station. Naked."

"This time next year, you'll look back on this and laugh," another said.

And another, "A kiss and more from Stardust. Hard to complain too much."

"You think they'll ever find the one who did this? Cripes, give me the shivers just thinking she could still be out there."

She laughed and waved all of them off, taking her customary spot at the end of the bar. She immediately fixed Rochelle with a stare, although it wasn't a very serious one. "That your doing?"

The mouse shrugged and smiled. "I can't make it disappear, but I can make people not care. They're treating it like the paparazzi got a compromising photo. It wasn't your fault all that happened, so outside of a few video clips going around, no one cares."

"And they don't recognize you?"

Rochelle just grinned and shook her head. Then she leaned over the bar, whispering conspiratorially. "So, how'd the second date go?"

Midnight sputtered for a moment. "Don't read my mind like that."

"Actually that was just a good guess. I figured you two, once you got a good push towards each other, would be inseparable."

"Oh." Midnight fidgeted on her seat for a moment more. "Second date went well. So did the third."

"Third date already. Sister, are you going to reveal your secret identity yet?"

"Did that already. I mean, after being that intimate, what's a little thing like our real names?" She blushed. "Anyway, I still owe you for that. I don't want you doing that any time soon."

"No worries. I don't have any intention of making a spectacle out of myself or my abilities again soon. Although it could be fun…" Doctor Midnight shot her a glare so dark that Rochelle took an unconscious step back.

"Oh, fine, no more making you get down with the new girlfriend. Don't think I'm needed for that anyhow."

Midnight's blush was all the answer she needed.

Rochelle jerked her head. "You don't need to hang around here on my account. Go on. Get back to her."

The skunk slid off the stool and made her way back sheepishly to the door. But once there, an idea seemed to strike her and she popped the hood back over her head, spun round on the spot and stared imperiously back down at the mouse behind the bar. "But let it be known," she announced. "One day, revenge will be mine."

Rochelle grinned and said to herself, "Looking forward to it."

SMOKEY AND THE JAYBIRD

Slip Wolf

We're both hungry. The Peterbilt's gas needle nestles near empty as dawn creeps over the East Appalachian's green shoulders. The Cummins engine block isn't growing as loud as I am, not on the down slopes anyway, and I'm looking for two birds to kill as the land straightens out a bit and the exits of West Virginia get closer together.

I see the twin silhouettes and know what they say before I read them. A Waffle-Den shares a parking lot with a full service Texaco truck stop. I'm in double luck.

I park, I fuel, ring near a hundred bucks on the pump as the Stones bitch about satisfaction from a radio inside the station. I know what they mean. The same four country songs mumbled off the radio for miles while disco crowds out every other channel. That bubble-gum shit can't go away fast enough. This bear likes her punk like she likes her waffles: hot, fast, and bad for you. Speaking of which...

I move the rig off pump and move my ass to the yellow hut's door, ringing the tiny brass bell as I enter. Cream and leavened batter tease my nose with prostitutional sweetness inside. Heaven from as far as Belgium, as close as a pork farm and with that zesty sugar dash of Canadian maple. My stomach applauds pretty loudly.

The otter in the black server's bib looks up. "Seat yourself sir," she says in her accommodating Virginian lilt.

"That's ma'am." I mutter indifferently. Bears my frame fool a lot of folks and this in particular doesn't anger me at all anymore. The linoleum creaks as I find a booth and slide in, disgruntled belly daintily tucked. The otter blanched a bit at the gender misappropriation and I don't wanna hear an apology. "Save you time. Coffee. One cream. Two gridiron Belgians, just syrup's fine. Eggs scrambled, double the thick-slab bacon and sub the toast for a buttermilk biscuit."

"Of course ma'am, right away." The otter's tail slaps a stool as she hastens and brings my scribbled order back.

"I heard her," a disaffected, patient voice says to the server and things start to sizzle. My coffee is there right away and the otter is gone again.

There's a crumpled sports section. I don't follow baseball and the Richmond Flying Squirrels had a dud game. Outside the rising sun is kissing Redstone's fibreglass hood, Redstone being my truck's name, and I'm feeling that weird anxiety that comes from hunger pangs and road weariness all at once when the sizzling gives way to something my ears miss at first. Then they pull the sound from the ruckus of the kitchen like a jewel from dirt.

A voice in song, low in register at first but rising high, lifting off above the bacon pops and flapjack burns and clattering of haphazard cookware. The fragment of verse is lost in the melee but the chorus rings true as I hold my breath and listen. "A spring we'll make together, no hearts under the weather, cause a blue sky's wide and smiling down for you. You and me we're tempting fate, and the devil may as well take the bait, cause no dark ain't fallin' on love I have for you."

"April." The otter cuts in. "Sweetie, I'll watch the eggs. Go get the hashbrowns from the freezer, would ya?"

I turn in my seat, and behind the stove I catch a flash of blue, bright under the open bulbs that illuminate the place. Its around the flimsy door to the back and gone. My neck is craning back that way and starting to hurt as I curiously wait for the songstress to return. I'm interrupted by the slide of plate on formica. "All ready there. You want more coffee?"

Asked as a matter of course because I've hardly drunk a drop of mine. "Sure," I breathe and eat and wait. My sugar-cookie ears catch the door click over the meager sounds of the kitchen at standby—there's only one other customer here—and I turn to see her.

The bluejay is slender, wingtips delicate as they flutter pans from place to place, prepping supplies with a slender knife, separating the frozen hashbrowns she brought out. Her dark beak opens and closes thoughtfully, eyes I can't make the color of down on her task. I turn back, praying for her to sing something again, but she manages only a few hummed notes of something that's idle in her head as she prepares for the next order.

I just want her to sing anything. Quite unlike myself, I'm too bashful to ask. I'd have to shout across the space to ask or get up and lumber over and she'd just get self-conscious. I eat everything in front of me fast but quiet. The natural sounds of the place are like a babbling culinary brook where something's set to happen.

You know when something brings a calm to you that you didn't know you were missing before? The interrupted melody keeps hanging like a bright mist under the spring sun creeping in and then the otter orders the jay to the back for another random implement and gone from sight.

I'm out of time. Clock hasn't stopped ticking on my route. I finish, tip and get back in the saddle.

***

The manifest has paper products enough to sop up Lake Erie. I count off numbers in my head. I'm six hauls this size and distance and my payments will be done on Redstone. I've been seven years driving the Peterbilt as a freelance contractor and by year eight the rig'll be mine. Four of those essential contracts are with this company, PriceCo, which has its dull logo slapped on the trailer I chugged here. Store outlets are spread through eleven East-side states fed by warehouses in Georgia and West Virginia, the latter of which looms high over me as the weasel with the clipboard marks each pallet. He's smoking like a chimney. I'm still trying to quit so I take a walk to stop myself from bumming one.

The overcab Marmon rig I pass two bays over is black, decaled with a yellow silhouette of a falcon leaping into flight on the door, inexplicably prominent breasts perked. I recognize the truck a second too late.

"Smoookeeey Leee!" The mountain lion wheezes from where he sits on his cab step, a tattered Harlequinn Romance in his paw. "I didn't know you hauled for these guys."

Shit.

Grey teeth show in his muzzle as he slides himself up to leaning against his truck, then off, pushing his red mesh cap back with a sinewy limb. "You running for them long?"

"Not long," I mutter. With our history he should know what it means when I glare at him the way I glare at him.

With our history he still doesn't give a shit. "Woah, don't give me a smile or nothing, Smoke. I'm just being neighborly."

"Good for you, Stick." He doesn't know how. "I'm getting loaded, should be out of here soon."

"Really? Cause I could've sworn I saw the Redstone pull in half an hour ago. They giving you a different trailer to move? Don't think they'd leave you hitched while they pull the goods off if they wasn't just loading the same box again." His smile is grey and cold. "I've missed you, Lee, worry about you sometimes."

Worried about how rejection still makes him look, public as it was last time. He didn't even want me. I was the only thing that didn't have a dick in an isolated corner of a Phoenix roadhouse on a Wednesday, and letting him get as close as he did still stinks in the memory as bourbon and regret. But his paws learned where not to tread. "You should stop worrying about me, Stick. I'm doing just fine."

Stickley's cold look grows more sour. "I'm just trying to be a gentleman, Lee. Least I can do for somebody who wouldn't recognize gallantry if it rode a horse-drawn wagon. We don't *all* think you're so homely you know."

I keep myself from glaring, find myself staring at the unnatural side-boob on his rig's dark eagle silhouette. The nerve of this fucker.

"You can hold up on the plastic charm, cat. I'm doing just fine I said. Gonna go call my man, catch up on his day." That man is nobody right now, but if anything will end this encounter with dignity for either of us, I'll take it.

"That so?" His arms don't know what to do with themselves, so they fold. "Word around the lanes is you ain't let any man near you in years."

Silence is too potent. Wood pallets bounce with cracks in the building behind us. I just want to reload and go. "Too few good ones."

"Or maybe good ones don't amount to much either." He wants to smile but settles for a weak sneer. "Word is."

I'm suddenly aware of how fragile and spindly he looks. "Word is you can kiss my ass."

He laughs like an earthquake oil change, nervous and unpleasant, reaching a paw back to toss the ragged paperback through his cab's open window. "To close to the quick there. Well I'm sorry." I hold rock still as he saunters past me, his tail dragging my thigh. "I wouldn't wanna take a woman away from her gallant man. He's a lucky one in'ne?"

The feel of a paw slapping your ass is distinct in that the surprise and shock are nine-tenths of the sting. That it's done so tenderly makes what happens next kinda inevitable, like gravity.

My right arm is up like a hand signal, dark fur under the rolled up checked shirt, muscle all but hiding the joint. I pivot fast, shoulder and hips together. His head is like a bad-fitted speedbag when my backhand connects. His hat ejects like a classroom spitball and the mountain lion's arms semaphore on their way to the pavement. The thunder of blood in my ears almost drowns out the distant tingle of laughter.

I turn, ready for more confrontation, but the laughter is clouded by a couple paws applauding and one authentically lupine wolf whistle.

Other truckers we mutually know from our circuitous routes are clustered round a picnic table outside a burger joint across the lot.. They laugh and point, bellies shaking. They all know Stickley and they all know me. Word will be across every CB wave before the mountain cat even gets his ass off the asphalt, but I know I'm not a hero to anybody watching. I'm just a diverting spectacle showing up a fool. My cheeks get hot and I huff as I go on my way. Whatever Stickley sputters with his bell rung doesn't make it legibly to my ears.

I walk around the whole building, thirty square acres of warehouse before I come back to sign for the new consignment they've loaded. I check the load with a sideways squeeze up the trailer's aisle, sign my name, and push off quick, feeling like a mugger. In my side mirror I catch just one glimpse of Stickley's parked cabover, the stupid cat leaning again, surrounded by three or four other truckers he knows, circle tight.

***

I avoid the usual motel stops that night, avoiding radio chatter and replaying the moment I struck Stickley over and over again in my mind before I finally find an out of the way place along my new route. There's a half-decent diner and gas station where I grab a redeye grilled cheese sandwich and take it back to the sleeper. The space is tight for a bear, but I've made it comfortable and fall fitfully to sleep with unsympathetic laughter crowding my mind. I'm still angry, at Stickley, at the other crew who just witnessed and laughed, and at an empty house somewhere in New Jersey that has nobody waiting for me, nor anyone in my travels I'd want to put there.

The morning comes with the rumble of an engine squealing out and receding, some other trucker behind schedule. I get a coffee and a donut and have the majesty of the Appalachians ahead of me once again when I hear the dull thud and the Peterbilt's steering goes wonky on a curving incline.

I don't panic. Panicking is every crash's best friend. I get off the gas, don't stamp the break. On a curve doing over forty that can be deadly. Everything goes into keeping steering so that I and my load hold the lane. Hazards on, ignore the honks, use the left turning bank to ease myself into the right lane. I get straight again as the road does, then the breaks get tapped. It takes a lot of time and gravel shoulder to get myself stopped a quarter mile short of a rest stop. I realize when the engine cuts that my heart was trying to beat itself out of my chest. Could be fear, could be too much salt in my diet.

Sure enough, the feedback didn't lie. I lost an outside left tire on the third axle. Some carcass hangs on the rim, more of it lays like flayed hide far back on the highway where the bend kinks the flattop out of sight. Winter's cramps, what a fuckin' mess. I take an expansive breath that flutters my jowls. I coulda gone off back there. Getting myself calmed down, I move back to the spare in the trailer's undercarriage, rolling up my sleeves and wishing for more coffee. It's then that I see something in my peripheral, jagged and ugly. Eyes are dragged back to the steel liner on the trailer's tip above the gone tire. The etching is deliberate, each letter carved in with score after score so it's permanently into the steel; FAT DYKE.

I stare at it, arms hanging limp, a chill setting in slow but certain. I mechanically get the full spare out of the trailer stirrup, get the kit, jack it a couple inches, crow off the naked rim, get the spare on, lug it tight. Arms are burning but as hard as I try to keep focused, I'm burning too, a heat that makes me pant through teeth that want to close and grind.

Don't know if it takes me a half hour or longer, but I'm back at the wheel, knuckles cracking around it as I roll up the road and hit the rest stop. I swear I can smell that mountain lion in the stale piss that bleeds out of both bathrooms and I just want to imagine his throat filling my paws and those eyes popping out. In the ladies' room, vision finally narrows to an inevitable crimson point. My closed fist meets metal of the first bathroom stall and behind the crack of the impact is a dent that'll stay in this place until they tear the whole shitty thing down.

A stall down the lane creaks open. The doe in skinny jeans gives me a heart-breaking terrified glance and her hoof clops are frantically close together as she rushes out, purse swinging, not washing her hands for mortal safety.

I haven't cried in forever. Dad wouldn't have it. Mom would, but without a word. Memories that need to keep hibernating stir; the disdain at seeing my first long-haul license, the dripping sense that something's just too different about me. And there was the passive aggressive worry from both those frowning jowls that I wouldn't be accepted among the boys who moved the machines I craved to command. I wash up and go back to my rig, stopping for a second to take a long look at the cigarette machine next to the soda. I've put the coins in and the Luckies drop before I realize what I've decided to do. There's matchbooks in the tray and I take my first puff in weeks. Fury turns to cold calculation as anxiety ebbs away behind the wheel. I won't report Stickley. I won't pass word around neither, don't know who's ready to take his side. I summarize things plainly in as flat as Nebraska and cold as an Alaskan ice lane to the open CB channel. "This is Smokey. Threw a shoe on seventy-seven south, just before exit 290. Alligator tread all over the place so eyes out. Over"

"Y'okay, Smokey?" I recognize the voice, a ferret named Raymond out of Dayton.

"Musta hit something needle-y as a *mountain lion's dick*. There's a lot of mess someone's gonna have to *clean up*. Over."

Silence on the line for a bit. So Stickley bragged. Stickley bragged and nobody dropped me a line to warn me that I had a tire about to go. That or nobody believed the insufferable shit. The mind seeks dark alleys of conspiracy and I snap myself out of it. The figure of speech I used probably confused everybody on the channel. Soon enough normal chatter resumes. I get on my way. Still angry, now hungry. A void under a storm. The place I pull off next is familiar.

The Waffle-Den is always open at its appointed hours. Snow storms, hurricanes, hell a Ruskie nuke would have to hit one directly to make a flapjack two minutes late. America thrives on so few reliable things. I'm in and seated. Over behind the grill, digits flying from sausage link to home fries is that same bright blue jay, feathers like a window to purest sky.

The otter who comes to take my order recognizes me. "Couldn't get enough huh."

I could tell her it's been a long day and men are fucking pigs and I could swear that God hates us each in our own special way, but I bury all that in a "No."

"What'll ya have?"

"Steak and eggs. Buttermilk pancakes on the side." Just the thought of butter melting down the stack of gold puts my fretting mind at a modicum of ease. I remember something that can get me the rest of the way there. I turn to watch slender feathered limbs at work, eyes fixed in concentration, dark beak parted just enough for a slender black tongue to poke out and recede as my dinner is poured, pressed, sizzled. She hums, a meandering ditty almost lost under the grill's purposeful hiss. Then she sings, slow and personal, almost under her breath, the melody winding from a beak nearly closed. I catch a mournful call for summer not to end, a trinket on a windowsill that waits for warm hands never coming, "and a heart won't break for waiting, if it's for you," is all I make out as she comes to a close. I realize I'm staring at the jay around the same time she does, meeting my hang-dog ursine sadness with her bashful avian eyes.

There's nobody here but me right now, breakfast rush being over and lunch a ways off, so I don't have to shout when I say, "Love watching you work."

The bluejay swallows as she slowly pours batter. "Thank you."

She places my steak with delicacy upon a grill further downrange and cracks two eggs. I realize the otter never asked me how I wanted them. She's out of the serving area, in the freezer or outside a minute.

"So," I say above the meager sound of frying things, "worked here long?"

That delicate swallow again; "Couple years about." The air is getting fluffy with the buttery aroma of my pancakes coming into the world.

"You sing pretty good."

She looks from me into the grill and her feathers fold in embarrassment as she works.

"No really. I was here yesterday, heading south to drop off, uh, it don't matter," I scratch behind an ear. "I heard you singing at the grill and I really liked it, t'was like spring in a dewdrop, best part of my day." After the warehouse and all after, it's a weak compliment to say anything was better, but she doesn't need to know about that.

She turns my steak. Raw meat burns. "Thank you."

"You write them yourself? The songs, I mean."

"Uh, yeah. Some of 'em." She swallows a white throat and I wonder if this is the longest conversation she's had here that didn't involve burnt bacon in a long time.

"You ever think of going into singing fulltime? I mean, you're really good."

"Oh I dunno. Once, but—"

"You're gonna burn em, April," The otter pokes her thick nose over the jay's shoulder, coming from nowhere. The jay, her name is April, flusters and gets the flapjacks and eggs on a plate. The steak goes on last and the feast is set before me. "Thanks," I mutter to the otter. But my back's to the plate and my eyes are still on the jay. "You thought of singing pro once, and…"

"Life kinda happened. I had responsibilities," by her gaze on the empty hot plate the sum total of those responsibilities is right before her eyes. I know the blunt end of that story well, a dream seems abandoned right where I'm sitting.

"You sing as well as you probably fly and for that voice not to soar is a sad thing. Take a break with me."

That surprises her. "I'd like that. Um," she looks disappointed. "I've got work to do."

"And I've got a fabulous meal to eat but we'll both have some time coming up." I catch the otter's eye. "Won't we?"

The otter's expression is unreadable.

"Yeah, sure," April says, sounding what I hope is amused. She tinkers, I eat the steak and eggs and flapjacks with gusto. About ten minutes later with only one tortoise passing through who just wants coffee, the bluejay, in her stained apron, is at my side, wings tight and nervous practically bouncing on her slender-toed feet like she's about to jump off the here and now to where-ever.

"You smoke, April?"

"No."

"My name's Lee. Short for Lee-Anne. Chat with me downwind." A luckie is already between two knuckles. Just because I'm not furious anymore doesn't mean I don't have anything to keep at bay.

"I wanna go outside," she says. When she follows me out, she has a light, springing hop to her steps.

"So where's home?" I ask when I'm down to a nub and she's got all the nerves bundling.

"Georgia. Originally."

"How'd you wind up here?"

"I needed to get away." She looks off. "I was good on the grill and… and, uh, you?"

"Mom's from Jersey, Dad's from the Bronx. Two far apart, very different worlds."

If April caught the humor in that she didn't let on. "Were they truckers as well?"

I watch the last ember of ash die in my fingers. "Mom's a store clerk, Dad's an actuary."

"Did they help you get into driving big rigs?" April says the last two words like they're a foreign language.

"They did not." I flick the butt halfway to the highway. "Nuff bout me. What about your folks? They know you're flinging flapjacks instead of buttering up souls at the Grand Ole Opry?"

The jay is silent a long time and I want to take back the question when she finally says, "They pretty much put me here."

"What, you mean, literally?"

"I needed to get out." The look in her eyes and the set of her beak want to change the subject.

"I guess if you get sick of a place, you can fly away right?" I put a chuckle on the end of that, but it ruffles her feathers. Her wings shove deep into the pockets on her dirty apron and for just a moment I see a flash in her eyes. I've a hard time reading bird expressions, but it looks like anger to me.

"So how long you wanna do this for? Cooking instead of singing?"

"Its not up to me," she says flatly. Her wings leave her pockets and droop limply to her sides. "Won't ever be."

Her gaze is dragged dejectedly to parking lot pebbles and flattened cigarette butts and when mine goes down to follow hers that's when I notice.

The digits that end her wings just behind the tip feathers are visibly clenching and it occurs to me that I shouldn't see those fingers. Nobody should. The feathers on her wing are jagged and flat-ended where careless shears have pared them down, all the way from past her finger-tips to her elbow and past. She hasn't flexed her limbs for a pre-flight stretch even once out here, away from the heat of the grill and the reason is as apparent now as my own black plug nose.

Her wings have been clipped.

"How did that happen?" I ask. "Who did that to you?"

"What?"

"Your wings. Who cut 'em?"

She looks at her own forewings and lets them droop again. "What's it matter? Veronica says it's for my own good."

"Veronica?" I remember the name tag on the otter. "Your manager? Here?"

"Yeah."

"Why would she clip your wings?"

"So I can work the grill better," April digs the gravel with a thin claw. "Why else."

In a hazy moment, I'm feeling unsettled and already putting together implications here. Today is a day for those, and they aren't good. "She clipped your wings right here in this kitchen?" Another cigarette is in my hands and I'm looking at buried hurt in the jay's eyes that she isn't good at hiding. My fingers are starting to tremble.

"No, she does it at home. I'm living with her. Working here pays my room and board." Her flat reply tells me how she feels about that. Just like that, things make sense.

I throw the unlit smoke away. "Stay here a minute."

I'm trying for a poker face as my anger rises and it doesn't stay on well. "What're you doing?" April hops aside as I march back inside.

Nobody's in but coffee tortoise and Veronica the otter, sitting on a chair behind the cash, Tiger Beat magazine on her lap in front of her. My shadow falls over Burt Reynold's grinning muzzle. Veronica looks up at me.

"Why are April's wings clipped?"

"Pardon me?" Her whiskers twitch.

"Her wings are clipped. I got a good look at them outside. Care to tell me why?"

She sets the magazine down next to the cash, dawning quickly to my disposition with her lips forming an 'oh.' On a day like today, when I'm already spoiling for a fight her silence just hardens my glare even further.

"I find it a little odd that a bird would need to lose her power of flight to be able to make breakfast for people, 'specially when they are getting room and board instead of a salary."

"Excuse me but what business is it—"

"I'm making it my business. Song-singing bird, slender defenceless thing, trapped over a stove all day making hashbrowns and scrambling eggs for big lumbering folks like me. Seems like you've got yourself some cheap labor, don't you?"

"I don't see what business our arrangement is of yours."

The tortoise pokes his head above the paper he's reading with his coffee. It's gone again fast. "Then I'll help you see it by asking again. What good is it for a blue-jay to have her wings clipped, where working at a diner is concerned? Why don't you want her out and about under her own steam? What, are you afraid she might fly away from your amicable arrangement? Room and board and what else? Bet she doesn't eat much."

The otter is off her chair and standing tiptoed to get her muzzle up under mine, pushed by her thick muscular tail. She wants to start something. I'm in just the mood to accommodate. "It helps her keep from—"

"Escaping, right?"

"From burning herself again!" She shouts and the growl from her teeth is plain.

The door opens behind me and shuts. I barely register it in the silence. "What?" I ask.

"She burnt her feathers on the grill several months ago, grease fire. Had to rush her to the hospital. Her feathers are too long for working a grill, dangerously so. We either had to clip those wings or find her another job. And there was no other job or she wouldn't have been here, starving, begging—" The otter gets a glance past me where April stands, sullen in her apron.

I turn around and meet the blue jay's downcast gaze. My anger caps so hard and fast it almost hurts. "This true?" I grunt.

April looks around, sees the trembling newspaper spread by tortoise fists and, thankfully, nobody else. "I left home," she says. "I'm not welcome in the family roost anymore." She opens her beak again and closes it. "Nearly clawed my Dad's eyes out. Why ain't none of your business."

Its quiet enough now that I hear Veronica swallow. "April, honey, go out back and take another five, okay sweetie?"

"Is this what you want," I blurt out, even though I already know the answer. I realize a second too late I've just idiotically shamed this bird into holding back an answer she can't speak aloud.

"You should leave," she says, and trudges heavily past the counter and into the back.

Veronica gazes daggers at me. "She doesn't want this life, who the hell would? But I'm all she's got now. Her father and mother both abused her, put her down and put her out when she rebelled. So I'm keeping her safe and putting a little away from each pay she's not collecting, so she can string a life together and do something else. If you reported her to the authorities they'd take her away, stick her in a state home where things happen I don't like talkin' about. She'd get worse abuse heaped on her than her folks did."

I'm growing embarrassed by the whole thing but only know how to be angry about it. I instinctively seize on what she's said. "What did they do to her?"

"I've seen a scar or two. But mostly with words. Women like us, in a world like this, know that's the cruelest weapon they got. Made her feel worthless, feel like nothin'."

That feeling that follows every snicker and taunt rolls down my back and I feel smaller than I have in a while. "I'd have a word with them if I could."

"Well you can't. And it wouldn't help. It's best you just move on."

I want to wait for April, verify it all, say I'm sorry, do anything at all. But I know I'm just gonna rub the wound raw. I pay, mutter an apology to the otter and I'm on my way.

***

Another day south, two different PriceCo outlets get their lawnmowers and garden shed parts. A new tire gets fitted and I stare at guns in the sporting good section for a while before realizing that some problems in this world only had ways to get worse.

It's a bleary two days and I'm back through the Appalachians again as dusk encroaches.. I stop at a half-decent burger joint I know to put down a cheddar stacked monster and a platter of fries. Then it's back in the saddle and I'm high enough in the Appalachians to pop my ears when the sun is gone completely. It's a dangerous trek down and I'm tired, but I forge ahead. I want to stop for the night as soon as possible, but these shoulders are dangerous places to park a rig so I head to the only open lot I know well enough. I'm just there to slumber, will use the gas station bathroom. They'll never even know I was there. The waffle-den is low lit, finally closed for the night. I park off in the dark between the gas station and the hut, heading out to use the bathroom just once before setting my pillow, undressing to my nethers and setting down to sleep. It's relatively cool here, night sounds drift in through a low vent and I'm just passing that velvet threshold into slumber when I hear a song drift in.

Sly, smoky notes caress the air, rising and falling, something jazzy and slow. It's the sin-drenched melody you'd hear over speakeasy high-balls or roadhouse Miller drafts, a promise of love passed across any space anywhere. I'm coaxed back awake and listening. The song pauses once, broken by a rusty hinge and a loud bang. Something unwieldy groans and hits metal and then the follow-up squeal makes itself out as a dumpster lid closing. Then the song returns, a little more breath-less and sounding rawer for it. I can make out words as the melody approaches.

"That time we lovingly shared, a feeling like a breath left me hop-ing and scared. And will we find love on a current of air, or will you still care." She breaks out into wordless song, the natural ethereal outlet of that slender feathered throat. I feel something stir, turning to catch each note with an ear to the vent as the sound approaches and starts to recede. I hold my breath to hear it better, one paw on the vent, the other reaching low to find an itch—

I hear a car door open, and I remember the lone Chevy that was parked here, closer to the gas station that I'd assumed was the atten-dant's. The singing is cut by the slamming of that door, then comes back presumably freed by a rolled down window. It's just cool enough for the air to make for a pleasant drive to wherever.

The engine starts over her song. Then both stop. I hear the jay swear. All alone, she's got quite the vocabulary. Tries again, engine fails to turn. She swears again. A horn is pressed during a cavalcade of curses and she settles down. My mind races. Is she going back in to call a tow? Is she going to try to flag down somebody for a jump? The solution is obvious, but so is the reason for hesitation. I contemplate quickly and resolve myself to do the right thing and wrestle on my jeans and shirt.

The idea of jumping out of the rig in my underwear is funny when I imagine it, but I get butterflies again as I slowly unlatch and open the sleeper cab hatch. She's staring straight ahead, beak whispering foul, unmelodic things to the night as I approach.

"You need a jump?" She jumps, feathered head softly hitting the VW's roof.

"Sorry," I mutter. "Really didn't think I was the type who could sneak up on you."

"What're you doing here?"

I'm embarrassed, but it's too dark to see. "This is my regular route. Didn't I say as much before?"

"No."

"Well I do runs through here, stop in cause I…like the waffles. Not now though because you're closed and I'm tired." I sigh. "It doesn't matter. Engine won't start?"

"This car is a piece of shit. It's Veronica's. I'm only back here without her because I forgot to take out the garbage and the stink hangs around if you leave it till morning."

"So…want a jump?"

April says nothing for a long time. "Sure. I'd be grateful."

I root around, find the jumpers and roll the rig forward. April lets me do the work, unsure about how to get this done, unsure about me too, no doubt. Twenty minutes later, the car finally turns over and twenty minutes after that, the battery has juiced up. The bluejay is bleary-eyed.

"You okay to drive?" Want me to take you home, bring you back in the morning?"

"We live off a country road that this rig would have trouble with." Her shoulders are as heavy as the whole night's sky. "It's a couple miles off, I'll make it."

"Naw, you look like you've got the blinks. Tell you what—" I close her hood and go open my sleeper, feeling pretty tired myself. "You go ahead and get some shut-eye. I'll sleep up front in the cab, give you some privacy. You can go back into the restaurant, let Veronica know you've got a place to shack up for the night, you can head home in the morning whenever. I'm on an empty trailer so you won't be holding me up."

April blinks and her beak opens for an instant. "Hell with it. There's something about you."

"I'm almost too tired to guess what that is."

"You just have one of those faces."

"Yeah?" I try to keep my expression neutral.

"You just look like you have a lot of good to give but aren't sure who it's safe to give it to." April's smile is weak but sincere. "I feel that all the time."

I don't know what to say. April leans against the battered Chevy, looking slender and fragile and yet hiding a reservoir of something her singing barely taps at. I finally break the silence with, "let me get you a fresh pillow from the top rack." And I do. I help her up, the touch of her uncut wing feathers on my paws like the dry smoothness of rose petals. I get her a fresh blanket and pillow, and drag the other stuff up front with me. I pull the Peterbilt's shades and nestle low as the moon spreads its dull silver. There's a portal to the back cab that's open, one my ursine frame is too big to slip through, forcing me to leave the driver's cab and enter the sleeper outside. It's open, and I listen for awhile to April's whistling breath, a lullaby that rises and falls through whatever dream eddy the bird is riding. The more I listen, the more I find myself recalling that touch as I helped her up, the slide of those tail feathers under my thick pads as she hopped inside. There was a bright spark that thrilled me there. And there's another now.

I imagine what else she feels like under that smooth beak and white throat, along those clipped slender wings. I'm wide awake now, listening to her sleep, feeling myself tingle. I'm hot, so hot in this closed cab. I open my shirt, hearing her melody in my head, unzip my jeans as I imagine the slender taper of her waist. I know I'd glimpsed it when I followed her out. She's a formidable but fragile seeming work of art and I'm a brutish beast given to righteous fits of anger. I can only hurt her, so I let the angel slumber as I slip my pants down and away. Cotton underwear follows and the hot air of the cab touches my sex directly. I gasp as a finger finds it, thick claw lightly dragging the pearly nub upward. I can smell myself in this closed cab, primordial and thick. Would a bird's dry tongue find me potent? Strange? Enticing? Shame shivers my loins, but she only keeps breathing steady on the other side of the steel wall and I hope I'm right that birds can't smell worth a damn. I give myself to her soft song.

My finger traces my curl-furred sex plucking bright strings of lust that float back and up. I let out a sigh as my finger presses within me, instinct seeking to fill the burrow. I draw the finger out, see it glisten in the meek gathered moonlight, then back inside, twisting restlessly as the rest of me. I groan a bit louder, the bird sleeps on.

I imagine a beak I could touch without roughly dragging it, limbs I could caress without fear of bruising them. An overwhelming, amorous calm follows close on the orgasmic shudders. I can love her. I can be loved in return. I can protect her from the sly, lying mountain lions and the grease burns of this life. The scent and taste of buttered pancakes prepared by a grateful lover presses into my subconscious for a second and I could laugh as I push it aside. The dry oil of soft blue feathers undulates under my nose instead as I imagine slipping a muzzle low, finding the nest of mystery that waits between slender legs and a caress of great black bear tongue that will make those smoothly scaled toe claws curl in delight April never knew existed.

My finger is in, out, up and around and back to my swelling nub as I ride bliss like a rocket. The Redstone rocks just slightly as my hips buck. No, don't move. Fragile things inside. I set my feet flat on the clutch and break like stirrups and brace my broad shoulders on the cab's back and hold my body still as I rub and slide and enjoy the musk of my wet spreading out of me and bite back a cry as I reach crescendo and fly off into the eddy's of slowly circling bliss,. I settle gradually, landing back in a pool of wet that dries underneath my fur as the last of the shudders recede.

There's a moment of silence as I catch my breath again and listen.

The somnambulant song carries blissfully on. I get myself decent once again and let sleep settle over me at last.

***

Sleep peels away in layers, the dawn just a lip of embers on the horizon. She's sitting next to me in the cab and I'm not startled or surprised. "Good morning," I rumble and stretch my thick arms to the sun flaps. "Sleep well?"

"Better than I have in a long time," April says. "Thank you."

I clear my throat and rub the sleep from my eyes, wondering if she was disturbed at all last night. I let a paw drift to my hips where I feel the jeans snuggly done up. "Least I could do after making things so awkward for you a couple days back. Last thing I wanted."

For a second it seems like she'd forgotten, then she looks at me in a way that wakes me up. "I liked that. I really did."

"Really? You're kidding, right?"

"All the time I've worked there, only three customers asked about my feathers. None of them ever bothered to ask Veronica about it, just let it be. It just wasn't their problem. You're the first who ever did."

"I get nosy."

"No. You care. You saw something that didn't look right, and you decided to get answers." She looks me up and down as if seeing me for the first time and smiles in that remarkable bird's way. "You seem like you don't take shit from anyone."

I manage not to sigh. "Seems that way." I want to ask her to sing me a song, or say nothing at all and just stay awhile but I realize what her fidgeting has her figuring out right now. "Veronica's probably gonna go dry enough to shed if you don't get her car home." I really don't want her to go. Then again, she'll probably be back to open up in an hour. "We might need to jump it again actually."

"You're right. She's likely worried. Will you be back when we return to open the place? Make you a double stack on the house. You really helped me out last night."

I feel fidgety too, remembering last night, all the things that went through my heart as I thought of April and imagined her staying right here and drawing the shades—

"I might have to get rolling but you know what, let me uh, radio dispatch and find out what time they need me back to get the next load."

My heart starts beating faster. What am I doing? I don't even know there's a next load available today. Hell, a haul to pull is one of the few things that are waiting around the corner that absolutely won't slip away if I let it wait. But the words come unbidden. "I might be gone before you get back."

April's beak closes, and she blinks. There's disappointment there, just below the surface. I can see it. "Well, I hope you'll be back this way at some point. I'd like to get to know you better."

"Maybe. I mean, yeah, that would be great." I smile and it hurts. Why does it hurt?

April opens the cab door on her side with a grunt and a push, she must have slipped through from the back effortlessly when she woke. Her wings spread and she hops, the meager air under them making her land gently. I idly click in my mind that the blue jay would never handle any vehicle bigger than a compact. The eggshell Chevy turns over just fine and she drives off the lot.

All the things I can possibly say roll through my head and all the things that she can reply apologetically or sympathetically roll right back and I drive away numb. The CB is on and chatter passes around speed-traps, gas lines, and bitches brewing trouble back home in Wichita. Those spreading the most chatter are rebels or a misunderstood poets or kings disrespected with hell to pay. The ones who don't know what they are keep quiet. I turn it off after a while, not even bothering to call in the highway motorcycle wolves who've pulled over some lion on a racing bike and obviously have a trap a half mile back.

***

There's the depot again, dock after dock yawning to puke middle-class bric-a-brac across a retail wasteland. I take direction and back the rig in. A dozen trucks have finished runs and returned. There's one in particular I see coming in and I get out to stretch my legs, feeling stiff inside, my anger strangely missing as I see that ridiculous big-titted-eagle silhouette, those knobby mountain cat knees and that ragged Harlequin Romance.

I remember the tire clear as day, the swerve on the Appalachian bank. The tattoo is still scratched like a scarlet letter into the trailer and my wallet is a hundred light. He doesn't see me coming. I'm faster than they all think I can be. I could be on top of him in a moment. Grab his arm, swing in into his rig, slam his head into a headlight and break both. I could drag him across this parking lot and punch the stuffing out of him in front of the whole yard and pass word of my enemies' fate that would fill the airwaves for days. Or I could quickly and quietly place my broad foot across his, break his toes, then apologize with a remorseless smile for how clumsy he must know I am.

I walk around his cab, block his sun, meet his eyes as he pushes his cap back. For a long space neither of us say a word. The recognition burgeons in his eyes that says he knows I know what he did.

"Nobody died," I say as clinically and calmly as a doctor. The fury is hanging right between us, enough to kick his callous ass up and down this lot and I find I have it at arms length, a squirming thing I can scrutinize. "Nobody died and I made it to where I was going."

"Dyke bar?" He snaps back and then swallows whatever would

come next as his brain overrides whatever was going to roll off his tongue next.

I feel his barb distantly, like an insect clicking itself against a window pane as I realize what I want to do and should do and it's very far from here. First things first. "You read a lot of those?" I nod at the Harlequin. "I know those are written by women and for women. And I know the women in those aren't the swooning sex-toys you treat women like, so I figure the only thing you try to identify with are the men who get to be with them. That's it, isn't it, Stickley? That's your draw."

His mouth tries to remember how to sneer. A nerve's been touched. "Why?"

"I wanna know when you decided exactly that the dashing man you always want to pretend you are became impossible and the sadist fuck you are became what's acceptable, became the real you. We both know that those books never got a woman in your bed yet, so you read them for you, not for us. When did you give up on yourself?"

His muzzle drops its sneer and he transitions to shock, then anger and finally I see hurt, deep and abetted by the simplest truth. I could savor it for a long time and watch him twist for the usual bag of gay-bashing tricks or women's-lib jabs but nothing in his arsenal is geared for bald truth, only slick slander. "You don't know a Goddamn thing about me," he growls but the grit in his teeth weakens quick. He knows I've decoded him and he's been shamed.

I take a moment, bury my anger just a little deeper. "And you know Goddamn well nobody wants to, not when you know you aren't *that*." I point to the pages trembling in his paw. He's stock still, pride smacked hard.

He definitely doesn't expect what I say next. "Here's just a thought, Stickley. Have you given a thought to trying to be that man? Have you ever thought that the women you can't have, are just clearing out for the one who someday just *might* want to have you? I mean, *if* you can be somebody that anybody else would want to have in their life, then maybe you won't be cutting women's tires and carving insults, and settling for a never-ending loneliness you don't have to deserve. Ever think that can happen?"

A mess of emotions cover his face and he takes his red hat off, taking a deep breath and blinking up at me, waiting for something physical to happen that isn't going to. He's trying to make sense of what's rolling over him, but he wouldn't know what the start of forgiveness even looks like, not yet. It's possible he may never, so I sign off. "You're gonna stay out of my life in every way for as long as it takes you to fix yourself. Just maybe you'll manage to do that. Good luck, Stickley."

With my final words delivered as neither recrimination nor lament I turn and head back to the Redstone. My anger is on its way down the drains on this lot, coolly setting me apart from all the curious eyes that trail me back to my truck. A weasel stands with a clipboard and pen in front of the Peterbilt's grill. I swallow. "Don't start loading."

"We can't till you sign for—"

"I'm not taking this load. Dropping off the trailer. Get me unhooked."

"Oh." He shrugs. "Okay." I help the dock-hands unplug and stand the trailer so I can de-link and roll free. When they care to check later, they'll see I still have another load on my contract. If I come back later and I've lost it to another hauler, then so be it. There are other jobs to take.

I roll off the lot, and a hound rolling in on an old Ford rig meets my eye. Hats tip, horns call out and I'm back on the Southbound again, feeling giddier by the second, aim true. I'm where I need to be in an hour. Veronica sees me first, pot of coffee in hand over a rabbit couple. April looks up and beams at me in that bird's own way.

I clear my throat. "Come with me."

April turns something over, smells like hashed potatoes. "On break?" she says?

"Yeah. That'd be alright wouldn't it?" I look over at Veronica who's taking an empty plate from one of the smattering of late breakfast diners. "Go ahead, April. Donny's coming in soon. I can hold the fort down."

I try not to fidget as April hops around the counter and with me out the Waffle Den's door. I want to light a cigarette, but I want her to be close even more. She is. I can almost smell the oil in her feathers, my senses electrical. "Thanks again for last night," she says and hops closer. Her arms part and she hugs me, like good friends meeting after a long stretch apart and I immediately get the sense of what it will be like to spoon her, get her beak nestling in my shoulder.

She nuzzles my neck for a moment and I get the distinct sense she's wondering the same. Questions for later. After this one: "Will you come with me somewhere?"

We part and she cocks her head curiously. "Where?"

I swallow. Moment of truth. "Nashville."

April freezes, meets my gaze, looks away at the pebbles on her Waffle Den's open, dusty lot and back to me again. She sees I'm serious and looks excited, terrified, disbelieving, all of it together.

"It would just be for a few days, just to show you some of America you haven't seen before, a place where singers go to be discovered. You take a number from Veronica, get a hold of her every day while we travel, give her some peace of mind. You have another person working here right? He full time or part-time?"

She blinks. "He's part-time, just Fridays and weekends. Wants to go full."

"Think he'd do it for a few days? You get vacation here?"

The implications are settling in and she's shivering now. "I think I'm due some."

I turn my head from where April is all but hopping up and down, and spot Veronica's broad nose all but pressing against the glass as she gazes out. Something in my happy eyes communicates something to her wary ones, and she sees April's tail feathers jitter in the noon light. The look she gives back to me somehow feels like long suffering acceptance, like she's been waiting for what is transpiring right this moment even though she can't hear a word. The chime rings with celebratory loudness as April bounds into the Den and takes Veronica into a corner.

***

Dark falls, the land past Knoxville a green basin garlanded by buckeye trees and shallow rivers. April is tired and nestles into me, warming my right flank as the open air cools my left. Glances we've stolen promise things we've never said but a peck on my cheek out of the blue, just past Wyndale says a lot all at once. I feel buoyant and giddy and free and I want to share her gift with the world. "You think you can sing the road a song?" I pass over the CB receiver and its crackle reaches waves into the ether. "Tell the rest of the free world you're coming."

She laughs beatifically, the golden pipes in her white throat coming alive. My Blue Jay sings into the open CB, filling the static of the open road with angelic bliss. The angry, squabbling chatter of the tireless fleet dies off, hundreds of transient souls raising an ear as heaven comes to everyone on the open channel, rolling long into the folding warmth of the American night.

Frontier Living

Jeeves Bunny

"Well now... what's this I see before me?"

Tabitha's blood ran cold as those words reached her ears. Her back stiffened, the tip of her tail twitched within the water, and her hands gripped tighter at the pan clutched between them. The forest remained quiet as the voice faded, only the rustling of leaves, birdsong, and the babbling of the river around the cougar's bare knees. Even then, before any more information beyond those first few words was made clear to her, she felt sick to her stomach. Terrified and furious at those words, at the gruff tone in which they were spoken, and what they almost surely meant for her. Trouble. Sure enough, her ear twitched as she heard it. The unmistakable click of a pistol being cocked.

Tabitha's voice quavered, her body slowly rising from where she had been bent almost double. She lifted the pan over her head as she did so, ensuring her hands were visible and entirely non-threatening. Slowly, with cold river water dripping from the pan onto her head and down the back of her neck, she began to turn on the spot.

"Please, sir. I don't want any trouble."

Her eyes widened. A flicker of frustration crossed her features as she saw not one, but two figures standing near the river's edge, at the centre of the camp. A badger stood, gripping his revolver in his left hand, flanked on his right by a rabbit in a long tan duster, arms folded across his chest and a sneering grin displaying just one solitary buck tooth. The rabbit's head turned, eyes darting furtively around the camp. A solitary tent. A campfire with its embers still smouldering in a stone circle. Some clothes lying out upon a rock some distance away to dry in the morning sun. His voice, the same which had addressed her before, brimmed with glee as he regarded the pan clutched between her fingers.

"You out here alone, girl?"

Outnumbered, Tabitha felt her heart rate quickening. For a moment her face creased in concern, but she forced it back to a state of neutrality. Panic would only serve to get her killed. She couldn't let that happen. She stood silent, motionless as the rabbit spoke. Only when he in turn fell silent did she give a curt, submissive nod. Revulsion surged through her, and she cringed as he smirked and extended a hand, twitching his fingers in a come-hither gesture.

As calmly as she could, Tabitha did as she was commanded. The gun in his companion's grip made perfectly clear that this was not a friendly chit-chat, and that nothing he asked of her was anything less than a divine commandment as far as she was concerned.

Tabitha stepped out of the river, dragging herself to her knees upon the bank before rising shakily to her feet. She left the pan upon the grass, but as she moved closer to the rabbit, she could see that his gaze was lingering upon that circle of pierced, sieve-like metal. The badger's eyes remained rooted upon her, though not with the gaze of a marksman. He regarded her bare legs, clad only in loose cloth undergarments hand sewn, and the damp, dirty shirt clinging to her upper body as only the most ungentlemanly of individuals could. His desire was shameless. She had met men like him before. She had seen that look in their eyes. Tabitha wanted to gag, her throat closing up and every muscle in her body growing tense. She wanted to snarl and scream at him not to look at her. But she didn't. She couldn't. Not without risking everything that she was so desperate to protect.

Thankfully she didn't have to think about him for much longer, for soon enough she was standing before the rabbit and had a whole different manner of hell to contend with. She kept her posture poor, hunched and downturned as he stood before her, not wishing to appear impudent by revealing how much larger than the rabbit she would have been standing at her full height. He spoke, slower than before, enunciating each word.

"You soft in the head? I asked you if you were alone. A girl like you, by herself, in the uncharted North-West? Now, I'm no Oxford scholar, but that don't track true. Would you let a pretty thing like this wander the great outdoors without a man to keep her safe, Ed?"

The badger leered at Tabitha, her skin crawling in revulsion, though she dared not show it. Hell, even the rabbit's smirk faded as he saw the look Eddie was shooting her way.

"Yeah, I thought not. So, why not tell me and Ed the truth my dear. I know you are not alone. Where is your husband? Where is the poor asshole who's doing such a bad job of keeping his lady safe? Be a good girl and tell me and Fast Eddie where he is. Tell us when you expect him to return or so help me God..."

His hand shot out, back of its palm raised, but stopped a fraction of an inch away from Tabitha's face. The cougar didn't flinch, but when she saw the surprise upon the rabbit's face, she let slip a forced whimper and stumbled backwards a step, feigning the terror he no doubt expected. She let herself fall flat on her backside, and however delayed it may have been saw the smirk return to the man's face as he folded his arms once more and stepped towards her, now looming large and domineering over her fallen figure. Tabitha could see in his eyes that he believed he didn't need to say another word, and just stood there as she told him exactly what he wanted to hear.

"Please, sir. Don't harm my beloved. We came out here seeking our fortune, just like you and Mr. Edward there, I'm sure. We don't mean no-one any harm. We just want to live a quiet life."

She watched the badger and rabbit share a look, her face twisting in renewed disgust as the badger sloppily licked his chops before turning his gaze to her. They stepped away from her, the rabbit turning to keep one eye on her as she rested there on the grass, trembling and grasping at clumps of grassy earth beneath her palms, fighting not to let her rage show over her feigned fright. They kept their voices low as they talked, but not low enough to keep Tabitha from hearing most of what they had to say to one another.

"You give the camp a look through. Keep it light though, we don't want the bitch's man coming back and getting the drop on us. I'm gonna have a talk with her about that gold-pan of hers. Looking at that there fire, this camp's been here a week or more. You don't stick around in a single spot for a week if there ain't nothing worth panning. And unless her man's smart enough to carry their findings with him always... well, we might be able to get out of here before he even gets back."

Tabitha shuddered as for the first time she heard Fast Eddie talk. It made her skin crawl just as his smile had, and that was before she heard what he had to say.

"We gonna take her with us too, boss? Something to keep us busy while we head to town and cash in the gold?"

She saw the rabbit frown and roll his eyes, but to her dismay he shrugged mere moments later. Bile rose in her throat, and she could feel the blood pounding through her temples as she heard his offhand response.

"It's a free country, Ed. You do whatever the hell you want with her, so long as you ditch her before we hit any real signs of civilization. But you know the rules. She's your fucking problem, so if she causes problems for us, that's on you."

Thankfully, when they finished their conversation, it was the rabbit who approached her once again while Ed began his search of the camp. He headed straight for their tent and Tabitha scowled as she saw him sticking his head and shoulders inside, carelessly tossing out loose items of clothing and parts of the bedrolls housed within.

"Eddie there thinks you've got gold hidden away in your supplies. It'd make things a lot easier for you and your man if you told us where it was. We'll take it and be on our way, and maybe when your fool of a beloved gets back from hunting breakfast or whatever the hell he's off doing, he'll figure out that maybe he's not cut out for a life on the frontier."

Tabitha's eyes darted away from the rabbit and scanned the tree-line of the camp. She barely managed to make her gaze half way along the edge of the clearing, before she felt the rabbit's hand grasp her roughly by the chin and tilt her head up towards his gaze. Crying out in discomfort, she fought with all her will to look terrified, rather than the fury boiling within her in that moment.

"Come on now. You've been smart so far. Do you really think you can outrun me? And even if you could, do you think you'd make it to the edge of the forest before Eddie put a bullet through your pretty skull?"

The cougar sagged where she was knelt, and her bottom lip trembled slightly as the rabbit caressed her cheek with his thumb.

"Tell me where the gold is."

Tabitha whimpered.

"P—please, sir. I don't know. My beloved does the work. I was just fooling around with the pan while he was away. I'm not to be trusted with things of value, that's what my man tells me. The first gold I've ever seen was what I was just panning up when you and your friend found me. That big chunk, it was so shiny..."

She saw him grin in triumph, as though all of what he expected of her had been proven correct. And then, as the latter part of what she'd said permeated through the man's brain, she saw his eyes widen. She saw his gaze dart away from her and towards the pan seated upon the river bank close by. In that moment her own eyes returned to the remainder of the tree line, and for the briefest moment she smirked to herself.

"A big chunk of gold, you say?"

He let loose her face, pushing her back and causing Tabitha to topple onto her side. She nodded up at him, gesturing towards the pan.

"Yes, sir. It's right there. Clear as day, so big and shiny and…"

The rabbit grunted greedily, cutting Tabitha off before she could say anything more.

"Bring it to me."

And hurriedly, crawling across the grass and clasping one hand around the pan's lip once more, she did so. She brought it back to the rabbit, swirling her free hand around in the muck still present in the bottom of the pan while her eyes watched Ed stalking away from the tent and towards one of the leather satchels resting against a makeshift log seat near the camp-fire. Beyond him, beyond the tree-line, she saw something glint. The cougar smiled, peering up with wide and innocent eyes into the rabbit's grinning face.

"It's right here. Don't you see it, sir? My lover has found dozens of chunks just like it, but this one I panned must be the biggest yet."

He looked closer. He frowned and grabbed her by the wrist, dragging it out of the muck as she continued to swirl it.

"Idiot, I can't see anything with you messing everything up like that. Give it to me!"

He grabbed the pan on its far side and tugged. It didn't leave Tabitha's grip. His eyes widened slightly, and he tugged again, more forcefully. Again, it didn't so much as move a fraction of an inch. Sneering, the rabbit raised his free hand once more, threatening to strike her. But gone was the fearful, subservient girl whom he had been easily able to threaten into doing as he wished before now. In her place knelt a fiercely grinning cougar, lips curling back to turn that grin into a savage snarl.

"You want it?"

She growled to him under her breath, the last part of the last word unheard by either of them as the loud crack of a gunshot rang out through the camp.

"Eddie, what the fuck?!"

The rabbit whirled around, forgetting about the defiant cougar as he tried to see what, or who, the hell his companion had shot at. Tabitha looked too as she sprang to her feet, eyes shining with triumphant glee and vindicated fury all rolled into one. She delighted in the dumbfounded look upon Ed's face as he slowly turned towards her and the rabbit, and let loose an audible grunt of satisfaction when she saw his gun unfired, hanging from his grip by a few loose fingertips.

The badger coughed, choked, and belched thick bloody bile down his front. Ed tumbled forward, eyes glazed as he fell face-first into the smouldering embers of the camp-fire, revealing a spreading bloodstain upon the back of his checked shirt. Beyond him, at the far edge of the campsite, the glinting rifle-barrel was still smoking as its stock was pulled away from the shoulder of its shooter.

"You fucking who—..."

The rabbit began to howl in rage as he saw the weapon's owner staring at him across the camp, and his hand went to his own weapon upon his belt. He never made it to his gun though, and his muzzle never finished that last, pathetic attempt at an insult as Tabitha swung the heavy iron pan square into the side of his skull, knocking him sideways with a thick, wet crack and sending him reeling and tumbling to his knees. In a moment, Tabitha was upon him. Kicking him in the gut as he landed upon all fours, dizzy and spitting blood, soon standing with one foot squarely planted upon his chest as she darted downward, dropping the pan and plucking his gun from its holster.

She cocked the weapon, holding back the hammer as she stepped away from the bleeding, semi-consciously groaning rabbit. In a matter of moments she felt movement at her side, and the warmth of a blessedly familiar touch upon her arm.

"You okay?"

Without looking away from the rabbit, who groaned and tried to steady himself, Tabitha smiled and nodded. She felt her lover's paw trembling, and clasped it tight within her own.

"I wasn't worried. I knew you'd be back in time, and I knew you'd help me when you were. I knew you'd never let anything bad happen to me, just like I wouldn't let anything happen to you."

Maria had never been as good at this, at the more violent parts of living on the frontiers of civilisation, as she was. She was a great shot, and every bit as strong and capable as Tabitha herself. When it came to this though, to making sure they stayed safe by whatever means were necessary, she never relished doing what needed to be done in the way that Tabitha did. It was Maria who would have done anything for a quiet life, a world where they were the only two sapient creatures in all of existence. Tabitha, meanwhile… well, for her such a life would have been immensely dull.

"Anyway, it's all okay now. I'm safe, you're safe, and this little problem…"

Clutching tighter at the cougar's arm, the coyote jumped as the revolver's release echoed around the forest and the rabbit's form fell limp once and for all.

"…is all in the past."

The next thirty minutes weren't exactly the relaxing start to the day that the two women had planned. Instead of eating breakfast together, the young boar which Maria had secured for them lay untouched at the camp's edge while the two women cleared up the mess that had been made.

Thankfully they already had a waste pit dug for the bones and other detritus they'd produced while camping here, so burying the bodies wasn't too difficult. After that, it was simply a matter of gathering up what had been cast around the camp by the badger during his search for their supposed riches. The final task was gathering some fresh firewood, and letting whatever of Ed's blood had dripped onto the embers burn off before finally they could begin to prepare their food.

It was, as a result of the delay, closer to lunch time than breakfast when the two women found themselves seated side by side, ripping flesh from bone and relishing the silence that came with good food and hungry bellies. They ate heartily until their stomachs couldn't handle any more, and only then, with yet more meat cooking and drying out to be preserved for later consumption, did they find themselves in a position to talk.

"I'm sorry," Tabitha sighed as Maria lifted her head, frowning in clear confusion.

"Sorry? Tabby, what the hell do you have to be sorry for?"

The cougar gestured towards the far end of the camp, towards the former waste pit, now double-grave.

"Them. I tried to think of a way to deal with them before you got back, but with one of them already having his gun on me before I even realised they were there—god, I was so dumb. So fucking greedy. I could have waited till you were back to start panning. I just, I had this idea. This dumb fantasy that I would find some huge nugget of gold, and when you got back I'd find some way to surprise you with it. Put it under your bedroll or in the bottom of your satchel or something. Instead, I ended up putting you in a position that I know you didn't want to be in. I'm meant to protect you from crap like that, not force you to wade headlong into it."

Maria smiled, reaching out between them and placing a hand upon Tabitha's still bare thigh. The cougar was mostly dry now thanks to the midday sun and the heat of the fire close by, but she was still only dressed in her hand-stitched undergarments and her dirty shirt, now streaked with a few smears of blood.

"You're sweet, but... don't treat me like a child. You always do this. Just because I don't like getting into fights or getting blood on my hands, it doesn't mean I won't. It doesn't mean I can't handle it when I do. You act like I'm so fragile. I might not be as strong stomached as you, but I'm not fucking fragile. Okay?"

She never raised her voice, never twisted her tone into something more grim or serious, and yet every word Maria spoke cut into Tabitha like knives that had been resting in hot coals. She winced visibly, shaking her head as frustration and guilt surged through her.

"Fuck. I know that. Y—you've told me that before. Again and again. And, I believe you, I really do. It's just..."

Tabitha felt Maria's hand leave her thigh and instead slide over to one of her own arms. She felt the coyote's hands encircle an already clenched fist and slowly begin to prise it open, to slip her fingers between the cougar's own. Tabitha took her lover's hand and squeezed, tight.

"I want to protect you. I can't lose you. I can't lose this."

The coyote sighed heavily. She leaned in against Tabitha's broader, taller figure and brought their heads to rest together, feeling the cougar's tail sweeping anxiously from side to side behind them and brushing against her own.

"You won't. But not because you're gonna be working twenty-four hours a day to protect me. This is a partnership. We help each other, right? And so when I show up out of the forest and shoot some hick in the back to save your life, don't apologize to me. Don't act like you've put a burden on me. But, y'know what you could do?"

Tabitha turned her head towards Maria's own, body trembling, face flushing as the other woman pecked her upon the lips.

"What?"

Maria rolled her eyes playfully, kissing Tabitha once again.

"Thank me. It'd be really kinda nice if you'd thank me."

The cougar's eyes widened. Her head pulled away from Maria's own, and her free hand rose to her muzzle in horror. Surely she'd already thanked Maria. She couldn't have completely skipped over that and gone straight to all this; to apologising, to playing the unwanted role of protector just like so many of the men they'd known. Anger coursed through her, directed solely inward as she realised that she was being just like them. Just like those men they'd both known before escaping out West and finding that they had minds and skills and lives that reached far beyond the role of wife, mother, or goddamn damsel in distress. The more she tried to find any moment in the last couple of hours when she could have possibly done so though, the more her mind drew a complete and total blank.

She stared at the coyote, slipped her hand free from Maria's grasp, and then lunged forward. Tabitha flung her arms around her lover's torso in a tight, frantic embrace, and half whispered, half sobbed the words that should have been the very first ones to leave her lips after putting the rabbit to rest.

"Thank you. Oh god, Maria. Thank you."

She said it perhaps a dozen times over as she clung to the woman she loved, ensuring that Maria heard it and knew that she meant it with all of her heart. Even when she stopped saying it aloud, she didn't stop showing it. She peppered the coyote's face with light, urgent kisses. She removed her arms from around Maria's body and clutched at her face, holding it in place for yet more kisses as they grew more rapid to begin with, then slowed in their frequency only to grow longer, deeper instead. Every so often a trembling whisper would still slip through…

"T—thank you…"

Even as the pair sank into more deep and indulgent kisses, hands trembling as they began to roam, cheeks flushing as eyes met and two minds realised in one moment that they were no longer just talking out their situation.

Maria's face burned beneath her rusty grey coat as Tabitha slipped down off the log upon which they had been seated together, shuffling into position between her lover and the flickering fire from which the scent of crisp roasting pork was still rising. Tabitha felt her lover's hands upon her face, stroking, touching, shaking slightly not in nervousness any longer but now in anticipation as the cougar's own hands fell to her lover's waist. She pulled loose Maria's belt. She tugged the coyote's shirt up, pulling it loose from where it had been tucked into the coyote's dark, muddy trousers, and kissed her lover's stomach. She nuzzled into the soft fuzz upon Maria's belly as the other woman squirmed happily, giggling and blushing more openly, more joyously now while her lower garments were unbuttoned and began to be peeled down, away from her hips, down past her buttocks as Maria purposefully lifted herself from her seat to aid in her own disrobing.

With a shared shriek of laughter, the pair tumbled as Maria over-balanced and toppled forward, Tabitha catching her in her arms and pushing them sideways together to avoid them tumbling into the fire like one of their uninvited guests. They landed in a heap of entwined arms and beaming smiles, but as Tabitha rolled over to place herself atop her lover she paused despite Maria's continued and clearly apparent delight. Her breathing was slightly fast, slightly ragged now just like Maria's own. But she paused, she gathered herself, and she looked down at Maria with a devoted growl.

"Tell me."

She saw Maria's eyes widen. She saw the coyote's blush deepen, and she smiled as Maria feigned innocence.

"Tell you? Tell you what, Tabby?"

The cougar growled again, more seductively than before.

"Tell me what to do to you. For you. Tell me how I can make you— how I can satisfy you to the best of my abilities. I want to hear it from your own lips, so I know I'm doing the best I can to give you everything you deserve and more."

Maria whined happily, squirming beneath the cougar in obvious desire. Despite this however she shook her head, face flushed crimson and sharp teeth nibbling upon her bottom lip.

"Y-you don't have to do that. N-not because of what I did. This isn't-I don't need that kind of thanks. That kind of reward."

Smirking, Tabitha shook her head. "I know. This isn't for that. Not just for that, anyway. It's… it's what you said before. I don't have to always protect you. I don't always know what you want, what you're thinking. I can trust you to tell me when something's wrong. When you need help. Or when you want something from me. So please. Please, Maria. Tell me what you want. Tell me what you want me to do to you. Because what I want... all I want right now is to make you happy."

She paused for a moment, blushing, frowning all at once.

"No. Not, not happy. To hell and back with that. I want to make you scream."

Maria's face was burning so bright beneath her fur that Tabitha swore she could have used it to navigate through the forest at night. Somehow though she still managed to speak, albeit a little tongue tied.

"Y—you already know how to make me do that."

Tabitha purred proudly. "I know a dozen ways. But this time, I want you to pick which one. I want you to tell me exactly how you want me to make you scream."

For a few seconds Maria trembled in silence. Then her muzzle opened, then closed again, then opened once more like a fish out of water. Finally, she found her voice, and bashfully croaked an answer.

"Kiss me."

Tabitha's purring grew louder, and shamelessly now she grasped the exterior edges of her lover's trousers, hooking her thumbs around both them and the linen underwear beneath. She was already kissing down the very base of Maria's stomach, lower and lower towards her crotch as it was exposed by the garments being slid hurriedly down her legs, when the coyote squealed with laughter.

"Tabby, oh god, not like that. I mean kiss me. Like, actually kiss me."

Smiling playfully, making no effort to pull her lover's clothes back up and planting one final peck upon the now bare, soft fur-clad mound of her lover's crotch, Tabitha relocated her muzzle further north. She crawled up Maria's body, planting a series of further delicate kisses along the way and unfastening a few buttons as she did so. Her gaze lingered upon Maria's modest but beautiful breasts for a few moments as the buttons holding her shirt closed sprang apart at her touch, before finally proceeding onward and reaching a murmuring, happily and lengthy lip-lock with the coyote.

They kissed, and kissed some more, and it was as they continued to make out heavily with no sign or desire to cease that Tabitha felt her partner's hand grasping at her right wrist. Their eyes met, their heated exchange faltering for just a moment as Maria whimpered pleadingly and Tabitha nodded, letting her arm fall limp and remain entirely under her lover's guidance. She felt her arm being pulled down once more, retracing the path south that her mouth had taken just minutes before, and the cougar growled happily as before long she realised where her hand was being led.

Once again, just before their kissing resumed, Maria whispered to her, panting breathlessly between each word.

"Kiss me," she begged. "T-touch me," she moaned, back arching as she pressed Tabitha's hand just a little further south before releasing it, the cougar's fingers now roaming through the delicate fur upon the coyote's loins.

"I want you to look at me. To see-ahh, to see what you're doing to me, Tabby. I need you to know you don't have to protect me. You don't have to coddle me. All you must do- all I've ever needed you to do, is love me. Love me, like you know I love you. Enough to die for. To kill for. And with god as our witness, everything in between."

Tabitha tried to think of something to say in answer to that. To think of any response, anything she could possibly convey to come even close to explaining how happy hearing that made her, and how much she mirrored those same feelings in return.

She tried, but in vain. Short of echoing her lover's own words, there was nothing more to be said. Thus, there was only one recourse left available to her.

Not words, but actions. The very actions Maria was asking of her, given shamelessly, openly, and with all that she had to give.

Her fingers sprang into motion between Maria's legs, questing, exploring, seeking out those spots she knew so well upon this woman whom she loved tenderly and craved savagely in equal measure. Her lips pressed to Maria's own once more just as the coyote's back arched, a strangled cry of pleasure erupting from her muzzle and out into their little camp, many hundreds of miles from the nearest settlement and hopefully almost as far from any further forces that might seek to disrupt the life they had fought so hard to share undisturbed.

They might not have had gold, this part of the river offering up nothing but the smallest and most occasional flakes. They might not have had anything more than a tent to call home, no land, no claim to any of the wilderness in which they slept, hunted, travelled and loved day to day, challenge to challenge. They might not have had anything more than their guns and their wits to keep themselves and one another safe way out there on the frontier. But that was far more than they needed.

All they truly needed, all that truly mattered to them, was right before their eyes in that moment. Moaning. Gasping. Blushing and beaming in increasingly euphoric elation. Giving each of them all the reason they would ever need, not just to live, but to thrive.

ROSES

Searska GreyRaven

Iknew the man for what he was the moment he set foot on my doorstep. Oh, the velvets and gilded cloak were fine indeed, but I have a beast's nose, and a beast's intuition. I'd learned long ago that beneath such finery, true monsters lurked.

So when he broke the only law of my keep, I was hardly surprised.

I caught him thieving among my roses, the only things that grew in the endless winter that blanketed the enchanted keep. The sight of anyone—let alone this crass fool—violating my roses set me howling in rage. As the shadow of my twisted form—neither wolf nor hart but a little bit of both—fell upon him, and he recoiled in horror.

One of my precious roses hung from the gilded merchant's clutched fist, ruby petals dripping to the snow. I glared at the fallen petals and snarled, the hackles upon my back rising. My wolfish tail lashed, swiping the snow from the path behind me as I stalked closer, closer. Cloven hooves whispered against the stone, almost hidden beneath the snow-white cloak I wore. I raised my head, tines of my antlers glistening in the moonlight. The merchant thief backed up another step, his eyes wide, wild, and locked to mine.

"Who…what are you?" he stammered.

I sneered, baring fangs. "The master of this place. You were warned, thief. It's there, written in gold upon my front door, and you agreed to those terms when you stepped inside my keep. And yet, here you are, with one of my roses."

"I'm sorry," he said. "I didn't think anyone would notice!"

No, I seethed, you didn't think anyone was here to catch you.

It always ended the same for these thieves; my roses feasted. But never before had one tried to steal my roses.

I snarled, lowering my head to strike.

"I have a daughter!"

I paused.

Perhaps he did have something.

"I have a daughter," he said again, begging. "Please, take her instead of me."

"I don't see her here," I rumbled.

"I'll send her. On my honor, I'll send her to you if you spare my life."

I paced, weighing the deal. Finally, I nodded.

"A life for a life," I growled. "And your debt is repaid. Bring her to me before the dead moon rises."

He nodded, stammered a meaningless thanks, and fled. My rose withered on the path, blackened petals falling to ash even as the wind grasped them.

I lifted my face to the moon, full and gleaming against a starlit sky. He would return when he realized he could not sacrifice his daughter. The magic of the keep would compel him to keep his word.

Or, perhaps, his daughter would arrive. I grimaced and hugged my cloak tighter.

Foolish to hope, I thought.

But hope I did.

***

The dead moon rose, and the merchant didn't return. Instead, a girl walked the stone path to my keep. No, not a girl. A woman who'd seen a score and more years pass her by, if a day. A red cloak hugged her shoulders, hood dusted with new fallen snow. A homespun skirt licked her ankles, bare to the cold. Raven-dark hair shot with silver fluttered about her face as she looked around, gazing up at the castle spires, through the wrought iron gate and down the cobblestone path. Her eyes lingered on my roses, and she nodded.

From my hiding place among the drifts of snow, I canted my head, curious. When the merchant had said "daughter," I assumed someone very young, barely more than a child. But this was a woman, well past marrying age. I snarled silently, realizing the merchant's gambit. He'd bargained a daughter he couldn't marry off upon me, throwing her life away to save his own.

Perhaps, if I'd been a man, I would have been insulted. Instead, I felt only a cold sort of kinship.

"Hello? Beast?" she called.

I blinked, startled. Her voice was soft, sweet. Soothing in a way that nothing else had been since the day I'd—

I growled and stepped toward her, compelled by the word that had become my name. Something soft and sweet like the first breath of summer passed my nose. *She carries the scent of wild roses with her.* I took another step, and another, drifting toward her as if in a dream. Suddenly, my hoof snagged a branch, snapping it.

She saw me and gasped. I froze, one hoof poised.

"You summoned me?" I said softly, bracing myself for the inevitable.

I expected horror, disgust, but I saw neither in her eyes. Amazement, yes, and surprise. But wonder I didn't expect, nor relief. Not a hint of fear, not so much as a shudder. I watched her gaze travel from the antlers atop my head, my wolfish visage, clawed hands and curled tail, split hooves in the snow, and she stood as steady as a sunbeam. She hesitated twice in her appraisal of me, at my chest and hips, and I shifted uncomfortably. *She's human. She can't tell by sight alone, not with how I'm dressed, and even if she suspects, she'll dismiss the idea as impossible.*

"I'm sorry, I mistook you for a snow drift," she said at length. "Or a gargoyle. Your white fur and cloak nearly had me convinced you were a hart or a wolf who'd wandered into the courtyard of this strange place. I...wasn't expecting you to be a little of both."

I bowed low, sweeping my hoary cloak aside. "No need to apologize. What brings you to my keep this evening?" I asked.

She swallowed, squared her shoulders and faced me proudly. I could see another question in her eyes, but she buried it. "I am here to repay the debt my father owes," she said instead.

I nodded, unable to trust my voice. Her lips were every bit as lovely and red as the petals of the rose her father had stolen, and I found myself wondering if they were as soft as well.

Foolish to hope.

But hope I did.

She took a step forward, and I marveled at the cervine grace from so small a motion. She tilted her chin back, baring her snow-white throat, and closed her eyes. Around her throat, I saw a single pendant glisten, a rampant hart cast from silver, with golden antlers and a single sapphire for an eye.

"I am ready," she said calmly.

I tilted my head to one side, puzzled. "Ready?"

"A life for a life," she said, and I understood.

I should have felled her, should have swept my claws across the soft expanse of her throat and left her to the roses. Though the compulsion of the geas urged me on, something stronger still stayed my hand.

Hope.

Foolish, foolish hope.

She opened her eyes and glared, her expression fierce. "Why do you delay? Do you toy with your prey? I thought you a wolf, not a cat."

Hope withered. "Are you so ready to die?" I growled, exasperated.

She hesitated. "No. But it's the only good I can do for my father, and it's all I have to offer."

I breathed, let mercy temper my wrath. I didn't want to send her to an early grave for her father's mistakes. The geas wouldn't be satisfied with simply letting the poor woman go, but...

There's more than one way to pay the debt, I thought. *The geas is a cage, aye, but there's room enough to move about within.*

"What if I offered to spare your life now, if you'd live in this keep for the rest of your days?" I asked. "You'd still pay the debt with your life, eventually, when old age took you. But not this night."

She looked at me sidelong, eyes narrowed. "Why would you do such a thing?"

I shrugged, brushing snow from my shoulders. "A whim, perhaps."

"I make a frigid bride." She said it bitterly. I'd heard winter winds with more warmth.

"I offer you hospitality in lieu of death; 'tis not an offer of anything more. The choice is yours," I said, stepping aside and gesturing to the marble steps. "If you still wish to pay your father's debt in blood, so be it. But I refuse to slaughter a maiden on an empty stomach."

"Do you not devour them, my lord?"

A weary smile tugged my lips. "I may be a beast, but I'm a civilized one. Come, if you will. Or let the endless winter claim you on my doorstep."

And as my hand touched the door, I heard her climb the steps behind me.

Foolish, foolish hope.

Still, my heart leapt.

I showed her the castle, from the front foyer to the tallest tower. She followed, mostly mute, asking only a simple question here or there. I answered, my heart fluttering every time I turned and saw her there beside me.

It won't last. No one can ever learn to love a beast.

"The castle sees to your needs," I said at last. "You have but to ask, and it is granted. At your leisure, choose a room. They are all open to you."

"Even yours?" She arched one ebon brow at me.

"Except mine," I replied, taken aback.

"And how will I know which one is yours?"

"The castle knows," I said. "It does not offer an occupied room to guests."

She nodded, satisfied. "If I should need you, what shall I call you?"

"Beast."

She looked at me, incredulous. "That cannot be your name, surely."

I smiled again, a crooked twist to the corner of my lip. "It is now." I bowed, excusing myself.

"Rose."

I turned. "Hmm?"

"My name, m'lord. It's Rose. Rose Villeneuve."

Of course it is. I nodded, bowed again to hide my face. "Goodnight… Rose."

***

Ten days passed, and I saw no sign of my new guest. I wasn't worried; the castle would see to her needs. Food, water, warmth, whatever she pleased. It provided and cleaned up after, leaving no trace behind. I almost wished that it would, that there was *some* proof that it hadn't all been a dream.

I drifted through the halls restlessly.

Another man became lost upon the road and stumbled upon my castle. He came and went, none the wiser of my presence. But he left behind a strange flier on the table next to his bed, and before the castle could attend to it, I snatched it up.

"A broadsheet," I murmured, settling down in a plump armchair. I skimmed the pages, devouring every scrap of news from the outside world. Around me, the castle tidied up the room. Dishes sailed to a rolling cart, sheets pulled themselves taught, and the drapery fluttered. I barely noticed it anymore.

"Oh! There you are!"

I yelped, flying from the chair and throwing the paper aside. I managed to grab it just before a dust pan could. I swear, the thing looked sullen that I'd stolen the paper from it.

Behind me stood Rose, wearing the same homespun dress she'd arrived in, although the keep had laundered it for her. She looked radiant, even in something so simple. She'd added a green velvet vest with gold thread, from one of the wardrobes no doubt. It matched her eyes. The silver pendant with a rampant stag hung low upon her chest, as if it were bounding over two perfect—

I composed myself, folding the broadsheet over and tucking it under my arm. "My apologies, my lady. I didn't hear you approach."

"No, please, it is I who should apologize. I didn't mean to startle you. I wanted to find you, to tell you that this castle is truly a marvel. Anything I want, anything at all, it simply appears. I've never tasted such wonderful pastries or seen such a marvelous greenhouse. Every turn, I find a new surprise! I can see why you'd never want to leave."

I grimaced, backed my ears, but said nothing.

"Why do you do it?" she asked, settling upon the newly made bed.

"Do what?"

"Help them. Travelers who have lost their way on the road through the forest. Why do you help them?"

"That is a long story," I said with a sigh.

She shrugged. "I have time."

I hesitated. "Why do you wish to know?"

"I don't know anything about this place, except for the stories and for what my father told me. I'm going to be here for the rest of my life, however long that is. I'd like to know about it. Why are you here? Who enchanted the castle? Is it really always winter here? What happened to y—" She bit back the rest of her words.

What happened to you? Why are you a Beast? Were you always a Beast?

I found myself glad that the geas could only compel me to act on demands, not questions.

She glanced at the broadsheet under my arm. "Is that from the village?"

I handed it to her. "Just don't drop it. The castle will assume it's trash, and I would like to learn what little I can of the outside world before the keep disposes of it."

She took the paper, her gaze flickering from page to page. "It's like I never existed," she said. "Even my step-father, damn his bones, has forgotten about me. No mention of my disappearance, or that I might have died. Life goes on as it always has, and I'm forgotten."

"I'm sorry," I said.

"I'm not," she said tartly, handing the paper back to me. "I'm glad to be free of him *and* that life. He's tried to marry me off since I was ten. The last one was this horrible, hulk of a man, with a shaggy, unkempt beard and he *reeked* of fish. He kept trying to reach up my skirt when my step-father wasn't watching. He'll have to force his attentions on someone else, now. This castle is a blessing. I can run through the halls howling like a wolf and no one cares. It's lovely!"

I grinned. "Yes. Yes you can," I said, tail wagging.

"And laugh as loud as I like, and wear pants! And...and learn to fight!" she exclaimed breathlessly.

I laughed and agreed.

Rose looked at me, judging my reaction. "No indulgent chuckle? No scornful sound from my dear host? M'lord, you *are* cut from a different cloth."

"So I've been told," I replied with a shrug. "There is an armory and sparring room here. I can even teach you, if you'd permit me to. I am no master, preferring arcane arts to that of the sword, but I know enough to help you begin."

Another sidelong look. I knew that look, had worn it often enough myself and it was strange to see it reflected on another's face. *What's the catch, what's the game?* the look said.

"No game, no catch," I said. "You're welcome to figure things out on your own, as you'd like. The castle can provide simulacrum that mimic a man's movements. They lack imagination, however, and become repetitive after a time."

"You've sparred with them yourself, I take it."

"I have been here a very, very long time."

She mulled it over for a moment and finally nodded. "Teach me, please."

I bowed to hide my elation and led Rose to the sparring room.

She marveled at the wall of practice weapons, picking up or setting down this blade or that staff until she finally settled on a short sword and a round shield, one with a rampant hart upon it. I watched as her fingers played along the hilt or scabbard of each weapon, caressing leather and steel with such care. I wondered how those fingers would feel twined through my fur, against my skin, between my—

I grimaced, blushing, and turned away.

I chose a falchion and a dagger. And for the rest of the afternoon, I taught Rose how to use a blade. By the time we finished, we were both panting, exhausted, and she was glistening with sweat.

"It's been far too long since I sparred with an actual person," I said, collapsing to the floor. "I've gone soft."

"Soft! I think my legs shall be sore for weeks!" She laughed, her whole body shaking with mirth and exhaustion. "But did that ever feel wonderful! I shall definitely sleep well tonight!"

I laughed weakly. "Same time tomorrow?" I asked.

She swallowed, suddenly anxious. "I...I think tomorrow I'd prefer to try against the simulacrum, if you don't mind," she replied.

My ears flattened, and I nodded. "As you wish. You know how to find me, should you have need of me." I bowed and left her in the sparring room.

Foolish, foolish hope, I cursed myself. I had been too rough, too forward, too eager.

And some part of me wondered if she suspected that I was more than just a beast beneath this cloak, and it made her wary.

I carried on the rest of the day on my own, wandering into the dining room just as the sun set and expecting to dine alone. But there she was at the end of the table, a silver goblet in one hand and a half-full bottle of wine on the table. *Rose red,* I thought. *Fitting.* She had changed clothing. Now she wore a red doublet with a linen shirt, tight ebon leggings and, over one shoulder, a dashing crimson cape. Her legs dangled over the arm of the chair, soft red leather boots hugging her calves.

"Good evening, m'lord," she said, grinning from ear to ear. "I was hoping I'd find you here. Would you care to join me for dinner?"

My heart stuttered, and for a moment, it was all I could do not to race to the table and sit down beside her. "As you wish," I said at last, settling down into a chair next to her. My tail slipped through the opening between the ornate backrest and the seat, and I couldn't stop it from wagging with joy. If Rose took notice, she didn't show it. "You are, after all, my guest and your wish is my command."

With a grin, I snapped my fingers, and the feast began.

The platters floated from the kitchens, and for the first time I could recall, I truly appreciated the scent and taste of the enchanted keep's fare. A first course of pottage: cabbage, leeks, onions, and celery in a thick broth and spiced with coriander. More silver platters appeared as we finished our soup. Succulent roast pork studded with cloves and orange slices, dark bread hot and fresh from the oven, sweet honeyed yams, meat pies with golden crust stuffed with venison, peas, and carrots. We dug in, both of us famished after our sparring. A baked chicken filled to bursting with stuffing passed Rose's way, and she tore a drumstick from it with animalistic glee.

I raised one eyebrow, and she took a defiant, savage bite from it. "There's no one here to tell me to take lady-like bites, unless you mean to start," she said.

I laughed, and tore off the other drumstick, ripping into it with equal gusto. Rose laughed and raised her half-eaten drumstick in a salute. Outside, the snow began to fall again in earnest, hissing against the glass.

Rose shivered and took a long sip from her goblet. At the end of the room, the fireplace shifted and stoked itself. A wave of warmth washed over the dining room, and Rose ceased shivering. Shadows danced across the plush curtains, which drew themselves closed over the frigid windows.

"How do you do that?" Rose asked.

"That was not me," I said. "The castle sees you as its guest and responds to your needs. You were cold, so it stoked the fires and drew the curtains."

"Amazing," she murmured.

I chuckled. "You've been here nearly a fortnight, and it's still a wonder to you?"

"I think it will always be a wonder to me. To have everything you could ever want at your fingertips the moment you wish for it...it's magic."

I smiled, in spite of the ache in my heart. "All magic comes with a price," I said.

Rose sobered. "Yes. Everything I could ever want, so long as I stay here. Was that the deal you made too?"

I grimaced and shook my head. "No, I came by this place a much darker way."

But before she could ask more, the next course arrived, and her question remained unasked. Salmon poached in white wine, mashed potatoes as fluffy and white as the snowdrifts outside. Hard-boiled eggs sprinkled with saffron set in a ring about a roast capon.

The wine poured itself all evening, topping off our glasses each time they dipped low. The third course ended, and dessert began. Peach tarts, cakes topped with creamy frosting and sugared strawberries, and endless parade of candied and brandied fruits, and a tray of different cheeses settled across the vast dining room table to await our pleasure.

"Where does all this come from?" she asked.

"The keep has been stingy with that secret," I said, popping a sugared plum into my mouth. "The larder is always stocked. And no matter how much you watch, it never seems to run low or diminish, even while meals are being prepared. Wherever it comes from, there is always more."

"Surely you have some idea," she said, examining the dark wine in her goblet. "This castle is yours. Did you not enchant it?"

I shook my head. "No."

Rose finished her wine, and we settled into silence for a time.

"If you didn't enchant this place, how did you come by it?" Rose asked, helping herself to a scoop of ice cream spiced with cinnamon and ginger. She lapped a spoonful from her silver spoon with slow, swirling motions of her tongue, clearly lost in the pleasure of the dish.

Heat rushed under my fur, and I found myself wondering again if her lips were as soft as they appeared. She must have sensed me looking, and she glanced at me, a wicked gleam in her eyes as she took another languid lick from the spoon.

I rose, knocking back my chair. The dull tips of my claws scored the table. "I'm sorry, it's late and I am most tired," I said. "I bid you good night, Rose."

And I fled before something worse than hope could compel me to tell the tale: desire.

***

Days passed, and I didn't see Rose again. I stalked the halls, my mood foul, and slashed several tapestries simply for being there. The castle mended them in minutes, and I slashed them again in savage frustration.

I refused to eat, snatching a bite or two from the larder only when I swooned. I didn't dare enter the dining room for fear of seeing Rose. Didn't dare approach the sparring room, or the green house, or even the library. Didn't want to hope anymore. I lingered in the belfry and brooded.

"Beast?"

Lucifer's balls. She'd found me. "On the balcony," I said through gritted teeth.

Rose stepped onto the balcony, pulling her crimson cape close and shivering. "I'd been looking for you," she said. "I wanted to apologize. I shouldn't have—oh my."

Rose came up next to me and gazed across the horizon. "The forest goes on forever!" she said. She stepped to the edge, grinning from ear to ear. It made her cheek dimple, her eyes light up. *I could love her. I could spend the rest of my days trying to make her smile like this and be content.*

I smiled in spite of myself. "It certainly seems to."

We watched the sun set, the moon rise, and she finally spoke again. "Would…would you care to spar with me again? Or dinner. We could do dinner. Not now, it's far too late now and I'm sure you've already eaten but I wouldn't mind a snack if you're up for it."

"I…yes. Yes, I would like that," I said. My tail wagged far too much and made my cloak swish awkwardly. "Dinner, I mean. Or sparring. Either? Both?"

Rose laughed and touched my paw. She was warm. Even here on the balcony covered in frost, she was as warm and alive as my roses. I felt something in my chest ease, melt. *Perhaps,* I thought. *Perhaps I can hope, just a little.* I offered her my arm, and together we walked down from the belfry.

Behind us, in one of the barren flowerpots, a snowdrop pushed through the ice and bloomed.

***

If more travelers partook of the castle, I didn't notice. Rose and I spent every waking minute together, either in the sparring room or the dining room or simply walking the endless halls together, enjoying each other's company.

Rose moved from practice weapons to steel, and I loved teaching her. She was lithe, clever, and moved like she was born with a blade in her hand. Before long, I found it harder and harder to get under her guard or around her shield.

"I believe we should call this a draw," I panted. My white tunic was slashed through in places, revealing my pale fur. So far, Rose hadn't drawn blood, but two of her strokes had shorn fur.

One had come dangerously close the slicing open my doublet.

"Getting tired, old man?" she laughed, her sword darting under my dagger. The rampant hart pendant on her bosom danced and gleamed, distracting me. Too slow, I tried to parry and the edge of her sword caught me across the chest. My doublet fell open. But Rose was already following through, and I fell on my backside to the ground, defeated.

"Ha! Got you, Beast! I win at last!" she crowed. "Are you alright? I didn't mean to—"

She froze. I tried to hide it, but it was too late. She'd seen what I had under the doublet.

"...is that...?"

I grimaced and struggled to my feet, tucking my wayward breast away. Like the rest of me, they were covered in soft, white fur. They were small, easy to hide under a doublet laced tight. Between the pants and the antlers, most people simply assumed.

As Rose had assumed. As I had *let* her assume.

"You're a woman." An accusation.

I nodded.

She glared at me, furious. "You never...I thought...all this time, and you *lied to me.*"

"Rose, I—"

Rose threw down her sword and shield and ran from the room, fuming. After a minute, once I was sure the castle had reshuffled its corridors, I too left the sparring room.

Thus ends my foolish hope.

I spent the night in the dungeon. It felt fitting to deny myself the light of day. I was a beast, after all. What better place for a beast than in a cage, in the dark?

***

I expected weeks or even months to pass before Rose sought me out again, if ever. But barely three days passed when she found me in one of the lower crypts. I was reclining on an old sarcophagus, reading a book by candlelight when the sound of footsteps roused me. Before I could flee, she was in the doorway, blocking my only exit. Her pants were dusty, her hair wild, and her white shirt clung to her skin. She panted heavily, as if she'd been running, and I tilted my head, curious. There was nothing in the castle to alarm her, surely.

Well, except for me, I suppose.

For a long moment, neither of us spoke.

"I'm sorry," she said at last, breaking the silence.

I swallowed slowly, my mouth dry. "For what? You have nothing to apologize for. T'was I who deceived you."

"For assuming. For getting mad at you," she said. "For...I don't know. All of that."

"You don't need to apologize—"

"No, I do. I should have guessed. Your doublet always seemed a bit full, and your trousers always seemed to lay a bit too flat in the front. You were too understanding, too quick to accept things I'd learned made men furious to suggest. Something about you was just...*softer*, even for a beast. You don't act like any woman I've ever known. I thought...I thought I'd finally met a man I could love, only to find out you aren't even male."

"No," I said softly. "I'm not."

"And...God! All my life, I've been told I couldn't do something because of my sex, but here you are, doing all the things I'd been told I couldn't. And you've shown me how to do them too. You're free."

I snorted. "Hardly."

"You aren't forced to do, or to not do, things just because you're a woman."

I sighed. It was both true, and not.

"Why keep it from me?" she asked, accusation gone from her voice. All that remained was a calm, quiet question.

"I was afraid," I whispered, backing my ears in shame, "that if you knew the truth, you'd hate me.. I didn't expect...well. I should have told you, and for that, I am deeply sorry."

She smiled and nodded. "Apology accepted," she said, and stepped into the room. She hopped onto the sarcophagus and scooted close.

"There's no name," she commented, examining the lid.

"No. No one is buried here. This part of the castle is all for show. Or for guests in a particularly morbid mood."

She picked at the marble, running her thumb along a dark vein in the stone. "Why don't you just leave this place?" Rose asked.

"I cannot."

"Why can't you leave?"

"It is not a pleasant tale."

"Still, I'd like to know what was so horrible that you'd lock yourself away in here forever like this. It's a lovely castle, but a pretty cage is still a cage."

I opened my mouth, closed it again. *Foolish, foolish hope.*

And yet...

And yet, hope I do.

"I wasn't always like *this*," I said, gesturing to my bestial form. "I was on my way through the forest to see my family, when a great snow storm drove me off the road. I wandered, I don't know how long, until I came to this castle. And inside, I met the most wonderful man. A prince, he claimed. I was smitten, enthralled. I didn't question what a nameless prince was doing in the middle of nowhere, didn't wonder where his castle came from or why it was always winter here. His charm and glamour drove the questions from my mind. We danced and drank and made love, and I forget the world for a time. He showed me magics denied to me because of my sex, taught me spells I never could have dreamed of, and I loved every minute of it. His touch was ecstasy, his kisses intoxicating. Nothing else mattered but his arms wrapped around mine. He didn't care that I had no interest in embroidery or feminine things, or that I loathed dresses and preferred pants. I should have known something wasn't right, but I was so enraptured to find someone willing and eager to take me as I was, that I failed to see the truth: that I was a prisoner within a gilded cage. Every time I approached the castle gate or walls, he found some reason to draw me back, to pull me within the keep once more.

"He proposed one night, told me of his grand plans for a wedding and a life with me by his side, and for the first time since I'd come to the castle, his glamour upon me cracked. I remembered where I needed to be, remembered my family and my home. I knew I had to leave. I promised to return when I knew my family was well, but he wouldn't let me go. He wouldn't take no for an answer, and so, I tried to run."

Rose took my paw in her hand and held tight. I took a breath and continued. "I didn't get far. He bewitched the forest, made the trees grab and hold and cage me, and I saw him for what he really was: a faerie prince. He dragged me back to the castle, threw me in the dungeons, and demanded that I marry him. And when I refused again, he cast a spell, cursing me, turning me into…this. He said that if I chose to play at being both male and female, stag and bitch, I ought to look the part." I snarled. The memory burned even now.

"Wolf and hart," Rose murmured, tracing a finger along one antler. Her fingers were still cool from the stone, and I shivered.

"He told me that I knew forbidden things, that no man in their right mind would ever want me now, and that my only choice was to stay with him forever," I continued. "I spat in his face from between the bars of my cage, and he went mad with rage. He began to cast, and I knew what was in his heart before it passed his lips: he wanted to take from me my freedom, my magic, my name. I'd seen him do this to those who displeased him before, and now he meant to inflict it upon me. With the last of my strength, I was able to banish him from this place, just as he set the geas upon me. I'm bound to the keep, to obey the will of any who enter it, but with the barrier, the prince is forever banished." I paused, took a deep breath. "In a way, I suppose I won."

"That's why you hide, why there were no stories of a beast here, just an enchanted castle for weary travelers," Rose said.

"I learned early on to avoid those who came seeking shelter," I said. "Thankfully, the keep carries on tending anyone who steps inside because the prince cannot pass the barrier to dispel it."

"Why aide travelers, then?"

"Because I can," I said. "Because it enrages the prince to know I allow mortals into his castle while he is barred from entering it."

"Why punish those who break hospitality, then? Why not let them loot this place, if it all simply reappears?"

"Part of the geas was that I was to serve any who entered the prince's domain, so long as they did not break hospitality. Once they trespassed, I was to be the instrument of their punishment." I snarled and backed my ears. "He intended to use me like a trained hound. A leashed beast at his beck and call."

Rose's hand tightened around my paw. "That's…sick."

I nodded. "But it is common enough, among the fey."

She fussed with her hart pendant. "How do you break the curse and become human again?"

I sighed. "I don't know that I can. I've been this way for so long that I can't remember what my human face looked like. Transformation spells become permanent after a while, and it's been a very long time since the prince cast this upon me. I've become used to this form. Even enjoy it. The world is so much more alive to me now. I don't know that I'd ever want to give this up."

"What about the geas?" Rose asked. "How do we break that?"

"By killing the prince," I said. "Not an easy thing, given that's he's a prince of the fey. But it could be done, with luck and cold iron."

"But since you can't leave the castle, and he can't enter..." I watched as Rose worked out the truth of it. She bit her lip, and suddenly wrapped both her arms around me and squeezed tight. "At least you won't have to be alone now."

I smiled sadly. "Sooner or later, old age will claim you."

"And never you?"

"I'm bound to an immortal fey through that geas. As long as he lives, I'll never die."

She shuddered and held tighter. "Until old age claims me, we won't be alone."

I swallowed back the sob aching in my throat. I hoped, still desperately hoped, but for now, the summer-warmth of Rose in my arms was enough.

It wasn't until much later that I realized, she'd said, "we."

***

More travelers came and went, but I hardly took note of them. Whenever I could, I spent time with Rose exploring the castle. We found a ballroom with black marble floors, and another with rose-tinted white. We found a parlor with an enormous fireplace fashioned after a great lion, a fire burning merrily in his jaws. We even found a library so vast that we couldn't see the end of it, and spent weeks romping through the volumes we found there.

One day, Rose came to me with a mischievous look upon her face and led me down a hall of grey-green stone. I hadn't seen this hallway before, and I wondered what my companion had found. She drew me to a door carved with wolves and deer romping through rose bushes and held out a blindfold to me.

"Please," she said. "I want it to be a 'surprise'".

I frowned, but put on the blindfold.

Rose took my hands, mindful of my claws, and gently pulled me through the door.

"Tell me about the geas," she said. I could feel her fingers trace the laces of my doublet, felt when the knot finally gave. Her hands slid up the back of my shirt, raked furrows through my pelt and drew a gasp from my throat.

I swallowed, wary. "If you wish for something from me, you have but to ask."

"And you can't refuse?"

"I can," I replied. "But only in word. I cannot stop you from forcing me to do something."

She wouldn't. No, not my Rose. I stood, fists clenched, and begged that it not be true, that she wouldn't do this to me.

"But if I ask, is your answer true, or what the geas thinks I want to hear?"

Oh my lovely, clever Rose. You found a loophole. "The geas controls my body, not my heart," I replied, my tension easing. "My words are my own."

She let go and embraced me from behind, pressing her body against me, and I swear my knees nearly buckled. Bare skin against my back, one hand on my hip and the other wrapped around my chest. Her lips brushed my neck, her breath ruffled my fur. Heat pooled low in my belly.

"So if I ask if you'd like me to kiss you—"

"Yes," I breathed. "Yes, I'd like that."

She nipped the tip of my ear and whispered softly, "And if I did something you didn't like, you'd tell me?"

I had to try twice to get the words out, my mouth suddenly dry. "Yes."

She tilted my head back until it rested on her shoulder, baring my throat to her. My knees bent, threatened to collapse, but hours of sparring had made her stronger than she looked, and she held me effortlessly. "Promise me," she murmured softly, planting a row of kisses up my neck, across my cheek. "Promise me that if I do something you don't want me to do, you'll tell me to stop."

"I promise."

The words had barely left my mouth when she pressed her lips to mine.

God above, she was sweeter and softer than I'd even imagined. Soft as my roses and just as demanding, she tasted of summer and honey and I couldn't get enough. I returned her kiss, lost myself in the taste of her.

Eventually, she came up for air and broke the kiss. And while I was still reeling, she released the blindfold and revealed the room to me.

It looked like a summer meadow. Plush green carpet dotted with embroidered flowers covered the floor. A bed with a dappled blanket sat in the middle of the room, the headboard carved into the likeness of a great tree. On one wall, a fountain trickled from the mouth of a gargoyle that looked very much like myself, a wolf with antlers. Candles glowed softly within hollows in the stonework walls, and a few hung from the carved branches in the ceiling, glimmering like fireflies. Chilling in the bowl of the fountain were two crystal glasses and a bottle of golden mead.

"I've never seen this room before," I said, amazed. My cloven hooves sank into the plush carpet as if it were moss.

"I wanted to surprise you," said Rose.

"Why?" I asked.

"Because." For a moment, I thought that was all she intended to give me as an answer, but she spoke again. "Because you have taught me so much, and I want to thank you. Because you're alone and deserve to be happy. Most of all, because you are the most beautiful creature I've ever seen, and I love you. And I want to show you that." She ran her fingers through my antlers, the pads of her fingers lingering over the pointed tines and sending a spark of pleasure down my spine.

"Because I want to make love to you, but I need to know you want it too. Not because the geas demands it, but because *you* want it."

I did. God help me, I did.

"Do you…do you want me to make love to you?" she asked, almost shyly.

"Yes," I said, barely more than a whisper. "I've wanted it since I first laid eyes on you."

"You don't mind that I'm…?"

"No," I said. "As long as you don't mind that I'm…?"

"A woman too?" Her hand cupped my breast.

I inhaled, feeling that heat kindle brighter. "…I was going to say a beast."

"You aren't a beast."

I made a wry face and pointedly looked down the length of my body.

Rose returned my look with one of her own. "Alright, fine. You aren't human. But I'd wager our parts aren't all that different."

I barked a laugh. "And what makes you think I'm not a wolf or a deer where parts are concerned?"

She grinned, a wicked gleam in her eye. I felt my knees go weak again. "I'll bet I'm right."

I smirked and didn't answer.

"If I'm right," she said. "I get to be on top." Rose unlaced my breeches, taking her time to pull the strings loose.

"And if I'm right, what do I get?" I asked.

"If you're telling the truth," said Rose, slipping her hands under the cloth, "you get bottom."

"I—wait, that's—" I gasped as her fingers found what she'd been seeking. A knowing smile lit up her face.

"You seem like every other woman I've known," she murmured, caressing me. "Soft lips here and there, slick and ready, and right here—"

My knees really did buckle as her fingers delved into me. But she held me and kept me from falling to the floor.

The mighty Beast, slain by a woman's touch.

"Yes, right *here*, right where it's supposed to be." She slid out, then back in again. I moaned wordlessly, pressing myself into her touch.

Rose grinned and withdrew, sliding her hand up a little farther. "There's still one more thing, to be sure," she murmured, and pressed the pad of her finger *just so.*

I cried out, clutching her tighter. I had mind enough to keep my claws from breaking her skin, but barely.

"I think that means I win," she murmured into my ear.

"I'll concede defeat," I panted, "as long as you don't stop."

She walked me backward towards the bed, her fingers still playing. The back of my legs hit the mattress and I fell, Rose giggling atop me. I tried to roll over, but she stilled and pinned me, one hand on my chest.

"You lost, remember? Bottom for you."

I grinned and relented. Rose peeled my pants down and settled between my legs, that knowing grin growing wider. She dipped her head, tongue red between her teeth, and kissed me thoroughly. And still, her fingers delved and played, driving me mad with pleasure. I moaned, bucked, writhed until finally she drove me over the edge and I howled her name.

I came back down, panting, boneless.

Rose reared back and knelt, her expression smug. She slipped one finger into her mouth, licking it clean before moving on to the next.

"Beast or no, you still taste like a woman," she said.

I cheered weakly, too spent to do more. Rose crawled up my body, nuzzling my belly, throwing the unlaced doublet aside to lay me bare. Her touch against my fur stirred me again. I wanted her, every inch of her. I wanted to make her moan and writhe and scream my name.

But I couldn't. Desire cooled as I looked down at my hands, half-lupine paws with claws I didn't trust anywhere near the softer parts of a lover. *But I have a tongue that works just fine*, I thought. *And…one other thing.*

It was my turn to wear a wicked grin.

"I have something I'd like to try, if you're open to the idea," I said.

She tilted her head and looked at me curiously.

"I was a magician before…this," I explained, gesturing to the keep. "And I learned to enchant things. Several things. I don't know if it'll work now that I'm *this*, but…one moment. Let me find it."

The castle made a wardrobe at the far end of the room, its form shimmering into existence like sunlight upon a rippling pond. I opened the doors and rummaged about inside, hoping the thing still existed after all this time.

"Ah ha!" And I withdrew from the wardrobe holding a simple leather belt.

Rose looked at me dubiously.

"It's more than a belt, I promise," I said. I wrapped it about my hips and buckled it. And like the wardrobe, magic shimmered and granted me a new way to pleasure Rose.

I frowned.

Rose giggled.

"Oh, my. Grandma, what a big cock you have!" Rose laughed.

"The better to rut you with, my dear," I replied, grinning lewdly. I sobered. "Or not. Probably not. It was just a plaything I'd made when I'd first learn to enchant things. It's supposed to look human. I didn't expect it would do this."

"You made a detachable phallus?" she said, sounding impressed.

I nodded sheepishly. "It seemed like a good idea at the time."

"I think it's still a good idea," Rose replied, eyeing my new member. "It's...canine."

"It's yours," she said. "Is it real?"

"Real enough," I replied. "I mean, it can't get you pregnant, if that's what you're asking. But it can do everything else. And it doesn't, ah, flag like a real man will."

She grinned and bit her lip. "I'd love to try it."

I climbed back on the bed, and Rose gestured. "You still lost, remember? Bottom."

I nodded and rolled on to my back. Rose straddled me and examined my length. It may not have been real, but it was still magic, and it *felt* like a real phallus. I could feel the cool touch of her fingers as she curled them around me, the heat of her breath as she flicked her tongue across the tip and the soft, slick warmth of her mouth as she—

I moaned and arched my back. My antlers caught the comforter and tore it, and I hardly noticed.

Rose withdrew and I opened my eyes just in time to see her slip my length into her. She threw her head back, moaning, and worked her way down.

"Oh yes, that's *nice*," she panted.

She bent down and kissed me soundly, her tongue playing along my fangs. "This was a wonderful idea," she murmured, kissing down my cheek, my throat, between my breasts.

"I might...be a bit out of practice with this," I panted.

Rose giggled and nipped my ear. "I've never done it like this with a woman before," she said. She sat up and gave my body an appraising look. "The view is infinitely improved."

I blushed but couldn't reply. Her hips had stolen my ability to speak. Rose rocked back and forth atop me, her body gripping me, wet and tight. I caught her rhythm and moved with her, adjusting myself a little at a time, watching her reaction as I sought just the right spot until she cried out.

"*There*," she gasped. "Right *there*."

"Rose, if you…take me much deeper…you might…I think there's a danger that—"

"Oh god, *yes!*"

With a cry of triumph, Rose took the full length of my faux phallus, all the way down to the canine knot at my base. I howled, my back bowed, and Rose rode me all the way over the edge. She slumped, finally, and I was forced to roll over to my side and catch her or risk her taking me off the bed with her. She draped one leg over my hip and grinned, her eyes glassy with afterglow.

We lay, catching our breath, and she finally spoke. "I think I like this toy of yours," she said.

I laughed. "It might be a bit before you free yourself from it, if it acts anything like a real wolf's cock."

She kissed my nose and wiggled, squeezing me inside her.

I moaned and gasped. "Longer if you keep doing that!"

She squeezed again, and I groaned.

"Oh yes, I *really* like this toy of yours!"

I don't know how long we spent in that room, pleasuring each other. But eventually, we both curled up on the bed, exhausted and satisfied.

***

The sound of my true name woke me. I resisted, the embrace of sleep so much more inviting, but the call insisted, then demanded. I rose from the bed, laying a kiss on Rose's forehead as I left, replacing my pants and doublet as I padded down the halls of the castle to the front gate. It was still dark, but the sky was clear. Starlight glinted across the stone path, played along the edges of the snowdrifts which seemed strangely diminished to me. I didn't have time to ponder it, though.

I knew who would be waiting there at the gate. Only one being on the face of creation knew my true name now and could summon me with it.

Standing there at the edge of the path was my tormentor, the faerie prince. He wore green leggings, green boots, and a green tunic. Atop his brow were a pair of smaller antlers, covered in fine, fuzzy down. Summer antlers to my winter ones. His hair was fiery, his eyes cold.

"Hello, Beast."

I curled my lip and growled.

The faerie prince frowned. "No greeting for your prince and bridegroom?"

"I would, if there was such a thing. But you aren't, and there isn't," I replied.

"I beg to differ," he said, pointing to the cobblestones. "Are those snowdrops I see beside the path?"

I glanced down, and to my amazement, there was green poking through the hardened ice. Delicate white flowers hung like bells, glistening in the moonlight.

And my roses, my beautiful winter roses, had begun to wilt.

"Your heart is finally melting, my love." He paced at the edge of the stones, one hand tipped with ink-black claws reaching out a breath from the gate but never, never touching it. He didn't dare try to cross so much as a toe over the edge of the path. The prince gave me a guileless smile, his expression a mask of innocence. "Will you not let me inside?"

I snarled and recoiled. "Never."

"Winter would melt for no one other than your true love, and we both know who that is."

No, only one of us knows.

The faerie prince sniffed the air like a wolf, and his look became truly vicious. "There is another. Another has laid hands upon you." He paced faster, like a trapped animal, and still he didn't dare approach. "It's not possible."

"Those who break hospitality are *mine*," I snarled. "I do with them as I please! Those are, after all, your rules. You bound them to the keep and to me."

"The geas demands you kill him, Beast," he said, his gaze fiery with rage.

"Old age is still a death, and it satisfies the geas."

"But not me!"

"I care nothing for satisfying you," I growled, lip curled in disgust.

The prince's smile was a thing of horror. Sharp teeth, like those inside a pike's maw, marred what should have been a handsome face. "Oh, but you should. You may have found a loophole to the geas, but I will not tolerate it."

"You cannot enter this place!"

"No," he purred. "But he can still leave it."

He?

I clamped down on the thought the instant it crossed my mind. The prince's wit must be slipping, if he thought my guest was male. But then, most were. It was natural that he would assume. *His madness clouds his senses, or he would have known the scent upon me was from no man. Or else my wonderful toy has muddied the scents enough that he is tricked.*

"I will tempt your lover away from the safety of your barrier, and slaughter him," the prince continued.

"Never," I growled, my hackles high and my fangs bared.

The prince sneered. "Finish it, Beast. By sunset. Or I will." He faded back into the forest, his eyes gleaming red.

I howled and bolted for the castle, thundering down the halls on all fours like the animal I was, shredding tapestries and shattering tables as I went. *No! No, I can't do it. I won't!*

Either I took her life, or the prince would. There was no other choice.

No, that's not right either. There is a third choice. There has always been a third choice but hope always convinced you never to take it.

I slowed, ceased my rampage and went still, breath heaving in ragged gasps. I'd come to the dining room, where a bottle of rose-red wine was already set upon the table with two silver goblets.

You always knew it would end this way.

I'd hoped it wouldn't. I'd hoped to find another way to thwart the damned faerie prince, any other way than that.

Foolish, foolish hope.

I couldn't save myself. But I could do one last thing. I could spare Rose from my fate.

I stood upright, straightened my doublet and smoothed my fur. I could do this. I had to do this. And I would face it with as much grace and dignity as any beast could muster.

Rose was still sleeping in the summer room, her chest rising and falling gently and her expression peaceful. She smiled in her sleep, and my heart shattered.

You have to do it.

"Rose," I murmured, nuzzling her gently. "Love, awake."

She grumbled and rolled over, her eyes slowly fluttering open. "Beast? What's wrong?"

I wanted to lie. I wanted to tell her everything was alright, but despair tore the truth from me. "The faerie prince I told you about has returned. He…he intends that I kill you, or he will."

"No," she said firmly, now fully awake. "I won't let him. I'm not leaving you."

"You won't have a choice! He's a prince of the fey. If he wishes it, no mortal can resist his charms. You must run, run *now*. Please!" I begged. "I won't watch him kill you."

"But—the curse—"

"GO!" I roared.

Rose bolted from the bed, tore from the room and down the halls. I didn't follow. I'd know when she'd left the castle.

I tipped my head back and howled, pouring my broken heart into the sound.

She was safe.

She was safe and I was damned, and maybe now, at long last, the nightmare would finally end.

It was hours, or maybe minutes, but I felt the first pulse of the geas as it squeezed my heart. I stumbled down the hall, every step weaker than the last. I forced myself to go towards the pain, away from Rose and peace and hope. I staggered out to the gate and finally collapsed. All around me, I could see where the snow and frost had begun to recede. But the sky was darkening again, blotting out the sun. When had it risen? How had I lost track of it? It didn't matter. Nothing mattered. A few heavy flakes fell to the earth around me, then a few more.

I didn't care.

No matter what happened, I could die happy, knowing I'd touched Heaven just that once. Bands of pain tightened across my chest, squeezing with every breath. The snowfall thickened, blanketing the world in deathly white. I closed my eyes, bracing for the next squeeze which would almost certainly be the last.

"What have you *done?*"

I opened one eye to see the faerie prince standing behind the gate, fists clenched at his sides. The snow never fell upon him, simply billowed around him and left the summer green of his clothing untouched. He glared at me, furious. Impotent.

If I'd had the breath, I would have laughed.

"The geas will kill you!" he shrilled.

"Yes," I rasped. "It will."

"I forbid it!"

The geas closed my throat, and I couldn't speak. But I curled my fingers into a fist and extended my middle finger in his direction. So much time had passed since I first met that ghastly fey, but the gesture was timeless.

His face purpled and he screamed. Fire sprang from his fingertips and he assaulted the gate, punching it over and over and over until I could feel it begin to give. I prayed to whatever god might still listen that the barrier hold until I'd truly died.

Foolish to hope, even now, at the end.

The prince screamed again, a banal animal screech, and I felt the barrier shatter. The gate sheared off its hinges and melted, ending the fey prince's banishment at long last.

I saw him step over the boundary, saw him gather flames between his hands, pull back his arm to throw it, his eyes bright with madness.

I held his gaze, refusing to let him have the satisfaction of seeing my fear.

He threw the fireball.

I inhaled.

It never connected.

Something stepped in front of it. Something lithe and tall, with a red cloak and raven hair. Something bearing a shield and short sword.

Rose?

She'd returned. Leather armor sheathed her, and she carried a shield embossed with a rose and a rampant wolf-hart-beast upon it.

"You can't have her." Rose held out her sword and pointed to the prince. "Not one step closer."

The faerie prince laughed, mocking her. "As if you could stop me."

Rose shrugged. "I'm sure as hell going to try."

The faerie prince's face became a study in rage. "Do you have any idea who I am?" he demanded.

"A monster," Rose said. "And I know what to do with monsters."

The geas eased now that she had returned, and I could breathe again. But the barrier was down and I still had no magic to call. All that remained to me were my teeth and claws.

And one iron short sword.

If I could pin him, Rose could finish him off. The fey couldn't bear the touch of cold iron.

I staggered to my feet and took a long, deep breath.

"Beast?" Rose didn't take her eyes off the prince.

"I'm here," I said. "The heart. Aim for the heart. Anything else will just make him mad. Keep him off the path, and he can't order me to stop."

She nodded once, and together, we charged.

The prince bellowed and the falling snow around us blackened, became as ash. Flames coursed along his flesh, and he threw another ball of fire at us. I ducked. Rose went high and blocked it with her shield. I darted around behind the prince, paws scrabbling in the slick ash.

He tried to turn, tried to reach for me, but Rose slashed and the prince was forced to turn towards her. She slashed, and he parried with his antlers, trying to snap her wrist and make her drop her sword. But she'd learned to fight someone with antlers, and the prince's attacks did no good. She forced him back, back, and back again, while I harried him from behind, slashing and distracting him, enraging him past reason. His green leggings and tunic hung in charred tatters, blood dripped from countless cuts, and still he stood and fought.

"I am a *prince* of the *fey!*" he shrieked.

"And you *still* haven't the power to force me to do your will!" I crowed from behind him. The prince whirled and tried to grab me, and Rose took the opening. She struck, sheering his antlers completely off. They clattered to the stones and shattered. Blood as black as pitch trickled from the stumps on the prince's brow.

Finally, he staggered off the stones and stepped over the ruined slag of the fallen gate.

He was off the castle grounds, and fair game.

With a mighty pounce, I leapt upon him, wrapped one arm around his throat and the other around his waist. Rose screamed and thrust her sword up under his ribcage. The blade cleaved his flesh, surged up and through his heart. I screamed as the tip of the blade bit into my arm, through it, and pierced the prince's chin.

He gurgled, red-black blood trickling from between his lips. And finally, his bloodshot eyes rolled back, and he went limp. Dark blood coursed down Rose's arm and the prince's chest, pooling on the stones and flowing towards the rose bushes.

"The roses," I gasped. "We have to give him to the roses!"

We dragged his dying carcass to the bushes. With a mighty heave, Rose yanked her sword free and we dropped him in the bush. Thorns and vines sprang to life, shredding the prince to pieces. Red-black blood rained down the stems, and my roses feasted.

I felt it, when the geas finally lifted. An ache in my chest I'd grown so used to eased and faded away. The prince's eyes clouded over and finally, *finally*, it was over.

"Is he...?"

I nodded, panting. My arm ached from the sword wound, but I held my hand over it and muttered a spell. The flesh mended without so much as a scar. Even the blood that stained my white fur faded away.

My magic had returned.

My form, however, had not.

"You're still...Beast."

The geas had been broken, but my transformation could not be undone.

"I think...I think this is me, now," I said. "Is that, I mean, do you still—"

Rose flicked her blade a few times, cleaning the prince's blood from the steel. She sheathed it and kissed me soundly.

"Is that a yes?" I said breathlessly as she pulled back.

"Yes," she said. "What about your name? Does this mean you can remember your name again?"

I nodded. "Dahlia," I said. "Dahlia Beaumont."

"I knew you had a lovely name," she said. Behind us, the castle crumbled. Without the prince's magic to sustain it, it collapsed and fell to blackened ash. Rose offered her arm to me, but I hesitated.

"Where shall we go?" I asked.

"Anywhere but here," she said. "There's a whole world out there, with dragons, ogres. There's got to be something for a couple of faerie prince-slaying adventurers, right? But first, a drink."

I smiled, waved my hand and made a pair of silver goblets filled to the brim with rich, rose-red wine. She laughed, offered me her arm, and I took it. "As my Rose wishes."

THE TUTOR LEARNS

Skunkbomb

I twisted the cross necklace in my fingers. The room had two male names on the door, but I knocked anyways. For some reason, she had insisted on meeting here instead of her own dorm.

"Yeah, come in!" a female voice said from behind the door.

The room was a mess. Both beds weren't made, and textbooks were left on the floor. A skateboard, half of its artwork of fish bones scratched off, leaned against the wall. Above one of the beds hung a small black and purple flag, even though those weren't the school colors.

"I'll be out in a minute," said the voice again from the bathroom. "Make yourself at home."

"Okay." My bushy tail whirled. Since both beds were a mess and there weren't any chairs, I elected to stand.

A sea of blankets rose from one of the beds. "So, you're the tutor or whatever?"

I squeaked. When I stepped back, I stumbled over someone's backpack.

"Shit, my bad." The covers lifted up to reveal a coyote dressed in nothing but shorts. "You okay?"

The bathroom door opened. "Mark, if you kill my tutor, I'll flunk out and you'll be all alone here."

"It was your backpack."

Webbed hands grasped under my arms and pulled me up. Behind me stood a tall otter. With her baggy graphic t-shirt, I almost mistook her for a boy, but her slim jeans hugged her wider hips.

I stuck out my hand. "I'm Julia."

The otter shook with a firm, warm grip. "Ramona. That's Mark. His roommate moved in with his frat, and my roommate's got me permanently sex-iled, so I just crash here."

I nodded. "Shall we head somewhere a little less distracting?"

Ramona picked up her backpack and the skateboard. "You hear that, Mark? You're distracting."

"Oh, I didn't mean—"

Mark scratched his bare stomach. "My Adonis-like physique is too much for mere mortals."

Ramona wrinkled her nose. "I think tutor squirrel meant you smell like dog."

I held up my paws and chittered nervously. "No, that's not—"

"I don't smell like dog," Mark said, turning his PlayStation on. He pulled up Netflix. "I smell like coyote. It's more exotic."

When we got on the elevator, Ramona glanced at my chest. "So, you're part of the Jesus squad?"

"Jesus squad?" I touched my cross. "Oh, you mean—yes, I'm Catholic."

"Oh." Ramona stared at the numbers over the door as they lit up in descending order.

It had been a bit of an adjustment going from a Catholic high school to a secular college. Sure, there were some students who didn't take their faith seriously in high school, but only a few students at college seemed to be religious. Jesus preached acceptance, charity, and love. What was so bad about that?

Once we were outside, Ramona hopped onto her skateboard, and she didn't say a word to me until we arrived at the school library. She at least sat next to me at one of the offices on the first floor. Students could reserve one of these special study rooms in the library ahead of time, which was perfect for tutoring.

"It's okay," I said as Ramona got another question incorrect. "We'll go over it again."

The otter slapped her tail against the ground. "When am I ever going to need to use math that has letters? I have an app on my phone that calculates a tip. Isn't that enough?"

I closed the textbook. "Let's take a five-minute break."

"That's barely a break."

"Well, we only have this room for another 30 minutes," I said. "So what's your major?"

Ramona shrugged. "Art, at the moment. I don't know. It's the only subject I liked."

"That means you only need to pass this one math class."

"But I already flunked it last year as a freshman," Ramona said, flopping her head on the table. "If I don't get at least a C this time, I'll get kicked out."

I placed my hand on top of hers. "I'm here to make sure that doesn't happen. How about we—"

Outside the door, a red squirrel walked by. I remembered the ruddy tint of his fur and his preacher-like tone when discussing Jesus.

"Spill it."

"I'm sorry?" I looked over at Ramona.

The otter leaned forward in her chair. "I saw the way you looked at him. Did you fuck him or something?"

I held a paw over my chest. "I'm saving myself for marriage."

Ramona rolled her eyes. "Of course, but seriously, you know him, don't you?"

I pulled the textbook back out. "We dated in high school. Now we're not dating. Let's get back to studying, okay?" I remembered his athleticism on the lacrosse field and his confidence when talking to other people, but I also remembered what happened in that hospital.

The last half hour dragged by, and when we left the study room, Ramona had gotten through a couple more problems. It was slow progress, but it was progress.

Rain pounded the ground in fast, fat drops. Students walked by wearing galoshes and holding umbrellas.

"Where did this come from?" I said.

Ramona snorted. "You're not from Florida, are you?"

I shook my head. "Connecticut."

The otter picked up her skateboard and held it over my head.

"But aren't you worried you'll get wet?" I said.

Ramona shrugged. "I'm an otter. Wet is second nature to us. Which dorm do you live in again?"

Ramona's snapback hat did nothing to protect her from the downpour. It was only a five-minute walk to my dorm, but by the time we made it inside, the otter was soaked.

"I've got a fur dryer in my room," I said, grabbing her wrist. "At least wait out the rest of the storm here so you don't get wetter."

"I mean, okay," Ramona said as I led her onto the elevator. "But you really don't have to. A little rain won't hurt me." A droplet of rain fell from her whiskers.

"That was more than a little."

When Ramona walked into my dorm, she whistled. "Nice shoebox."

She wasn't wrong. The room was a narrow rectangle. A small kitchen lined the left wall while the bathroom was immediately to the right. Past the kitchen/bathroom area was my dresser, desk, and twin-sized bed. I could walk from the door to the desk in about seven steps.

"So how loaded are you?" Ramona said.

"I'm sorry?"

"You've got a single in an upperclassman dorm," the otter said.

I gathered up the top blanket of my bed. "A single works best for me. Now, you get unchanged in the bathroom and then I'll take your wet clothes to the laundry room downstairs. It'll take half an hour at most to get them dry. I'd offer you some of my clothes, but you're a bit taller than me."

I left Ramona wrapped up in a blanket in my room while I tossed her clothes into the dryer: baggy gray t-shirt, jeans with tears in the knees, and striped underwear. It wasn't the heat in the laundry room making my ears feel this hot. I paid with my laundry card and pressed my head against the dryer's door. I had a naked girl in my room. What was I doing? I had a single to avoid moments like this.

I had a roommate my freshman year. Rosy, a mouse, was one of those girls who had strict parents and was tasting freedom for the first time. I made the mistake of letting her drag me to one of those frat parties and mixing my drink. I couldn't taste the alcohol. It was a great night. We just chatted about how overbearing our parents could be, complained about professors, and I kept calling her cute. She's a little feisty mouse. Of course she was cute. But then I kissed her. I'm a girl and I kissed a girl. She laughed it off that night, but she didn't speak to me the same way afterward. At the end of the semester, she didn't even tell me she was moving in with some other girls.

I took a deep breath and walked out of the laundry room. The laundry wouldn't take long to dry, and I was helping someone in need. There wasn't any ulterior motive to getting Ramona out of her clothes. The Lord would forgive me.

When I got back to the room, Ramona was lying on my bed glaring at the crucifix above my desk.

"I think Jesus is trying to check out my tits," the otter said.

I wasn't sure how to react to that, so I just chuckled a little and sat down in my desk chair. Ramona's webbed feet hung off the side of the bed, and the blanket slid up, revealing the side of her outer thigh.

"Jules?"

My ears perked up. "Sorry, yes?"

"You were spacing out," Ramona said. "So, where's your TV?"

I shook my head. "I don't watch a lot of live TV. I watch Netflix sometimes on my laptop."

"Sweet," Ramona said, sitting up. "Let's watch an episode of something. You pick."

I picked out a comedy from my list of shows to watch since comedies tend to be 22-minute episodes. I clicked on the pilot episode and turned the laptop toward Ramona.

"The screen's tiny," the otter said. She patted the space next to her on the bed.

My tail went rigid. "But you're sitting there. I don't want to crowd you."

Ramona looked at the several feet of space next to her and then back at me. "Dude."

I nodded and climbed onto the bed. Thoughts fluttered back to high school dances. *Leave some room in between for the Lord.*

The show was pretty amusing. Two sisters, one of them adopted, end up moving next door to one another when they're in their 30s. One's a divorced businesswoman with a kid and the other's a hippie artist. As the Netflix description promised, hilarity ensued.

Warmth radiated in my face and neck. I don't think I was coming down with a fever, but I didn't feel right. I glanced to my left. Ramona had leaned toward me to get a better look at the screen. I leaned closer. Her whiskers brushed against me, and my face tingled.

Ramona turned. "Shit, my bad." She didn't move, and neither did I.

The alarm on my phone buzzed.

I hopped up, almost knocking my laptop to the ground. "That's your laundry. I'll go get your laundry. Then you can get dressed." I glanced at my phone. "And I have class in twenty minutes, so you have to leave."

"Oh, yeah, sure," Ramona said, shrugging.

I took deep breaths all the way down the elevator. When I returned to my room with Ramona's laundry, she changed in the bathroom. On her way out, Ramona rested her hand on the doorknob. "Let's catch the second episode after our next study session, okay?"

I nodded. Words felt too dangerous.

When Ramona left, I breathed a sigh of relief. When I stepped into the bathroom before I left for class, I found Ramona's blue bra hanging from the towel rack. A drip of rainwater dropped onto the teeny puddle beneath it. My head felt hot and thick all over again.

***

The university may have been secular, but there was a church a few blocks away. I came every Sunday for mass, but sometimes I'd stop by when my mind was unsettled and I needed peace. Kneeling in the pew, I asked the Lord to help me find the way to guide Ramona, to be the tutor she needs, and only her tutor. Though, I wouldn't mind watching the rest of that show with her. It'd be a good way to pass a rainy day, all snug under the blankets and—

I lowered my head further. What was wrong with me?

The pew creaked as another squirrel, a red squirrel, sat down and scooted next to me.

"Peace be with you, Julia," the red squirrel said.

"Peace be with you, Tyler."

He held out his hand. "Come. Let's pray together."

We were in God's house. It seemed wrong to refuse, so I took his hand in mine for the first time since we both entered college. I prayed for my younger brother, who had a soccer game in a few days. I prayed for my American Literature professor, who had cut her hand open and had to get stitches. Mostly, I prayed for Tyler, in hopes he would come to understand that we would never be together again.

I had a feeling Tyler would follow me out, and sure enough, when I stood, he did too. He walked silently behind me until we were walking down the front steps of the church.

"The Christian Students Association's planning a trip to one of the retirement homes in the area," Tyler said. "It'll be a good time."

I shook my head. "We both know that's not a good idea, Tyler."

Tyler chuckled. "How is helping the elderly a bad thing?"

"Not that," I said. "Us."

"That was high school," Tyler said as he placed his hand on my shoulder so I wouldn't walk into traffic, as if I needed a reminder not to do that. "That was a lifetime ago."

The walking symbol popped up, and I walked ahead of Tyler. "I haven't seen you with a new girlfriend."

"And I haven't seen you with a boyfriend," the red squirrel said. "Though there was that otter in the library."

"Ramona's a girl," I said, and then added, "I'm tutoring her."

"Huh," Tyler said. "Hard to tell with the butch ones. Wait a minute." He bounded up to me and grasped my hands. "I see what you're doing."

I tugged, but I couldn't get out of his grip. "What are you talking about?"

"You're showing Ramona the error of her lifestyle."

"Are you serious, Tyler?" I said, my tail all puffed up. Raising my voice in front of other students was enough to get Tyler to release me. "You say high school was a lifetime ago, but you haven't changed."

Tyler glared. "Seems like you're changing for the worst."

I walked away. With the other students walking by watching our fight, if Tyler ran after me, that would make him look like the bad guy. I had escaped, at least for now.

"Our trip's on Saturday," Tyler called after me. "I'll save you a seat in my car."

***

Ramona's bra sat in my backpack. It was only a bra, but it felt like I was smuggling drugs. I had a plan before I got off the elevator. I'd discreetly return the bra to Ramona. Then, after the tutoring session, we'd go back to my place and sit a respectable distance from one another as we watched Netflix.

Walking out of the elevator, I wondered if Ramona was even a lesbian. Yesterday could have been a complete misunderstanding, and even if it wasn't, it's not my business who Ramona was attracted to, and I wasn't a lesbian. I was probably just going through a phase, like when I wore a tutu at home everyday for six months as a kid. I was being ridiculous.

I opened the door. "Ramona, I—"

Ramona sat on her bed clutching a pencil and a sketchpad. Mark was reclined on his bed. He wasn't wearing shorts this time. Or underwear.

I shrieked and ran out the door.

Ramona and Mark, now wearing shorts, found me by the elevators a couple minutes later.

"I'm sorry for freaking you out like that," Mark said, his ears flat.

I held my hand up, cutting off the rest of his apology. "I should have knocked. Sorry for interrupting whatever you were doing."

"Art homework," Ramona said, a little giggle in her voice. "I like using live models when I can get them. I should have been watching the clock, but I got carried away."

"We should get to the library," I said, pressing the down arrow by the elevators. A part of me held back a smile. Tyler had been wrong about Ramona. Even though I had assumed she was a lesbian after yesterday, she was just a tomboy. I should have seen it the moment I met Ramona and Mark. A boy and a girl unofficially sharing a room with one another? Of course they must have been in a relationship.

***

"So, all I have to do now is divide 38 by 2x, right?" Ramona said.

I tried to keep my face neutral, but my tail tip flicked nonstop in my chair. "And …?"

"That means X is 19."

"Yes! That's right!" I patted her hand. "See? You're getting this."

Ramona squeezed my hand lightly for half a second. "I think I can feel my brain growing, or maybe the math's giving me a headache."

I looked at my phone. "I think our room time is just about finished."

Thankfully, it wasn't pouring outside like yesterday. Ramona stepped onto her skateboard and rode ahead.

I jogged after her. "Do you always ride around campus on that?"

Ramona shrugged. "It's faster than walking, and it's more fun too." She stopped and stepped off her board. "You want to try?"

I looked at the four wheels. "I'm not sure if I could if I wanted to."

"Come on," the otter said. "At least you'd be tall for once."

I crossed my arms in mock seriousness. "Being short gives me a better center of gravity."

"Awesome," Ramona said. "Then you'll do fine."

I placed one foot on the scratchy black top of the skateboard and then hopped up. My arm flung out and Ramona grabbed it.

"I got you," the otter said, holding onto both my wrists.

I didn't ride the skateboard so much as Ramona guided me along the sidewalk to the crosswalk before my dorm. We weren't going that fast, but there was still a nice breeze from the momentum. It did little to cool me off.

"So," Ramona said. "How's it feel to be taller than someone for once?"

With me on the skateboard, her nose came up to my lips. All she had to do was stand on her tiptoes and we'd be even, her lips up to mine.

"Wow, just remembered I have a quiz to study for," I said, stepping down from the skateboard. "I have to go study for that. It's a big quiz."

Ramona released me, her whiskers drooping. "Oh, okay. Do you still want to watch Netflix later?"

I nodded, and the walking symbol popped up. "Of course. Bye!"

When I returned to my room, I chucked my bag aside and slid onto the cool floor. What was wrong with me? Why wasn't I following the plan?

I had long since planned out my life's path, or at least a plan I thought God would approve of. I would go to college, get my teaching degree, teach at a Catholic school in the northeast not too far from home, settle down with a nice squirrel, and have four kids (three through birth and one through adoption).

Ramona wasn't part of my plan. I buried my head in my hands. If God was testing me, I had a feeling I was failing. Why was I even attracted to Ramona? I always imagined myself marrying someone a little more put together. Her clothes were baggy or had tears in the knees. Sure, she was tall, and the otter had lean muscles that suggested strength with a hint of delicateness, and Ramona's fur was a lovely dark brown except for around her mouth, neck, (and maybe her chest), and the pads of her paws were a little rough, but the hint of scratchiness would feel wonderful on my—

I fingered the button on my pants as a new plan formed in my head. This was just an impulse, a random infatuation I had to work out, like an illness. I just had to take care of it. Once it was out of my system, I'd go to confession and then everything would be better.

I stood in front of my full-length mirror as I dropped my pants around my ankles, followed by my underwear. In my American Literature class, one of the books had a woman who compared her vagina to a wet rose. I used two fingers to spread myself. Mine looked like some dark, foreboding cave. I bit my lip and placed the pad of my finger against my slit. A shuddering breath escaped from me as I slipped my finger inside, teasing one of the lips. Oh God, why did this have to feel so good?

Someone knocked.

"Hold on! I'll be right there if you give me a minute!" I hoped it wasn't a fox or some other species with good hearing on the other side of the door. Otherwise, my shouting might not have covered the sound of me pulling up my underwear and pants.

"Hey, it's Ramona."

My breath caught in my throat. When I didn't reply, she continued.

"I know you're studying or whatever," the otter said. "But Mark was feeling super guilty that you saw him naked, so he made you cookies. They're white chocolate macadamia nut, but I don't know if you're allergic to chocolate. I mean, I heard white chocolate isn't actually chocolate. Also, I know you're a squirrel, but I didn't want to just assume you liked nuts in your cookies."

I took a deep breath and opened the door. "Thank you very much for the cookies. That was very nice of Mark to—"

"Shit, are you okay?" Ramona said, her voice softening.

I touched the fur under my eyes, brushing away dampness. "Oh, I'm…" My jaw wouldn't open the way I wanted it to and my throat closed up. Fresh tears ran down my face.

The otter pulled me into my dorm room and shut the door. After handing me my box of tissues, she sat down on the bed with me. "So you're obviously not okay. What's wrong?"

I took a moment to breathe, staring into my lap. Looking Ramona in the eye didn't feel like a good idea. "How do I put this? I think I don't like nuts with my cookies."

Ramona held back a chuckle. "Mark can make different cookies. His chocolate chip ones are pretty damn good."

I bit my lip. She was going to make me say it out loud. I buried my eyes behind my palms. "I'm supposed to marry a guy, but I can't stop thinking about girls. I was never tempted with guys, but now with girls I just feel feverish and thickheaded, like I'm sick."

Ramona grasped my wrist, and I looked at her. She looked like the angels I read about: stern tempered fury.

"You're not sick," Ramona said. "There's nothing wrong with you."

"But how do I stop feeling like this?"

"Have you tried getting off?"

I hid my face with my tail. Was I hiding from Ramona or the cross on my wall? It was probably both at this point, or just the entire world. "I'm not supposed to."

"What, were you taught that touching your pussy's like ringing the devil's doorbell or something?" Ramona said. "First, if your vagina's a portal to Hell, that's badass. I'd put that shit on my resume. Second," she grasped my shoulder. "This is your body. You can do what you want with it."

"I know I can," I said, sniffling like a cub. "But I'm not supposed to."

"Look, I haven't read the whole bible, but I know parts of it," Ramona said. "I'm pretty sure the line about touching yourself mentions not spilling your seed or whatever. It doesn't say anything about women getting off."

Even if that was true, the idea of touching myself still felt wrong. I gripped my sheets. I didn't think I was strong enough to stop from trying again.

Ramona placed her hand over mine. "If you've got questions about what you're going through, I can help. What do you want to know?"

Since I started having these feelings, there was something I wanted to know about Ramona. How soft were her lips? Would her whiskers tickle me when we kissed? Would holding another woman feel different than holding a man?

I leaned forward and learned.

Maybe Ramona could have used a little chapstick, but goodness, those lips were warm. Her whiskers tickled my fur, shooting shivers through me. Maybe the shivering was just nerves, but as she held me tightly against her, I calmed.

I brushed fresh tears from my eyes as we parted. "Will Mark be mad about this?"

"Why would he?" Ramona said.

I looked away from her. "I mean, I saw you two earlier, and he was naked, so..."

The otter burst into laughter. "What? No, we're not dating, fucking or anything like that. We're just friends."

"Do you draw all of your friends with their clothes off?"

"Play your cards right, and you can be my model next time. And speaking of getting naked," Ramona fingered the bottom of her shirt. "Do you want to try this with our clothes off? I know you're going through a lot, so I don't want to do more than you're ready for."

I clutched a clump of my shirt. "Am I…am I supposed to be sexy when I do this?"

Ramona snorted. "If that'll make you feel good."

The otter must have had practice doing this. I'd only taken off my shirt and unbuttoned my pants when Ramona had already stripped down to her bra and underwear. Her breasts weren't large, but they fit her athletic build. Her underwear had polka dots this time. The cream-colored fur of her inner thigh peeked out.

"You seem a little stuck," Ramona said, grabbing my zipper. "Can I help?"

I lay back on the bed so she could tug my pants off, and then she unhooked my bra much more slowly than necessary.

After Ramona tossed my shirt away, she did this weird eyebrow wiggle. "Damn, you're pretty stacked."

I placed an arm over my chest. "My bra straps dig into my shoulders. It's not as great as you'd think."

Ramona's hands disappeared behind her back. With a flick, her bra loosened, and she pulled. Her breasts were the same creamy color of the nape of her neck.

It usually felt good taking my bra off after a long day, but this was a new kind of naked for me. The air conditioning felt colder against me. We fell into one another again, though this time Ramona kissed me under my chin and on my neck. I leaned back onto the bed, and the otter's kisses trailed down my body, only detouring to kiss my nipples. It never occurred to me so many parts of my body could be kissed.

When her lips reached my belly button, Ramona's fingers slipped around the waist of my underwear and pulled down. I've gone to a gynecologist before, and she was a woman, so I just pretended Ramona was examining me. To be fair, I did need some attention down there. I wasn't quite sure what was going to happen next. Normally, the guy would stick his penis in the girl, but I was pretty sure Ramona didn't have one. How were we supposed to—

My gasp evolved into a moan. I clasped my hand over my mouth.

Ramona licked her lips. "You okay?"

I nodded.

The otter's fingers spread me. "Good."

Her tongue darted in and out of me. Every now and then, she would run the flat of her tongue slowly from the bottom to the top of my lips.

The story of Noah's Ark came to mind. The flood began as a steady rain that grew heavier and heavier until the great wetness overtook the world. I bit my hand. A flood barreled through me.

Ramona licked her wet muzzle. "Damn, you really were pent up."

Whatever came out of me had dribbled onto the sheets. I fought the urge to pull them off the bed and throw them in the washing machine.

"That's got me going," Ramona said, shifting onto her rear. She spread her legs. Her vagina glistened. "I could show you how to touch me, but if you just want to watch, that's okay too, or …" Her whiskers drooped. "Oh shit, did I hurt you?"

I rubbed dampness from my cheeks. "This was just a lot."

When the otter leaned forward and reached for my cheek, I pulled away. "I should really go to that class with the quiz I mentioned earlier."

Ramona nodded, and we both changed with our backs facing each other. I spritzed some light perfume on myself. I didn't want anyone sniffing out what I did. Would it really matter though? God saw. He wouldn't be fooled.

"I'm so sorry," Ramona said. "If it's too awkward tutoring me, you can stop. I'll understand."

I shook my head as I locked my door. "It's fine. I still want to help you." I hurried off, but we ended up waiting together for the elevator anyway, so my retreat was useless. The reflective surface of the walls made it look like everyone was staring. Ramona didn't stop me when I walked away from campus and toward the church.

***

I broke down the moment I sat on the pew. I didn't feel self-conscious crying here. People from all walks of life who were fighting their own battles come here everyday, and Jesus allowed them to lay their feelings out in the open. If a priest was available, I could ask to go through confession.

The weight on the pew shifted. Tyler, looking beatific as always, grasped my hand. "Come on, let's pray."

We sat in prayer as my crying calmed to sniffling. Being around Tyler still made my tail stiff, but praying with someone who shared my faith was comforting. After a while, we left the church as I wiped the last of my tears from my eyes.

"What's wrong?" Tyler asked.

I shook my head. Even though he was helping me, I couldn't give him the full details. "I may have damaged a potential friendship with someone I'm tutoring."

Tyler nodded stiffly. "The lesbian?"

"Yes."

Tyler shrugged. "Maybe it was never meant to be. I think I know what will make you feel better. The CSA will be at the Sunset Shores Retirement Home tomorrow, so why not come with us? Sharing my faith with someone has always made me feel better."

Going with him would be a bad idea, but at least I'd be doing some good talking with lonely grandparents. "What time?"

"We leave at 2:30 and get there by 3:00."

"I'll be there."

Tyler's tail whirled. "Fantastic! Hey, if you're getting hungry, how about we grab a bite to eat?"

I shook my head and sped up. "Sorry, but I've got class in fifteen minutes, and I have to run back to my dorm to get my books." When I configured my schedule for the semester, I didn't realize how easy it would be lying to people about having class on Fridays.

Back in my dorm room, I closed the door and flopped on my bed. All this guilt about my attraction to other women and Tyler's presence was like going back to high school. I thought stepping out of my hometown would help me figure myself out, but all I was left with was a mess. Why did Tyler have to follow me to Florida? The thought of having dinner with him stole my appetite.

My knee rubbed against a damp patch on the bed, and my nose twitched. Maybe I was a little hungry. I picked up one of the cookies Ramona brought over and took a bite.

***

I went through the motions with tutoring Ramona the following day. She tried problems, I helped her where she struggled, and neither of us mentioned what happened the day before. I threw my books into my backpack the moment the session ended.

"Do you want to grab lunch?" Ramona said, rubbing the back of her neck.

I shook my head. "I already ate. I'm meeting up with some people to go visit Sunset Shores Retirement Home."

"Christian stuff?"

"It's with the CSA, yes." I pulled on my backpack. "The library's closed on Sundays, so we can take a break tomorrow, if that's good with you."

"We can study somewhere else," Ramona said. "Maybe we can watch some Netflix after. We can watch it in my room, or I can bring my laptop and we can watch it somewhere else on campus if that's better for you or—"

I looked at my phone. "I really should get going. We can text later." Ramona didn't follow me on my way out.

Tyler had this nice SUV with enough seating for the two of us and three other CSA members. I wanted to sit in the back so I could chat with the other members, but Tyler claimed I had already reserved shotgun. I had to crane my neck back to talk with everyone else on the ride over: a raccoon, a groundhog, and a ferret. They were nice. We talked about innocuous meeting-for-the-first-time subjects: what year they were in college, what major, and where they were from.

The retirement home was painted a sunbaked pink and had a front lawn shorter than a driveway. The CSA came once a month, sometimes to help throw a birthday party or play bingo, but today was more casual. We split off to chat with someone who looked lonely.

"I've been talking with this husky who was in the marines," Tyler said. He put his arm around me. "I'll introduce you to him."

I wiggled out of his grip. "Maybe before we leave. The badger over there looks lonely."

Tyler shrugged. "Good luck. She's a grump."

I sat on the couch next to the badger. The black of her fur was more of a gray and her white fur was yellowing at the edges. She stared with an analytical eye at the spinning Wheel of Fortune.

"Hi," I said. "My name's Julia. What's yours?"

"Salted Caramel Ice Cream," the badger said. Only a third of the letters were revealed on the screen. "Jesus, these contestants have rocks for brains." Her gaze flitted briefly in my direction. "Your boyfriend's an ass."

I stuttered briefly before I could untie my tongue. "We're not dating."

"You kids are the Christian group at your college," the badger said, her attention back on the TV. "But he was ogling you in a very unchristian manner."

"He knows we're not together anymore."

The badger chuckled dryly. "'Anymore'. Your not-boyfriend presses his faith on Walter over there whether he wants it or not. I'm guessing your not-boyfriend is the same way with women."

"Ah, we didn't know more of you were coming," the woman at the front desk said.

Mark, who was wearing a full set of clothes for once, and Ramona, walked in. I gripped the side of the couch.

Tyler walked over to the worker. "They're not with us, but they're welcome to stay."

"Sweet," Mark said. The coyote wandered over to the husky, Walter.

I hurried over to Ramona after Tyler walked off in search of another elderly person to chat with. "What are you doing here?"

"Making sure you're okay," Ramona said.

"But I'm fine."

"You're a Jesus fangirl, but you don't hang out with the Jesus fans," Ramona said. "And you avoid the guy who's head of Jesus' fan club at our college. I'm not sure why you're hanging around with him because even though I haven't even met Tyler, I can tell he sucks."

I held her hands and rubbed the webbing. "You didn't have to do this."

"Hey Ramona!" Mark said, waving at her. "This dude does watercolors. You have to check them out! Don't be mad, but I think he's better at it than you."

The otter slipped her hands away. "Let me check them out!" She hurried over to the coyote and the husky.

I wandered back onto the couch with the badger. She gazed at me like a solved puzzle. "So, you and the otter?"

"I've been tutoring her in math," I said, staring at the TV. "I've only known her for about a week, but I think it's safe to say we're in that realm of friendly—"

"My girlfriend's name was Edna," the badger said. "I called her Ed. It was safer back in the fifties talking to family about Ed instead of Edna. Everyone called me Dolores, but to Ed, I was Dot. Could you imagine a big girl like me going by a name like Dot?" She shook her head. "It sounded perfect when she said it."

"What was she like?"

"Adventurous, sweet, loyal," Dolores said. "One time, a boy was giving us trouble, so she hatched this plan. I swiped his keys when he wasn't looking, and Edna lured him into the bathroom. Then she climbed out the window—she's a rat, so that wasn't a problem for her—I met her around the front, and we took this boy's motorcycle for a joyride."

I covered my mouth as I held back a laugh. "That's illegal."

"Felt like justice to us," Dolores said, her grin sharp and toothy. "Ed and I rode that motorcycle all the way out of town to Daytona Beach. Then we sat on the shore and watched the sun rise over the water."

I nodded, but I stared at my lap. "How did you know you and Edna were more than friends?"

Dolores placed her hand on my shoulder. "When I was with boys, it was like two puzzle pieces that didn't fit right. It could work if I forced it, but it never felt good. Women though, it felt like our pieces fit just right."

Ramona was kneeling by Walter and Mark, pointing at something on the husky's painting. She wasn't a canine, but she had a little bark to her laugh after Walter had said something.

On TV, Vanna White applauded as the solved puzzle flashed on the screen.

***

It was tradition for the CSA to go to Steak and Shake after their trips off campus. Tyler, smiling tightly, invited Ramona and Mark to join us. We got a booth, and Ramona and Mark pulled me between them on one side of it. Tyler had to pull up a chair to sit at the end of the six-person booth.

No one said much at first other than putting in our orders. For a minute, I actually thought it would be a normal, if awkwardly silent, dinner.

"So Ramona," Tyler said in his preacher voice. "When did you decide to become a homosexual?"

Somehow the quiet table became even quieter.

"It's who I am," Ramona said. "It's the same way you're a squirrel. I was born this way."

"So, right from birth you somehow know you're not attracted to men?" Tyler asked. He looked around the table. The other CSA members looked away.

"No, not at all," Mark said. "Sometimes it takes years to piece together who you're attracted to, but that doesn't mean you suddenly wake up gay or 'decided to be gay.'"

"And what are you supposed to be?" Tyler said.

Mark tapped the pin shaped like a black, gray, white, and purple flag. "I'm the A in LGBTQIA+."

Tyler shook his head. "It's not enough that the homosexuals have all the colors on their flag. Now they want all the letters."

"Tyler, leave them alone," I said, my hands balled up in my lap. "What does it matter that they're not straight? They helped with the elderly just like the rest of us. The least you can do is be civil."

"I'm not the one raising their voice," Tyler said, his hands up. "I'm all for having a civil conversation, but we can't have that if you shout the moment you become uncomfortable."

"Oh please. You just want to give a sermon."

Tyler looked to me, then to Ramona, and then back at me. "What is she to you? You were never this combative until you started hanging out with that otter."

"She's my math tutor," Ramona said. She scooted herself so she was facing Tyler. "And not that I'd recommend this, but for someone who's got a boner for Jules, being a douche isn't a good way to convince her to get back together with you."

"You said you two were dating," the raccoon at the other end of the table said.

"We're on a break," Tyler said.

"I made it clear that evening in that hospital that we were done," I said.

Tyler leaned forward, his preacher voice becoming more of a growl. "You don't just stop seeing someone without telling them 'I'm breaking up with you' or 'it's over.'"

"And you don't just tell someone in the hospital they'll get better if they stop being gay!" I clapped my hand over my mouth. Diners at the tables next to us were starting to stare.

"Oh fuck no," Ramona said, shooting up to her feet.

Mark grabbed her by the hood of her sweatshirt. "We're leaving. Julia, hold Ramona for a second, okay?"

"I was doing him a favor," Tyler said, a hint of an uncomfortable chuckle in his voice. "He wouldn't have gotten beaten up if he hadn't been gay."

Mark slipped twenty-five dollars on the table. "That should cover all three of us plus tip." He nodded to the three other CSA members. "I wish you three good luck on the ride home."

"I can't believe I wasted a whole year of my life on you," I said to Tyler, holding the thrashing otter in my arms.

"You'd have a better future with me than her!" Tyler said. "What is she giving you that I can't?"

I swallowed. "An orgasm."

Ramona stopped thrashing and flopped against me in a giggling fit. "Oh shit!"

Mark, biting his lip to keep the smile from forming, placed his hands on our backs. "We're, like, five seconds from being kicked out. Come on."

I climbed into the back seat of Mark's car while Ramona rode shotgun.

"Sorry about not actually getting food," Mark said as he pulled out of the parking lot. "I'll make you something back at the dorms. I mean, I'll cook you anything after that sick burn on Tyler."

"I'm so sorry," I said. I hid my face behind my tail as I brushed tears away. "Even in high school, he wasn't that bad." Or perhaps he was. I just hadn't realized it until the end of the relationship.

Even though we were in a moving vehicle, Ramona unbuckled herself and climbed into the back with me. After I insisted she buckle herself in, I buried my face into her shoulder.

"What happened with that gay kid?" Ramona said.

I sniffed. "Jeffrey went to the same high school as us. Everyone always suspected he liked boys, but he never talked about it until senior year. He started admitting he was gay, and he came to a football game wearing a rainbow bracelet. Later at the game, someone found him unconscious behind the snack bar, all bloody and beaten up. He ended up missing the rest of the school year."

"Was it Tyler?" Ramona said.

I shook my head. "He fights with words, not fists. After the attack, Tyler suggested we visit Jeffrey in the hospital. I was running late, but when I got there, Tyler was holding Jeffrey's hand, telling him if he stopped being gay, God would forgive him."

Mark accelerated. "The scary part is that I honestly think he be-lieves that was the right call for the situation."

"Tyler must have heard me behind him," I said. "But I wouldn't let him hold me. I just told him to get out and to leave me alone." I shook my head. "I was mad, but I didn't understand why I was so mad at the time. I think I know now."

"What was it?" Ramona said, stroking the fur on my head.

I brushed the last of my tears away. "Ramona, after dinner, do you want to go back to my dorm and watch Netflix?"

***

My laptop remained off.

Ramona and I sat on my bed, our tongues exploring each other in a deep kiss. The otter pulled away. "Okay, but are you sure?"

"Yes, I'm sure," I said, fighting the giggle coming into my voice. "I want to know how women touch each other. I've spent the last few days tutoring you, so think of this as returning the favor."

Ramona leaned back and pulled her jeans and underwear down. "I'm guessing you Catholic school kids didn't get a lesson on how to work a pussy."

"They taught you to masturbate in public school?"

The otter snorted. "No, but I'm guessing I've got some more com-prehensive knowledge here. You've got more than just the vagina down there."

I nodded. I took health and Sex Ed in high school, but the dia-grams were mostly names and the first Sex Ed class ended with the teacher giving out pamphlets on the dangers of oral sex.

Ramona slid her fingers along the edges of her vagina. Slickness coated her fingers. "So right now, I'm working my labia, and it's a good sign if it's nice and wet like this."

"Is it because you're masturbating?" The word still felt weird in my mouth.

"That, and we were making out," the otter said. "Not everyone gets me wet just from kissing. You're fucking hot. You know that, right?"

My cheeks were feeling pretty hot at the moment. "So are you, even if you swear like a sailor."

The otter barked her laugh, and she slid her finger up her opening of her vagina until she reached the top of it. "Now under this little bit of skin is my clit. The clit is awesome. You're going to want to work it." She pulled her finger away and spread her vagina further with two fingers. "Want to try?"

I crawled closer to the otter, the scent of her musk thick in the air. I slid my fingers slowly along the labia until I reached her clit. I touched it.

"Oh, fuck."

I pulled my finger away. "Did I hurt you?"

Ramona grabbed my wrist and pulled my hand closer to her vagina. "Keep doing that."

I switched it up a little, sometimes trailing up the left side of the labia, and sometimes trailing up the other side or sliding my finger straight up to her clit. Ramona didn't so much moan as swear breathily. I think she would have let me know if she had an orgasm, but she was already dripping on the covers.

"Can I undress too?" I asked.

"Go for it," Ramona said, slipping her finger back into her vagina. "I'll show you what to do next when you're done."

Ramona's toes curled with each press of her clit. I wanted to be where she was, and clothing wasn't helping that. When I fully un-dressed, there was a wet patch at the crotch of my underwear. Slickness slid down my thighs.

"Ramona," I said, sitting back on the bed. "I think I might be at-tracted to women."

"You don't say," Ramona said, licking her lips. "Now that I'm all turned the fuck on, it's time to dive right into the pussy." She slid two fingers inside of herself and curled them upward. "You don't have to use more than one finger if you don't want to, and you don't have to jam it in as far as you can. My finger's not all the way in, but I've found my g-spot." She slid out of herself. "Try it out."

I slipped one finger in, but I met resistance.

"That's my urethra," Ramona said, pushing back. "Go a little lower."

This time, when I slid into her, she melted onto the bed.

"Do the come-hither finger thing," she said. She covered her eyes with one arm and did the motion.

When I started, the otter arched her back. "Work it just like that, but faster. I'm close."

More and more slickness covered my finger. I pressed just a little bit harder against what I hoped was her g-spot. Just as her breathing began to quicken into panting, I rubbed her with two fingers.

A gasp escaped the otter, and clear liquid coated my hand. She collapsed against the bed.

When Ramona didn't say anything for a while, I spoke up. "Was that good?"

The otter picked herself up and held her hand up. "You fucking rocked it."

I laughed as we high-fived.

Ramona licked her slick hand and climbed off the bed. She waggled her rear in my direction as she dug through her bag. "I thought I'd show you something cool since you had a crappy day. If you don't want to do it, that's okay, but if you do, I promise I've cleaned it."

Before I could ask her what she cleaned, Ramona pulled out what looked like a computer mouse. She pressed on it, and it buzzed in her hand.

"Imagine that, but on your clit," Ramona said. "This bullet gets me cumming in under five minutes."

"It doesn't hurt or anything, right?" I said.

Ramona shook her head. "If it does for some reason, I'll turn it off. Lie back."

I was beginning to associate this view of my ceiling with a whole new set of feelings. I gasped as something warm and wet ran along my vagina.

Ramona licked her lips. "Sorry, I wanted a taste. Now buckle up."

I gripped my sheets. The vibration was a buzz against the fur around my vagina. Ramona trailed the bullet in a circle between my thighs, the circle shrinking smaller and smaller. As the bullet pressed against the fleshy part above my clit, the buzz grew louder and stronger.

I grabbed my pillow and held it over my face. Waves of pleasure rocked my body. I pushed my hips down against the bullet, and I had this feeling like I needed to use the bathroom. Something tapped against the pillow, and I looked up from underneath it.

"How are you doing under there?" Ramona asked, a flirty smile on her face.

When I opened my mouth, the buzzing intensified. I made some noises, but they weren't any recognizable words.

"Holy shit, you're fucking wet," Ramona said. "Sorry about your sheets. You want to go a little further?"

I nodded. Whatever "further" meant would finish me. I was barely holding on from sprinting over the edge.

"Just let me know if it's too much."

The bullet slipped lower onto my clit. I was able to slam the pillow over my mouth before my body locked up and I moaned. It didn't feel like I had to use the bathroom anymore.

Ramona turned the bullet off, and she licked the slickness that dripped from it. "That was under two minutes, and I didn't go above level three. There's five levels on this thing."

"I'm sorry," I panted.

The otter leaned down and kissed me. Her saliva tasted odd, tinged as it was with my slickness. "No, that was just me bragging about the toy. You did awesome." She lay down next to me, becoming the big spoon.

I shifted my tail so it wouldn't tickle her nose. "Is this normal for lesbians?"

Ramona shrugged. "I guess it depends on who you're with, but this could be our normal."

"Tutoring, Netflix, and then actually watching Netflix?"

"I don't think I've ever been so motivated to learn algebra."

"In that case," I said, getting up and grabbing my laptop. "We can study after I come back from church tomorrow."

Ramona sat up. "You're still going?"

I nodded. "Not to the same one Tyler goes to. I know Christianity doesn't have the best record when it comes to homosexuality, but I still want God to be a part of my life. I'm sure there are resources out there for lesbian Catholics."

"Just tell me if some priest says something's wrong with you so I can beat him up," Ramona said.

I sat back against Ramona and started up a new episode. This was the part where I was supposed to ask if Ramona wanted to be in a relationship with me, but after the events of today, I think I already knew the answer to that question. I snuggled up against my new normal.

About the Authors

Skunkbomb currently lives in McLean, Virginia with his family. When he's not working an office job in Washington, D.C., he enjoys reading, going to the movies, and playing tabletop games. This is his first time writing F/F erotica, but his other erotic writing, which is M/M, can be found in *FANG* 7 and 8. He is also published in *What the Fox?!*, though that story is not erotica. Skunkbomb was part of the first class of RAWR, the Regional Anthropomorphic Writers Retreat. He can be found on FurAffinity at http://www.furaffinity.net/user/skunkbomb123/ and on Twitter as @Skunkbomb123.

Potentially a cryptic, Holly Morrison haunts the woods around New York City, where she spends most of her days pretending to be a lawyer, against her own better judgment. She's been telling people on the internet she's a winged horse since the previous millennium, and writing stories involving talking animals for just as long. A fan of Dungeons & Dragons, 80s cartoons, and Overwatch, the little time she has that isn't spent writing or working is usually wasted in a potentially futile pursuit to play all of the Legend of Zelda games in order of release. Holly's twitter is @rolypwny, a pun of which she is inordinately fond, and while she doesn't update frequently, she does check her feed every day. Promise.

Slip Wolf has been long haul writing for several years in the fandom, moving narratives from port to port and hitting writer meets from Pittsburgh to Chicago whenever he gets a chance to cross the border from Canada. You can rate his freight by stopping into the garages of Sofawolf and FurPlanet, with a stint or two with Rabbit Valley and Weasel Press, all places from which fine writing is shipped from to docks across the world. His dream is to converge on one of the furry fandom's mecca's of mayhem one summer or fall, laptop in hand and start a creative convoy. Hopefully coffee and flapjacks will be on hand for all.

MADISON KELLER is the author of the epic fantasy *Flower's Fang* series of young adult fantasy novels, the humorous fantasy *Dragonsbane Saga* novella series, as well as numerous short stories. Madison originally hails from the great state of Utah, but for the last eight years they have made the Pacific Northwest their home. When not writing Madison enjoys bicycle riding, knitting, and playing Dungeons and Dragons with their pals. They live in Oregon with their partner and their pack of adorable Chihuahua mixes. They can be found on twitter @maddiekellerr and at http://www.flowersfang.com

JEEVES has been writing furry erotica as part of the fandom for over a decade, and has made his living as a full-time writer-for-hire for the last three years. When not working on his latest story he enjoys playing Dungeons and Dragons with friends, cooking, and spending time walking in the Scottish countryside that he calls home. You can find his work on Furaffinity.net, username: jeevestheroo, and support his writing via patreon, username: jeevesroo. To keep track of his writing on social media, follow @storiesbyjeeves on twitter.

DWALE is a semi-sapient congeries of dross and shadow-play who walks the path illumed wherever the moon touches the sea. Producing works at once abstruse and aggressively pretentious, its stories have received critical acclaim and various award nominations. You may follow it on twitter: @ThornAppleCider

TENZA is a writer, editor and long-time member of the furry fandom. He's a former collegiate English instructor and served as a fiction editor for a small publishing company. After a long hiatus from writing, he's now back in the groove of things and makes his furry publication debut with "She Who Wears the Mask" in this volume of *CLAW*. He's got some very ambitious plans for future creative endeavors! When not writing, he is a wonk of many, many things but areas of particular interest include coffee and tea, motorsports, and gaming. He maintains a presence on Twitter (@hyoufox).

SEARSKA GREYRAVEN has been writing since someone left her unattended with a crayon and a blank surface. Her previous work can be found in the anthologies *ROAR 8*, *Arcana*, and *What the Fox*. When she isn't scratching out a new story, she can be found cavorting under the Floridian sun, tending her bees, or trying to coax plants into growing. Follow her on Twitter @SearskaGreyRvn.

CRIMSON RUARI is a wolf-shaped function for turning folk songs into smutty stories. He has entirely too many hobbies and a lingering theory that he can apply Agile software development methods to writing. Previously published works can be found in a couple of con books and *Heat 14* from Sofawolf Press. Additional works may be found on SoFurry at crimsonruari.sofurry.com. Additional ramblings may be found on twitter at @crimsonsign.

BLUESEIRYUU is a British author specialising in all kinds of fiction, after beginning her writing career in fanfiction she has branched out to produce all genre of fiction content, having produced a series of moderately successful short stories online, she has settled on furry content. She can be found behind her Crocoyeen fursona on Twitter @Crocoyeen and her content can be found on her FA pages BlueSeiryuu and CritterCreativeIndustries.

KRISTINA "ORRERY" TRACER has always had a love of transhumanist, transformation, and transformative works of fiction. She's a member of the Furry Writers' Guild, ran the Cóyotl Awards for two years, and has published three novels to date. She's a graduate of Kyell Gold and Ryan Campbell's RAWR 2018's class, and her most recent work appeared in Madison Scott-Clary's *Arcana*.

In addition to her better-known works, Orrery's been published under both her pre- and post-transition names, served as the second coordinator for the Metamor Keep shared universe, and has two stories hosted on the Transformation Story Archive under her maiden name. She's helped launch two different spiritual temples, practices spiritual alchemy, and studies magical narrativism. She has essays featured on Wikifur's Postfurry page and is one of the founding members of the Seattle postfurry community. Her writing and essays, and links to her other creative works, can be found at *orrery.prismaticmedia.com*.

Dark End is a quiet writer from the American Midwest who drinks entirely too much coffee. He is the managing editor of *Heat* magazine and the *Hot Dish* anthology. His stories have also appeared in *Will of the Alpha*, *Purrfect Tails*, and the upcoming *Fur 2 Skin* anthologies. Even more stories can be found at his website at www.furaffinity.net/user/darkend and his editorial ranting can be found on twitter at @DarkEndWrites.

Erin Quinn is a trans-femme skunk who lives in Austin, TX; when not writing, she fixes phones and computer and consumes too many energy drinks. Her writing has appeared in the Furry Fiesta and RMFC conbooks, and her debut novel *Tailless* is published through Rabbit Valley. She insists she sprays lavender.

About the Artist

Teagan Gavet is a professional illustrator, graphic novelist, and freelance rambler. Find more at: http://www.teagangavet.com
http://www.furaffinity.net/user/blackteagan

About the publisher

FurPlanet Productions publishes original works of furry fiction. You can explore their selection at www.furplanet.com and find their e-books at www.baddogbooks.com.

About the editor

Kirisis "KC" Alpinus is a passionate and deeply sensitive writer who can usually be found with her nose buried within a book. A Magna cum Laude graduate of Tuskegee University and veritable goofball, most of her current free time is spent reading and judging for the Leo Awards, and being a member of the Fury Book Review. When she's not doing that, she can be found painting CMON games miniatures, playing Magic the Gathering, or wandering around in circles trying to catch something random in Pokemon Go.

Her written works can be found in the Coyotl-winning anthology *Inhuman Acts, Bleak Horizons, Dogs of War II: Aftermath*, and *ROAR 9* from FurPlanet; *Infurno* from Thurston Howl Publications; the upcoming *This Book is Cursed* and *A Sword Master's Tale* from Armoured Fox Press; *Fur to Skin: Ladies First* from Rabbit Valley Comics, and *Furnicate* from Weasel Press. Her editing works include the upcoming *Species: Wildcats* and *Breeds: Wildcats* (read it for the tigers!), and the anthology you're holding now. She can be found between the warm, sandy beaches of St. Petersburg, FL and the snow-capped mountains of Calgary, AB, where she lives with her loving boyfriend, Ocean Tigrox, (whom she spends most evenings debating the pronunciation of *quinoa* with).

Find her at @Darheddol or @Swirlytales on Twitter

To everyone that encouraged and worked with me: Thanks!!!

CPSIA information can be obtained
at www.ICGtesting.com
Printed in the USA
FSHW020348230721
83405FS